The Roar of the Lost Horizon

K.N. Salustro

NOVA DRAGON STUDIOS, LLC

For Mom and Dad

who, when presented with my own wild dream, said,
"Do it."

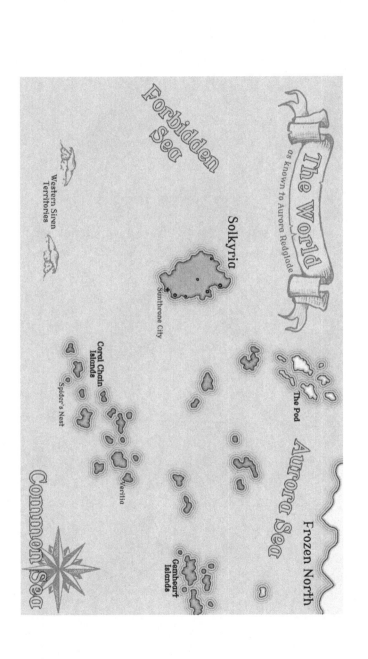

Contents

CHAPTER ONE

A Life for the Empire

TRY AS HE MIGHT, Nate could not blow out the candle. The tiny flame swayed in the gentle air currents that itched at the edge of his awareness, mocking him with its flickering. He could feel the potential in the element, the chance to stir the air into powerful gusts or a small yet precise breeze, but that was all the element had ever been for Nate: unreachable potential.

Sweat ran down his face as he strained for the wind in the dark room. His arms ached from stretching into the uncooperative air. The muscles from his fingers all the way to his shoulders were locked and straining. The wind was there. Nate *knew* it was there, feathery at the tips of his fingers, and if he could just grab it, he could snuff that horrible little fire out of existence and save himself. He was almost there. If he could reach just a little further...

"Enough," a shadow said from the corner of the room.

"I can do it," Nate said, shifting his stance for what must have been the hundredth time. He reached for the wind with every fiber of his being, stretching his hands and his mind as far as they could go. It was there. It was waiting for him. He sensed it so clearly. He could do this.

"No," the gruff voice of the shadow said. "You're done."

The shadow moved to the windows and threw back the heavy curtains. Weak autumn sunlight spilled into the room, blinding Nate for a moment before revealing the cluttered office of the imperial academy's head wind working instructor. The lean, dark-haired form of Tobias came into focus soon after. The head instructor wore the flowing black robes and four-sided cap of the academy's teaching staff, with a sky blue tassel hanging off the cap and a matching sash around his waist to mark him as a wind worker. Unnecessary adornments, really, given the tattoo across his brow. The design was similar to Nate's, but Tobias's tattoo was more ornate, and had an extra flourish in the middle to signal his position as a teacher at the academy. And Nate, still trying in vain to catch the wind even as he blinked away the sting of the light, found himself focusing on that blue ink. If he looked at the tattoo, he did not have to meet the pitying gaze of the man who bore it.

Tobias sighed and sank into the padded chair behind his desk. "Gods below, Nate, enough."

For a moment, Nate considered arguing. Only a moment. Then he let his arms fall and winced at the needling pain that raced up from his fingertips. His sense of the wind faded to a dull thought at the back of his mind, a familiar but useless presence. Nate collapsed into the plain wooden chair across from the head instructor and buried his face in his hands. "I'm sorry," he whispered.

"I know," Tobias said, "but there's nothing you can do. It's time to accept that."

That brought Nate's head up again. He was breathing hard as he met Tobias's unblinking eyes. The pity was there, highlighted by the cheery candlelight, but Nate refused to accept it.

"I know I can't harness the wind yet," Nate said, the words a rush as they left him, "but I can sense it better than anyone else. You know I can. That has to mean something."

Tobias sighed again and shook his head. "A wind worker telling you a breeze is coming but who can't do anything to catch or turn it is about as useful as a weather vane." He reached for a pen and a sheet of clean paper. "Perhaps even less so, as you don't need to feed and clothe the weather vane."

The words stung. Nate had heard worse throughout his life, and he'd known coming into his final Skill evaluation that he was unlikely to succeed, but this was his last chance, and now, just like the wind, it was slipping through his fingers.

He swallowed as Tobias began to write. "I could teach," Nate said. "I could explain proper techniques and evaluate student performances and—"

The pen paused as Tobias peered at Nate from under his thick brows. "The academy isn't taking new instructors. You know that." The pen resumed bleeding ink across the paper. "You also know that you need to demonstrate a special aptitude for your element before you can be considered. A Lowwind is not going to be able to do that."

"But you're a Lowwind," Nate said, "and the head wind working instructor."

This time, Tobias's gaze was sharp enough to pin Nate to the hard chair. Then Tobias raised his hand and, with a flick and twist of his wrist, summoned a small gust that immediately snuffed out the candle. It wasn't as precise or as graceful as a Highwind could have done, but it reminded Nate that Tobias could do what Nate could not, and so much more. His Skill may have lacked power and depth, but Tobias Lowwind could tap into every kind of wind working technique known in Solkyria, and twist it to his will. Nate had seen him use the dancing motions inspired by the tide workers just as efficiently as the slicing gestures favored by most wind workers. Tobias could even turn a breeze with his mind alone. Not a strong one, but he could do it, and he had proven time and time again that he could connect with every kind of wind worker and hone them into the tools the empire needed.

Every kind, except for Nate.

"Let me rephrase," Tobias said. "A Lowwind *like you* is not going to be able to do that." He held Nate's gaze for another long moment, the pale smoke from the snuffed candle drifting between them.

Nate knew that Tobias had tried with him, more than he had tried with any other trainee. Nate's Skill had manifested early, and given what his older siblings could do with their magic, hope and expectations had shaped Nate's future. Tobias had been particularly eager to train him, but as time wore on and it became all too clear that Nate was nothing like his brother and sister, Tobias had tried to find a new way for Nate to serve the Solkyrian Empire. Oh, how he had tried. But Nate could never do more than sense the winds, and Tobias finally had to give up. There were rumors that Tobias's position was in jeopardy because of Nate's failure to master even the easiest of wind workings, and while Nate had never been able to find out if they were true or not, Tobias's patience had worn thinner and thinner as Nate had grown older, and the hope had finally faded from the instructor's eyes. Nate wasn't ready to give up, but Tobias was. All that disappointment had taken its toll.

The head instructor looked much older than his thirty-seven years, with heavy streaks of gray in his thinning hair and in the neat, square beard on his face. His eyes drooped with long lines at their corners, and his skin, once the deep bronze of a healthy Solkyrian citizen, had paled to a sallow hue.

It was not uncommon for the Skilled to burn through their lives quickly in service to the empire, but an academy instructor should have had more time. Among wind workers, it was a comfortable, coveted job, one that only went to those who had demonstrated particularly broad or impressive abilities that could extend beyond service on a ship. Nate felt worse than foolish for thinking he could ask for a similar privilege, especially after all of the time and resources that had gone into his failed training. Now approaching his nineteenth birthday, Nate had been at the academy longer than any other trainee, including those who had undertaken additional work to hone their Skills into unique specializations before they went into service. Nate knew that he should have been kicked out a long time ago. It was time to accept that he'd finally reached the end.

"Where am I going?" Nate asked softly, although he already knew the answer.

Tobias tapped his finger against the pen before resuming his writing. "When a Skilled cannot serve the empire the way they intended, there is only one course open."

Nate shut his eyes. His stomach clenched around the cold certainty that his suspicion was correct.

He was going to the mines.

It was a fate that had haunted him ever since his ninth birthday, the third year that his Skill had refused to shape itself into anything useful since manifesting. Hopes that he was simply a late bloomer had begun to die, and with it went the support around him. Still, Nate had known that if he could just catch a scrap of a breeze, he would be safe. Weather working Skills were highly desired across Solkyria, especially in the navy where Nate's older brother and sister had gone to serve, both at remarkably young ages. That should have been the first sign that Nate would never measure up to his siblings; by the time his brother Sebastian and sister Lisandra had reached their respective ninth birthdays, their Skills had firmly manifested, and they were learning techniques typically reserved for trainees in their early teens. Just after his fifteenth birthday, Sebastian was lifted out of the academy and placed in the navy as an important wind worker. Lisandra had followed soon after as a tide worker, aged fourteen. Nate, meanwhile, kept losing his grip on the wind.

Somehow, even falling short of his siblings, and even after receiving the plainest Lowwind tattoo the academy could bestow on his brow, Nate had held on to the hope that he would, someday, catch the wind and secure a place for himself in the world. He was Skilled, after all, with unclean blood that bound him to the air element. Not so long ago, people like him had been killed for their dangerous, supernatural abilities, but the previous emperor had put a stop to that and found a way to safely integrate the Skilled into society. Now, in exchange for feeding, clothing, and properly training the Skilled to keep their wild magic in check, the Skilled went into service to the empire in order to repay their debts.

Nate was so willing to pay his. Just not in the mines, where men and women dove for the precious and semi-precious metals that were the lifeblood of Solkyrian society. He was a wind worker. His Skill should have afforded him a better fate than being locked away beneath the surface of the world, away from the wind and the open sky. And what good could

Nate possibly do there, if he could not bring fresh air down from above, or turn away the deadly gases released from the depths of the world?

As though he'd heard Nate's thoughts, Tobias said, "They might find some use for your Skill, but if I were you, I'd start learning how to properly use a pickaxe." The instructor finished off his writing with his curling signature, then flattened his palms in the air over the paper. He gently pushed down, and Nate felt the stirring in the wind element as it responded to Tobias's command, pressing the moisture out of the fresh ink and leaving the letters crisp and dry against the white paper. Tobias folded the paper over twice, then reached for the light blue sealing wax on his desk. He relit the candle that had gotten the better of Nate, held the wax over the flame, and then let it dribble on to the folded paper, sealing the letter. Tobias pressed the silver academy signet ring he wore on his left hand into the wax, making Nate's doom official. "You are to leave for the mines at first light tomorrow," Tobias continued. "When you get there, give this to the overseer. We'll send a bird ahead, so he'll know to expect you, but I'm giving you the rest of today to get your things in order and say your goodbyes. Your parents will want to know." Tobias cleared his throat and extended the letter across the desk. "The wagon drivers heading north should not give you any trouble, but if they do, show them the seal and they'll let you ride with them." He gave the letter an impatient shake.

For a fleeting moment, Nate saw himself grabbing the letter and tearing it to shreds, or throwing it out the window, or holding it over that cursed candle flame and watching it burn. But then he had the letter in his hand, and he marveled at how such a light thing could feel so heavy, and he knew that destroying the written orders to report to the mines would change nothing.

He was Nate Lowwind, and this was his fate.

With a heavy sigh, Nate pocketed the letter and rose from his seat. He had his hand on the doorknob when Tobias said, "Nathaniel, wait."

Nate froze, his breath caught in his chest. He turned back to the head instructor, and saw the man standing with two fingers over his heart in the traditional Solkyrian loyalty pledge. "The empire is my life," Tobias said.

Nate's hand shook as he raised his fingers to his own heart. "My life for the empire."

Tobias nodded his approval. With that, Nate was dismissed.

THE DOOR OPENED OUT on to the small courtyard that all the instructors' offices shared. It was a luxury afforded only to them; the rest of the wind working academy was a smattering of tight buildings squeezed into the mercantile sector of Sunthrone City, crammed into the spaces that the merchants and higher class shop owners had not already claimed. Trainees took their basic academic lessons in the small classrooms, where they learned the ways of the empire and how they could use their magic to serve. As they grew older, they spent less and less of their time in the classrooms and more of it practicing and perfecting their Skills higher up on the mountain or down on the coastal beaches where they were unlikely to accidentally destroy a citizen's property or otherwise make a nuisance of themselves. They lived in the dormitories provided by the empire and ate the food provided by the empire, until they were old enough to catch the attention of a sponsor to take on the debts they'd wracked up over the years. It was ideal; this way, the wealthy took on the financial responsibilities of the Skills they purchased rather than the original—and often poorer—families that had borne the tainted children.

Sebastian and Lisandra had both received full sponsorships from the navy, all debts forgiven when they'd gone into direct service for the Solkyrian Empire. Nate had also received a naval sponsorship when he was younger, but it had been revoked. Then the merchants had recognized that he was a bad investment, and then no ships had wanted him at all, and his debts had passed back to his parents. They could have asked that Nate's training be terminated the moment his sponsorship was gone, sending him to the mines and sparing themselves the burden. That was usually what the families of the weakest Skilled did, no matter if the tainted child was from a poor family or a wealthy one. Nate's parents had chosen differently. He suspected that his parents were dangerously dedicated to proving that all three of their children would be vital to the empire, and that their shameful bearing of three Skilled babes from their otherwise untainted bloodlines could be atoned given enough time.

Nate had failed them horribly.

He wished he could tell his parents that all of the years and money had bought him a better life than one set to end in the mines, but at least now there would be no more pretending. This was the end, and it was worth nothing.

The admission tasted bitter in his mouth.

Nate shivered in the light breeze that pushed through the courtyard from the street as he made his way back to the dormitory. The sun was beginning to sink behind the mountains that crowned the island, leaving a chill in its wake. Sunthrone City would fall into the shadow of the mountain soon, and the night would not be long behind. Nate's steps quickened as he thought about being caught out in the cold without his coat, and he went faster still when he remembered that he needed to pack his things. It would be infinitely better if he could prepare for his doomed journey north while the other trainees were still out.

He did not have far to go, but at this time of day in the mercantile sector, threading his way through the streets was difficult. People swarmed the shops, trying to get the last of their purchases in before the sun set and the shops closed down. The Dancing Skies Festival was not far off, and many were seeking gifts for friends and family, tokens that promised unity and love even in the darkness of winter. Nate sidestepped a man coming out of a coppersmith shop, wrapped parcels of jewelry and knickknacks bundled in his arms. Nate caught a glimpse into the shop before the door swung shut, and saw the neat shelves of copper workings glowing warm and pretty in the store's lamplight.

He briefly thought of the copper shop his parents had once owned, but that was long gone now.

Nate ducked his head and hurried along.

He respectfully stepped around the clean-faced Solkyrian citizens, and avoided eye contact with the Skilled attendants who served the wealthiest of them. None sported the blue tattoos of the weather workers, and were happy to give Nate a wide berth when they saw his own mark. Plain as it was, Nate's blue tattoo afforded him a few last shreds of dignity; all Skilled were tainted by magic, but wind and tide workers could serve the empire far more directly with their practical Skills. The light benders and animal speakers who attended to the wealthier citizens recognized that, and they'd always bowed their heads to Nate and any other weather workers who'd crossed their paths. Had they known what now sat inside Nate's pocket, even the lowest Grayvoice would have scoffed at him instead of stepping aside. The thought quickened his feet.

Nate made it to the dormitory without incident, and he bolted inside and up the stairs to the third floor, where the male trainees slept. Nate shared a room with three of the oldest boys. They were all younger than him by at least two years. He knew from overhearing their excited talk over the past few days that their aptitude tests had gone considerably better than his. They were now waiting for finalization of their ship assignments before they packed their things and began their new lives at sea with the wind on their skin and the sky over their heads and the pride of the empire on their shoulders. They were also blessedly absent from the room, just as Nate had hoped.

He pulled his worn bag down from the hook beside his bed and shoved his possessions inside: a few shirts and trousers, a couple pairs of thick socks, and the carved wooden bird he'd managed to hold on to from childhood. The paint had long since worn away and there were scratches and chips in the wood from the times it had been stolen and hidden and abused by academy trainees over the years, but Nate had always managed to find it again. It was small in his hand and looked so fragile, but it had survived the academy alongside him. It deserved a better fate than the mines. Perhaps his mother might like to have it. Nate placed it in his pack, tugged on his coat, and grabbed his worn cap from the edge of the bed. He pulled it low over his eyes and stepped out of the room without a glance back. He hurried down the steps, hoping to make it outside and away from the dormitories without anyone seeing him.

Luck was not on his side. He was just stepping off the stairs when the front door banged open and five of the younger trainees raced inside, faces red and raw from their run up from the beaches. They saw him immediately, and Nate felt their eyes lock on the pack over his shoulder. They knew he was leaving for good, and Nate had no choice but to gather the remains of his dignity and walk past them. They were all younger than Nate by far, with only two of them old enough to have received their Skill marks. That did not guarantee that they'd let him leave with any of his pride intact.

Nate kept his eyes on a point over their heads, banking on his indifference to the children and their hunger after their exercise to let him slip past with minimal interaction. Two of the girls and the youngest boy in the group moved silently aside as he approached the door, but the older trainees looked hard at Nate, and he felt their eyes clawing at the plain tattoo on his face. A sideways smirk spread over the older boy's face, mean and ugly beneath the blue Lowwind tattoo on his brow.

"The Nowind's finally leaving," he said, his voice pitched low but easily loud enough to carry to everyone in the room, Nate included.

Nate's mouth went dry.

"You think he finally got a posting?" the older girl murmured back, also a Lowwind, and also too loudly to be considered discreet.

Nate brushed past them and reached for the door.

"Don't be stupid," the boy snickered. "Who would ever want Nate Nowind?"

Nate closed the door behind him with a hard click. His eyes burned as he walked to the transportation office a few streets over.

Years ago, he'd tried to fight back against the nickname, both mentally and physically, but it had passed itself down the generations of academy trainees like a plague. First, the Highwinds had adopted it, using it as an extra reason to look down on him for his lesser Skill. It did not take long for the Lowwind trainees to latch on to it with gleeful malice, ecstatic to have found a way to call out the weakest among them and offer a clear target for the torment of the Highwinds. Then one of the instructors had accidentally called him by the name, and then there was no going back. The name had not left Nate alone as he'd grown older, and he'd learned a long time ago that there was no dignity or purpose in picking fights with children over it. They continued to use it as much as they could, and sometimes teased each other with it as they struggled to control the wind in their early training days.

Have we got another Nowind? the older trainees would say, and without fail, that pushed the struggling child to tame the wind with a righteous fury, and then look at Nate with a relieved smirk.

Perhaps Nate would have the chance to rid himself of the horrible nickname in the mines, if there were no other abysmal wind workers around to revive it. Or maybe he would die before someone had the chance to call him that. That was a very possible outcome. Either way, the torment would be over soon. Nate took no comfort in the thought as he skulked up to the transportation office.

Securing a wagon ride north was easy, and Nate had no trouble with the official who took his information down. She told Nate that his wagon would depart from the northern gate an hour before dawn, and he would be riding with three Solkyrian citizens hired to work in the mines, now that they were of age. No other Skilled would be going, so Nate would need to mind himself around the citizens and make sure they had no reason to complain about his presence. She glanced at his tattoo then, and with obvious surprise told him that it was a rare thing to see a weather worker of any sort heading for the mines. Then she shrugged and said, "The miners will be glad to see a Lowwind instead of another one of those weird Grayvoices. Your Skill is useful, at least. It'll help them a lot, having someone to bring fresh air down from above."

Nate pulled his cap lower over his plain Lowwind mark and tried not to let the transport official see his shame.

With that done, it was still too early for Nate to say goodbye to his parents. Neither of them would be home from their jobs yet, and he did not want to spend what little remained of the daylight idling in the factory district while he waited for them. His legs burned with the need to move *some*where, but each way he looked, there was something that stood as a barrier to him.

Turning west and making his way up the gently sloping streets would take him into the wealthier neighborhoods and, eventually, the noble district and the home of Emperor Goldskye himself. Sunthrone City wore its palace like a crown, at the crest of the highest hill it could reach before the vast mountain claimed the land and rose too steeply for building. The wealthy flocked to the area, placing themselves well above the smog of the factories and the smell of the fisheries down by the coast. Nonthreatening lesser Skills could be put to work up in the noble district as personal servants, and charming, dazzling Brightbend entertainers and demure Clearvoice animal handlers were common sights up there. For Nate, a journey to the western heights of the city was a quick ticket to scorn and potential bruises. Some of the uphill gentlefolk were all too quick to find creative uses for their walking canes when the Skilled crossed their paths, no matter the color of their tattoos.

If he headed south, Nate would return to the coppersmith neighborhood, and eventually come to the small but comfortable home his parents had owned before they had squandered every copper mark they had on Nate, trying in vain to coax a stronger Skill out of his blood after his sponsorship had been revoked.

If Nate went north, each step would bring him closer to the mines. He would face that terrible fate first thing tomorrow. He could not do it today.

So, with no other choices, Nate braced himself with a heavy sigh and turned east, heading downhill towards the harbor. From the city's main thoroughfare, Nate could look out over the roofs of the low buildings and see the curving arm of the harbor down below, with ships nestled safely inside and the vast, wild horizon stretching far beyond. He kept his eyes on the street.

When he was younger and still believed that he would be a Highwind like his brother, Nate had often looked out at that hard line between the sky and the sea and imagined sailing over it, twisting wind into the sails of an imperial navy ship and sending the craft racing over the waves. As the years wore on and Nate stopped dreaming, the horizon started to look harsh and mocking, much like the crisp, curving lines of the tattoos stamped across the faces of his worst tormentors. The horizon was often the same color as those tattoos: light and clear, blue as the sky.

That day, Nate did everything he could to avoid looking at the horizon. He turned down the much narrower side streets as often as he could, keeping the sight of the harbor and the line of the sky crashing against the sea away from him.

He passed all sorts of people as he walked, although as the sun set and he descended further downhill, his worn clothing began to stand out less and less from the other pedestrians'. He also saw more faces with the tattoos of the Skilled as he went: there, a sailor with the elaborate, deep blue tattoo of a Goodtide on his face, carrying a large parcel as he walked behind two clean-skinned sailors; passing Nate and heading back uphill was a horse-drawn carriage driven by a woman with the black tattoo of a Clearvoice; a pair of men with the white marks of light benders rushed out of a bakery and headed towards the factory district; and there was another Lowwind with a slightly more complex tattoo than Nate's, marking her Skill as the stronger one. He dropped his eyes and gave her a wide berth as they passed each other. She did not look at him.

Soon, the sky was deep orange with the last light of the day, and Nate was far enough downhill that he could no longer see the horizon over the roofs of the city, let alone the harbor. The wind was obstructed by the buildings, but that was far from a blessing. Without the winds to whip them away, the smells of the city were thick. Nate was used to them, but coming down from the clearer air of the merchant and financial districts always left his nose and his stomach threatening to rebel, especially when he turned his feet in the direction of the fisheries and started for the place his parents now called home.

The smell of dead fish mixed with the realization that he would need to show his parents the letter in his pocket was enough to propel Nate further than he'd meant to go. Rather than turning down the street that would take him to their apartment on the very edge of the factory district, he kept walking, delaying his killing of their hopes just a little longer. If they had loved him less, if they had sacrificed less, it would have been easier to face them. So Nate turned down a different street, figuring he would circle the block once or twice before knocking on his parents' door.

He did not get the chance. Instead, Nate walked into a duel.

CHAPTER TWO

The Duel

AT FIRST, NATE DID not think much of the people squeezed into the narrow street between buildings. Solkyrian citizens often gathered in the final light of the day to wish each other well and make their plans for the morrow. Perhaps such a large crowd was unusual, but Nate ducked his head and wove his way through the citizens as respectfully as he could. This close to the harbor, citizens tended to be a bit more forgiving of the presence of the Skilled, and the people he passed did not pay him much attention at all. He was careful not to push or step on anyone's toes as he threaded his way towards the wall, and the crowd thinned a bit as he skimmed his way along the bricks. He came up short when he heard a rough voice growl a promise to decorate the streets with someone's innards.

For a heart-stopping moment, Nate feared that they were speaking of liberating *his* internal organs. It had not been legal to kill a Skilled on the street for a long time, but that did not mean that it did not happen, although usually it was the Grayvoices that bore the brunt of those attacks, not weather workers. Still, Nate's gaze darted over the crowd, searching for a quick escape. He thought that, if he launched himself off the wall and rolled past the man with the sword, he might be able to slip away.

Then Nate paused and looked again at the man with the sword, and the duel came into focus.

The duelist before Nate was massive, with thick shoulders and arms that sloped like a bear's. His face was a hard plane of sharp angles and square bones, with a bulbous nose and thick brows hanging low over clear, bright eyes. He had the bronze skin and dark hair of a Solkyrian citizen, but those eyes were pale and predatory and sharp enough to draw blood. He lazily tugged open the collar of his shirt and rolled up his sleeves, pushing the fabric over his bulging muscles and taking time to flex them as he moved. Whether that was to bolster the confidence of his supporters or intimidate his opponent, Nate could not say, but he knew that he did not envy the poor fool lined up to fight the bright-eyed bear man.

The poor fool turned out to be a woman, fit and lean but so small compared to the bear man. Like her opponent, she had dressed down to a loose, long-sleeved shirt and pair of black breeches. Her boots were old but finely made and well cared for, and the red sash wrapped around her waist added a striking splash of color to her form. Especially when she drew a pistol out of the sash. Instead of doing what Nate deemed the only intelligent thing and leveling the weapon at the bear man, she passed it to a boy behind her, who already had his arms full of what must have been her coat and hat and at least three other pistols.

"Blades only," she called in a strong, clear voice. "First blood ends it."

"You can keep all your blood if you hand the little thief over," the bear man snarled back.

She cocked a dark eyebrow and considered him with wolfish intensity. "That wild accusation is what landed you opposite me in the first place," she said. "Don't make this worse for yourself."

The bear man flashed a wicked grin, displaying teeth as large and square as his jaw. "Bold talk from a woman about to have a new scar." He sank into a combative stance, the weapon in his hand more like a dagger than a sword against his raw size.

The woman turned her back to him, and placed her hand on the shoulder of the boy who held her things. The boy looked up at her, and Nate was struck by the pure terror in his eyes. But the woman gave his shoulder a firm pat, and the boy swallowed and stood straighter.

The gesture was nothing more than a small moment, but it made Nate look closer at the female duelist, and the people that clustered behind her. They were sailors, Nate saw, although not from the imperial navy, nor from any merchant ships. Likely not any of the independent Solkyrian fishers, either, he suspected. There was a roughness to them, men and women alike, with their well-armed postures and wind-worn faces. There was also an unexpected unity to them as they pressed forward to place themselves closer to the terrified cabin boy. He seemed to draw further comfort from their presence, and some of the fear left him. Not all, but some.

Nate looked at the other crew, the one behind the bright-eyed bear man, and saw an equal sense of danger and unity among them. Nate decided that it would be best if he slipped away before someone noticed him, but a bespectacled sailor had stepped into the space behind him, watching the duelists with a grim intensity and blocking his escape. Nate pulled his hat lower over his Skill mark and shoved as far as he could against the bricks at his back, praying to the gods above to protect him and keep the duel away from his little part of the wall.

The woman finally turned back to her opponent. She drew her sword and swung the blade in a glittering arc in front of her. Her eyes were dark and angular against the sun-browned skin of her face, highlighted by high cheekbones and the gentle slope of her nose. Her long, straight black hair was tied back with a simple band. She stretched almost lazily as she considered her opponent, rolling her shoulders and shaking her arms out one at a time. "Ready, then?" she called.

The bear man smirked and flexed his arms again. "I'll try not to scar your pretty face, darling."

"As you like," she said with a shrug. And then she was across the gap between her and her opponent, driving her sword straight for his heart.

The burst of speed took almost everyone on the street by surprise, and the bear man only just managed to throw up his own sword to turn her blade aside. He stumbled back and fell into his crew mates, who murmured and growled as they caught and steadied him. They rallied behind the bear man as the shock wore off. Just in time, Nate saw, as the woman was already closing in for another swing.

"Cut the bitch's heart out, Ed!" someone shouted from the bear man's side.

The swords rang together again, but Ed the bear man was not laughing now. He gave more ground under the woman's onslaught, and low cheers sounded out from Nate's side of the crowd. They grew more frenzied as the woman pressed her advantage, and kept Ed the bear man dancing back on his heels.

"Get him, Captain," the sailor next to Nate murmured.

Captain? Nate thought. *Dueling on behalf of a cabin boy?*

He did not have time to dwell on the realization. The fight circled around to his side of the street, and Nate found himself stumbling sideways to avoid the edge of a sword. He fell into the bespectacled sailor, who took a firm grip on Nate's arm and tugged him further out of harm's way, just in time to avoid Ed the bear man crashing into the wall and leaving a Nate-sized smear on the bricks. Ed caught his balance on the wall and pushed off of it with a snarl, trying to meet the female captain's onslaught with his own brute force. She countered his wild swing, then slashed her sword across his chest. Ed fell back, clutching at the cut in his shirt, but his hand came away clean.

The hand on Nate's arm tightened in frustration before releasing him. "She'll get him," the sailor growled before turning his attention on Nate. "All right there?"

Nate nodded and risked glancing away from the duel for a moment to thank the man. His voice dried in his throat when the man's eyes fell on Nate's tattoo, and a deep frown settled over the sailor's features.

The man peered at Nate over the circular spectacles perched on the tip of his hooked nose. "Who are you?" he asked, his tone suddenly wary.

Nate did not have the chance to respond. There was another ring and rasp of metal as the duelists' swords came together again, and then Ed the bear man yelped and pushed away from the captain, a red stain blossoming where her blade had bit into his flesh. He looked at the wound with a savage light in his eyes as cheers erupted from the female captain's side of the street. Ed's glare shifted from the shallow cut on his arm to the captain as she turned to take her possessions back from the very relieved and smiling cabin boy. Then Ed rushed at her, and the cheers gave way to cries of warning. The captain whipped around just in time to throw up her sword and block Ed's slash, and then they were back in the thick of the fight, blades slamming together once more. People from both sides of the crowd drew their own weapons, but before anyone could rush in to kick off an all-out brawl, there was a sudden pressure in the air off to Nate's left, just at the edge of Ed's side of the crowd, followed by a loud bang, and then something small and deadly ripped across the air and grazed past the captain's bicep to shatter into the bricks of the far wall.

The captain cried out and fell back, clutching at her injury. Blood seeped through her fingers as smoke from the pistol shot wafted through the alley, and everyone went still. Even Ed, who had missed being shot by no more than a hand's breadth. Fury and confusion warred on the bear man's face as his gaze slipped over his own crew, trying to puzzle out where the shot had come from as the female captain did the same.

Nate's magic was warm in his blood as he followed the creased trail of the gunshot back to its origin, trying to fathom why one of Ed's crew would have taken such a risk. The gunman—who, Nate saw, had already hidden his weapon and slipped towards the back of the crowd—could all too easily have been jostled by one of his neighbors, or planted his foot wrong on the uneven stones of the street, or overswung the barrel of the pistol as he'd drawn the weapon and cracked off the shot. One tiny mistake, and it would have been Ed the bear man with the gunshot wound instead of the captain, whose face was contorted with anger and pain as the blood seeped between her fingers.

A shrill whistled sounded from somewhere up the street, the Solkyrian enforcers finally coming to see what the commotion was about.

Ed gave the wounded captain one final look of scathing hatred and snapped, "We'll finish this another day, if you live to see it." Then he turned and ran, chasing the rest of his crew down the street.

Nate's side of the crowd hesitated just long enough for the captain to look at them all and bark, "What are you waiting for? Run!" Then they broke, most of them disappearing into the twilight.

The cabin boy and a broad, pale-skinned man stayed to help. The boy took a firm grip on the captain's belongings and trotted after her as the pale-skinned man stripped off his own coat and draped it across her shoulders. It was far too large and nearly drowned her in the fabric, but it hid the blood. The pale-skinned man took hold of her uninjured arm and started to lead her down the street. They started fast but the woman grimaced and had to slow.

"I gave you an order," she growled as they passed Nate.

"Fight's over, Captain," the pale man returned. "And Dax would kill me if we came back short a captain."

The cabin boy nodded in fierce agreement as he followed them.

The enforcer's whistles came again, piercing the darkening air as the last of the crowd scattered.

Nate hesitated. He knew that, with the way those three had just gone, the alley would take them in a slow curve back to the main street. The enforcers were coming from the opposite direction, but those were the ones that were intentionally making noise. The other enforcers, the quiet ones waiting in ambush, would pounce as soon as the whistles had flushed out the fighters. Some of bear-man Ed's crew may have already tripped into the trap; they'd gone the way of the main street, and if they weren't quick enough to turn around or duck down another side street, they'd be caught. Nate could not say why, but his stomach soured at the thought of imperial enforcers arresting the captain who had dueled to defend a cabin boy. He ran after her. She and the others jolted in surprise when Nate cut in front of them.

"This way," he said, his voice low, and gestured to another alley so narrow, the pale man would have to go through sideways. Nate dove into the shadows and moved quickly, bursting out the far end and scanning the street for signs of the enforcers. All was quiet, and Nate moved to let the others out.

For several moments, no one else emerged from the darkness, and Nate wondered why he had expected them to trust him. Then the captain stepped out, clutching the oversized coat around her. The cabin boy came next, still holding on to the captain's possessions as if they were made of solid gold, and then the pale man stumbled out after them, huffing and grumbling about apparitions leading them down tight spaces. He stopped when his eyes fell on Nate.

"Oh, he *was* real," the pale man said. "Good, I'd much rather be murdered by a human than a ghost."

"Quiet," the captain hissed. She looked at Nate. "Which way?"

Nate waved them down the street, opposite the way they'd been heading, before cutting down another alley and bringing the small group away from the shrieking whistles of the enforcers. It was full dark when they finally came to a stop beneath a flickering street lamp several blocks away. Nate got a better look at the captain then, and he blanched when he saw how much the pain and blood loss had ghosted her complexion. She needed a doctor, and soon. Nate told her as much, and then flushed at his own stupidity. She had a gunshot wound in her arm. Of course she knew that she needed a doctor.

But to Nate's surprise, the captain chuckled, if dryly. "Solkyria's as likely to arrest me as stitch me up, but don't you worry. I have a substitute." She tilted her head at the pale-skinned sailor, who grimaced.

"Just once," he said, "I would like to step on this island without getting someone else's blood on me."

The captain smiled more fully and turned back to Nate. "I would normally shake your hand," she said, "but I don't think you'd appreciate that right now." She waggled her blood-covered fingers at him. "But know that I mean it, boy, when I say you have my thanks."

Stunned, Nate could do little more than blink and nod in response.

The sailors turned to leave. "I'd love to know who shot me," the captain said as they stepped away.

"I know who," Nate said. He swallowed hard and dropped his eyes to the ground when they all turned to look back at him. "I suppose that doesn't do you much good now, though."

"Nonsense," the captain said. "That would let me know who I need to stab the next time we see that crew."

Nate started to smile, but it occurred to him that she was being serious.

So Nate told them about the shooter. He had been a lanky, thin-haired man with a straight, narrow nose and the weathered, wind-scarred skin of someone who had been at sea for years.

"Gray hair, or black?" the captain asked.

"Gray, mostly," Nate said, and the sailors nodded grimly.

"Whiteleaf," the pale man spat. "Probably could've guessed that one. No one else stupid enough to try something like that with their quartermaster in the line of fire."

"You're certain that was the man who shot me?" the captain asked.

Nate nodded.

She looked ready to take her leave, but then her eyes locked on the spot just over Nate's left eye, where his Lowwind tattoo sat on his brow. Her breath hitched for a moment, and a strange intensity came over her. "How?"

The pale-skinned man looked at her sharply. The cabin boy looked mildly confused, but said nothing.

Nate's mouth went dry again under the close scrutiny of the captain. He gestured to his tattoo, figuring that would suffice.

It did not.

The captain took half a step closer. "*How* did you know?" she asked, her voice low.

Nate tensed, ready to bolt. Whatever this captain wanted of him, it was nothing good, and likely nothing that Nate could actually do.

But the captain froze, her gaze sweeping over Nate's posture, and then she drew back. "There's no need to be scared, boy." She extended a hand to him. "I have no wish to hurt you."

Nate let his attention drift to the blood on her fingers before snapping his focus back to her face, and then to the broad, pale man behind her. He could probably outrun them both. Probably.

The captain grimaced and withdrew her hand. "Mr. Novachak," she said over her shoulder, "why don't you and Kai head back to the ship and I'll be there shortly."

The pale man shook his head. "Can't leave you like this, Captain."

"Nikolai," she said firmly, turning to him.

The pale man held her gaze for a long moment before heaving a sigh and tapping the cabin boy on the shoulder. "Come on, Kai, we'll go slow and double back to make sure our frost-touched captain hasn't collapsed in the middle of the street."

The captain waited for them to move out of earshot before speaking again. By then, Nate had edged away, and the gap between them was noticeably larger. She did not try to close it. Instead, she simply gazed thoughtfully at Nate's tattoo.

"Those fools gave you the lowest mark they could, didn't they?" she said. She stared at him a moment longer before murmuring, "Self-righteous idiots." Louder, she said, "I am Captain Arani, and I have reason to be interested in your Skill. *Very* interested."

That made Nate pause. Part of him bristled at hearing someone call the academy instructors fools and idiots, least of all a Veritian. He knew the name Arani came from that island deep within the Coral Chain, where its inhabitants were said to spend their days lazing on lush beaches and idling away their lives. Supposedly, that was some form of passive defiance against their rulers. Veritia had been an imperial colony for hundreds of years now, but its people did little to merit the resources and education brought to their island, choosing instead to reap the benefits of their status as part of the Solkyrian Empire for far less of the work than Solkyrian-born citizens put in.

This woman, however, was a ship captain, and she had just faced off against a bear-man for the sake of a cabin boy. That did not quite match up with what Nate expected of Veritians.

What was more, she'd said that she was interested in his Skill. He doubted that she was familiar with Skill magic, but he knew he should correct her mistaken belief that he was a Lowwind of any use before it got him into trouble. She clearly wanted him for her ship, whether he was willing to join her or not.

"I'm not strong enough to help with your sailing," Nate said warily.

Arani waved him off before pulling the oversized coat tighter around her shoulders. "My crew can sail just fine without a wind worker spoiling them with easy breezes, but that's not why I want you."

Nate threw an uneasy glance over his shoulder, wondering if anyone from the Veritian captain's crew was sneaking up behind him in the dark. No one came. When he looked back at Arani, the intense gleam in her eye had not faded.

"What's your name?" she asked.

"Nate, ma'am," he said.

"Well met, Nate." The corner of Arani's mouth twitched. "You didn't really see who shot me, did you?" she asked.

"I wasn't lying," Nate said quickly. "It was—"

"No, I'm sure you correctly identified him. What I mean is, you didn't *see* him fire the gun. But you knew it was him." She tilted her head. "Am I right?"

Nate nodded slowly.

This time, the captain took a step forward, but she stopped herself when she saw Nate tense again. She glanced up and down the empty street before saying, "Tell me how."

Nate frowned and wondered if he should leave. No, he *knew* he should leave, but for reasons he could not fathom, he stayed. "There was a crease in the air from the pistol shot," he said. "Sharp, leading back to where that man was standing. He tried to slip back into the crowd, but it definitely led to him." Nate swallowed and cleared his throat. "But that's basic wind reading. Any Lowwind could do it."

"Not like that," the captain said. "Maybe they could sense some strong gusts from an approaching storm, but what you just did..." Her brows twitched together thoughtfully. "You're not just any Lowwind."

Nate opened his mouth to argue, but closed it again. He did not understand what this woman wanted from him, but he had the sense that disagreeing would get him nowhere. And she wasn't wrong; unlike other Lowwinds, Nate could not turn, stop, or summon the wind. Somehow, he did not think that she wanted to hear that.

Arani shifted under the massive coat, wincing when her injury rolled against the fabric, and then again when another enforcer's whistle sounded from a few streets over. "I'm afraid I need to take my leave," she said, sounding genuinely regretful, "but I would like to speak with you again." She peered at his tattoo one last time, as though trying to memorize the shape of it. "Come to the harbor at ten bells. I have an opportunity for you, and from what I know of the Solkyrian Empire, you'll want to hear me out." She gave Nate another smile, this one grim. "Ten bells," Arani said, turning away. "Don't be late."

Nate stared after the captain long after she had disappeared into the dark. He felt very strange, now that he was alone. Obviously, he was not going to sneak through the city in the dead of night to meet with what was clearly a gang of sea criminals that were more likely to kidnap or kill him than offer him a job that "not just any Lowwind" could do. That would be stupid. Arani the Veritian captain was lying to him, and he would not get himself caught up in whatever mess she was trying to spin. He turned and firmly set himself on course for his parents' home.

But his heart was beating hard against his chest, steady and persistent as it asked, over and over again, *What if? What if? What if?*

CHAPTER THREE

The Captain's Confidants

THERE WAS VERY LITTLE dignity in being carried aboard your own ship no matter how much blood you had lost, Iris decided. She doubted she would forget the panicked look that passed among the crew as they watched the boatswain haul her up on to the deck, or the sly calculations from a few of the less loyal ones. Unfortunately, Iris was in no condition to throw her shoulders back and saunter across the deck as though it would take far more than a wounded bicep to fell Captain Iris Arani. She had lost too much blood for that. Far more blood than the ship's boatswain and substitute doctor was comfortable with. She knew that, because he kept saying it.

"At some point," Iris said to Nikolai Novachak as he prodded at the back of her arm, "you should maybe try stitching it closed."

"I'll do that when I know for certain there isn't part of a bullet in here," the boatswain retorted. "How you southerners have survived so long without basic medical training, let alone conquered half the archipelago, is beyond me."

There was a snort from quartermaster Dax. "The empire has plenty of educated doctors," he said. "Just not among its Skilled or colonials."

Iris grunted. "Remind me to conscript one of them the next time we run across a Solkyrian ship."

"Happily," Novachak grumbled. "You're lucky this is just a graze, not a full bullet hole in your arm."

"Doesn't feel so lucky," Iris murmured.

She grimaced as the suture needle finally jabbed into her skin. Novachak had mixed a little sleeping draught into some tea to help dull the pain, which Iris had tried to refuse at first, but he had insisted and would not stitch her up until she'd downed it. Even though the herbal mixture made her head fuzzy, she did have to admit that if she'd thrown the stuff overboard like she'd originally threatened to do, the minor surgery would have been agony. Still, she hissed in pain as Novachak clumsily stitched her wound closed.

The man may have received basic medical training while growing up in the Frozen North, but basic training was a far cry from professional finesse.

"This would be easier," Novachak noted, "if you'd let me do this out in the open with proper lanterns around us."

They were in Iris's private cabin at the stern of the ship, shut away from the eyes and ears of the crew. Usually, momentous decisions on the *Southern Echo* were put to the vote of everyone, not made in secret.

This was one of the rare exceptions.

"I needed to talk to you two alone," she said. "You're the only ones I trust with this."

"That's going to be a problem when you need the crew's cooperation," Dax remarked.

Iris waved him off with her uninjured arm, which prompted a stern tap from Novachak. "If I tell them what I mean to do, they'll never be able to keep it to themselves," she said. "They'll know our intent when we're on a firm course with a comfortable head start."

"And when we've confirmed that the boy can really do what you think he can," Novachak added dryly.

Iris narrowed her eyes, but she smirked down at the wooden floor of her cabin as she thought back to the boy's explanation of how he'd known who the shooter was. The excitement bubbled in her chest once again. "You were there," Iris said to Novachak. "You know what he can do."

The boatswain shrugged his massive shoulders. "I know he can lure us down alleys so cramped and smelly, not even the enforcers dared to follow us."

Iris's smile was a bit more biting this time. "I fit down that alley perfectly fine," she said. There was a brief pause before the needle stabbed into her arm again, a bit harder than necessary.

"You're the one who knows what we need for this frost-touched adventure of yours, Captain." A suture pulled taught as the boatswain knotted it off. The stitching felt uneven over the wound, but at least it would hold. "But that boy's going to need a lot of training before he's ready, I think."

Dax's expression turned grim. "Another fail out of the imperial academy, I take it?"

"I'd be shocked if he wasn't," Iris said. The wound at the back of her bicep stung as the boatswain dabbed at it with a damp cloth before moving in with the bandages. "The boy's nearly a man," she continued, "and he was terrified to look any of us 'citizens' in the eye."

Novachak grunted. "If he shows tonight, I'll eat my own socks."

"He'll come," Iris said, although her confidence wavered a little as she remembered Nate's skittishness. "But tread gently around him," she added. "I think he'd run from his own shadow if it looked vaguely threatening."

"We'll need to put a friendly face in front of him, then," Dax mused.

"Wouldn't hurt to bring a pretty one, either," Iris remarked as she tugged her shirt back into place over the freshly bandaged wound.

"All right, all right," Novachak said as he hopped off from his perch on the table. "I'll go."

There was a light pause as Iris and Dax looked at the boatswain.

"Oh, northern winds freeze the pair of you," Novachak growled, "that was funny."

Iris offered him a thin smile before turning to Dax. "Humor aside, we'd better take Rori with us tonight. I think we can use Luken to test this boy's Skill, and Rori will be a lot calmer about all of this if she's there from the start."

"You'd trust her with the secret, then?" Dax said.

Iris paused for a moment. "I don't plan to tell Rori everything," she finally said, "but she's too smart for her own good. She'll know something's up if we bring a Lowwind aboard, and she'll question every heading I give her. Besides, if anyone can help keep the rest of the crew from pushing after a secret, it's her."

There was a heavy silence.

"Someday," Novachak murmured, "they are going to find out what she did to that ship."

Iris pressed her lips into a grim line. "Maybe," she said, "but not today."

Dax crossed his arms and frowned at Iris. "Rori *is* a Goodtide, though. I don't think putting her in front of this boy is going to have the effect you're hoping it will."

"Doesn't matter," Iris said. "Even if they end up hating each other, this boy will see a weather worker his own age living free of the empire. He needs to know that he could do that, too."

"If he shows," Novachak muttered, "and doesn't report us to the enforcers."

"He won't," Iris said. She was confident in that much, at least.

The boatswain glanced at her as he gathered up the rags he'd used to staunch the bleeding of her wound, dropping them into a bucket of boiled sea water that swirled pink with Iris's diluted blood. "You really think he'll go to the docks tonight?"

Iris considered this for a moment. The boy really had been jumpy, but Iris knew she had not imagined that spark in him, that hunger for the freedom to make his own choices about his own life. "I saw the look in his eye," she said, "when I said he wasn't just any Lowwind. He'll show." She caught the glance exchanged between the quartermaster and the boatswain. "And if I'm wrong and he can't do what I think he can," she allowed, "we'll at least get another hand to help with the ship. But I am not wrong."

She was projecting more confidence than she really felt, considering how long it had been since she'd seen a wind working Skill like this, but if she was right...

She'd been waiting for this chance for a long, long time.

Finally, Dax sighed softly and scrubbed a hand across his face. "You told him to be at the harbor at ten bells?"

Iris nodded.

"I'd better get going, then."

She frowned. "Why do you sound like you are under the impression that I am not coming with you?"

"Because you have a hole in your arm," the quartermaster said.

"Novachak said it was a lucky graze," she countered, but Dax shook his head.

"You wait here and get some rest. I'll bring the boy back, and we'll see what he can do."

Iris considered arguing, but Dax did have an irrefutable point, and the weak sleeping draught Novachak had given her was fuzzing the edges of her mind. It was hard to resist the idea of taking a brief rest before starting off on a new adventure, excited as she was. In the end, she agreed to wait and even sleep a little, but she made Novachak swear that he would wake her well before Dax was due back with the boy. She promised to run him through with her sword if he did not, injured arm be damned.

"Aye, Captain," the boatswain said as he and Dax took their leave. His voice was colored by exasperated affection.

After the two men were gone, Iris sank down into her hammock. She thought that she would be too excited to sleep, but her eyelids grew heavy under the pull of the sleeping draught. Before she fully succumbed, she tugged at the thin chain around her neck and pulled the pendant out from her shirt, where she always wore it close to her heart and hidden from the eyes of the world. Its edges had dulled over the years, but the black surface danced with smoky whorls in the soft light of her cabin, just as it always had. She curled her fist around the black scale and brought it to her lips.

"Soon," she promised herself, and drifted off with hope running wild through her mind.

CHAPTER FOUR

Truth and Treason

THE COPPERROSES LIVED IN a tiny apartment on the fourth floor of a small, dark, stone building crammed into the very edge of the factory district, close enough to the harbor to bathe in its smells but without the luxury of a direct line of sight to the open sea and the winds that would have cycled the air. They had moved in over five years ago, after selling their home in the mercantile district to fund Nate's extended time at the academy. He owed them the knowledge of what their desperate scrapings for funds had bought: the failures of a Lowwind son so weak the whole world could sneer and call him Nate Nowind.

What would a pirate captain possibly want with him?

Ransom, perhaps, but she had to know that no one, not even a family as stubborn as the Copperroses, would have paid to recover a Lowwind marked for the mines. Wind workers were valuable, but as Nate knew firsthand, they were not rare in Solkyria. And if a crew of pirates were going to ransom him, or force him into servitude on their ship—which would have been extremely disappointing for them—why not just kidnap him on the spot instead of letting him walk away? Why take the chance that they'd never see him again?

Nate ultimately decided that the pirates only wanted a laugh at his expense. He could not imagine any serious job offer for a Lowwind who couldn't turn aside even the softest of breezes. He was as useless to pirates as he was to the empire. Most of all, he was useless to himself. He could not harness his Skill to save his own life. And now he had to tell that to his parents.

Nate did not visit them often. He used to, when he was younger and still so certain that he would get a Highwind mark. His mother and father had always been warm and kind and encouraging, and that had made it so much harder to face them once the academy instructors had determined that he was not a Highwind, once he had lost his sponsorship, once he had begun to understand how truly weak his Skill was. The quiet disappointment in his father's eyes and the devastation in his mother's had been too much for Nate the last time he'd visited them. That had been nearly five months ago, when he'd come to tell them that his final Skill evaluation would take place in autumn. Now, here he was again, preparing himself to rip their hearts open once more. At least this would be the last time.

Nate climbed the three steps that separated the building from the street. The main door was unlocked to allow the laborers easier access to their homes after long days at work, and Nate slipped inside without trouble. The narrow hallway was lit by dingy candles, and Nate shot them a begrudging look as he headed for the steep stairs at the far end. Despite all his walking up and down the hilly streets of Sunthrone City, Nate's thighs were burning by the time he reached the fourth floor. There were four apartments crowded into that top level, only one of which was lived in. Few Solkyrian citizens wanted to live in such cheap lodgings if they could have afforded even a little better. Under the burden of Nate's debts to the empire, the Copperroses had not had a choice.

Nate took a moment to even out his breath and let the muscles in his thighs relax before moving to his parents' door. He heard voices seeping through the cracks as he drew near, a man and a woman. He was surprised that his father was already home, but supposed that his self-indulgent detour to help the pirates escape the enforcers had delayed him enough for that. This was a good thing. He could talk to them both now, and then take his leave from their lives. Nate raised his hand and knocked lightly on the thin door.

The voices paused. Footsteps creaked over the wooden floor as someone stepped closer. Nate took a deep breath to steady himself, and tried to muster a weak smile for the sake of the parent that came to answer.

It slipped away when the door opened and Nate found himself face-to-face not with his father or mother, but his brother Sebastian.

Nate's mouth went dry, and he took an involuntary step back. His brother quirked an eyebrow and looked at him with open disdain. It was the same expression he'd worn a year ago, when they'd last seen each other during Sebastian's brief shore leave and visit back to the wind working academy to observe and encourage the young trainees.

As he had been then, Sebastian was dressed in his imperial navy uniform of a crisp, white shirt and breeches and shining black boots, all decorated with silver buttons stamped with the Solkyrian crest. He wore his heavier coat, long and deep blue with more silver buttons running down its length and the embroidered patch of his rank and Skill on the shoulders, a special affordance for a Highwind as strong as him. He held his three-cornered hat in his hand, and with his head bare and his long, dark hair gathered back from his face and tied neatly at the nape of his neck, Nate got a good, clear look at the intricate, elegant Highwind tattoo on his brother's brow.

When he was younger, Nate had idolized that tattoo, and sworn that he would get one just like it once his own Skill had fully manifested. Now, it was a grim reminder that while Nate shared Sebastian's proud, straight nose, angular jaw, black hair, and dark eyes, he would not and could not be like his brother.

Sebastian held himself straight, his broad shoulders filling the doorway with ease. He was a little taller than Nate, just enough to look down at him, and that combined with the imperial uniform gave Sebastian enough of a regal air that Nate tipped his gaze to the floor.

Sebastian snorted, and Nate caught a whiff of stale alcohol on his brother's breath. Nate grimaced. He knew better than to ever hope for a good encounter with his brother, but they were always worse when Sebastian had been drinking.

"Who is it?" the thin voice of their mother asked.

"It's Nathaniel," Sebastian answered in his rich, deep voice as he stepped out of the doorway and swept his arm in a gesture of mock greeting. "Nowind," he added, softly enough that only Nate could hear it as he moved past Sebastian into the apartment.

Sometimes, it was possible to forget that Sebastian had been the first to call Nate by that hated name. But only sometimes.

"Nate!" their mother called, the affection in her tone hitting Nate like a hammer. She was there a moment later, pushing herself up on to her toes to wrap her arms around Nate's neck. He could hear the smile in her voice when she said, "Both my boys, home. What a wonderful day this is."

Sebastian reached up to give their mother a gentle touch on the shoulder, a smile on his lips, but his eyes were cruel as he looked at Nate.

All at once, the room felt too close, and the letter in Nate's pocket threatened to rip a hole through him. He squeezed his eyes shut and hugged his mother back, realizing that this was one of the last embraces they would ever share. When she released him, there was a coldness deep inside his chest.

"Oh, forgive me, Mother," Sebastian said. "I almost forgot. Lisandra sends her regards. She would have come herself, but she has a special new assignment, and her ship was at sea again before I had the chance to do more than blink."

"Of course," their mother said. There was a tinge of sadness in her voice, but it had been a long, long time since Lisandra had come home.

Sebastian's imperial expression softened as he looked at their mother. There was genuine affection in his gaze, and for a moment, Nate felt reunited with the brother of his early childhood, the brother who had pulled Nate along on adventures and played at being navy sailors with Lisandra, all three of them certain that they shared the same bright future in the empire. Then Sebastian reached into his coat and withdrew a small pouch that tinkled softly with the sound of copper marks. "From Lisandra and I," he said as he passed the money to their mother.

She drew in a small, sharp breath and hesitated, but only for a moment. There had been a time when she had tried to refuse the meager salaries of her two elder children, but she accepted it now, a flush racing up her neck and over her cheeks as she murmured her thanks and regrets that her children had to provide for her.

"The navy sees us fed and clothed," Sebastian informed her, stoically and unnecessarily. The silver buttons on his coat gleamed in the dim light. "This is the least we can do for you and Father. We know that you've had difficulties." He cut his gaze to Nate on the last word, and Nate squirmed under that unpleasant stare.

Their mother did not see. She had her head bowed as she pocketed the marks, and Nate could see the relief in her shoulders as she thought of all the things they would be able to afford that month.

"This is more than you ever should have felt the need to give us, Seb," their mother said. She reached up and placed her hand against her older son's cheek, humbled gratitude winning out over her pride.

Nate did not know just how far into debt his academy training had thrust his parents, but even without Sebastian's pointed reminder, he was acutely aware that the Copperroses would be working it off for years to come. The empire would never let its own citizens starve, but training the Skilled was expensive. Even if Nate survived working in the mines for a while, it would not be anywhere near enough to cover his debt. Watching his mother now, with Sebastian sneering at him over the top of her head and the orders to report to the mines burning in his pocket, Nate felt a deep and aching rage take root in his gut.

"Are you here long, Sebastian?" he asked tightly.

His brother gave him a languid smile. "Sadly, no. My ship only returned to Solkyria to restock, but we're out on the next tide. I came to visit with Mother, but I'm afraid I must be leaving." He waved his hand loftily through the air. "Lots to do before I summon the wind to take us back out to sea, you know."

"A shame you can't stay longer," their mother said wistfully as she hugged Sebastian again.

Nate did not share the sentiment. The last thing he wanted was to break the news about his fate in the mines in front of his older brother. The sooner he was out of the apartment—and the remainder of Nate's life—the better. A soft sweat broke out on Nate's forehead and his stomach tightened unpleasantly at the sudden thought that Sebastian would find some reason to stay longer, and Nate would be forced to unveil the letter in his Highwind brother's presence after all. He swallowed and tried to sweep the anxiety from his face, but he need not have worried. Sebastian was not paying him any attention at the moment.

"Now, Mother," Sebastian chided gently, "when the empire calls, we must go. Lisandra and I are proud to serve, and we are so honored that the empire not only forgave our debts, but also pays us our own salaries. Not many Skilled are so valued, you know." Sebastian did not look away from their mother, but Nate felt the jab of the comment through his gut. He watched his brother adopt a faux look of remorse as he said, "I only wish we could give you more."

"Perhaps you could," Nate said before he could think better of it, "if you weren't so eager to drown yourself in ale."

There was a stunned silence as both Sebastian and their mother looked at Nate with wide eyes and slack mouths. His older brother's vice had been known for years now, as much as their parents tried to pretend otherwise, but even Nate was surprised that he'd spoken so boldly about it.

Their mother recovered first. "Nate," she began, her voice stern, but Sebastian stopped her with a hand on her arm and a smirk at Nate.

"Ah, Nathaniel," Sebastian said, his voice smooth and cold, "I see you still don't know how to speak to your superiors. I'd warn you about where that can land you, but I think that's a lesson you'll need to learn for yourself." He donned his hat and brushed a nonexistent wrinkle out of his coat sleeve. "I suspect that will happen soon enough." He stepped forward, letting his slight height advantage crowd Nate out of his way. "If it hasn't already," he added, flexing his fingers in a seemingly careless gesture that sent a small ripple through the air, which bounced playfully against Nate's coat.

Right over the letter in his pocket.

Nate drew in a quiet but sharp breath. The rage inside him withered as he realized that Sebastian already knew about the mines, and had probably known that would be Nate's fate for a long time. Nate looked away.

Sebastian had the door open and one foot outside before he paused and turned back. "Oh, and Mother," he said, almost as an afterthought, "I'm afraid I cannot do what you asked of me." He gave Nate one final, scathing flick of his attention. "I can't think of a single ship that would ever want the Nowind." His smile was sharp enough to draw blood as the door clicked closed behind him.

"Well," Nate's mother said after several long moments, "are you staying for dinner?"

"No," Nate answered. He was still looking at the door, and his blood ran cold as it became clear that his mother was not going to acknowledge that Sebastian had just called Nate "Nowind" in front of her. "I already ate at the academy." It wasn't untrue, as he had choked down a meager breakfast that morning. He hadn't eaten since then, but the thought of eating now made his stomach clench and threaten to rebel. And he heard the soft sigh of relief that escaped from his mother. Tears blurred his vision, but he blinked them away as he reminded himself that he wouldn't be a burden to his family for much longer. "I only came by to speak to you and Father about something," Nate said, straining to keep his voice steady.

If his mother noticed, she did not comment on it. "His factory should be letting out soon," she said. "Come and sit with me until then."

He did not have to follow his mother far to the small kitchen near the front of the apartment. Beyond that lay the single bedroom, with a window that faced the wall of the neighboring building and managed to only let cold into the apartment during the winter and heat in the summer. It was dark at the back of the apartment, the few candles his parents could spare to light sitting in various spots in the kitchen. Nate took a seat at the tiny table against the wall while his mother set about carving thin slices off of a severely diminished loaf of dark, stale bread and reheating a pot of an even thinner fish stew that had been watered down long past its prime. His parents kept the apartment as clean as they could, but it was still close and cluttered and if Nate turned his head, he could see warm glints of candlelight off of metal amid the clutter; the last traces of his parents' earlier life. The one they had loved.

After they had sold the coppershop to keep Nate in the academy, the Copperroses had tried to continue their business. It had worked for a time, with them selling their intricate pocket watches and pots and jewelry from their home, but they lost many clients when the legitimacy of the storefront disappeared, and more dropped away when they could not work quickly enough in borrowed smithies to meet their outstanding orders for custom pieces. Then the house in the mercantile district went away, and no one would buy copper pieces from someone on the edge of the fishing district. Even the gentlefolk who knew the

Copperroses by name and admired their work would never have made the journey downhill to buy from them, and those who did not know the Copperroses assumed that their inventory had been stolen. It took Nate's parents a long time to find a trusting enough buyer for a single piece, and even then, they had to sell far below the market value. Eventually, it had made more financial sense for them to find work in the factory district, with his mother taking a job in a textile factory and his father in the iron plant, where he toiled alongside other workers smelting the ore brought into the city from the northern mines. The same ore Nate would be digging up for the rest of his life, however long or short that would be. The thought settled over him like a shroud.

He could not help but wonder how much longer his parents could hold on to their copper name status. They'd been on the cusp of becoming the Silverrose family before Nate had lost his sponsorship, and they didn't have much further to fall before they'd be required to take on the color of a common name. Between Nate's academy debts and the looming expiration of the five-year status renewal they'd purchased back when they'd still been able to afford it, it would be a long, bitter struggle for them to reclaim the Copperrose name.

When his mother joined him at the table, Nate was morose. His mother failed to notice as she began asking him mild questions about his time at the academy, if he was eating enough, how his friends were doing. Nate did not see much point in reminding her that his few loyal friends had been sent off to their respective postings years ago, and the others had grown distant the moment he was branded as the Nowind. She knew this, surely, but she was distracted, and clearly trying not to ask Nate about his aptitude testing. They would have to face that subject eventually, and Nate could not stand the thought of holding it inside until his father appeared.

"Did you ask Sebastian to find a ship that would take me?" Nate asked.

His mother did not immediately respond. Nor did she look at him when she finally nodded.

"Why? You know the navy won't take me as a sailor."

She waved a hand in negation. "There are other positions on ships. You don't need to be a sailor." She worried her bottom lip between her teeth for a moment. "And it would not necessarily have been a navy ship."

For a moment, Nate was too stunned to say anything. A future with the navy had eclipsed his whole life, with Lisandra and Sebastian setting impossible expectations. No one had ever mentioned the possibility of him going anywhere else. "You would support that?" he asked.

"Of course, Nate." His mother turned her head towards him. The candlelight softened the hollows in her cheeks and the harsh lines around her eyes. "As long as your Skill is in service to the empire, that's all that matters."

Nate had not realized that a bubble of hope had risen in his chest until it burst, leaving him heavy and cold all over again. He had not expected her to turn to him and say she'd like for him to join a pirate crew, but for one moment, he'd thought, he'd *hoped*, that someone else had true faith in his Skill. But no. All he had ever been was the useless Nowind, so the empire was going to seal him underground. Anger rekindled in his gut, and the words of the Veritian pirate captain drifted through his head again.

You're not like other Lowwinds.

Nate traced a knot in the grain of the table with his nail as he said, "What if I did not serve the empire? What if... I found something else?"

He felt the shift in the room as his mother tensed and gasped. The breath lanced into her, drawing a sharp line through the air. "Nate, hush." She did not completely keep the edge out of her voice. "They've hung Skilled for saying less. Do not even think of it."

"Why not?" he pressed, digging his nail deeper into the rough wood. "Why should my life be determined by what I can't do with my Skill? If it's so weak, why can't I just find other work?"

"Because you're not a citizen!" his mother spat. She jerked back and slapped her hands over her mouth, but the words were already out.

Nate scratched at the wood and did not look at her.

His mother took a few moments to steady herself. She lowered her hands and stretched them across the table, catching Nate's hand and lifting his nail away from the wood knot. "Nate," she began, her voice soft and gentle, "you know the law. 'Those that bear a Skill—'"

"'Are marked for service to the empire,'" Nate finished for her, "'and to the empire must dedicate their lives.'"

Tears rose to his mother's eyes as she looked at him, at the Lowwind tattoo over his left eye. "If I could have stopped the magic from tainting your blood, I would have," she murmured. "I don't know why the gods chose to curse our bloodline after so many pure generations, but I would have given anything to have a child of my own, just one child that the empire would not claim." Her fingers tightened around Nate's. "But it was not to be, and I have to accept that." She released his hand and wiped the tears from her face. "As do you."

Nate considered her for a long moment. "Would you have wished you could keep me if I had been marked a Highwind?"

"Of course," she said fiercely.

"But I'm a Lowwind, and so I have to wonder, would you rather I went to the mines and died within the month than committed treason and lived to see my next birthday?"

"Nate—"

"Would you?"

They stared at each other in silence, a candle flickering between them. The moment broke when the door opened, and Nate's father stepped inside.

His voice filled the small apartment, deep like Sebastian's but with a naturally rough cadence to it like unpolished metal. He called for his wife, apologizing for being late and telling her about a misbehaving bit of equipment all in the same breath. Nate heard him shuck off his work boots and shrug his way out of his coat as he asked if Sebastian was still around.

"No," his wife called softly, sitting stiffly at the table, "but Nate's here."

The pause that followed was just a little too long for Nate to pretend it did not happen, even when his father quickly shuffled into the kitchen. Time and stress had been unkind to both of Nate's parents, though his father had fared a little better than his mother. Years of squinting over fine fabric stitching that the coal-powered machines were not delicate enough to handle had left Nate's mother with eyes that strained to see over distance, and a slope to her shoulders and neck that had not been present earlier in her life. His father, on the other hand, still had keen eyesight, and physical labor in the iron factory meant that he'd kept his fitness. When Nate's father folded him into a hug, he smelled of sweat and coal smoke underscored with a metallic tang from the ores.

"Good to see you, son," Nate's father murmured before releasing him and stepping back.

His clothes and bare hands were filthy, but where the protective mask he wore over his face at the factory had blocked the soot and fumes, his skin was the same copper brown as Nate's. Sebastian and Nate had inherited their father's angular jawline, but they'd gotten their noses and rounder eyes from their mother. Nate's father had a flatter nose with a bump up on the bridge, and smaller, narrower eyes. There was gray in his hair, but most of it was still lustrous black. Lines were etched into the corners of his mouth and around his eyes, which darted from Nate to the pot of thin stew on the stove and took on a fearful glint as he ran the calculations in his head.

"I'm not staying," Nate said. "I just came to tell you and Mother something."

His father tried to hide the relief that washed through him. He did not fully succeed, but Nate let it pass without comment. This would all be over soon enough.

Nate's mother came to stand next to her husband, and he wrapped an arm around her shoulders. The coal dust would leave a long smudge against her shawl, but she leaned into the embrace and lifted her chin. They both seemed to brace themselves as they waited for Nate to speak.

Nate's hand drifted into his pocket, and he found the sealed letter. The wax was cold and hard against his fingertips as Nate fiddled with it, delaying the inevitable just a little longer. They must have known what was coming. He was a Lowwind, the *Nowind*, and there was only one way he could repay his debts to the empire.

His heart began to quicken in his chest, whispering that rebellious chant again.

What if. What if. What if.

Nate's grip tightened on the letter.

Then he released it, and withdrew his empty hand from his pocket. "I actually found a ship that wants me," he said. "Not the navy, or a merchant. An independent fisher. He can't afford to keep a proper wind worker, but he said my Skill could help him steer clear of storms and follow the good winds whenever he goes out to sea."

For a solid minute, neither of his parents looked like they believed him. His father changed first, a broad smile splitting across his face and melting away some of the toil and stress of the past several years. He clapped Nate on the shoulder, said, "That's wonderful, son!" and pulled Nate into another hug.

Nate worried that his father would feel his traitorous heart thundering against his chest, and broke the embrace quickly. He stepped back to see his mother looking at him suspiciously, fearfully.

"A fisher," she said. "What is the good captain's name?"

Nate's mind gave a panicked flash, reaching for the first name it could find. "Novachak," he said, and then almost winced. Arani would have been the better choice, even if it was unusual for a Veritian to have command of a ship, but no, his brain had given him the extremely foreign one.

"Novachak," his mother repeated, testing the name with a frown.

"His father is from one of the northern colonies," Nate said, surprised at how easily the lies were spilling out of him now. "One of the islands in the Pod, I think. His mother is full Solkyrian."

His mother's frown deepened, but his father laughed.

"Well, try not to hold his uncivilized half against him," he said. "A colonial is just a citizen who couldn't help where he was born."

Nate tried to smile, but his mother's expression was tightening his chest until his heart threatened to explode out of it.

"I'm sorry," he said to her quickly, "for earlier."

His parents blinked at him, and now his father was frowning too.

"It was a near thing," Nate said. "I went in for my final test and I thought I was going to walk out headed for the mines, but this man was there and he said that I could help him and..." He willed his mother to believe the lie with every scrap of his being. "It didn't feel real, until now, when I said it out loud."

A long moment passed before his mother slowly said, "This Captain Novachak found you at the academy?"

Nate nodded vigorously. "He said he'd nearly lost his boat to a bad storm and was desperate for a Lowwind, but he didn't know if he could afford to pay the empire for one. But the head instructor—you remember, Tobias Lowwind?—he introduced us, and I showed the captain what I could do, and he bought my Skill on the spot." He offered a crooked smile. "Lucky that my Skill comes cheap, right?"

Another silence followed his words, and Nate swore that his father suddenly looked a little disappointed. But his mother smiled in earnest, and she said, "Gods above be praised for colonial fishermen," and then his parents were laughing and happy and Nate felt weak with relief.

The next few minutes passed in a whirl, with Nate's mother disappearing into the bedroom and coming back with a small pillow wrapped in a ragged blanket, along with three needles and a precious spool of thread. She insisted he take all of it.

"Lisandra wrote in her first letter of how much she wished she'd brought her own pillow and blanket for her hammock," his mother said as she reached for his canvas bag. "And Sebastian's told me that he should have learned mending earlier. It might have saved him an embarrassing hole or two."

Nate accepted the bundle, although he tried to argue against the thread. His mother would hear none of it, and into his pack it went, which was now considerably fuller with the pillow and blanket included.

Then his father took off the gold ring he wore on his right hand. It was set with the seal of the Solkyrian Empire, the fine sun seeming to pulse with life. Nate knew that ring was the last object of any real value in his parents' lives. It had been a gift from an aide to the emperor, who had commissioned a custom watch from Nate's father years and years ago, before Nate had even been born. His father had refused to sell it, instead holding on to this one last keepsake from the life he'd led before pouring everything behind Nate's Skill.

Nate stared at the cold ring as it sat in his palm. In the candlelight, he could just see his own warped reflection in the band. The ring stretched and exaggerated the blue tattoo on his face.

"Wear that proudly, son," his father said. "No matter how far you sail, never forget where you come from. The empire is your life."

Nate's mouth was dry once again as his parents looked at him expectantly.

"My life for the empire," he said. His parents mistook the raw note in his voice for excitement.

They did not question Nate leaving immediately after that. Sebastian and Lisandra had both slept aboard their new ships when they had been drafted, and the Copperroses knew that it was better to already be aboard the vessel than racing over the docks at first light, trying to reach the ship before its anchor left the water. They embraced him one last time, wished him well, and then saw him out the door. Out on the landing, Nate paused long enough to slip his hand back into his bag and pull out the little wooden bird. He remembered his intent to give it to his mother. He could not bring himself to go back inside the apartment. Instead, he placed the wooden bird on the handle of the door, where it would fall and clatter to the floor when his parents left the next morning. It seemed a fitting end to this part of his life.

It was time for something new.

As Nate left the building and started towards the harbor, he took a small bit of comfort in the knowledge that, somewhere between his parents' warm but strained smiles and the cold night outside, he had stopped lying to himself. He wanted to know what would happen if he met with the pirates.

And if they killed him, at least Nate would die under the stars, and not underground.

Chapter Five

The Test

WITH THE WAR AGAINST Vothein raging far away and the seas around Solkyria quiet and safe, there was no curfew in effect, but as the tenth bell rang out, Nate was one of very few who were out and about, even at the harbor. Once, this part of the city had been dangerous after nightfall, even with the chill of the dark warding off a good number of people. The desperate and those looking to exploit bad situations had dominated the area, but the empire had erected more shelters and set up programs to help keep the poorest citizens off the streets, and the enforcers were usually enough to stop any violent trouble before it began. Duels between pirates had proven to be the exception.

Nate's footsteps sounded too loud in his own ears as he traipsed up and down the docks, and he felt the eyes of the sailors on the night watches settle on him every time he stopped to scrutinize one of the ships at anchor. Belatedly, it occurred to him that he had no idea what the pirates' ship looked like, or if it was even anchored in the harbor. Most of the vessels docked in the harbor were smaller, being mostly sloops and cutters with two frigates anchored next to each other on the far south, where there was space for them to claim. But further out, galleons and an imperial man-of-war rested on the water. Lights burned on the ships' decks, illuminating the bright canvas of their furled sails. Nate idly wondered what kind of ship he would have served on had he been a proper wind worker, but stopped when he realized that he was gawking and giving the night watchers more reason to pay attention to him. Twice, Nate was warned away from a docked ship with the promise that the captain executed stowaways. Another watcher mistook him for an imperial inspector until she saw the tattoo on his face and chased him off. One more thought that he worked for a clandestine pleasure house and tried to invite him aboard. Nate quickly excused himself from that conversation.

Finally, shivering in his worn coat, Nate stood on the last dock at the southern tip of the harbor, in the shadow of one of the frigates. The soft peal of the city bells announced the hour, and as the eleventh one faded away and no one emerged from any of the boats, Nate had to admit defeat. Either he had missed the pirates, or they were laughing at him from the hold of their ship with no intent to bring him aboard. Nate was disappointed by the realization more than anything else; he should have known better than to get his hopes up. The lies he'd told his parents had been for nothing after all, but at least for a little while, he'd held on to the thought that he would not die underground.

His traitorous heart told him that he wasn't ready to die at all.

He took a deep breath to steady himself, then shifted his pack on his shoulders and turned away from the sea. He would not go north. He'd go... somewhere else. Get out of the city and run off into the Solkyrian wilds. It was a large island, with rolling hills, steep mountains, and forests with leaves that would be fiery and beautiful this time of year. Perhaps he could survive out there for a while, until winter came and the cold claimed him. If he did not starve first, or get eaten by one of the gryphon colonies that plagued the wildlands.

It seemed his life was doomed to end soon, no matter what Nate did. His hand dipped into his pocket and withdrew the crinkled orders to report to the mines. His heart was quiet as he looked down at the letter. He picked out the shape of the academy seal in the wax, a reminder that he would have food and a place to sleep if he went north. He could not serve with his Skill, but the empire would still provide for him as long as he could work. His pride was a bitter, difficult thing to swallow. Nate put the letter away and turned his feet to take the first step.

And then a bird stole his hat.

It was not the most successful of thefts, as the hat was a good deal larger than the bird. The creature only managed to get it off of Nate's head through a combination of surprise, speed, intense flapping, and Nate yelping and pawing at the hat himself. Once it was clear of his head, the bird managed to sail a few paces away before the ancient cap proved too heavy. The bird dropped it and landed with an indignant trill on one of the dock posts. The animal fluffed its feathers at Nate in what could only be irritation.

Baffled, Nate cautiously retrieved his hat and jammed it back on his head, never once looking away from the bird.

Now that it was not flapping around his head, Nate could see that it was a striking creature. Its wings were striped with thick bands of bright and deep blue, with black feathers on its body that gleamed in the moonlight. Its tail feathers and the crown of its head were marked with the same blues of its wings, but what really caught Nate's eye were the long, pennant-like feathers that trailed off of each wing. When the bird's wings were folded, the trailing feathers were long enough to extend well past the tail. When the wings were open, showcasing their startling size and angularity, the pennant feathers waved emphatically. Especially when the bird trilled at Nate again and began to hop around the post. It clearly wanted something, but without an animal speaker with avian inclinations to translate, Nate had no idea what that could possibly be.

The bird did not consider this an acceptable excuse. It flew at Nate's head again. He yelped once more and tried to swat the bird away. It pecked his hand, sank its small but sharp talons through the thin fabric of his hat to scratch against his scalp, and then took off into the night.

Nate rubbed the top of his head, relieved when his hand came away free of blood. He felt as though he'd had more surprises and unpleasantries packed into this one day than the rest of his entire life, and he was quite ready to be done with it all. Muttering a curse on the attacking bird's entire species, he turned and started north.

He slowed to a halt as he realized that he had never seen a bird like that in Solkyria before.

What if...?

He hesitated a few moments longer, looking at the harbor full of ships to his right and the sleeping city on his left and the fate that awaited him if he went forwards, into the north. Then Nate turned south and followed the bird.

He had to step off of the docks and on to the beach. He stumbled a little as the soft sand shifted under his boots, so he stuck closer to the water and left his footprints in the wetter sand, which the waves dutifully erased. The water chilled his feet whenever it washed over his boots, but they held and kept him dry.

The glow from the lanterns around the harbor faded behind him, and soon Nate was making his way by the light of the twin moons hanging overhead.

After a few minutes of walking, the bird made itself known again by darting past Nate's head and swooping off along the shore, its wings flashing in the night. Nate kept a firm grip on his hat and followed.

The bird led him further and further south, past the beaches where the academy students often trained and Solkyrian citizens sometimes lounged in warmer weather. The city kept pace with him for a while, following the curve of the shoreline, but it dropped off until the only man-made structures were the watchtowers that poked up from the surrounding trees. The tall, dark towers faced the sea, and on sunny days, the figures of watchers could be seen through the long, narrow gaps in the stone. Once, the watchtowers had held living men and women who had glared out at the horizon, searching for enemy ships. Now that the Solkyrian navy had dominated the western seas and spread out to conquer more of the archipelago, there was no real need for the watchtowers. Yet they remained, and the emperor ordered their yearly upkeep, which included cleaning the stone carvings of the warriors that stood in the windows and stared out to sea with blank eyes. If the tides of war turned again, the watchtowers would at least make Solkyria's enemies pause.

After passing the fifth watchtower, the bird trilled ahead of Nate, and he saw it alight on a rock on the beach. Nate slowed as he approached, glancing about for anyone that might have come to meet him.

The rock moved, and Nate stumbled back.

"Are you the Lowwind?" a feminine voice asked.

Nate squinted in the moonlight, and just managed to resolve the figure of a person kneeling in the sand.

He'd mistaken them for a rock in the dark. Hastily, Nate straightened and nodded. "I am," he said. "Are you a pirate?"

The person did not answer.

Nate had a few moments to start feeling uncomfortable before something descended over his head and plunged him into total blackness. Nate yelled and flailed his arms, feeling his elbow connect with something soft before a strong set of hands pinned his arms to his sides.

"Easy, now," a man said in his ear. "Better if you stay calm."

Nate struggled harder.

There was a soft sigh before the man shifted one hand to the nape of Nate's neck. Nate made to swipe at whatever he could reach with his free arm, but the fight went out of him as his heart rate slowed and his breathing deepened. The panic receded, and Nate stilled.

"There you go," the man said. "Calm and easy, that's all we need."

Nate's eyes swiveled, searching for any spots in the hood over his head that would allow a little light to filter in, but there were none. His heart quickened with the discovery, but the stranger pressed his hand a little firmer against Nate's neck, and the calm returned.

"We're not going to hurt you," the man said.

"Why would I believe that?" Nate asked, louder than he'd intended.

"Because if we were going to kill you, we wouldn't have bothered with the hood," the female voice responded. Nate could not tell the speaker's age from voice alone, but he was pretty sure it was a younger woman, closer to his own age. She'd drawn nearer while Nate had flailed against the darkness.

The man that held Nate chuckled lightly. "That is the truth of it." He eased his grip on Nate but did not fully release him. "And we can't risk you seeing where our ship is before we know if we can trust you."

Nate swallowed hard. "What happens if you decide you can't trust me?" he asked slowly.

"Then we kill you," the woman said.

Nate tensed immediately.

The male pirate groaned. "No, we'll put the hood on again and walk you back here. *If*," he added, "you understand the consequences of reporting what you see and hear tonight to imperial enforcers, and why that would be a terrible idea."

"He's a Lowwind who walked off alone to go meet with pirates," the young woman remarked dryly. "What could he possibly say to the enforcers that wouldn't put him first in line for the gallows?"

"I'm less concerned for him than us," the man said.

"I won't tell," Nate said. His voice was steady now. "No matter what, I won't tell."

"Good." The man patted Nate's shoulder before giving him a gentle push forward. "Let's go."

Nate tried to measure the distance they walked, but it was impossible with the hood over his head and his steps uncertain. The sand squelched under his feet for a while as they moved along the shoreline, but then the pirates abruptly turned him inland and took him through the forest. The woman stayed ahead of them, picking out their path while the man carefully steered Nate through the trees and murmured warnings about treacherous obstacles. Nate stumbled his way through underbrush and over fallen branches, but the pirates let him find his footing every time and they did not rush him. They stopped once when the whooping call of a gryphon rang across the night, but while Nate flinched in fear, the pirates merely halted and waited until the animal had moved away before pressing on. Finally, they emerged from the woods and Nate felt the soft touch of a sea breeze against his skin before his boots hit sand again. Wherever the pirates had brought him, it was quiet, with waves that only whispered against the shore. They came to a halt on what Nate assumed was the beach, and the hood was pulled off of his head.

After the total darkness of the hooded journey, the moonlight was almost blinding. It illuminated the hidden cove the pirates had brought him to, shining on the fine sand and glinting on the gentle waves. A dramatic sweep of a cliff walled in the cove on its southernmost side, casting a shadow across the shallow water. Anchored halfway in the shadow and facing out to sea, the moonlight silvering its bow, was a ship.

It was too dark for Nate to determine the colors of the vessel or any fine details, but he could see the two masts that stood proudly on the main deck. Sails were rigged from the masts along the length of the ship, all the way to the tip of the bowsprit, but they were tightly furled while the ship was at anchor. Even so, it looked to be a fast, nimble vessel. It was small compared to the navy ships that his siblings served on, but Nate had the feeling that this one, with the sails unfurled and swollen with a good wind, just might be able to outrun the big imperial ships. The sight thrilled him, and Nate couldn't help imagining himself standing on that deck with the wind roaring all around him as the ship sprinted over the waves.

He was so lost in the fantasy that he did not realize another pirate had come to join them until a match flared and a lantern glowed to life. Nate jumped, and the pirates chuckled.

"A nervous one, isn't he?" the female pirate asked.

"You weren't much better in your early days," the newcomer said, and Nate recognized the voice of Captain Arani.

Her injured arm was bound in a sling and her eyes were a little puffy with disrupted sleep, but she smiled easily at Nate. "Glad you could join us." She hefted the lantern higher, bringing the rest of the group and their flashing smiles into the light.

To Nate's left was the male pirate who had steered him through the forest. Nate had to look up to meet his eye, and he was struck by the easy authority the man carried in his frame. He may have been dressed in simple, older clothing, but he held himself as straight and proud as any imperial officer Nate had ever seen. His teeth were very white against his dark, sun-browned skin, and his head was shaved clean of hair. The style accentuated the elaborate, multicolored tattoo that stretched across his brow, mirroring itself on each side of his face and reaching back to follow the sweep of his ears and dip of his skull. Nate had never seen a tattoo like that before. On Solkyria, it was illegal for anyone to mark the skin where Skill tattoos were meant to be branded, so this man and the ink decorating his head must have come from outside of the empire. The mirrored designs were mesmerizing, accentuating the fierceness of the pirate's dark eyes. Nate remembered the pain of getting his own simple Lowwind tattoo, and was awed by the sheer amount of willpower it must have taken to endure a mark like that. The pirate grinned under Nate's scrutiny.

"Captivating, aren't they?" he asked, jolting Nate out of his hypnosis.

Nate flushed and mumbled an apology for staring.

The pirate laughed and clapped his hand on Nate's shoulder, sending him stumbling a little. "It's good to know that they're so distracting. Keeps people from noticing this." He turned his head and ran his finger along part of the pattern over his left eye.

Nate followed the gesture, tracking the deep blue lines that wove in and out of the black and white of the rest of the tattoo. He would not have recognized the pattern without the pirate tracing it out, but Nate's breath caught when the design snapped into focus.

"You're a Malatide," he blurted, and the pirate smiled again.

"Daxton," he said, extending his hand to Nate. "The crew calls me Dax, or 'sir' when I'm giving them orders. I'm the quartermaster."

Numbly, Nate shook Dax's hand, his gaze still locked on the disguised Malatide tattoo. Even now that he knew what to look for, the Skill mark slipped in and out of focus, losing itself in the intricacies of the symmetrical design that blazed across Dax's skin.

"The dumbstruck boy is Nate," Arani supplied.

Nate managed to close his mouth and nod in agreement.

"And this," Arani said, gesturing to the last member of the little group, "is our navigator."

"Rori," the remaining pirate said, extending her own hand.

Nate took it, and found himself staring all over again. Rori was by far the prettiest girl he had ever seen.

She was a bit shorter than Nate, but not by much, and barely had to tilt her head to send her dark eyes piercing into his. She had the clear brown skin of a Solkyrian, just like Nate's, and her thick, wavy black hair was braided back from her angular face and studded with a few decorative wooden beads. Her lips were full, her nose straight and proud, and under dark eyebrows, her eyes were large and round, equally ready to narrow with laughter or with anger. On her left brow and trailing down her fine cheekbone was the deep blue tattoo of a Goodtide, nearly as curling and elaborate as the one Nate's sister had received.

That broke the spell.

Nate quickly withdrew his hand, wary of what this Goodtide would say once she learned how weak his Skill was. The empire placed equal value on wind and tide workers, but after everything Nate had endured at the hands of his brother and the other wind workers, especially the Highwinds, he did not trust a Goodtide to be kind. He ripped his gaze away from her face, but he could not help looking at the rest of her.

Rori Goodtide wore a loose gray shirt befitting a sailor, a long black coat, breeches, and a pair of high-topped boots. The belt at her waist secured a pair of pistols and a small wooden box painted with an intricate design. Perched on her shoulder was the blue-banded bird that had tried to steal Nate's hat. It fluffed its feathers against Rori's cheek and chirped contentedly as she reached up to lightly brush her fingers against its breast.

"Well," Rori said, her dark eyes growing less and less friendly the longer Nate stared at her, "shall we see what he can do?" She gave a soft whistle, and the bird flew off of her shoulder, pennant feathers trailing in the air.

Nate swallowed past the dryness of his throat. Anger abruptly ignited in his gut, and he promised himself then and there that he would die before letting a Goodtide and a Malatide laugh at him. He'd swallowed more than enough of that to last him ten lifetimes.

"I'll save you the trouble," Nate growled. "I'm the Lowwind all the others laugh at. You have no use for me."

Rori's eyebrows arched in surprise, pushing the mark of her superior Skill against her hairline. It stayed there for a moment, and all three pirates stared at Nate in silence.

Then Arani stepped forward, handing the lantern off to Dax. "You're right," she said, "we have no use for a Lowwind. There's enough wind at sea to keep our sails full, and I can take us around the world twice over before we run into danger. We have no use for a Lowwind's Skill." She stepped forward, bringing her face close to Nate's in an open challenge. "But as I said before," she said, her voice low and hard, "you're not just any Lowwind. Now tell me where the bird went."

Nate blinked at the captain. "The... what?"

"The bird. Small, feathered, makes chirping noises. Where did he go?"

Nate decided that Arani was either mocking him, or insane. Neither boded well for him.

"Why would I know where a bird went?" Nate asked, trying to meet the intensity of her challenging stare but failing beneath the weight of his confusion and growing unease. The anger had fled from him as quickly as it had come, taking its strength with it.

Arani's hand came to rest on his arm, firm and expectant. "Earlier today, you told me that you tracked a bullet through the air. A bird should be easy compared to that." She paused, and the faintest flicker of doubt came into her eyes. "Shouldn't it?"

Nate wasn't sure if she was asking him, or the tide workers standing behind her, or simply posing the question to any gods or spirits that happened to be listening at the moment. He was certain, however, that he was not walking away from this meeting without doing *some*thing with his weak Skill to appease the pirates.

He risked a glance over the captain's shoulder, and saw that Rori Goodtide and Dax Malatide were both watching him, but with that unenthusiastic glaze that accompanied the certainty that Nate was going to fail. He'd seen that look from the academy instructors enough to recognize it in an instant, and his anger flared again.

They're not going to laugh at me this time, he thought. *They want me to follow a bird? I'll follow the godsdamned creature to the sixth hell and back.*

Nate took a step back, small enough to let Arani know that he was not trying to run away, and glanced around. There was no sign of the bird anywhere in the cove. Nate took a shallow breath and reached for the wind element, and let the natural patterns of the air flood his awareness.

It was difficult to pick out the faint burst of a wind shadow that rippled out from Rori's shoulder, but after a few minutes of hard concentration, Nate managed it. Luckily for him, the embrace of the cliff protected the cove from the harsher winds blowing in from the sea, and Nate could still follow the bird's trail of disturbed air through the night. That trail would fade and scatter as stronger winds came through the cove, but for now, Nate caught the impressions of the hat thief's wingbeats angling up into the sky. He followed the trail with half-closed eyes, squinting at the places where it broke whenever the bird had tucked his wings and allowed himself to fall for a few moments before snapping them open again, his pennant feathers streaming out behind him and adding a distinctive flair to his prints. The trail angled towards the anchored ship, and Nate took a few steps in that direction. He stopped, confused, when the trail became muddled, as though the bird had somehow doubled himself. Nate eventually puzzled out that the bird had changed his mind and flown back the way he'd come, heading for the western side of the cove. By then, the trail was blurry at best, smearing away into the softer winds. Nate hurried after it, struggling over the soft sand until he came to firmer footing at the edge of the tree line. He lost the trail there. The swaying trees disrupted too much for Nate to follow the bird any further, and his shoulders slumped in frustrated defeat.

Nate Nowind had failed yet another test.

His face burned with shame as he turned to head back to the pirates. He came up short when he saw that they had followed him, and not one of them was looking at him with disappointment or amusement or disdain.

Rori reached him first. She stepped up next to him and peered into the trees, then raised her fingers to her lips and gave one sharp, short whistle. Her eyes widened in surprise and something else that Nate could not identify when a high trill answered her, and the bird came fluttering out of the trees. He alighted on the pirate's shoulder once again and twittered insistently. Rori fished a small berry out of her pocket and fed it to the bird.

"You really can do it," she said. And then she gave Nate a strange look, but it was not cruel or mocking. "Be careful," she murmured as the others moved to join them.

"That's incredible," Dax said, bringing the lantern up to illuminate the bird on Rori's shoulder. The bird greedily devoured his berry and ignored the people staring at him. "I knew it was possible, but I never thought I'd see it."

"I promised you would," Arani said. Her smile was wide and sincere, and Nate could not remember ever seeing anyone looking so happy after witnessing his Skill. "Did you really doubt me, Dax?"

"It was a mistake I shall not repeat," the Malatide said, "until the next perfectly reasonable thing to doubt comes along."

Arani scoffed and cuffed him lightly on the shoulder with her uninjured arm before turning to Nate. "I've been looking for someone like you for a long time," she said. She smiled again, and swept her uninjured arm in a grand gesture across the cove, to the ship anchored in the water. "Come with us," she said, "and see the world from the deck of the *Southern Echo*."

Nate stared, his mind gone blank and still from shock.

"Although," Dax put in quickly, earning a more irritated glance from the captain, "before you agree, you should know that we're not exactly... legal."

"You're pirates," Nate said numbly.

"See?" Arani said. "He had plenty of time to figure that out, and he came anyway."

"But he still hasn't said 'yes', Captain."

"Hence the invitation."

The captain and quartermaster traded a few more words, but Nate barely heard them. His eyes were locked on the ship and the horizons it promised to let him cross, and his heart was rising to a frenzy in his chest, but this couldn't be right. *No one* wanted Nate Nowind.

"I don't understand," he finally blurted, cutting off the exchange between the two officers. They looked at him in surprise, but Arani nodded for him to continue. "You said you don't need me to harness the wind for you, and all I've shown you is simple wind reading in closed areas with almost no breezes." His hands clenched at his side as he tried and failed to calm his racing heart. "What do you want with me?"

Dax Malatide and Rori Goodtide both looked to their captain, who drew in a breath like she was trying to gather her patience.

"You have a very special Skill, boy," Arani said. "It's extremely rare, enough so that the empire hasn't even thought to try to understand it yet." Her expression darkened. "There are a lot of things the empire doesn't know about the Skilled."

Nate did not try to hide his disbelief. He'd spent most of his life in the imperial academy, and those years had all added up to the undeniable conclusion that Nate could not and would not ever be a proper wind worker.

Arani sighed. "I think a demonstration would help the boy understand."

Nate cut his eyes to Rori, but the Goodtide was studiously fussing over her pet bird and not looking at him. He was surprised when Dax stepped forward.

"I'm not going to hurt you," Dax said as he lifted a hand towards Nate. He moved slowly, as though dealing with a frightened animal, which wasn't all that far of a throw from the current situation. "I promise."

His hand came level with Nate's chest, and he began to flutter his fingers. They moved fast, very fast at first, beating the air in a one-two rhythm that was erratic but familiar. Dax gradually slowed the rhythm, bringing it down to a calmer beat, and Nate realized that his own heart rate was dropping to match the pace Dax was setting. A jolt of panic hit him, but Dax made a soothing sound and continued the steady fluttering of his hand until finally, Nate's heart was under control. It was still beating a little fast, but it was no longer frenzied or terrified.

"I didn't know Malatides could do that," Nate said, and there was a tinge of wonder in his voice as he placed his hand over his own heart and felt its steadied rhythm.

"They can't," Arani said. "Not usually."

"I'm like you," Dax said. "My Skill did not meet imperial standards, and they didn't know how to measure me any other way. The empire wanted to know what I could do with water in its purest forms, but I could not turn the currents to my will, I could not separate pollutants from rivers, and I could not make a cup of water boil. For the longest time, I thought that I was the weakest Malatide to have ever drawn breath. Then I learned what I could actually do with my Skill."

Nate lowered his hand, frowning. "And you think I'm like that?"

"Somewhat," Arani said. "Obviously you're not a blood worker, but I believe you're Skill is far stronger than the empire understands."

Even in the face of Arani's confidence, Nate could not shake his doubts. "How do you know?" he asked quietly.

There was a subtle shift in Arani's stance then, becoming a little more guarded, a little more distant. "I met someone like you a long time ago," she said. "He served on a lower class merchant ship, but..." Her expression hardened. "He did not survive his service."

Nate swallowed and nodded. He'd heard of such things happening on smaller merchant ships that tried to maximize their profits with cheaper wind workers. He understood that it wasn't common, but it was one reason he'd been so determined to follow in his siblings' footsteps and join the navy. There, at least, lay respect and a chance for true glory.

"I don't tax the Skilled among my crew with using their magic as the empire does," Arani said. Her voice was firm now, the weight of the past shaken clear. "Dax uses his as he sees fit, and Rori here has chosen to never use hers."

Surprised, Nate glanced at the Goodtide, but she was standing with her arms crossed and her head turned to the ship anchored in the bay. Her eyes narrowed when Nate's gaze touched her face, but she did not say a word.

"You could make that choice, too," Arani said, "but I believe you can do something incredible, and I want you to try."

Rori made an ugly sound then, something like a growl crossed with a scoff, and Arani paused long enough for something dangerous to begin to form in the air.

"Rori," Dax cut in quickly, "let's you and I ready the rowboat."

The Goodtide looked ready to protest, but she closed her mouth under Dax's stern stare. "Aye, sir," she grumbled instead, and followed the quartermaster as he led the way back down the beach. They left the lantern with Arani and Nate, and were quickly lost to the darkness.

"You'll have to forgive Rori," Arani said after a moment, and Nate wasn't sure if she was talking to him or to herself. "She's a damn fine navigator and fiercely loyal to the crew, but she has certain opinions about Skill use, and sometimes forgets that not everyone would make the same choice as her." The pirate captain shifted her grip on the lantern and turned back to Nate. "I want you to understand, boy, that this *is* a choice, so listen well.

"If you sail on the *Southern Echo*, you won't have an easy life. You won't be comfortable, you won't be coddled, and there will likely be some days when you won't go to sleep with a full belly. You will be wanted by the empire, and you're just as likely to be killed by a

Solkyrian sailor as you are another pirate's blade. This is not a safe life.

"But if you sail on the *Southern Echo*, you will have a free life. You will be a part of the crew and have equal say in all matters of council, your vote counted equally on all decisions. You will have a share in this magnificent ship's duties, and in all treasures we take. And above all, you will come to understand yourself far better than you ever could have under the Solkyrian flag." Arani took a step back, opening up the path back to the ship. "What say you?"

Nate stared at the pirate captain blankly, then turned his eyes to the ship in the harbor and a horizon suddenly flooded with possibilities. He was paralyzed by the sheer openness of it all, but as he began to think about it, he realized he could not see any positive outcomes for himself. If he joined a pirate crew, he'd be turning his back on his parents, the empire, everything. Earlier, he'd thought that he had nothing to lose, but now that the chance was real and dangling in front of him...

"What if I'm not strong enough?" he asked.

"I don't think that's going to be a problem," Arani said.

"What if it is?" Nate pressed. "What if I can't do what you think I can? Do you abandon me on an island or throw me overboard in the middle of the ocean?"

The pirate captain regarded him for a long moment. "I'm a *pirate*," she said with a hard edge in her voice, "not some Solkyrian merchant. If there's one thing I've learned, it's that any idiot can learn to mend a sail and swing a sword. I'm sure we'd find some other use for you."

Nate ducked his head and dropped his eyes to the sand. That wasn't what he wanted at all. He *wanted* to use his Skill to help the empire. He *wanted* the tainted magic that made him less than Solkyria's clean-blooded citizens to be worth something. He *wanted* the empire, his parents, his *brother* to finally say, "We are sorry we ever called you Nowind."

But before that could happen, he needed to find the true worth of his Skill. He could not do that on his own. He did not think that a Veritian pirate captain would be the one to show him, but his heart was beating its rebellious question again.

Nate raised his eyes to the anchored *Southern Echo* once more. "Do you really think you can teach me something the empire couldn't?" he asked.

Arani was silent for so long that Nate thought that she had not heard him. When he glanced at her, he saw that her gaze was fixed on his Lowwind tattoo. She was frowning, but she was nodding slowly. "I do," she said quietly. "But before I can, you need to make your choice, and do it with all of your heart behind it. This is no time for uncertainty."

Nate hesitated. He sensed that he was losing the chance before him, but he could not say that he was ready to turn away from Solkyria forever. It was his home, and he wasn't ready to give up on it yet.

I could come back, he suddenly thought. *I can learn from Arani, and then come back.*

He risked another glance at the pirate captain, who looked back at him placidly, but her eyes burned with an intensity that suggested she wanted to pick him up and carry him aboard the ship herself if that was what it took for him to come along. He wondered if Arani would willingly let him go someday, once he'd learned enough and could return to Solkyria. His mind raced through possible confrontations with the captain, all of them ending with his blood spilling. But if he could play pirate for a while, keep his head down and do as he was told while he learned, perhaps he could find a way to escape and return to Solkyria. If he came back with new knowledge of his own Skill and a tale of his kidnapping at the hands of a pirate crew, surely the empire would forgive his absence from the mines. And perhaps that new knowledge would secure him a proper fate, maybe even one on a navy ship after all.

What if? Nate's heart asked.

He promised himself then and there that he would find the answer to that question.

He took a step forward, towards the pirate ship in the harbor.

Arani seemed both relieved and pleased by his decision, and she walked with him down to the water, where the two tide workers waited with a small rowboat. On the way, she outlined what he would need to do that night before anything else, from getting a bunk assignment from Dax to leaving his signature on the crew's code.

"I can't read or write," Nate said.

Arani did not miss a beat. "You're not alone in that. I'll read the code to you with the quartermaster standing witness, and you only need to make your mark on the page." She slowed as they drew closer to the rowboat and the lantern light began to illuminate Rori sitting in the boat and Dax standing in the surf beside it. "One more thing," she said. "For a little while, we're going to keep your true Skill a secret. Dax, Rori, and I all know what you can do, as does the boatswain, but that's it. I'll speak with you more about this on the morrow, when we're clear and away from Solkyria, but for now, keep your head down. Tongues have the tendency to wag and I don't want the crew talking about you until you're good and ready to show them what your Skill can do."

"And what is it that my Skill can do?" Nate asked.

"You'll learn," Arani promised. "Soon enough, you will learn."

Puzzled but not seeing much harm in the request, Nate agreed, and followed Arani into the rowboat. Rori took up an oar and pushed it into the sand as Dax shoved his weight against the boat, and it slid forward into the surf. The rowboat rocked as Dax pulled himself inside, Rori and Arani both reaching to help him, and then the Malatide took the oar from Rori and began to row them back to the ship. Before long, they clunked against the side of the *Southern Echo*, and Nate got his first up-close look at the ship.

True to his first impression, the ship was not as large as he had expected of a pirate ship. Built from oak wood stained dark all over, the ship was seventy feet in length, if that, but the masts were tall and imposing, with large sails rigged all around them. Seeing the ship at night made it difficult for Nate to understand much of what he was looking at, but he caught a glimpse of a figurehead positioned beneath the bowsprit. Its odd shape and the way it seemed to erupt from the wood caught his interest, and he made a promise to himself that he would survive his new life as a pirate long enough to get a better look at the figurehead, preferably in the sunshine when he could see the rest of the ship, too.

Ropes came down over the side railing, and Dax and Rori secured the lines before following Arani up a short ladder to the main deck. Nate went last. He nearly slipped on his way up, his wet boots sliding on the rung. He fell hard against the smooth hull, and was surprised by how warm the wood felt beneath his hands. He laughed after a stunned moment, and scrambled up the rest of the way.

There were two pirates at the railing, and they gave Nate little more than cursory glances as they went to work hauling up the rowboat and returning it to its proper place of storage. Nate did not have much time to watch as Dax had already given the order to raise the anchor and set sail. He and Rori vanished into the sudden chaos on the deck, and Nate found himself dodging out of the way as more than two dozen men and women set about their various tasks. Nate did not try to track what they were doing, and instead focused on every patch of open deck he could find. He danced his way through the bustling crew, only to find another pirate stepping into the spot to fulfill some mysterious task. Nate finally ended up at the stern of the ship, near the massive wheel of the helm. He did not feel out of the way yet, and he pressed himself as far off to the side as he could, until he was stopped by a staircase that led up to a small, elevated deck.

"Come on up," Arani called. Nate glanced up to see her leaning over a railing above him. "You only leave behind everything you've ever known once in your life, and I think you'll want a clear view of it."

Nate went up the steps to find Arani and another pirate standing on the top deck, consulting a complicated-looking sea map. Arani waved Nate to the very back of the deck. "Enjoy the view for a bit, and then we'll have you sign the code and deal with the rest, all right?"

Nate nodded and stepped to the back as the ship cleared the little cove, throwing a soft wake of foam across the waves as it ventured further out to sea. Soon, they were sailing on open water, and Nate watched the space between him and Solkyria grow wider and wider with each passing moment. As the land receded, Nate saw the distant glow of the lights of Sunthrone City, where he had spent his entire life until that moment. He leaned against the railing as he watched it all disappear, feeling the pure, salt-stained air of the sea around him. It was almost dizzying, being in such open space, and Nate took a few deep, intoxicating breaths. His hand dipped into his pocket and brought out the letter that had tried to secure his death. It fluttered wildly in the wind, the pale, unbroken wax seal boring into Nate like an evil eye accusing him of betraying his family, the empire, everything.

Nate opened his fingers and let the letter go. The wind took it immediately, sending the pale paper spiraling through the night before slamming it into the sea. Dark waves buried it forever.

I will return, Nate promised Solkyria as the island blurred into the horizon. *When I am better, when I can finally serve you with my Skill, I will return.*

CHAPTER SIX

New Blood

AFTER WATCHING SOLKYRIA DISAPPEAR over the horizon, Nate's first night aboard the *Southern Echo* was a whirl of formalities. Before he was allowed to do anything else, the captain read him the crew's code and Nate sketched his mark, agreeing to the allocation of shares of each prize the crew took, to never gamble money or other items of value while aboard the ship, to keep his equipment in proper order, and several other rules that promised cut rations, flogging, or worse if he stole from, deceived, assaulted, or otherwise betrayed his new crew mates. Nate had no money or valuables to gamble, no weapons to oil or sharpen, no interest in thieving from those who *did* have weapons, and no intent to do anything the crew could possibly find offensive. He was resolved to work on whatever menial tasks they gave him, keep his head down, and find out what, exactly, this pirate captain could teach him about his Skill that Tobias Lowwind could not. But when Nate was in his newly assigned hammock in the berth, the ship creaking and swaying underneath the snores of the sleeping men and women around him, Nate found himself remembering the adventures he had dreamed about as a child. The call for two watch changes went out before Nate finally fell asleep, his mind full of open horizons, exotic lands, and coins as round and gold as the sun.

He woke when someone upended his hammock and sent him crashing to the deck.

The pirates around Nate chuckled as they climbed out of their own hammocks with far more dignity, pulling their boots on and shrugging into coats as they prepared to face the day. Some of them were already on their way up to the main deck, and Nate flushed as he realized that he'd overslept. The night before, Dax had instructed him to report to the boatswain at dawn, before the main shifts began. Judging by the light slanting into the hold from the open stairs, Nate had missed his deadline by at least half an hour.

"On your feet, new blood," the man still holding Nate's hammock barked. "This is no pleasure cruise, and it's time you earn your keep."

Nate scrambled up, but he froze in surprise when he saw that the boatswain was the broad, pale-skinned man he'd met after the duel. Novachak, Nate recalled. The man had not been particularly friendly at their last meeting, and now he seethed with impatience as he waited for Nate to pull himself together. Nate hastily tugged his breeches and shirt straight as he dropped his eyes and mumbled an apology.

The boatswain made a displeased sound at the back of his throat and snapped his fingers in front of Nate's face. "Stand straight and look a man in the eye when you speak to him, boy," the boatswain growled. "Especially when that man is me." His words carried the rolling accent of the north. Not that of the Solkyrian colonies, but the distinct lilt of the nation that resided deep in the Aurora Sea, the one that continued to endured the war and resist both Solkyrian and Votheinian rule. His voice was deep and salt-weathered, underscoring the pale blue stare he pinned on Nate. The boatswain's white skin was a patchwork of sunburns and faded tans over his thick muscles, and a curling, white beard framed his face, turning his round head even rounder. When he spoke again, Nate caught a glimpse of three silver teeth behind his thin lips, on the left side of his mouth. "I won't stand for that downcast Skilled nonsense," Novachak said, "and I have no time to try to read your lips, so you either speak to me proper or keep your mouth shut."

Nate swallowed past his dry throat and managed to scrape out a "Yes, sir," before snapping his mouth shut.

Novachak gave him a critical look as he released Nate's hammock, sending it flipping and swinging against the sway of the ship. He hooked his thumbs into the belt loops of his breeches as he considered Nate. "What do I call you, new blood?"

"My name is Nate Lowwind, sir," Nate answered.

The boatswain frowned. "You intend to keep that name?"

Nate offered him a blank stare in response.

"Solkyria named you Lowwind," Novachak said. "You're not in Solkyria anymore. If you want to change that name, now's the time."

Nate hesitated. Once, before the magic in his blood had revealed itself, he had been Nathaniel Copperrose. Then he was Nate Blanc after his magic began to manifest and the academy poked and prodded at the limits of his Skill, right up until they understood those limits and gave him his tattoo, making him Nate Lowwind. Which, of course, had led to the name Nate Nowind, but he was determined to reject that one outright. But Blanc was a relic from a time of dangerously optimistic hope, and it wasn't right for him to try to claim the Copperrose name, which belonged to the clean-blooded man and woman who had brought him into the world. He would not shame them any more than he already had.

"Lowwind suits me," Nate finally said.

Novachak's frown deepened, but he did not press the matter. "Nikolai Novachak," he said instead, offering his hand. They exchanged a quick, firm shake, and then the boatswain turned for the wooden steps leading up to the main deck. "Come along, new blood. There's plenty for you to do. Thinking we'll start you off on something simple until..." Novachak trailed off, pausing with one foot on the steps. "You ever been off Solkyria before?" he asked.

Nate shook his head. "Does that matter?"

"It should," the boatswain said, his voice taking on a weary tone. He eyed Nate suspiciously, until his gaze snagged on Nate's right hand. "Ah, that would do it."

Nate glanced down and was surprised to see a metallic flash on his own finger, until he remembered that his father had made him wear the gold ring out of the apartment. With his thoughts occupied by pirates and treason, he had forgotten to take it off. He turned his hand over now, and the Solkyrian crest stamped into the ring twinkled merrily at him.

Never forget where you come from, his father had said. *The empire is your life.*

My life for the empire, Nate had answered, but it wasn't until last night and his pledge to return that he had finally understood what the words meant. He felt a sudden rush of gratitude towards his father, and he almost smiled down at the proud Solkyrian crest. He caught himself just in time. If he was going to make these pirates believe that he was one of them, wearing a ring stamped with the imperial sun was not the way to start. And against the pirates' code or not, Nate was pretty sure it wouldn't be long before someone tried to take the bit of gold away from him.

He winced at the thought, and he began to tug the ring off.

"Don't," Novachak warned.

"I shouldn't be wearing this," Nate said, pulling the ring over his knuckle. He dropped the ring into his pocket. "I don't—"

He meant to say more, but the moment the metal left his skin, the world tipped and spun around Nate, and a wave of nausea sent him reeling. Something caught and tugged on his arm, and Nate went stumbling back the other way, his limbs feeling like jelly. His stomach heaved and sent a burning jet of sick up his throat, and Nate barely registered the taste as it shot past his teeth. Then something cool was pressed into his hand, and Nate could breathe again, and the world slowly righted itself.

When his vision had cleared and his innards were only gurgling with mild discontent, Nate found himself leaning heavily against Novachak. The boatswain had caught him before he could fall, and Nate saw that, somehow, the man had managed to avoid getting splattered with Nate's vomit. Nate's boots and the deck were considerably less fortunate.

"Well," Novachak said after a long moment, "looks like we'll be starting you on cleaning duties."

Nate swayed on his feet and coughed at the acrid taste in his mouth.

Novachak thumped him lightly on the back. "You'll be all right, new blood, if you keep that ring on you. I think. I've never seen a Skilled get hit by the magic sickness that fast. Or turn that particular shade of green."

Nate groaned and opened his hand to find the gold ring twinkling in his palm. Novachak must have retrieved it and pressed it back into his hand. Soothing coolness seemed to radiate from the metal and calm the wild racing of his blood as he shut his eyes and closed his fingers around the ring.

"Perhaps he would prefer some agate," a new voice said.

Nate and Novachak turned to see the captain standing a few steps above them, eyeing Nate and the mess on the deck. Her right arm was freshly bandaged and resting in a sling, but she stood sure-footed, bracing herself easily against the rhythm of the ship.

"We don't have much to spare, Captain," Novachak answered. He cast a dubious look at Nate again. "And if he's got a ring of Solkyrian gold, that should keep the Skill sickness off him just fine."

"Then keep that ring on, boy, unless you intend to repeat that performance for the amusement of the crew."

Nate's face heated with shame as his stomach gave another unpleasant twinge, but with the ring back in his hand, the worst was past. He felt incredibly foolish. In the excitement of everything, he'd completely forgotten an important lesson he'd learned at the wind working academy about what happened to the Skilled if they left Solkyrian soil; without an anchor to tie them back to the island, their magic would rage freely through their bodies, bringing on the Skill sickness and rendering them completely useless until they either found an anchor, or succumbed. It was why the navy outfitted their wind and tide workers with silver-buttoned clothing. And it was one more layer to the curse of Nate's magic.

So much for hiding the Solkyrian crest.

The captain moved down the last few steps, revealing that a few pirates had paused on the deck above to peer into the hold and see what the commotion was about. Most of them had clean faces, but Nate caught a Darkbend mark on one of them. Nate pulled himself away from Novachak and forced his legs to hold him upright before the Skilled pirate could laugh at him. His head swam with the movement, but he pushed through the dizziness and steadied himself with a few deep breaths. He stumbled a little as the ship swayed beneath him, and he just managed to avoid stepping into the vomit splattered across the deck. His nose crinkled when he smelled his own sick at his feet, but the captain was before him now, watching him with her dark, steady gaze.

"I trust you slept well?" she asked him coolly.

Nate flushed again and the pirates watching from the above deck snickered.

Arani quirked an eyebrow at him, but all she said was, "Don't make a habit of it." Then she looked up at the loitering pirates and her gaze hardened. "If you have time to stand around," she barked, "you have time to mend those sails."

The pirates hastily began to retreat.

"Marcus," she called, and the broad-shouldered pirate with the Darkbend mark froze. He was not laughing now.

"Aye, Captain?"

"Dax has informed me that you've skipped your last two cleaning rotations." She pointed at the soiled deck. "Get a bucket and get to scrubbing."

The Darkbend's face twisted with disgust, but he nodded solemnly. "Aye, Captain."

"No," Nate said, "I should do that."

"You," Arani said, "are coming with me. I need to speak with you." She nodded for Novachak to follow, then led them up the steps.

Nate tried to catch the eye of the Darkbend as he climbed, but the light bender was staring at the mess below with open despair. Nate burned with shame as he trailed after Novachak and the captain. He was certain he had made a fresh enemy thanks to his blunder.

Arani led them over the top deck, weaving deftly around the pirates that were at their various tasks. Nate went more slowly, still unsteady on his feet, but his head turned every which way as he followed, fascinated by the activity despite his earlier embarrassment. Several pirates were on the deck, mending tears in spare sails. Others were up in the rigging, hanging perilously from the ropes and adjusting the wind-swollen canvas as the ship rushed over the blue waves. Wherever Nate turned, he saw pirates, and beyond them, the wide, open sea stretching to meet the pale dome of the sky. There was a purity to the sea winds around Nate, and he found himself breathing deeply and savoring the fresh, untouched air that not even a bird's wing had marred.

No sooner had Nate finished the thought when a trill sounded out, and something crashed into his head.

Nate yelped and swatted at the bird as it tried to steal his hat. He successfully fended it off, and it dashed away to perch atop a coil of rope, chittering softly at him. He recognized it as the same bird that had tried to steal his hat the night before, the one with the striking blue bands and the pennant feathers trailing from its wings.

Several pirates laughed as Nate brushed his clothing straight. One of them called for Nate to summon a solid gust and teach the creature some manners. Nate turned his flinch into a dramatic show of righting his hat and pulling the brim down low over his Lowwind mark, pretending he had not heard the suggestion. His stomach soured all over again.

Twice in one morning, he'd been humiliated in front of the crew, and his Skill had been entirely responsible for the first instance while completely failing to save any of his dignity in the second. He had a nasty feeling that he was not going to evade the Nowind nickname for long.

"Luken seems to have taken a real liking to your hat."

Nate turned to find the Goodtide girl—Rori—coming up next to him. She was smiling affectionately at the bird, oblivious to the problems he was causing for Nate.

"I am sorry about that," she said. "He's a spirited little thing." She pointed at Nate's cap. "He'll probably go for it again. You'll need to keep an eye out for him."

"Or," Nate said, "you could keep your pet under control, and put him in a cage if you can't."

Rori's eyes went wide for a moment and she looked genuinely taken aback. Then she frowned with stormy intensity. "I'm not going to cage something that should be free. I would have expected you to understand that." Her gaze flickered to Nate's tattoo before she turned away. She called the bird back to her with a sharp whistle, and it obeyed without hesitation.

Nate wondered if every pirate had such a terrible first day, or if it was him, specifically, that could fail so wondrously before he had even begun.

"New blood!" Novachak's rough voice called out, and Nate hurried to the impatient boatswain. He waved Nate through a door into a cabin at the stern of the ship, where the captain and quartermaster were already waiting.

The cabin was small, already feeling claustrophobic with Nate and Novachak squeezing inside to join the gathering, but it managed to hold all of them, along with a large desk, a number of books and journals, several writing tools, a chest full of equipment Nate could not identify, and rolls and rolls of maps and charts. Novachak closed the door behind them with a snap, and the room went eerily quiet without the roar of the wind or the shouts of the crew spilling inside. Nate could still hear them if he listened, but he understood that this was as close to privacy as one could get aboard the ship.

"Now that you've seen fit to join us," Captain Arani said from her seat at the desk, "there are several things we need to discuss." She nodded to the quartermaster, who stood off to her side with his arms folded over his broad chest. "Dax here has claimed the first topic, being that he believes you may not have fully understood what it is you signed last night."

"We live and die by those articles," Dax said. His tone was strict and allowed no room for argument. "Every member of this crew has made their mark upon the code, and pledged to follow it until they leave this ship for good, or death claims them." He fixed Nate with a hard, unblinking stare, made all the more terrifying by the twin tattoos that adorned his head. "You are expected to do the same, or you will face the consequences. Skilled or not, if you try to steal from your fellow crew, you will lose a finger. Accuse or slander someone with no evidence to base your claim, and you will lose your tongue."

"The punishment fits the crime," Arani cut in before the quartermaster could extrapolate further. "If you look, you'll find a few sailors who did not believe that, at first."

"Interestingly, they're some of our most loyal members now," Novachak mused.

Arani inclined her head in agreement before focusing on Nate again. "Do you understand?"

Nate swallowed past the hard lump in his throat. "I do," he answered. He meant it. He remembered the articles quite clearly, including the outlined infractions that would result in his death. He had no intention of violating them.

"Good," Arani said. "Moving on to the more important matter—" she ignored the sidelong frown from the quartermaster, "—we need to discuss your Skill."

Nate felt his stomach lurch again. This was it: the moment the pirates said they had no use for Nate Nowind. Maybe Arani had realized she'd made a mistake when she'd seen the Skill sickness overtake him, or the way he couldn't keep Rori Goodtide's godsdamned bird away from his hat. He'd be ordered to mend sails or untangle ropes or even serve as an officer's personal cabin boy, and Arani would say she'd been wrong, and she could not teach him anything about his Skill, and there would be nothing for him to bring back to Solkyria. He braced himself and waited for the words.

Arani did not speak them. Instead, she gave Nate a sharp smile and said, "I was very pleased by your demonstration last night. I had every faith in you, but there were some who needed convincing." She turned her grin on Dax, who chuckled lightly and rolled his eyes. She turned back to Nate. "I've been looking for someone with your Skill for so long, I was beginning to doubt we'd ever find you. Nate," she stood up and faced him squarely, excitement radiating off of her so strongly, the air nearly shimmered with it, "thank you for coming with us."

Nate stared at her. He was fairly certain he had not misheard her, and that this pirate captain had, in fact, just thanked him for joining her crew. She had to be joking, then. There was no other explanation. But as Nate looked from the captain to the quartermaster to the boatswain and back again, he saw that they were all serious. Arani was easily the most eager among the three officers, but their expressions were all earnest.

"I'm really not going to be much help with the sailing," he said, uncomfortable under their gazes. "My Skill doesn't... I mean, it's more for—"

"Tracking," Arani said. "And it's a good one, if you're already following birds and bullets. You're not great, but we'll fix that."

Dax and Novachak nodded.

Nate shook his head. It seemed he would need to explain this a few more times before the pirates accepted it. "What I can do is just a petty trick," he said, remembering the scathing evaluation that had come from one of the secondary academy instructors ahead of his final aptitude test. "It's basic element reading, nothing more."

"Oh, my boy, it is so much more than that." Arani looked out the windows at the rear of the cabin. "I told you that I'd met someone like you years ago. He could sense things in the winds that no other Lowwind or Highwind could. Things that no one else in the world could follow." She turned her gaze back to Nate. "That's your Skill. Or it will be, once you've had some proper training."

Nate did not know what to say. He knew that he was particularly sensitive to the element, but he had never heard of a wind worker doing what Arani was suggesting, of tracking something over the open ocean, where nothing ever laid down a trail to follow. He shook his head again, and did not care that his mouth was agape.

Arani tilted her head and gave him a wry smile. "All right," she said, "once you've had *a lot* of training."

"And some more convincing," Novachak added. "Which, Captain, quite a few people will need before they'll let you take us on this frost-touched quest of yours."

"They'll believe it when they see for themselves what Nate can do," Arani responded. Her confidence was like a knife to Nate's heart.

"I—wait," he said, stumbling across his voice once again, "what is it you want me to do?"

"Track something," the captain said before either of the other officers could speak. "Something no one else can."

That clarified nothing. "A ship?" Nate asked, his mind presenting no other possibilities. As he said it, he realized how useful a wind worker who could track enemy ships would be to the empire. His heart quickened as an image of himself in a naval uniform flashed across his mind, standing on the bow of a man-of-war and using his Skill to suss out Votheinian ships slinking over the horizon.

But Arani shook her head. "I have something else in mind."

Crestfallen, Nate waited for her to continue, but she offered nothing else. He looked to Dax and Novachak, but both men were watching the captain and taking their cues from her. Nate gave a sharp exhale and spread his hands in confusion. "I'm sorry," he said, "but I don't understand."

"You will," Arani promised. "I know that this is confusing for you now, but trust me, and I will show you that the empire made a terrible mistake when they tried to cast you aside. I am the captain of a ship full of men and women who have broken free from that same empire, and I stand before you and swear that you, too, will break free, and become far more than Solkyria ever let you dare to hope."

Nate saw no mocking laughter in the captain's eyes, or cruelty of any sort. She believed wholeheartedly in every word she spoke.

Nate did not. But if he wanted to return to Solkyria someday and prove himself useful to the empire, he had to pretend that he agreed, and give himself the chance to learn everything he could from Arani. And even if she did not want him tracking ships, that did not mean he could not try to develop that technique on his own.

That, certainly, was something he could take back to the empire, and present as the true worth of his Skill.

Nate tightened his grip on the ring still clutched in his hand, feeling the skin of his palm press against the rays of the sun crest, and nodded.

"Good." Arani's eagerness flared again, and Nate felt it infecting him with a steady warmth. "Now," the captain continued, "last night, I mentioned that we would keep quiet about your Skill. Right now, only the people in this room and our navigator know that your magic is unique. That's one too many for my liking, but we can trust Rori for now, and once we're done with our business on Spider's Nest, we can tell the full crew immediately."

"I still think we should tell them now," Dax said.

Arani shook her head. "Tongues wag on Spider's Nest. We shouldn't let word of what we intend to hunt slip out, especially not now, when we've just found our tracker. Believe me, if we could skip Spider's Nest completely and set out today, I'd much rather do that. But I do have important business there."

"And we need to restock and let the crew rest," Dax put in firmly.

"And the quartermaster says we need to restock and let the crew rest," Arani said as she turned back to Nate. "So we keep quiet for now, and wait until we're clear and away from Spider's Nest before we reveal your Skill. Understood?"

"They're going to wonder why I'm not helping," Nate said. "The crew, I mean," he clarified when the three pirates gave him bemused looks. "I don't know where Spider's Nest is, but I assume we're going to be at sea for a few days? That means the crew is going to see me, a Lowwind, not helping with the sailing."

"That I will leave up to you," Arani said. "If you want to use your Skill to help harness the winds, you can, but if you'd rather hold back and say you choose not to use your Skill the same as Rori, they'll have to accept that."

Nate felt unease flicker in his chest. "I can't," he said.

"If you're worried about them pressuring you, the crew knows that I don't tolerate that kind of talk on the ship. Dax can vouch for that."

Nate shook his head, wincing internally as he realized that he would need to kill Arani's confidence in him after all. "No," he said, "I *really* can't help with the sailing. I can't harness the wind at all. I've never been able to control the wind with my Skill."

Silence fell over the room, and Nate was very aware of all three pirates staring at him.

"You can't work the wind at all?" Arani asked, a skeptical frown deepening on her brow. "But you can sense it?"

"I don't mean to be disrespectful," Nate said quietly, "but I have been trying to tell you that since yesterday."

Arani went so still, she did not even blink for several long moments. Nate felt his gut clench as he watched her excitement fade under rising uncertainty. He was intimately familiar with that look, as with the shame that began to gnaw at his gut. It seemed that Nate was going to disappoint the captain after all.

Before anyone could speak, Novachak cleared his throat and turned a pointed look upon the captain. "I thought the other tracker you knew could do that wind magic stuff?"

"He could," Arani said slowly. "Not very well, but he could do it." Her frown deepened as she gazed at Nate, hope and doubt openly warring in her expression.

"Maybe he's more like me than we thought," Dax mused. "My Skill doesn't let me do anything with pure water. Maybe it's the same with Nate and the wind?"

Arani made a thoughtful noise, but she did not look convinced. She considered Nate for a long moment before leaning back in her seat. "I never saw the other tracker follow a bullet." Nate watched her turn this idea over in her mind, and then nod more firmly as she said, "So maybe Dax is right."

"And if he's not?" Novachak asked pointedly.

Arani reluctantly said, "Then I suppose we resign ourselves to the idea that we've found a new crew member, and nothing more." She gazed at Nate for a moment before adding softly, "I hope that's not the case."

Nate fought the urge to fidget with the gold ring as the officers talked about him as though he were not in the room. He promised himself again that he would unlock his true Skill, even if Arani could not, and take it with him back to Solkyria to help the navy hunt Votheinian ships, or perhaps even pirates.

He shook off the small flash of guilt that accompanied the thought, reminding himself that he was not like other Lowwinds, and that had to mean something. He had to make it mean something, no matter the cost.

Nate made himself stand tall and look Arani in the eye when he said, "I don't know what you want me to track, but I'm willing to try. I promise, I'll work hard." He imagined himself speaking not to the Veritian pirate, but to his parents and Tobias Lowwind and the entire Solkyrian Empire when he said, "I won't let you down."

Arani's brows twitched up. Then she smiled with subdued relief. "I'm pleased to hear that, Nate. And I promise you, we will figure this out. Trust me."

Nate did not trust her, but he made himself nod all the same. *He*, at least, would figure this out.

"Good." Arani gestured to Novachak with her uninjured arm. "Now, it's time to get you to your first duties. Who knows, maybe you'll be able to make yourself useful to the boatswain here, who has been screeching about needing an assistant for a long time now."

"I do not *screech*," Novachak said primly. "I *bellow*."

"Perhaps you can bellow your way to the mainmast and start teaching Nate which ropes to pull when we need to furl the sails."

A few more words were exchanged, but they blurred around Nate. He stood clutching the gold ring, and felt it pressing hard into the soft skin of his hand. Slowly, he opened his fingers, and stared down at the little hoop of metal and the red impression it had branded into his palm. He stared at it until Novachak drove him out of the navigation room and back into the bright sunlight.

"Come on, new blood," the boatswain said. "We'll get you settled, and then get you into the chore rotation."

Nate barely heard him. He was still gazing at the ring in his hand, feeling determination and defiance swirl through him. He had not turned his back on his family and the Solkyrian Empire for nothing. He promised himself that this would all be worthwhile, and no matter what, he would make it back to Solkyria in the end.

He slipped the ring over his knuckle, bringing the imperial crest to rest against the base of his finger, where it burned in the sunlight.

CHAPTER SEVEN

Doubts

AFTER NOVACHAK AND THE boy had gone, Dax turned a flat stare on Iris, letting the silence stretch between them. Iris knew what the quartermaster was thinking long before he said it, but part of her hoped that if neither of them spoke, they could pretend that she had not gotten her hopes up for nothing.

It's not nothing, Iris told herself sternly. *He* is *a tracker. I've seen him do it.*

But could he find what she needed on the wind?

"Well," Dax finally said, and Iris shut her eyes against his measured tone. "That's certainly not what you expected, is it?"

She leaned back against the table and sighed. "No," she agreed, "it's not. But I don't think he's lying."

"Agreed," Dax said. "I've just never heard of a wind worker who couldn't actually work the wind. I always thought that even the weakest among them could pull a light breeze from the sky."

"We saw him track Luken," Iris said. "That has to mean something." When she opened her eyes again, she saw that Dax was studying her closely.

"Do you think he can do it?" he asked.

Iris hesitated, thinking hard about what she'd seen Nate do compared to the only other Lowwind she'd known who could track through the air. "Not with his current abilities," she finally said. "But if he can learn to go farther than what he did in the cove, then maybe..."

Dax frowned as she trailed off, and she knew what was coming.

"If you really intend to propose this hunt to the crew," he said, a hard note of warning in his voice, "you need to be certain."

"I can't be certain until I know what he can really do."

"Then you can't send the crew chasing after this fantasy."

Iris looked at him sharply. "It is *not* a fantasy," she said, the words low and dangerous. "The empire may have tried to turn her into a fable because she wasn't Solkyrian, but Captain Mordanti was as real as I live and breathe."

The quartermaster sighed and nodded tiredly. "I know, but you have to admit, when not even Veritian history can say for certain what her hidden treasure is, it's hard to believe that it's really out there." He looked like he wanted to say more, but Iris had heard it all before, and he knew that.

Still, his doubts rankled her.

The legend of the Veritian ship captain Ava Mordanti was known throughout the Solkyrian Empire, but outside of Veritia, it had been reduced to just that: a legend. To Solkyria and the islands its people had conquered, Captain Mordanti was a fabled, foolish woman who had tried to steal from the gods and was struck down for her arrogance. To Veritia, she was a skilled and fearless captain who had taken a wondrous treasure not from the gods, but from enemy Solkyrian sailors, and then hidden it away before dying in battle against the sun empire's invaders. Because of Mordanti's skills in combat and her ultimate sacrifice in a key battle, Veritia resisted

Solkyria for another four long, bloody years before finally succumbing to the empire. Even then, Solkyria had needed to resort to desperate tactics that had cost the empire dearly and nearly resulted in their defeat at the hands of Veritian forces. Solkyria had never forgiven that injury to their pride, and they'd reduced Mordanti to little more than a children's story to warn future generations against rebellious behavior. Over two hundred years after her death, many Veritians saw Mordanti more as a myth than an actual figure from their history, but there was still evidence of her in the world. That much Iris was certain of, because she wore a piece of it on a chain around her neck.

That did not mean that Dax was wrong, however. Iris could not ask the crew to chase after Captain Mordanti's legend without the means of securing it. She so badly wanted to believe that the wind worker Nate could provide those means, but after what he'd said, she could not be certain. She'd been determined not to let the true depths of her doubts show in front of Novachak, and certainly not in front of the boy, but Dax was another matter. Iris and Dax had known each other too long and had saved each others lives far too many times to overlook false confidence.

"We need to see what Nate can really do," Iris said. "Start testing his limits and see how far his tracking abilities go, and build on his Skill from there."

"Iris," Dax said, and the warning note was not gone from his voice, "what if he can't do it?"

She frowned at the floor and drummed her fingers against the table. "Then I give this up," she finally said before cutting a hard look at the quartermaster. "We go back to hunting merchants and avoiding navy ships, just like we always have, and I go back to wondering if I'll ever have the chance to follow Mordanti, just as I always have. But I *know* that Nate's a tracker, and by all the gods above and below, Dax, I want to try."

Dax sighed and ran a hand over his head, right along the tattoo that disguised his Malatide mark. "The crew's patience is going to wear thin very quickly. We haven't had a good run lately, so the promise of a legendary treasure is bound to pique their interest, but if you set them on this path without a way to see it through..." He looked at her squarely, his dark eyes boring into hers. "I can't protect you if they turn on you."

"I would not expect you to," Iris said quietly.

They gazed at each other for a long moment, years of friendship and responsibilities stretching between them. Not for the first time, Iris found herself missing their younger days when the unseasoned crew was more forgiving of her new captainship and Dax had not yet been elected quartermaster. They'd been able to spend easy time in each other's company then, and they'd even started turning towards something more as they'd grown older. But circumstances had changed and demanded other things from both of them, and while they'd remained friends, they'd needed to set everything else aside for the good of the ship and the crew. Iris did not regret her life, but there were a few things that she wished could be a little different.

Dax was the one who finally broke the silence. "For what it's worth," he said, "I don't think you're wrong about that boy, but everything is going to come down to him."

"I know," Iris said with a grim nod. "Let's hope he's as eager as I am to prove the Solkyrian Empire wrong."

CHAPTER EIGHT

Friends and Enemies

NATE WAS ALLOWED TO rest for a few hours following his earlier brush with the Skill sickness, and then his duties aboard the *Southern Echo* began with menial tasks like untangling rope and scrubbing down the main deck, which kept him busy and tired all through the rest of his first day. Captain Arani and her quartermaster ran a tight, clean ship, and it seemed to Nate that someone was always running seawater over the wooden boards. He eventually learned that the daily soaking kept the boards tight and stopped moss and mold from growing in those empty spaces and slowly tearing the ship apart, but it was also to benefit the spirit that inhabited the ship.

"The ship's bonded with a dryad," Dax explained to Nate on his second day as they walked the length of the ship and the quartermaster introduced him to every nook and cranny of the *Southern Echo*. "Her spirit is mostly dormant now, but she keeps the sea worms out of the hull and a lot of barnacles off the keel so we don't have to careen nearly as much as other ships do. Our mainmast is her heart tree, and it's stood strong and sturdy even through the worst storms."

Nate wasn't certain if the Malatide was teasing him or not, but Dax insisted that it was true.

"How do you get a dryad to join with a ship?" Nate asked. "Don't they die if their trees are cut?"

"If you take the heart tree against the dryad's will, yes," Dax said. "But I was there when ours joined with the *Southern Echo*, and I promise you, she came willingly, trading her heart tree for all the adventures we would ever have, and a prime view of all the places she'd never have seen if she'd stayed in her grove."

He took Nate to see the figurehead below the bowsprit then, and while Nate still did not have a good line of sight, he could see that his initial impression of the carving had been correct; the figurehead erupted out of the wood of the ship, a gleaming head and torso facing the open sea and everything from the waist below melting back into the lines of the ship as though they were one. The arms were spread as if in jubilation, and even though he could not see the face, Nate had a strong feeling that the expression was one of pure joy.

Nate still wasn't certain that he fully believed Dax, but if it was a lie, it was a pretty one that only enhanced the beauty and allure of the pirate ship.

"Are there a lot of dryad ships out there?" Nate asked as he leaned over the railing to study the decorative wood.

It took Dax a moment to respond, and when Nate tore his eyes away from the figurehead, he saw a tinge of sadness in the quartermaster's eyes. "There are some out there made of dryad wood, yes. But not many are alive like the *Southern Echo*."

They left the matter at that, and after he'd learned a bit more about the ship and how the crew operated, Nate returned to the menial but time-consuming duties Novachak had assigned him. It seemed that, as the newest and least experienced member of the crew, Nate would be untangling ropes and patching holes in the spare sails for a while. He didn't mind. The work was tedious but simple enough even if the tears in the sails were oddly violent to have come from weather alone, and the tasks let him sit back and observe the lives of the crew.

What he noticed immediately was that for a ship that had so recently come from port—albeit a secret one in a hidden cove at least two miles away from civilization—the *Southern Echo*'s stores were oddly depleted. No one seemed overly concerned about the amount of food and water left in the hold, but it seemed sparse to Nate, and what was there was far from fresh. The water had gone stale in its casks, and the only one who seemed to prefer it to the dwindling beer and grog was Arani, who took it fiercely boiled and steeped with tea leaves. The hard biscuits were full of weevils, the salted meat was stiffer and drier than tanned leather, and if there had ever been a fruit or vegetable present on the ship, it had long since been consumed.

And for a pirate ship, the *Southern Echo* was distinctly devoid of treasure. There were plenty of ropes and cannonballs, and Nate was given his own cutlass and a small dagger from the ship's weapon reserves, but there was nothing of any real value to be found on the ship.

He pushed the gold ring more firmly against the base of his finger and wondered what Arani and her crew had been doing on Solkyria.

He learned the answer from Xander Grayvoice, who introduced himself by appearing out of nowhere and snatching up one of the sails Nate had just mended, examining the patch with exaggerated care, and grimacing.

"You're terrible at this," the Grayvoice remarked as he picked at the threads. They came loose under his quick fingers, and the hole returned in far less time than it had taken to patch it.

Nate, stunned by the pirate's unexpected appearance, gaped in bemused mortification at his undone work. He wasn't sure if he should be embarrassed, angry, or both.

The Grayvoice observed this for a few moments, and then laughed softly. He settled down next to Nate and grabbed the large needle from his hand. "Use this stitch," he said, demonstrating with a few quick passes of the needle through the canvas. "Won't come apart if you sneeze on it like that mess you were making." He handed everything back to Nate and looked at him expectantly.

Nate bent back to the work, a flush creeping up his neck. Novachak had given Nate the simplest task on the ship, and he'd proven himself useless at it, as was befitting of Nate Nowind.

This is only until I can unlock my true Skill, Nate reminded himself. *I am going to do something amazing.* He held on to that thought like a lifeline as he completed several unsteady but markedly stronger stitches in the canvas. *Better,* he thought when he held up the repaired sail.

He was surprised to find the Grayvoice still sitting next to him when he looked away from his shoddy handiwork.

The Grayvoice had his elbow braced against his knee, chin resting on his hand as he studied Nate openly. His dark hair was cut short, held out of his eyes by a red bandana tied around his head that partially obscured the plain black tattoo over his left brow. His face had the square, bold features of a man who did not take kindly to being told what to do or where to go, and it was easy for Nate to see that the imperial instructors for the animal speakers had completely failed to tamper down his spirit. The Grayvoice was a little older than Nate, more fully grown into his adult frame, and he was lean and muscled under his brown skin. His eyes were dark and intense, and Nate could not decide if they held the promise of friendship or calculated the best way to make use of him.

"You're odd for a Lowwind," the Grayvoice suddenly said.

Nate froze, remembering the captain's warning to keep his Skill a secret. Had someone already figured him out?

"You don't walk around like you're better than me," the pirate went on, and Nate relaxed a little. "Not like the other wind-puffing snobs I've met. You seem to know better than that." He grinned and thrust his hand forward. "I think you and I will get along just fine. Name's Xander."

Nate introduced himself, taking the Grayvoice's hand for a quick shake. He was relieved that his secret was safe, and that he seemed to have a new ally before him, if not a willing friend.

But before Nate could pull away, Xander twisted his wrist so that the golden ring on Nate's hand faced up and flashed in the sunlight. The Grayvoice examined it with open interest, but his eyes narrowed and his lip curled when he recognized the Solkyrian crest. He quickly released Nate's hand.

"Nice ring," Xander growled. "They give those to all the wind workers?"

"It was a gift from my father," Nate said, which did not seem to placate the Grayvoice at all. If anything, his expression darkened even further. So much for finding an ally. "The boatswain said I should keep it on to help with the Skill sickness," Nate added quickly.

Xander made an unimpressed noise and looked away from the ring. "Oh, that'll protect you well enough. Just too bad it's been tainted by that godsdamned sun crest."

A protest rose to Nate's lips, but he bit down on the words. He needed to blend with the pirates if he was going to learn what he needed to return to Solkyria, not pick fights with them. Nate moved his hand under the canvas in his lap, hiding the ring from the animal speaker's sight. "I don't have anything else," he said, putting what he hoped was a shamed note in his voice.

Xander continued to glare at nothing in particular, but he suddenly shook himself and his expression cleared. "Right, you're new, you wouldn't have had the chance to get some proper agate yet." At Nate's bemused stare, the Grayvoice turned his head and fiddled with the earring that hung from his left lobe. It was a large, sharp chip of dark agate, crudely wrapped in metal wire. He turned his arm and showed Nate a woven hemp bracelet with a similar piece of white agate secured in the knots, pressed against the paler skin of the bottom of his wrist. "Fresh from Solkyria," he said proudly. "Taken right out from under the empire's nose. Finest agate anchors you could find."

Nate peered dubiously at the agate as he recalled the ship's depleted supplies. "Is that why the *Southern Echo* was at Solkyria?" he asked, his curiosity overruling his caution.

Xander nodded. "We have a cache there, and we sometimes stop off to get fresh anchors for us Skilled." He pinched his agate earring between his thumb and forefinger, rubbing the stone thoughtfully. "Captain had us take more than we usually do this time. I think she means to sell some of it to make up for the bad run we've had lately."

That explained the disappointing lack of plunder in the hold. "Why didn't Arani restock the ship on Solkyria?"

Xander looked at Nate with genuine surprise. "We never restock on Solkyria," he said, as though

Nate should have already known this. "That's too dangerous."

"The captain was dueling a man the size and shape of a large bear when I first met her," Nate pointed out.

The Grayvoice huffed an amused snort. "Oh, *she* can venture into the capital to take care of a bit of business and collect a few scraps of gossip just fine, so long as she uses a false name." He bared his teeth in a snarl. "But we Skilled can't be seen there. They'd arrest us or kill us as soon as we set foot in that city."

Nate frowned. He'd seen all sorts of Skilled in Sunthrone City. Surely a Grayvoice, trained at the animal speaking academy on the western side of the island, could have moved unrecognized through the capital city's crowds, even if he was a runaway pirate. Nate said as much, and Xander's eyebrows arched in surprise.

"You really had an easy time at that wind school, didn't you?" The Grayvoice cut his eyes to Nate's hidden hand, seeking out the gold ring even with the canvas blocking it from view. "The empire branded you deep," Xander said. He narrowed his eyes, considering something. "You know, it would do you a lot of good to take that sun crest off and feel what it's like to really be free."

"I can't," Nate said. "Last time—"

Xander waved his hand dismissively. "You'd be fine with a bit of agate in place of it." His lip curled a little, and then he huffed a sigh. "If you want," he offered with clear reluctance, "I could trade with you, give you my agate for the ring." He looked ready to take the words back, but resigned himself to the offer with a visible effort. "Agate's the better anchor, anyway, and you'll have an easier time with it instead of pure metal."

Nate was mildly insulted but mostly amused by the Grayvoice's attempt to get a gold ring off of him in exchange for a few rocks. "You'd do that for me?" he asked. "Trade away your agate for a ring with the Solkyrian crest?"

Xander made an unpleasant face, but he did not fully keep the triumphant gleam out of his eyes. "Consider it a favor from a friend," he said.

Before Nate could respond, a step sounded behind him and a low voice said, "Don't do it."

Nate turned to see a tall, lithe pirate with an elegant Darkbend tattoo across his finely sculpted features standing over them. A short hemp necklace with a large bit of agate sat in the hollow of his throat. His shirt was open to reveal the smooth skin and muscles of his chest, which Nate suspected was meant to impress someone, perhaps one of the nearby female riggers who was giving him an appraising look that was far less subtle than she seemed to think it was.

"Xander's agate is worth a few silver marks," the Darkbend went on, "but not a gold ring, which works *perfectly well* as an anchor. He knows that."

"Sure I do," the Grayvoice said, "but *he* doesn't."

"Stop trying to swindle the new boy."

The Grayvoice gave a dismissive snort. "You never let me have my fun."

"Your idea of fun is annoying at best and dangerous at worst."

"But that makes for the best stories," Xander said with a sly smirk. "And I think you've flashed your pecs long enough to know that you're not going to have much luck with this one."

Nate and the Darkbend looked at each other for a moment, and Nate saw disappointment bloom in the man's eyes.

"It was worth a shot," he said with resigned acceptance. He buttoned up his shirt enough to hide most of his chest, but purposefully left the top two buttons undone. "I'm Eric," the Darkbend said.

"Nate," Nate said, "and I was actually going to suggest Xander bring me his weight in agate before I give him a gold ring."

Eric stared at him for a moment, and then a brilliant smile lit his face. "You're going to do just fine here," he said before he turned his grin on Xander. Nate turned to see the Grayvoice studying him with narrowed eyes again, as though reconsidering and recalculating his initial assessments. Nate offered him a tentative smile and a shrug. The Grayvoice did not return the gesture.

"Forgive my lack of finesse," Eric said as he reached down to shake Nate's hand. "It's been a while since we've had new blood on the ship."

"Are you suggesting the rest of us have somehow gone stale," the Grayvoice asked, "or that you've decided to raise your standards?"

Eric leaned against the railing, looking entirely unbothered. "Whichever upsets you more, Xander."

The Grayvoice chuckled darkly and nudged Nate's shoulder. "Eric here is the self-proclaimed champion of swooning hearts and pining glances. I'm always thrilled to find someone else immune to his charms. According to him, we're a rare sort, but I think that's a lie."

"He does seem to have his admirers," Nate noted softly. He nodded at the female rigger who was dawdling at the ropes across the deck, still throwing unsubtle glances at Eric.

The Darkbend made a puzzled sound in his throat. "Liliana knows that I strictly prefer men, right?"

"Doesn't seem to be stopping her from looking," Xander remarked.

Eric made a slow, grand gesture of sweeping his hand through his shining hair. "I suppose I *am* too pretty for that."

This time, Nate laughed along with Xander, and the three of them spent a good part of the afternoon talking.

HE WAS INTRODUCED TO Marcus Darkbend more officially that evening.

Nate was sitting at one of the small tables in the part of the ship that passed for a mess hall, talking with Xander and Eric when the other light bender slid on to the bench across from Nate, looking far more excited about dinner than anyone else. Nate recognized him immediately, and the blood drained from his face as Marcus looked back at him. The stout Darkbend frowned, as if trying to place Nate's face in his memory, and then his expression cleared.

"Ah, right," he said, pointing at Nate, "you're the one who painted the deck with his insides on his first morning." The light bender looked off with a traumatized shudder. "It took me two hours to get the smell out of my nose."

Nate flushed. "I am so, so sorry," he mumbled.

"Don't be," Eric said brightly, earning an irritated glance from the other Darkbend. "With Marcus ducking out of cleaning duties, the gods were bound to punish him eventually. You just happened to be the vessel of their divine wrath."

"Aye," Marcus agreed glumly, "I just really thought that was going to take the shape of me scraping the bilge, not scrubbing up vomit."

Eric eyed him sidelong. "You would have preferred that?"

"It would have smelled better."

Marcus, Xander, and Eric all laughed, but Nate dropped his eyes to the table, burning with shame. He looked up when a hand lightly cuffed him on the shoulder.

"Hey, don't worry about it," Marcus said as he settled back into his seat. "I've seen plenty worse, and we all started off bad when we left Solkyria." He pointed the remaining bit of his biscuit at Nate. "You got an anchor to keep the Skill sickness off you?"

Nate nodded.

"Good," Marcus said, "and with you all as my witnesses, I am *not* cleaning it up the next time someone leaves Solkyria without an anchor, I don't care how much I've pissed off the quartermaster."

"You think Dax would let you avoid it?" Eric asked.

"He'd have to," Marcus said earnestly, "because gods above give me speed, I will throw myself in the bilge and make him drag me out himself."

Dinner passed in that way, with Marcus teasing and being teased by Eric and Xander with equal good humor. Marcus was broader and blunter than his fellow Darkbend, squared where Eric was elegantly honed, but he had a rich, musical voice and an easy laugh, and he moved with more grace than Nate would have expected for someone with his build. He surprised Nate further when someone stopped to clap a hand over his shoulder and ask him if he would play a bit that night, with the weather being so fine. Marcus agreed, and he disappeared into the depths of the ship while Eric and Xander brought Nate topside along with several others. When Marcus returned, he had a fiddle in his hands, and the gathered crew cheered as he took up a dramatic pose near the mainmast, gave them all a haughty, overly dignified look, and then began to play a fast tune that had everyone clapping and stamping their feet, Nate included. Some took up the melody and sang a raunchy song to go with it. A few people locked arms and swung around in a dance, and Nate and Xander both laughed as Eric found increasingly creative ways to dodge Liliana's unsubtle attempts to bump into him. The fun lasted until the sun sank below the horizon and those not on watch duty retired for the night.

Nate could not remember the last time he had felt so genuinely happy.

IT DID NOT LAST.

As he settled into the ship's routines, Nate became aware of a tension across the crew. It rose up in the ways some of the pirates received their morning and evening rations, as though they did not quite believe that this was the best they could do. They'd go on to their assigned duties with dark expressions and bitter mutterings, and then bleed off their idle hours by staring out at the horizon, hungry for something that was not there. Nate suspected that more than the poor food was on their minds.

While nearly everyone found something to complain about in the biscuits and hardtack—Marcus being the only real exception, as he attacked each meal with gusto—most found reason to laugh about it, and their moods were further lightened by the promise of a place called Spider's Nest, which was the *Southern Echo*'s next heading. Nearly everyone was eager to make landfall, and Nate's curiosity flared as he listened to the crew's plans and eager daydreams.

Xander warned him not to get his hopes up too high.

"Everything on Spider's Nest comes with a price," the Grayvoice told him as Nate finished up one of his deck swabbing rotations. "You can find a good time no matter which way you turn, but whether you can afford it or not is another matter."

"And sadly," Eric added, "our pockets are a bit light this time."

"So what will you do, then?" Nate asked as he tipped the dregs of the bucket over the side of the ship. He leaned against the railing and took a deep, savoring breath of the clean sea air, happy to spend the next few hours lounging on the main deck under the sun with Marcus, Eric, and Xander. The days were growing considerably warmer the further they sailed from Solkyria, and Nate savored each and every moment he spent topside with the wind in his hair and the sun on his back. He was also surprised by how much he enjoyed spending time with the other Skilled. They were an easy going three, and while Nate never let himself fully relax and took care to hide his gold ring from Xander, he liked listening to the stories from their lives at sea and laughing along with them.

"We'll make our own fun if we have to," Eric said. His face was turned up to the sky, eyes shut against the bright sunlight but clearly enjoying the day every bit as much as Nate was. His white tattoo was soft in the light, looking far more elegant than the rest of the group's Skill marks, including the other Darkbend's.

"If we're smart about it, we could probably visit Madame Silverdale's," Marcus suggested.

Eric frowned and cracked open one eye to peer at the other light bender. "After last time, we are far from Madame Silverdale's favorites. You in particular."

Marcus shrugged. "I really did think it was a copper mark that I gave her."

"And the fact that it had holes in it and was still attached to some thread clearly told *her* that you were trying to pay with a button ripped from your coat," Xander said. "And now we have to pay upfront before we can even step inside the house."

"At least she'll let us in," Marcus said. "I hear she won't even let Novachak on the street in front of the porch."

"Actually," the boatswain said, passing by their group at exactly the wrong moment, "she'd love for me to visit her again, so she can separate my vital organs from the rest of me." He paused to examine the damp deck that Nate had finished swabbing, and gave him a satisfied nod before turning to the stout Darkbend. "Believe me, you don't want to get on the wrong side of Madame Silverdale."

Marcus offered Novachak a lopsided grin. "How'd you manage to do that again?"

"That's none of your concern," the boatswain said haughtily.

"Come on, I think we've earned the story by now."

"You absolutely have not," Novachak said, "and with the way you lot laze about, you can be certain you never will."

Xander waved a dismissive hand. "We're all done with our duties," he said. "And I've shifted that sail so many times, there isn't a scrap of wind left that I haven't touched." He kicked at the deck, leaving a faint scuff mark with his boot. "Gods below take this creaking tub and give me a faster ship."

"Don't let the captain hear you say that or she'll keelhaul you," Novachak warned. His tone and his frown were more serious now, enough to make Nate shift uneasily at the growing tension. "And you've been with us long enough to know how fine a ship the

Southern Echo is, Xander. She'll get us to Spider's Nest soon enough."

"We could get there even faster if someone would deign to use his magic," someone grumbled.

Nate turned to see a stocky, bespectacled pirate from the gun crew staring at him. He recognized the man from the duel between Arani and Ed the bear man. He'd been against the wall with Nate, too distracted back then to pay much attention to a stranger beside him. The bespectacled gunner didn't look like he recognized him now, even with his eyes riveted on Nate's Lowwind tattoo.

"Is everyone frost-touched today?" the boatswain growled. "We'll be there before the sun's overhead tomorrow. You can wait that long to go make fools of yourselves in Spider's streets."

"Aye," the stocky gunner said, still staring at Nate, "but we could have been there yesterday if the wind worker would just—"

"Shove off it, Jim," Xander cut in with a snarl.

The gunner passed his eyes over the Grayvoice as though looking at a particularly unpleasant rat. "And what are you gonna do, Sheep Lips? Bleat at me?"

Xander went very still, and Marcus and Eric both tensed, their attention locked on the Grayvoice. Nate wasn't certain if they intended to stop Xander should he spring forward, or follow him into battle. Nate didn't know what he'd do in that situation either, but with each moment that he spent in Jim the gunner's company, he found his preferences leaning more and more towards the fight.

"Enough, both of you," Novachak growled before anyone could move. "Unless you *want* half rations on our next voyage?"

Jim and Xander glowered at each other, but neither said a word.

"Good," Novachak grunted. "Jim, go check the cannons and make sure they're secure, and then do it again, twice more. Gun deck *and* topside guns. I want full reports after each pass. Xander..." he cast about for a moment, shaking his head, "go take over Liliana's duties for the rest of the day. She at least won't pick a fight in her off time."

Xander's breath hissed out between his teeth, but he stalked off to do as he was told. Jim the gunner gave Nate one final accusatory glare before doing the same. Nate swallowed past the dry lump in his throat, and knew that this was not the last he would hear of his nonexistent wind working.

It would be so much easier if he could simply tell everyone the truth, but perhaps it was for the best that Arani had insisted on secrecy. The less Jim and every other pirate like him thought of Nate, the better, and revealing that he supposedly had some special tracking Skill was bound to attract their attention. Still, the urge to prove himself began to simmer in Nate's gut. He wasn't sure he had the patience to wait, as Arani had told him to do.

A heavy sigh from Novachak disrupted his thoughts. The boatswain gave Nate and the two Darkbends a tired look. "Just stay out of trouble until we reach the Nest, all right? I really don't think it's too much to ask." He sounded almost pleading then.

"Aye, sir," Eric said, clearly taking pity on the man.

Marcus and Nate echoed his words a moment later, and the boatswain lumbered off, muttering something about a northern custom of feeding troublemakers to ice bears.

The afternoon felt spoiled for Nate after that, and he went below to get out of the wind, saying that he wasn't feeling all that well. Marcus looked alarmed, but Eric elbowed him in the ribs, and the Darkbends followed him without comment. They passed some time playing Liar's Farm with a deck of cards Eric procured from his possessions, betting nothing but imagined riches as they tried to outwit each other.

At the end of the second round—both of which Eric had won handily—Nate gave voice to a thought that had been bothering him since the altercation with Jim.

"What animal can Xander speak to?" he asked quietly.

The Darkbends paused and exchanged a look over the tops of their cards.

"He won't tell us," Marcus said.

"Or rather," Eric corrected, "he *will*, but it changes every time. Suffice to say, we have no idea, and he likes it that way."

"But it's not sheep?" Nate asked as he gathered the five cards Eric had dealt him for the new round. Two chickens, a silver-winged falcon, a gryphon, and a leviathan sea serpent stared back at him. A good hand, if neither Marcus nor Eric had drawn the deck's lone dragon.

"Not as far as we can tell," Eric said. "From what Xander's told us of the animal speaking academy, those that talk to sheep are the lowest of the Grayvoice lows. Jim Greenroot knows that, and he knows how Xander feels about being compared to them, too."

"Don't know why he won't just tell us what animal he can speak to," Marcus added. "It can't be much worse than sheep, and would stop the whole thing with Jim."

"Sometimes I think Xander likes having the excuse to be angry," Eric put in mildly. "But I also think it's his way of spiting anyone who would dare to ask him to use his Skill." He considered his cards thoughtfully before selecting one from his hand and placing it face-down on the table. "At the end of the day, it's his choice, and he chooses to keep everyone guessing. This is a dog, by the way." He slid the card forward.

"Liar," Marcus said before Eric had lifted his fingers from the back of the card.

Eric gave him a flat look before flipping the card to reveal a barking dog. "Gods below, you never learn, do you?"

"You lied on your first turn last time!"

"And now we're playing a new hand and you've just lost a turn. You're up, Nate."

Nate silently considered his cards, wondering how Xander and the others would react if they learned that Nate was keeping secrets about his own Skill. He doubted that any of them would like the part where he planned to take those secrets back to Solkyria.

THE NEXT DAY, NATE was off the chore rotation and faced with an abundance of free time while Marcus, Eric, and Xander saw to their own duties. He was surprised by how much he missed their company. They weren't his friends, exactly, and they couldn't be, given his plans, but they were easy to talk to and even the lulls in their conversations felt companionable. Now that he was alone, Nate found the day passing agonizingly slowly. He spent a good part of the morning seated in the galley, examining the cards Eric had lent him after he'd managed to win two rounds of Liar's Farm. Eric had won the other five, but he was eager to find a better opponent in Nate than Marcus could provide, and so Nate flipped through the deck, studying the painted animals and idly thinking about strategies for the game. He lingered over the silver-winged falcon that had given him his first victory when he'd claimed it was the dragon on the second-to-last round of the hand, and neither Darkbend had been willing to argue otherwise. The bird was shown flying high in a cloud-studded sky, mouth open in a delighted cry. Nate tried to imagine what it would feel like to be able to ride the wind like that, but that demanded far more control over the element than he had ever possessed.

I will get there, he promised himself. *With Arani's help or on my own if I must, I will work the wind.*

Nate gathered up the cards and went to return them to Eric's pack down in the berth. He had just buttoned the satchel closed when he heard voices drift in from the gun deck, just on the other side of the thin bulkhead.

"—brought aboard *another* Skilled brat to feed and lounge about while the rest of us break our backs doing work they could finish in a minute."

That was Jim Greenroot, the clean-skinned, bespectacled gunner that Nate was finding more and more reasons to dislike by the minute.

"He's a Lowwind," a woman's voice said. AnnaMarie Blueshore, Nate thought, another one of the clean-skinned Solkyrian gunners. "What backbreaking labor do you do that a *wind worker* could help with?"

Jim sputtered for a moment. "That's not the point!" he finally spat. "He could have us moving twice as fast, but he won't do it! And Arani will let him sit back and play with sailcloth instead of pushing up our speed."

AnnaMarie sighed. "Arani has a soft spot for the Skilled. We've always known that. If that boy doesn't want to bend the wind, there's nothing we can do about it."

"But he's a *wind* worker," Jim pressed. "What's a few hours' of magic to him if it means we make landfall a full day sooner? Unless you *like* foul water and weevil-infested food."

AnnaMarie made a displeased noise before saying, "How come you never get this way over the Goodtide?"

"Because at least *she* makes herself useful! Not like those other Skilled brats..."

Nate winced, caught on Jim's words like so many barbs. The man's voice faded away as he and AnnaMarie walked off, but the words stayed with Nate for a long while, and they would not be shaken off.

She makes herself useful.

He could only think of one way a Goodtide could be useful on a sailing ship.

After a few minutes, Nate crept to the gun deck, trying to keep his steps soft against the creaking wood. While he was never far from someone while aboard the *Southern Echo*, the gun deck was empty for the time being, and all was quiet with the cannons lashed down and away from the gun ports. Nate stepped past one of the cold, heavy weapons, eyeing the blocks wedged into the wheels that kept it from rolling. The blocks were holding and the seas were calm, so there was no risk of the cannon breaking loose and crushing him, but Nate still hesitated uneasily before kneeling in front of the gun port and easing the hatch open, letting the wind rush freely into the ship. It lifted his hair and pressed his shirt flat against his chest, and Nate allowed himself to savor a few slow breaths of the salty air.

Then he pushed up his sleeves, braced himself on his knees against the gentle swaying of the ship, and reached for the wind.

It was the first time he'd tried to use his Skill on the open sea, and away from Solkyria. The wind was stronger than he was used to, purer, and he could sense the raw potential in the element as it danced around his fingertips. It felt strange at first, as though he'd fallen out of synch with his own body, but a soothing feeling radiated out from the ring on his right hand, and he quickly found his rhythm again. He extended his hands as he'd been taught and tried to tangle his will with the wind, to push it in a new direction. It ignored him and went right on blowing as it saw fit.

Nate felt the familiar frustration bloom beneath his ribs, but he made himself take a deep breath and try again, thinking about what might be useful for a tracker. He reached further, concentrated harder, and tried to pull the wind towards him. His awareness flared with the power of the element, and he imagined he could see the pattern of the winds sweeping out from the ship and over the water. He crooked his fingers, bore down with all his mental strength, reached for the wind—

And felt it slip away from him as easily as it always had.

Nate grunted and tried again, and again, and again, but he never once came close to working the wind into a new shape. And with the sea empty all around the *Southern Echo*, Nate had no idea how to begin training himself as a tracker. What was worse, his magic let him sense everything that he *could* do with the wind if he caught just the tiniest scrap of it, if he reached a little further. He would not give up, though. He gathered himself to try again.

"What are you doing?" a soft voice asked from behind him.

Nate jolted as though he'd been struck by lightning, slamming his head against the lip of the cannon as he shot to his feet. The pain and surprise caused him to slip and go crashing back to the deck, spawning a fresh bout of pain in his rear as his hand tangled in the thin ropes that held the gun port open. The ropes came loose and the hatch thudded shut, cutting off the outside wind and making Nate's hiss all the more audible. His head and his tailbone smarting, he looked up to see Rori Goodtide standing next to the cannon, watching him with her brows arched in surprise.

"That looked painful," she remarked after a moment.

Nate groaned and pushed himself to his feet, not bothering to respond. It seemed that startling Nate and causing unnecessary pain was a trait the Goodtide shared with her pet bird, which was conspicuously absent for the moment. Nate half expected Rori to reach over and try to grab his hat since Luken wasn't there to do it himself, but she only took a step back, clearing the way for Nate to move away from the wall. She looked from him to the gun port and back again, and tapped her fingers against the thick spine of the small book in her hands.

"What were you doing?" she asked again, a little less gently this time.

Nate rubbed the sore spot on the back of his head. "Trying to be useful," he muttered.

Rori cut her eyes to the gun port once more, then glanced around to make sure they were in no danger of being overheard. A few footfalls sounded overhead, and Nate heard pirates calling to one another on the upper decks, but the gun deck only held the two of them.

"You shouldn't do that," she said softly. "Just leave it be."

She turned to leave, but Nate heard Jim's words in his head again.

She makes herself useful.

"I thought you didn't use your Skill," Nate said.

Rori stopped and frowned at him. "Excuse me?"

"I heard Jim Greenroot say you use your Skill to make yourself useful."

The Goodtide stared at him for several moments before her expression clouded. "No one here forces me to use my Skill," she said.

"But you use it voluntarily?"

"No!" Rori snarled with far more intensity than Nate expected, sending him an inadvertent step back. She swallowed hard and visibly struggled to control herself. "I don't use my Skill anymore. I never will."

It was Nate's turn to frown. "Never?" he asked.

"That's what I said," she growled.

"But you're a Goodtide," he pressed. "How else do you make yourself useful?"

"Do you think that magic is the only way to do that?" Rori looked at him as though he had sprouted a second head. "I'm the *navigator*," she said, each word slow and deliberate. "I read maps and keep us on a proper course." She turned away and started for the berth. "I don't use my Skill. You shouldn't either."

Nate followed her. "Why not?" he pressed. She did not answer, but he recalled something as he watched her put away the book in a small sea chest beneath her assigned hammock. "And why did you tell me to be careful, that night on the beach when Arani asked me to track your bird?"

Rori's frown deepened as she closed the sea chest. She straightened up and faced Nate squarely, her hands on her hips. "Because the captain is going to want to use your Skill so badly, it may burn right through you."

Nate blinked at her. "And you don't like that?"

Rori pressed her lips into a thin line. "I think you should have the chance to figure out what *you* want before you throw your life away on your Skill." She moved to pass him, heading back towards the gun deck and the stairs that would take her topside.

"What if using my Skill is what I want?" Nate asked before she'd gone too far.

The Goodtide halted. "Is it?" she asked without turning around.

"It's all I've ever wanted," Nate said with complete and total honesty.

Rori did not move.

"I don't know why you don't want to use your Skill," Nate said as he stepped up beside her. "If I had a high Skill like yours, I'd use it all the time."

"You'd use it as much as they told you to use it," the Goodtide snarled, "and not a moment more."

The intensity of her rekindled anger pushed Nate a step away. He blinked at Rori, surprised and at a loss for words. A taut silence stretched between them.

Rori broke it with a sigh. She visibly gathered herself before turning to him, calm and collected once more. "You have the chance to make a new life for yourself," she said, spreading her hands a little to gesture at the surrounding ship before pointing at his Lowwind mark. "You can be something other than what that tattoo says you need to be. That's what all of us Skilled have done, here on the *Southern Echo*. Dax Malatide is quartermaster. Xander Grayvoice is one of the lead riggers. Eric Darkbend is apprenticed to the carpenter. Marcus... is Marcus, but he lives his life to the fullest."

"And you're the navigator," Nate said softly.

"Aye," Rori said. He might have imagined it, but he thought that a hopeful gleam had come into her eye. She opened her mouth to say something else, but Nate suddenly realized with a rush that it should not have been possible for a Goodtide, for *any* Skilled, to be a navigator.

"How are you a navigator?" Nate asked abruptly. "They don't teach writing or reading at the imperial academies."

The question surprised Rori, and she glanced away, suddenly no longer able to meet his eye. "They do at the citizen schools," she murmured. "I didn't go to the tide working academy until I was thirteen."

So many questions rose up in Nate's mind, but the Goodtide shook herself and moved away before he could ask any of them.

"If you don't mind," she said with clipped efficiency, "I still have a lot of work to do." She practically ran for the stairs that would take her back to the main deck.

"I'm sorry!" Nate called after her. He wasn't certain what exactly he'd done, but he knew that he had hit a painful nerve, and in spite of the friction between them, he did not like the heavy sadness on Rori's face.

She paused halfway up the stairs. She glanced at him once more, working something through in her mind. "Jim, was it?" she suddenly asked. "The one who said some nonsense about being useful?"

Nate nodded.

Rori ducked down and kept herself low as she went up the next few steps. She stopped just below the level of the main deck, her face turned skyward. Curious, Nate moved closer as she began to move her hands in the signals she used to command her bird from afar. When Nate joined her on the stairs, he saw a flash of Luken's brilliant blue wings in the sky overhead. Rori told Nate to stay low. He followed her example, keeping his body below the level of the main deck, and watched with her as Luken flapped higher up into the rigging. Nate lost sight of him among the sails, and he gave Rori a quizzical look. She held up a finger to tell him to wait, and less than a minute later, a yelp of disgusted anger came from the middle of the ship.

Nate turned to see Jim kneeling with AnnaMarie next to one of the cannons, a large splotch of fresh white goo adorning his shoulder. Jim was shaking his fist up at the rigging, and then he shifted the gesture to AnnaMarie when she burst out laughing. Luken was perched contentedly on the ratlines overhead, shaking out his tail feathers.

Rori gave a sly smile as she watched Jim jump to his feet and attempt to wrestle his shirt off without smearing the bird excrement against his skin. "You know, some people consider that good luck," she remarked offhandedly.

Nate was too stunned to do more than just stare at her, but he felt a grin shaping itself at the corners of his mouth as he watched Rori smile.

The spell broke when a shout of "Land ho!" came from the crow's nest, and then there was an excited press towards the bow as the crew strained for their first glimpse of land in over a week.

"Spider's Nest," Rori said, straightening and moving up the last few stairs. "Watch your pockets and your back out there, new blood."

CHAPTER NINE

Bargains and Betting Men

IRIS HAD NO SPECIAL fondness for Spider's Nest. On a good day, she was indifferent to its carnal offerings and the smell of its port town. On a bad day, she detested the place almost as much as the man who ran it.

This was an unusual day. For the first time, Iris was eager to thrust her boots into the sand of the beaches and find Spider in his web.

Their arrival in port went as it normally did. The *Southern Echo* skimmed over the last stretch of open water before cruising easily into the harbor, the ship's shallow draft letting them cut over the jagged coral mazes that kept the bigger ships anchored well away from the beach. They steered into a clear spot a little ways from shore, where the waves rolled gently and their caps did not break. Their closest neighbors were the *Red Siren* and the *Gryphon*, both anchored far enough away that Iris could not make out the faces of the few men and women on their decks. She hailed them anyway and was given a polite salute in return.

When the *Southern Echo*'s anchor dropped into the clear blue water of the harbor, the crew raced to get the rowboats ready. They were so excited to go ashore that Dax barely had to give directions of any sort, and the first boat was ready within minutes. Iris threaded her way across the crowded deck, jostling familiarly with the crew as they argued over who would get a spot in the second boat. The first one was reserved for the captain's shore party, and whichever unlucky few had drawn badly in the lots and found themselves on rowing duty.

Nikolai Novachak was already waiting in the boat by the time Iris got to the starboard railing. She made to step up and into the suspended rowboat, but paused when her gaze caught on the newest member of their crew.

The boy's attention was riveted on the island, his eyes roving over the shoreline and devouring every detail. There was an eager glow about him, the kind that promised more trouble than was wise. He stood near the bow with Xander Grayvoice, Eric Darkbend, and Marcus Darkbend, trading excited whispers and laughing. Not far from their group, Rori Goodtide leaned against the foremast, idly petting Luken on her shoulder, but her gaze was fixed on Nate. She wasn't smiling, but there was an intensity there that also promised more trouble than was wise.

Iris pressed her lips into a grim line. The secret of Nate's Skill was still guarded and safe, but Iris knew that Rori would have strong opinions about him using that Skill, and Xander was the sort who, once he caught a whiff of something hidden, would scratch and dig and needle until he found the truth. She wasn't surprised that Nate had gravitated to the company of the other Skilled in the crew, but she did wish that there had been other options for him. The Darkbends were fine, if a bit on the mischievous side, but Xander's usually harmless yet insatiable curiosity was dangerous in a place like Spider's Nest where exposed secrets spread like wildfire.

What was worse, Nate's blue Skill tattoo would catch attention. Spider's Nest was meant to be a haven for all of pirate kind, including the Skilled, but someone less than honorable might try to snatch a wind worker for their ship. They would be in for a nasty surprise once they learned what Iris had, that Nate could not actually turn the winds, but that was something she wanted to avoid for several reasons. If Nate stayed with his friends or one of the officers while he was on the island, he'd likely be all right, but if he went off alone, he'd be a target. He wasn't ready to fend for himself yet.

With that thought in mind, Iris turned and sought out Dax's steady presence. The quartermaster stood at the stern of the ship, well away from the press of bodies fighting for the chance to go ashore. Their eyes locked, and Iris tilted her head towards Nate. Traditionally, a quartermaster would have gone ashore with the captain while the boatswain stayed behind to get the rest of the crew in order, but Dax's Skill often left him overwhelmed in large crowds, and while she knew he would have preferred to remain on the ship, Iris needed Dax to watch Nate and make sure the boy did not get into too much trouble, either of his own making or of any of the many varieties Spider's Nest offered. Dax followed Iris's gaze to the boy, then nodded solemnly to her. He knew what she was asking, and would follow Nate ashore.

Satisfied for the moment, Iris stepped into the rowboat. She felt that sudden chill and shudder that always settled over her whenever she left the warm, steady cradle of the dryad-infused ship, but it lasted only a moment, and then she was seated in the rowboat and moving ever closer to the greatest treasure hunt any of them would ever see.

Iris watched the faces of her crew slide above her as the rowboat was lowered into the water. Most were smiling and laughing with their neighbors, already picking out the places they would visit first on Spider's

Nest, but there was a hard edge to their excitement. They needed this, Iris knew, after that dreadful end to their last hunt, but if it were up to her, Iris would give them a day ashore at most, morale be damned. Once they understood what she meant to hunt, many of them would gladly trade a little time spent drinking and throwing money to games and the pleasure house for their next voyage across the sea, and she might even convince Novachak to hurry the negotiations of their supply restocking. But even if Iris was fully willing to risk her captainship over cutting the crew's leave short, she couldn't.

Not until she'd gotten a vital piece of information from Spider.

Idly, Iris ran her thumb along the chain around her neck. She stopped short of pulling the black scale pendant free from her shirt, knowing that the crew wasn't ready for that secret just yet, but she thought about Nate's Skill and excitement bubbled in her chest despite Dax's warnings. Iris adjusted the chain to ensure that the black scale was still hidden by her clothing, and caught Novachak watching her with an inscrutable expression. She gave him a sly smile in return, and the big man shrugged and turned to stare at the approaching shore.

Iris knew that she had never fully convinced Novachak that Captain Mordanti had truly sailed the seas all those years ago. While growing up in the Frozen North had given Novachak a more flexible outlook on what was history and what was nothing more than wild stories, the boatswain harbored his own doubts about Mordanti. But he'd believed Iris's own story when she'd shown him the scale she wore. Iris knew that Novachak would vote with her when the time came. That was all she needed for now.

By the time the rowboat approached the shore, Iris was impatient enough to jump over the side while the waves were still at her knees. Her high-topped boots protected her legs, but her coat began to drag against her shoulders as it soaked up water. A harsh pain radiated out from her injured arm, and she grit her teeth against it. She'd avoided infection, thank the gods above, but the wound from the bullet graze still caused her a good amount of pain if she moved the wrong way. She saw that Novachak and the two men on the oars were watching her, and she forced herself to take a deep breath before straightening her back and placing her good arm against the nose of the rowboat. Novachak splashed his way over to join her, and together they pushed the rowboat back until it was clear of the sand. The oarsmen gave a grateful salute before fighting against the waves and returning to the *Southern Echo*. By then, the second rowboat was already in the water and starting for the shore, crowded with more bodies than Iris had thought possible.

Novachak snorted beside her. "A copper mark says at least one of them ends up in the water before they get halfway to the beach. A second mark says the boat doesn't stop to pick them up."

"We're not even out of the water yet and you're already breaking the code?"

"Code says I can wager a mark or two while my boots are on land. This sand may be underwater, but it counts."

Iris gave him a dry smile. "And the day you wager only two marks is the day I eat my hat."

"Does that mean you take the bet?" Novachak asked, and he was serious.

She shook her head and turned to the beach. "You can gamble away what's left of your savings later. We have work to do."

Novachak reluctantly followed Iris as she sloshed her way out of the surf.

At this time of day, the beach was crowded with men and women trudging between the makeshift stalls that lined the sand, and the air was full of voices and laughter and curses as pirates bartered and gambled their way to new provisions. In bad weather, these tents and wooden huts would be packed away, the tools rushed into the town's storehouses for safe keeping. In good weather, with the sun shining down and warming the sand and everyone's moods, the beach was bursting with vendors. Iris and Novachak passed a clothing trader with a spread of old but clean and well-mended shirts, a roasting pit with a full boar spitted over a fire, and a metalsmith sharing tools and an anvil with a sword-smith.

Novachak turned a keen eye on the wares as they walked, and Iris practically heard him running calculations in his head as he weighed what the ship had in its stores against the goods on offer and what kind of prices he and Dax had agreed to expect from Spider. Iris did not think that the boatswain would like the numbers he ended up with, and she was in no mood to be reminded of the ship's sparse supplies. She lengthened her strides and led Novachak quickly over the beach, bringing them to the wide dirt path that would take them into Spider's Nest proper.

It wasn't much of a town, as far as the Solkyrian Empire's standards went, but for a little fleck of rebellion against imperial law hidden in the southern tip of the Coral Chain, the place served. While most of the independent traders set up along the beach, Spider had made the town for himself. A couple of squat, ugly buildings with heavy locks and stone-faced guards that patrolled at all hours served as his storehouses for supplies and valuables both. Spider's tavern rented out rooms with fairly clean beds to those who could afford to object to sleeping on their ships or passing out on the beach after a night of hard drinking, and that same tavern supplied the liquor needed for said drinking, along with what passed for a good meal if the meat was not inspected too closely. Across from the tavern stood the pleasure house, which charged a pretty coin but catered to the tastes of nearly every pirate who came to the island. Spider made sure of that. He knew how much money he could squeeze out of his fellow outlaws, and as long as they had full bellies and a willing companion for the night, very few pirates ever begrudged him his earnings.

Spider was shrewd, careful, and knew better than to slip under the influence of his island's vices. Iris had never seen a drop of liquor pass his lips, but that did not mean he spent every moment of sunlight hunched over a desk, making numbers dance and twist to his whims. Often, he could be found out among the crowds, encouraging their revelry even as he sipped black tea and absorbed every detail and secret that came to his shores. If he was ever to let himself be distracted, it would be by the piano at the pleasure house, and even that was a calculated indulgence.

As Iris and Novachak approached the tiny town, music spilled out of the open door of the pleasure house, accompanied by cheers and the rough voices of men and women singing along. Though she could not make out the words from the road, she heard one man's deep baritone holding the lead of the song, and the raucous laughter that followed every other line. That was Spider, then, working the crowds alongside Madame Silverdale.

Iris glanced at Novachak, who was scanning the front porch of the pleasure house. A few men and women lounged against the wooden railing, smiling at passing people and waving to entice them inside. Novachak's gaze flicked over all of them before moving up to the upper levels of the pleasure house. He looked uncharacteristically nervous.

"Really?" Iris asked. "Still?"

He shifted uncomfortably and hunched his shoulders.

"I'm sure the Madame has forgiven you by now," Iris said.

Novachak frantically shook his head. "You don't make a woman like her that angry and walk away without a visible scar."

Iris chuckled darkly. "You can't say it was entirely undeserved."

"Aye," the boatswain agreed, "but I got off the island before she had the chance to give me that scar. That's how I know she's still mad."

"And now you'd like to wait out here while I go extract Spider from his admirers?"

"May the frozen goddess bless you, Captain."

Iris rolled her eyes and set off for the pleasure house. One of the male companions tried to catch her eye as she ascended the wooden steps, but she waved him off and stepped inside alone.

It was dim inside the pleasure house, with gauzy curtains drawn to soften the light and enhance the allure of the workers. The still air was loaded with perfume, but that could not disguise the underlying smells of sweat and lust that pervaded the building. Upstairs, windows could be opened in the many bedrooms to coax cooling breezes inside, but down here in the parlor, the heat was driven directly into the soul, heightening the desire to down a drink before shedding clothing. The tactic did not work on everyone, but Madame Silverdale saw enough business to justify driving away the odd customer or two. Especially when the regulars loved coming back.

Companions slunk through the dimness, engaging patrons with artful smiles and invitations. A shyer patron might spend their first few visits in the parlor, chatting with the workers and being put at ease before allowing themselves to be led upstairs. An eager and braver customer could walk in, say aloud exactly what they wanted, and head upstairs with a willing companion within a minute, if there wasn't a wait ahead of them.

Iris, for her part, waited by the door, where the air was a little fresher and cooler and she could observe the room without anyone slipping outside under her notice. Not that she needed to spend much time looking. As she'd expected, Spider was at the piano in the corner, surrounded by a small crowd of patrons and workers alike, all laughing and singing along as his fingers flew over the keys. But abruptly, Spider launched into a heavier rhythm, and he began to sing in a steady, serious voice:

Bring forth the sun throne's golden way
Arise brave souls and strike away—

That was as far as he got before jeers from the crowd drowned out the next line.

"Oh, we don't like that one?" Spider shouted over their enthusiastic protests. "All right, what if I made a few changes?"

More jeers answered him, but they shifted to applause as the piano notes took on an upbeat, staccato tempo, and the Solkyrian anthem metamorphosed under Spider's creative license. The changed song filled the pleasure house, and Iris could not help but smile a little as she leaned against the wall and listened.

Come forth, my pirates, to the golden way
New adventures I'll grant you every day

The sun throne fears your deadly arts
Hel-lo I say to your black hearts

'Cross my island pleasure rings
Here I make you queens and kings

To mighty Spider's Nest you sail
By flag and blade and gun
Fine rum and pleasure to those who'll pay
With each new prize that's won

A good-natured groan went up from the crowd, followed by more laughter and encouraging calls for Spider to continue. Iris made to step forward before he could launch into the next verse and further remind everyone to spend their money on his island.

"Lovely to see you again, Captain Arani," a silken voice cut in before she'd taken more than a single step.

Iris turned to see that Madame Silverdale had swept up beside her, silent as a cat. She wore a low-cut dress of deep blue that matched the striking, oceanic color of her eyes, an odd hue that teased a non-Solkyrian ancestor somewhere in her lineage. Her dark hair was curled into an elaborate pile atop her head, held in place by several pins tipped with glass. Had they stood within the parlor proper, away from the light spilling in from the door, the lines at the corners of Madame Silverdale's eyes and mouth would have been smoothed away, leaving her seeming as young and striking as she'd been when she first came to Spider's Nest nearly fifteen years ago. In this light, the age lines were a badge of her experiences and the knowledge she'd gained in her time as a madame, and they added a sharp edge to her shrewd smile.

"What is the business of your pleasure?" Madame Silverdale asked, keeping her voice smooth despite the calculating look in her eyes.

"No time for pleasures today, I'm afraid," Iris said, keeping her own tone nonchalant. "I've business with the man currently abusing your poor piano."

The madame gave an airy laugh, but her gaze did not soften. "You might come back later, once he's drawn in a few more customers for me. Business is hard these days."

Iris kept her eyes on the madame and said nothing, but her voice itched to point out that there was already a crowd of patrons in the parlor, and more would be spilling in from the beach as the sun went down and wishful thoughts turned to warm places and warmer bodies.

"Speaking of which," the madame continued, "I am expecting Mr. Novachak to pay me a visit." Her gaze flicked out the door and scanned the road outside, but Iris expected Novachak to have had the good sense to hide. Madame Silverdale came to the same conclusion. She pursed her painted lips and made a disappointed sound. "If you would be so kind, Captain, do tell Nikolai that it's rude to keep a lady waiting, especially after what he did."

Iris sighed and withdrew a silver mark from her pocket. She offered the coin to the madame along with a smile that was not quite friendly. "For his troubles, Madame."

Silverdale lifted the coin and turned it so that the face of the Solkyrian emperor flashed in the light. "I suppose I could be patient for a little while longer," she mused. Then she did something with her hands that made the money vanish from sight, despite her dress having no pockets in any visibly accessible places. "But one silver mark does not begin to cover his troubles," she said, her voice taking on an icy edge. "He has a debt, and I expect his repayment in full."

"As is your right," Iris said. She thumbed the pommel of the saber belted at her hip and did not look away from the madame's deep gaze.

Silverdale held Iris's stare for a moment longer, then gave a dismissive wave of her delicate hand. "My regards to that handsome quartermaster of yours. Fair winds, Captain Arani." She turned and slipped deeper into the parlor without a backwards glance.

Iris let out a hard breath, uncertain which angered her more: Novachak's past foolishness landing him in trouble with the madame, or the idea that, somehow, Madame Silverdale had met Daxton Malatide and the encounter had warranted her remembering him. She wondered when that had happened.

In a considerably worse mood than when she had arrived, Iris turned her attention back to Spider. He had finished the marching song and was soliciting praise and requests from his audience. Perhaps sensing her glare, he suddenly swiveled around on the bench, and his gaze snagged on Iris lurking in the doorway. His smile did not waver but his head took on a knowing tilt, and he made a small gesture to her.

Iris took the cue and headed back outside.

She found Novachak across the road, crouching behind an empty mule cart waiting next to the tavern. He did not look the least bit ashamed as Iris stalked up to him.

"Well, you were right," she said as she came level with the boatswain. "She still hates you."

"Color me entirely unsurprised," Novachak growled.

He refused to stand, and only moved out from behind the cart once Spider had emerged from the pleasure house, strode over to them, exchanged a quick but pleasant greeting, and then led the way into the tavern.

At that time of day, patronage at the tavern was thin, with only a few scattered people taking up seats. Spider tossed greetings to them all, along with a warning to keep their boots off of the tables. A few curious glances followed Iris and Novachak as they went up the stairs after Spider, but they fell off quickly enough and the murmur of conversations returned.

Spider ushered Iris and Novachak into his office with a flourish, then shut the door snugly behind them. The sounds from downstairs cut off immediately, but the open windows let in a pleasant breeze and voices from the road. They were murmured snatches, though, and there was no real risk of them being overheard in Spider's office.

Novachak did not seem to agree. He gave the open windows a dark look, but a glance from Iris stilled his tongue. Together, they took their seats before the large, wooden desk, and faced down Spider.

He was almost a different man when he was behind his desk and not out charming the masses. Almost. If Iris had not known him better, she might have been surprised by the sudden chilliness in his demeanor, but everything Spider did was calibrated to turning the largest profit. This was no different.

"I hope you don't blame me for what happened on your hunt," he said, dropping all pretense of friendliness. "I had no way of knowing Prince Trystos's forces would be there."

"Now, you see, I find that fascinating," Iris said, lounging in her seat and throwing her good arm carelessly over the back. Spider's eyes did not so much as flicker to the sword or pistols at her hips, but Iris knew he saw them. "You knew that we had a run in with the brat's ships before I even had the chance to think of all the words I wanted to use to tell you that. A shame, really. That would have been one of my better deliveries. Damn near poetic in the rhythm of the profanity and my suggestions for all the places you could stick a sword."

Spider raised his hands in a placating gesture. "The *Southern Echo* wasn't the only ship I sent that way, nor was it the first one to limp back to my port. I know now that Prince Trystos is turning his focus to those waters, but I have plenty of whispers of fat merchant ships taking alternate routes. I won't send you there again."

"Provided we can afford the price of the next bit of information," Iris said.

Spider gave the slightest of shrugs. He did not offer so much as a scrap of an apologetic smile. "You know the risks when you go out. You buy the information, and you chase down your prize. Whether or not you succeed is up to you."

"And if we do, we come back here to sell our plunder safely, and you take a cut in exchange for that security," Iris returned.

"And if we don't," Novachak put in, "we still end up back here, scraping together enough to afford your next tip before another crew snaps it up."

Spider spread his hands over his desk, careful not to upset the stacks of papers or the massive ledger sitting open in front of him. "You're welcome to strike out on your own. I only offer a safe haven."

"And what's supposed to be reliable information on where to find unguarded merchant ships, not a roaming pack of imperial pirate hunters flying the brat's flag," Iris spat. "You failed to provide that."

Spider made a noncommittal noise, but his jaw was locked. He drummed his fingers on his desk as he weighed Iris's anger, and how far she'd be able to spread it across the island. His eyes narrowed, and Iris knew that he did not like the way the scales had balanced.

"Perhaps I could wave my fee for your next endeavor," he finally said.

"And reduce your charge for running the plunder through you," Iris added.

Spider's eyes narrowed, but he nodded in agreement. "Let's see what I have for you. I think we'll try for something a little smaller this time. The *Southern Echo* hasn't had the most successful of runs lately, even without Prince Trystos disrupting your efforts."

Iris stiffened. She knew that it was a calculated barb, and she saw the satisfaction in Spider's eyes as he took in her reaction. No good would come of her snapping back at him. They both knew that he was right, and Iris needed a successful hunt to keep her crew happy. She'd brought part of their agate cache to sell to Spider in order to pay her pirates this time, but it would not mollify them for long. For that, she needed to tempt them with something bigger. Something legendary.

Her thumb went to the chain around her neck again, and she thought about Nate tracking a bullet through the air, and a bird in a cove. He couldn't turn the wind, but he could follow those things, and Iris was more than willing to bet that he could do more. It was a risk, but as Novachak was so fond of saying, there were no great rewards without great risks. The boatswain may have used that bit of wisdom to justify his gambling habit, but if ever there was a time to agree with him, this was it.

She'd come to a decision by the time Spider was reaching for one of the papers on his desk. "As it happens," he said, "my sources have confirmed that a small merchant is on return from the Gemheart Islands. Not a grand prize, but the hold should be well-stocked with furs and provisions."

"I had something else in mind," Iris said.

Frowning, Spider rifled through another stack of papers. "I'm afraid that's the best I have for you, unless you want to take your chances against Trystos again."

"No," Iris said, "I aim to keep away from him."

"What, then, are you—?" Spider broke off when he looked up and saw that Iris had pulled up the chain around her neck, and was letting the black scale at the end sway in the breeze from the windows. His eyes widened, and then he shot to his feet and hurried to close the windows. When the final one was shut tight, he turned back to Iris and regarded her with fresh interest. "You've found a tracker," he said, and there was no room for doubt in his tone.

Iris ignored the sharp look Novachak was giving her as she slipped the chain back inside her shirt. The scale came to rest against her skin, warm and familiar. She leaned back in her seat again, met Spider's gaze, and nodded.

Scrubbing a hand over his face, Spider paced to the far wall and stared at the large map painted over the wood. The known islands were a cluster of whites, greens, and beiges, rendered in careful detail by the artist. All around them stretched wide, blue water, empty yet full of promises. Spider stared at that painted water for a long time before turning back to Iris.

"You're certain you have the right Skill?" he asked.

"He's rough," Iris said, "and green as they come, but he can already follow a short trail. Some proper training and he'll take us over the horizon."

Novachak shifted in his seat, but he did not speak. Iris kept her attention on Spider, who made a thoughtful noise before glancing once more at the empty blue stretches of the map.

"You could use some time, then, to let him get his feet under him," Spider mused. "If he's that untrained, I imagine a few weeks would be best, but the court will have moved by then."

"It would be best if we left sooner than later," Iris agreed. She winced inwardly at the idea of spending more time than was absolutely necessary on the Nest. They should be able to keep Nate safe from rivals looking to snatch a wind worker, but the idea of keeping his true Skill a secret for that long was exhausting on its own. And if it slipped out, someone was bound to start digging into Iris's intentions. As much as she burned to prove Mordanti's legend was true, Iris was not ready to share that legacy with others just yet. "How long will the court remain in its current location?" she asked.

Spider considered the map for a long moment. "You'll need to leave within a week at the latest," he said. "With the seasons changing, they'll be getting ready to begin their matings on top of their usual migrations, and you do *not* want to be in their waters when that happens."

"Could we wait for that to end before we visit them?" Novachak asked, and Iris caught the note of bleak desperation in his voice.

"From what my scouts have reported, siren mating rituals tend to last until spring," Spider said. "They're... dedicated."

Iris glanced at Novachak, who gave her a resigned look and nodded for her to go ahead. She resolved to scrape together a gold mark to give to Madame Silverdale on his behalf.

To Spider, Iris said, "We could be ready to sail before sundown tomorrow. The crew won't like their time on the island being so short, but they'll forgive me once they learn what we're seeking, and when they understand what our newest Skilled member can do. And we can train the boy en route." As she spoke, Iris felt her excitement growing. After so many years, everything was finally coming together, and her heart thrilled at the realization that soon, very soon, she would be sailing the same waters as Ava Mordanti, exploring the same wonders and chasing the same legends.

Histories, Iris corrected herself. *Veritian histories that Solkyria could not erase.*

Her smile was genuine as she focused back on Spider. "All we need is the court's location, and then we can restock and be on our way." She paused for a few pointed seconds. "This is when you give me that heading, in case that wasn't clear."

Spider looked at the map again, and a small knot of tension came into his shoulders.

Iris sat up straighter. "You *have* been tracking the exact locations of the court?"

A long moment passed before Spider spoke again. "Honestly, Captain, I had my doubts that you would ever find your tracker, and there were more profitable things out there to keep my eye on."

Iris was on her feet and stalking towards Spider with her sword drawn before he'd finished speaking. "We had an agreement," she growled. "And I've been paying you to hold up your end for *years.*" The tip of her saber swayed towards his heart.

Spider pressed his back against the map and held up his hands, but to Iris's irritation, he did not look the least bit terrified.

"Calm down," he said, "I was the one who suggested you go through the Court of Sirens to begin with. I wouldn't have done that if I hadn't already learned their migration patterns. I know where they should be at this time of year, I just need to confirm before you go ripping off after them."

"And if you're wrong?"

"I'm not," Spider said. "Every time I've ever sent out a ship to check, the court was where I'd expected it to be. More or less." His voice dropped low as he added darkly, "And they nearly sank the last two ships that went their way during mating season."

"Have you sold this information to anyone else?" Iris demanded.

Spider scoffed. "Captain Arani, you're the only one who will buy myths instead of solid leads."

"It's not a myth," Iris growled. "You know it's real."

"I know you found that scale somewhere," Spider returned, "and that Ava Mordanti holds a special place in your Veritian history. You're also the one taking on all the risk in this matter, so of course I am going to indulge you, and I am not going to sell your secrets, regardless of whether or not I believe them. That's bad business. But if you want my true opinion—"

"I don't," Iris said.

They held each other's gazes for a long moment before Spider sighed and shrugged. "We were due for a sweep of the southern merchant routes as it was, so I already have a scout out there. They know to look for siren signs, but it will be several days before they return and we can confirm the location. I consider that a good thing, as I'll need to teach you proper etiquette before you rush off to meet them." He shot a pointed look at the tip of the saber still hovering near his chest. "Behavior like *this*, for instance, will see your crew slaughtered outright." Spider pushed the sword away from him with a slow, disgusted motion. "You're also going to need quite the offering to hold the court's interest long enough to bargain for the information you want."

Iris sheathed her sword, but did not relax. "This is where you speak to Mr. Novachak about purchasing some of our Solkyrian agate."

Spider gave her an easy smile that did not touch his eyes. "A fresh store, straight from the island?"

"Aye," Novachak answered. "Strong enough to keep the sickness off the Skilled here for at least three years, and then some."

Spider moved back to his desk, and Iris turned to study the map while the two men began the negotiations. She tried to focus on the various islands that dotted the vast seas, but her concentration slipped elsewhere.

She seethed at the knowledge that Spider had been taking her money and only keeping a cursory eye on the Court of Sirens rather than the close one he'd promised, though she supposed she should consider herself fortunate that tracking the court aligned with Spider's own interests of keeping ships out of their territory. She supposed he could have mapped out their migration route as an area to avoid at all costs and then left the matter at that, giving her nothing more than a vague idea of where to look for them. At least he'd learned about their behaviors, including when their outrageously long mating season took place.

She couldn't quite bring herself to be grateful for that. She'd paid Spider a small fortune over the years, and now they needed to scramble to bring everything into alignment and set them on course to follow in

Mordanti's wake. That included Iris securing enough funds to buy her way into the court's good graces, and having to wait in agony for Spider to verify information from his scouts.

She turned around to find him and Novachak both frowning as Spider skimmed through a ledger from his storehouses. "Gods below, what now?" she asked.

Novachak glanced up at her, and Iris knew the answer before he opened his mouth. "It's not enough, Captain."

Iris sighed and ran a hand over her face. "Even if we sell all of it?"

Novachak shook his head.

"Your crew is going to want payment for their last few voyages," Spider said, flipping the ledger shut. "Even if you convince most of them to forgo their shares, which I think we all know is next to impossible, you're not going to end up with much left for the sirens."

Iris gave a sigh of defeat. "With the way our luck has been going, that sounds about right." She glanced out the windows of Spider's office, which offered a glimpse of the harbor and the sea. "We'll need another prize."

"And you'll need something better than the fur merchant from the Gemheart Islands," Spider added.

She thought for a moment. "Will your scouts have fresh news of merchant ships when they return from the south?"

"Naturally."

"Then we'll let the crew rest while we wait for the scouts to return, and we'll take a prize while we're en route."

Novachak's chair creaked as he shifted. "That's a bit risky, Captain."

"It's our best option," Iris said. "If we go now, the crew will be exhausted, and the best we'll get is something small. This way, we may find something that the sirens will want."

"Or we could sail right back into Prince Trystos's hunting grounds," Novachak remarked.

Iris looked to Spider, who shook his head. "This time of year, the sirens will be farther south. If you're clever, you may be able to do as Captain Arani is suggesting and make it back in time for the Dancing Skies Festival."

"And won't that have been the real treasure all along," Iris remarked.

Spider chuckled. "So if we're in agreement, I'll pay your asking price for three-quarters of the agate, and that should at least let you pay your crew well enough to keep them happy while we wait for my scouts to return."

Iris and Novachak exchanged a quick glance before nodding their agreement. With their business concluded for now, they shook hands with Spider, and then turned to leave.

Spider stopped them at the door. "A word, Captain, if I may?"

Iris waved Novachak on and waited at the threshold.

"You will need to be smart about this," he said. He was frowning and there was a note of genuine warning in his voice. "Legendary treasures have the tendency to draw out legendary foolishness."

Iris gave him a wry smile. "I've seen what my crew will do when they're chasing down a prize. This won't be much different."

"Actually," Spider said, "I was talking about you."

Iris blinked.

"Be careful out there," Spider continued after a moment. "This is bigger than a run in with the navy, and the *Southern Echo* can only carry you so far."

"You know," Iris said after a moment, "the beautiful thing about an echo is that it always comes back."

Spider's frown deepened.

Iris pulled the door closed behind her before he could say anything more. It shut with a soft click, and she stood outside with her hand on the knob for a while, brow furrowed. Then she reached up to touch the chain around her neck, and the scale moved against her skin.

Soon, she promised herself, and then went to rejoin Novachak.

CHAPTER TEN

A Day on Spider's Nest

"IF YOU KEEP GAWKING like that," Xander said, "they're going to think you're touched in the head."

Nate closed his mouth, but he kept turning as they walked, trying to take everything in. "I've never seen anything like this," he breathed.

"That much is clear," Xander said, but there was a smile in his voice. He gestured to their small group, which included Marcus, Eric, and—much to Nate's surprise—Rori Goodtide as a last-minute addition. "Come on," the Grayvoice said, "let's head into town."

Nate hurried after Xander, still marveling over the crowds and not caring who saw him staring.

Unlike Sunthrone City, there was a raw chaos to the set up, with vendors sprawled across the beach in no particular pattern, and yet there was a blurry harmony to it all. Men and women of all sorts flocked around the makeshift stalls, bartering for goods and supplies no matter how new their coats or worn their boots. They came away pleased or soured purely from the kind of deal they'd managed to strike, and the only hostility seemed to bloom when rival crews crossed paths. Even then, a few words and glares were exchanged, and then the pirates went their separate ways.

That included the Skilled among them.

There weren't as many Skilled on Spider's Nest as Nate had grown accustomed to on Solkyria, but the ones he saw walked with their heads raised and looked the world in the eye. They were dressed similarly to their unmarked peers, and they laughed and cursed with just as much abandon. Nate saw a Grayvoice walk right up to a sword-smith and immediately begin to haggle the price of a new cutlass. A trio of Darkbends traded stories with a woman who ran one of the roasting pits, and she carved off morsels of sizzling meat for the light benders as though it were the most natural thing in the world.

Everywhere Nate looked, he caught a glimpse of the Skilled mingling with clean-skinned pirates, and no one thought anything of it. After they'd gone a ways across the beach, it occurred to Nate that most of the Skilled on Spider's Nest bore lower level marks, including the weather workers. Rori's Goodtide tattoo was unique in its intricacy across all of the disciplines, and the few other tide workers Nate saw were Malatides. Lowwinds were even less common, and a Highwind was nowhere to be seen. Nate saw Clearvoices and even several Brightbends, but their tattoos were plainer than the ones Rori and Nate's brother and sister had received.

The realization made Nate look at Rori again, and he wondered what had happened to land her on the *Southern Echo*. No living ship captain would have let a Goodtide go, willingly or not. Especially not a powerful one. Something had happened there, and Nate wasn't sure if he wanted to find out. He looked away before Rori could catch him considering her.

The group made their way past the last of the beach vendors and turned up a wide dirt path that led to more permanent buildings. People moved with more purpose through the small town, striding confidently to set destinations. Nate's group was no different, although he had no idea where they were heading until they drew up in front of a three-story building with a wide front porch and a grand balcony on the second floor. Men and women in various states of undress lounged outside, smiling at nearly everyone who walked by. The smiles disappeared when they saw Nate's group.

"You bring money this time?" a woman in a low-cut dress called.

"Aye," Marcus called back, "and we brought it last time, too, but someone swiped it before we could pay you."

The woman exchanged an unimpressed glance with a man wearing dangerously tight pants and very little else.

Marcus gave them a cheerful wave before spinning around and pulling the group in close. "How much *do* we have?" he asked in a low voice. "We're definitely going to have to pay to get past the front door after last time."

The group began patting their pockets and fishing out a few copper marks each. Nate, with no money and no urgent need to satisfy himself, amused himself by watching the others frantically add up their funds. That was why he saw the surreptitious glance that passed between Xander and Rori even as they counted their own coins.

"I don't think we have enough," Eric said after a moment. "Copper marks may get us into the parlor, but not upstairs."

"Well, not all of us," Marcus said, his attention still on the few coins the circle had produced and the calculations he was running in his head. "But if we pooled it, one of us could go."

"Oh?" Eric asked. "And who is the lucky one?"

Marcus shrugged. "Well, it was my idea..."

Nate laughed as the others jeered and gave him playful shoves.

"Fine, fine," Marcus said, holding up his hands in surrender. "We'll get a hot meal instead and pretend we're enjoying it and not suffering together." He looked up and caught another glance shared between Rori and Xander. "Gods below, that's not fair!"

Rori leveled an unimpressed stare at Marcus, but Xander flashed him a wicked grin.

"You could go off and enjoy yourselves, too," he suggested. "Nothing's stopping you."

Marcus and Eric looked at each other.

"I've seen him eat," Eric said. "That is *absolutely* stopping me."

Xander laughed but Rori had caught his arm and was pulling him away. He hurried after her without another backwards glance. Nate could not tear his eyes away from Rori's fingers locked around the Grayvoice's wrist.

He stumbled when Marcus slung an arm around his shoulders.

"Don't get your hopes up there, Nate," the stout Darkbend advised. "Xander had to work hard to get Rori to look at him twice, and even then, it only happens when they go ashore."

"She seemed ready to look at a few of the men on that porch," Nate remarked.

"When they go ashore and can't afford the pleasure house," Marcus amended.

"But they're together?" Nate asked.

"Ehh..." Marcus tilted a hand back and forth in the air. "It's messy. Best as I can tell, Rori's all business on the ship, and she doesn't have much interest in anyone when we're out to sea. Might be she doesn't want to tangle with anyone she knows she can't get more than a ship's length away from the next day."

"But she'll go with Xander?"

The Darkbend shrugged. "Like I said: messy." He gave Nate a firm shake before releasing him. "But Rori's a good friend to have. It's hard to break her shell, but she's loyal to her core. Don't you go ruining that for any of us."

"I won't," Nate promised, and he meant it.

He had never thought that he would make friends among the pirate crew, and his heart told him to resist getting too close to anyone from the *Southern Echo*. He was used to being alone, so it should have been simple for him to continue on that path. But Marcus and Eric had slid into Nate's life with such graceful ease, it was hard to believe he'd only known them a week. Xander's edges were a bit rougher, and he cut in more than he slid, but Nate was beginning to learn how to navigate the Grayvoice's mercurial moods, and as long as their conversations stayed away from their Skills and Solkyria, Nate actually enjoyed Xander's biting wit. Especially when nasty Jim Greenroot bore the brunt of it. And Rori...

Well, Nate still didn't know much about Rori, but after seeing her smile, he wanted to learn how to make her do that every day.

"Besides," Eric put in, pulling Nate out of his thoughts, "if you really wanted to get into that kind of a mess with someone from the crew, all you'd have to do is ask for volunteers." He gave Nate an approving glance.

Nate's mouth twisted into a half-grin. Eric's teasing flirtations were familiar to him now, but apart from that first day, the Darkbend never made any move to act on them. Eric had even offered to deflect the rigger Liliana's clear interest in him over to Nate, although Nate had passed on the offer, secretly thinking of Rori. Having seen her hand wrapped around Xander's wrist, he knew now that he'd probably made the wrong choice on that front.

"Come on," Marcus said. "I'm starving and actually looking forward to some fresh food. We'll treat you on this one, Nate."

The three made their way across the road to the tavern, talking loudly to drown out the teasing from the pleasure house workers. Nate was smiling again when they stepped inside, and his grin broadened when he smelled the food coming from the kitchen.

"Boar stew," Marcus said, almost reverently.

Nate drank deep of the rich scent, and his mouth began to water. He started to follow Marcus and Eric as they made their way to a table. Then a hand closed on his shoulder.

"Excellent timing, new blood," Novachak said as he swung Nate around. "We were just looking for you."

Nate, too surprised to resist, found himself stumbling back to the door, where Captain Arani and Dax Malatide waited.

"I didn't do anything," Nate blurted, at a loss for any other reason why all three officers would be seeking him out.

Novachak patted his shoulder. "Oh, aye, and that's the problem, isn't it? You've been with us for days and no one's taught you how to swing a sword."

"Can't that wait?" Marcus asked. He'd followed Nate and Novachak, and now addressed the captain and quartermaster as much as he did the boatswain. "We're not going to have to fight our dinner before we eat it."

"But if you did," Dax said, "would you want Nate at your backs with a sword in his hand?"

Marcus hesitated and gave Nate a considering look, clearly thinking about Nate's early bout of Skill sickness and his total lack of grace when it came to hauling on sail lines and pushing mops over decks.

"Now imagine that at sea, in the middle of capturing a prize."

Marcus reluctantly agreed, but asked why Nate could not work on his swordplay later. "All he's got to do is swing it and poke people with the pointy end," the stout Darkbend said.

Arani quirked an eyebrow at Marcus. "Is that the extent of your ability to handle a blade?" she asked. "Perhaps you should join Nate for some training."

Marcus quickly backed down, but had the decency to shoot Nate an apologetic smile before hurrying back to Eric, who gave Nate a pitying glance before turning his attention to the tavern worker and asking for two bowls of stew. Nate heard Marcus thank Eric, only to be informed that both of the bowls were for Eric and Marcus would need to get his own. Their playful argument followed Nate as Novachak took a firmer grip on his shoulder and steered him out of the tavern, Dax and Arani following close behind.

"I'm still getting my sea legs under me," Nate said as they turned down the road and headed back towards the beach. "Shouldn't I settle that before I pick up a sword?"

"I see you've been learning from Marcus," Arani remarked dryly. "Best not make a habit of that."

A protest rose to Nate's lips, but he thought better of it and clamped his mouth shut. He let Novachak guide him back down the road, away from his friends. Disappointment pricked at Nate as he grudgingly accepted that he would miss the better part of the day and whatever antics the Darkbends got up to. He was sure they'd catch him up later, but he'd been excited to spend his first day on Spider's Nest with them, making memories of his own instead of listening to everyone else's. Apparently, learning how to stab someone was more important than that.

As he walked, Nate wondered what sword training would look like with the pirate officers. Maybe they would start him on the beach, then push him into the surf and see if he could keep his balance while the waves crashed into his legs. Or maybe they'd send him back to the *Southern Echo* and confine him to the decks, making him practice away from Spider's Nest and all the fascinations it offered.

He was surprised, then, when Novachak abruptly turned Nate off the main road and on to a thin, dusty path that led into the trees, so small and nondescript that Nate had overlooked it completely until he was walking on it. There wasn't enough room for him to walk next to Novachak, and the boatswain took the lead. Nate went after him, bewildered, with Arani and Dax close behind.

No one spoke much as they followed the narrow path, save for a few warnings from Novachak about protruding tree roots or a low-hanging branch. With the trees blocking the wind off the sea, the air was sluggish and sticky against Nate's skin. His shirt dampened with sweat and clung to his shoulders and back, and his breath grew heavy in his chest. When the path finally changed from dirt to sand and deposited them on a tiny beach on the southern side of the island, Nate's hair was plastered to his neck and he was panting. The salty breeze from the sea offered some relief, but nowhere near enough. Nate considered ripping his clothes off right there in front of the officers and throwing himself into the surf, the gods below damn anyone who tried to stop him. Then he realized that the water was rougher here, and peppered with rocks, and he was likely to be battered and broken by the waves.

Not a terrible *trade for some relief from the heat,* Nate thought.

He was about to say as much to Novachak, but stopped when he saw that the boatswain was breathing easily and barely sweating at all. The same went for the quartermaster and the captain, who, despite her healing injury, looked cool and unbothered by the trek.

She eyed Nate and pressed her mouth into a disapproving line. "I suppose they didn't see much use in keeping you fit at that wind working academy," she remarked.

Nate's exhaustion outweighed his embarrassment. It was true that his physical training sessions had diminished in frequency and intensity the longer he'd been at the academy, and it seemed slowly walking up and down the streets of Sunthrone City hadn't been an appropriate substitute.

"Come on, Nate," Dax said, gesturing to the center of the little strip of sand that passed for a beach. "Catch your breath and let's get started."

Reluctantly, Nate moved to the indicated spot in the sand. He drank deep of the salty air and worked his breathing down to a shallow pant, helped along by the steady wind off the water. As always, he felt the raw potential of the wind element whisper over his skin, but it danced beyond the reach of his fingertips.

When he was breathing easier, Nate turned to the officers and nodded his readiness. He expected one of them to hand him a sword. None of them did.

Instead, Novachak and Arani hung back while Dax stood next to Nate, facing the sea. He motioned for Nate to do the same.

"I expect this would go better if I was a wind worker," Dax said, almost apologetically, "but there should be enough overlap between our Skills that I can advise you."

Nate stared at the quartermaster for a long moment before glancing back at the captain and the boatswain. "I thought I was to learn sword fighting," he said.

"I'm less concerned with your ability to swing a blade and poke them with the pointy end," Arani said, "and more with you being at least a little competent as a tracker before we begin our next voyage."

Nate's heart quickened, and his irritation at being pulled away from his friends evaporated under the promise of finally, *finally* doing something useful with his Skill. "I'm to start training now?" he asked. He glanced eagerly around the beach. "Is there something you want me to track? What do I do? How do I start?"

There was a restrained laugh in Dax's voice when he said, "For now, we're going to start with the basics."

"I've had wind training," Nate assured the quartermaster. "I'm ready to try whatever you want me to."

Dax quirked an amused smile. "The basics," he repeated. "Shut your eyes and feel the wind element in your blood."

Nate started to protest.

"And shut your mouth while you're at it," Dax added, the words taking on the same firm tone he used to command sailors on the ship decks.

With a reluctant sigh, Nate did as he was told.

Shutting his eyes did not do much for his connection to the element. Nate knew from his academy days that it wouldn't, but if he had to indulge this for a few minutes before his training began in earnest, he would endure it. His mind raced with possibilities. What would his training look like? Was there a ship out on the horizon that Arani wanted him to find? How would he even begin to do that on this sequestered beach? Was there something else she wanted him to follow?

"You're heart is racing," Dax said, cutting across Nate's rushing thoughts. "Calm yourself, and just feel the wind. How it ebbs and flows in your blood, until your heart has been swept up in its rhythm."

Nate frowned and cracked open one eye to give the quartermaster a bemused look.

"It doesn't feel that way for you?" Dax asked after a moment.

Nate shook his head.

"Ah." Dax furrowed his brow and placed his hands on his hips, thinking. "All right, then do... whatever it is wind workers do to connect to their element."

Nate snorted and shut his eyes again. A sliver of doubt began to worm its way into his mind as he reached for the uncooperative element, and for a panicked moment, he imagined himself failing this test like all the others that had come before it. He shoved the thought away. Captain Arani had said his Skill was unique, and she'd promised that he would learn how to properly wield it. He focused on that and let his excitement bloom in his chest again.

"Feel the wind," Dax said again. "How it... blows over you... and... you know what, why don't *you* describe it?"

Nate couldn't stop another snort from escaping, but he did as he was told. "It's a solid flow from the sea," he said. "Steady and full of salt. It knows where it means to be."

"Good," the quartermaster said. "What else do you notice?"

Nate shrugged. "It's a clear day. No taste of a storm as far as I can tell."

"What about the wind right around you? Does it... taste strange?"

Amused, Nate shook his head. "It's bending around those rocks out in the water, but the shape is strong."

He braced himself, waiting for the quartermaster to ask him to try to change that shape to his whims, but Dax stayed silent. Nate waited, and then yelped as something sharp bounced off the back of his head. He spun to see Novachak holding a handful of shells and pebbles.

"Not so good with the downwind," the boatswain mused.

Nate brushed his fingers against the spot where the seashell had hit him and glared daggers at the officer. He was considering picking up the shell and hurling it back at the man to see how *he* liked getting pelted with debris when he felt something blur across the sea wind. He turned just in time for the next shell to hit his cheek.

"Considerably better with upwind," Arani said. She'd circled around Dax and Nate until she stood just off to one side and could hook pieces of the beach at his head. "Let's try again."

So far, Nate did not like how this training session was going.

IT DID NOT IMPROVE. By the end of the day, Nate had a few small cuts from various shells, and a budding bruise on his left bicep. He was exhausted physically and mentally from trying to sense the projectiles before they connected with his flesh, and the joy he'd felt at the prospect of finally using his Skill had evaporated under Arani's clear unhappiness with his progress.

"You'll need to do much better than this," she informed him, eyeing his injuries. "We need you to be able to sense more than just things that are upwind from you, and certainly further out than twenty paces. Report here tomorrow at first light, and we'll start working on your distance first."

Nate was too tired to protest. All he wanted was a mildly comfortable place to sleep, but his stomach announced to the officers that it would not be satiated with rest. The growl felt loud enough to shake the trees.

Dax took pity on him, and gave Nate a coin for a meal at the tavern. He and Arani left then to attend their own business, but Novachak stayed back to match Nate's slow pace back to town.

"As far as training goes," the boatswain said as they trudged along the narrow path through the trees, "that wasn't the *worst* I've ever seen. It wasn't the best either, but at least you swatted away a few of the shells before they hit you."

Nate grunted, frustration and resentment towards Arani simmering in his gut. She'd promised to train him, but this entire day had been a far cry from anything useful.

"Were I a betting man," Novachak said, "and happily I am, I'd say you likely couldn't get any worse." He lapsed into a thoughtful silence. "Unless you tried to throw yourself into the shells, but then you'd be better at sensing them, wouldn't you?"

"Is this meant to make me feel better?" Nate asked.

"That depends," Novachak said. "Is it?"

"No."

"Then no."

Nate groaned and halted. He turned his face to the sky, seeking out even the smallest of breezes to give him some relief from the heat. The sun may have been setting, but the air had been baked to a close, sticky mess the entire day, and Nate was soaked with sweat. At least at the academy, he'd been able to look forward to a bath after a long day of unsuccessful training. And the instructors had never made him bleed for failing to shape his Skill the way they'd wanted. They'd been cruel, but not physically so. Not like the pirates. Nate solemnly reminded himself that this would all be worth it in the end, when he returned to Solkyria and secured a place for himself in the navy as a tracker of enemy ships. But he allowed himself to indulge in a small, spiteful fantasy of standing on the deck of a navy ship bearing down on Arani's, with the sweet anticipation of justice dancing through his veins.

"New blood, the longer you stand there," Novachak said from over Nate's shoulder, "the longer you invite your stomach to sing."

As though hearing its name invoked, the organ in question rumbled and groaned.

Novachak gave Nate a wry smile. "It's not a pretty singer."

Nate did not laugh.

When they returned to town, Nate fully expected Novachak to leave him and head off on whatever business the boatswain had to attend to. Instead, Novachak accompanied Nate all the way back to the tavern, and, after a bit of awkward shuffling and sidestepping, made sure that Nate was walking on his left. Nate had spent long enough trying to avoid the attention of unmarked people that he quickly picked up on Novachak very pointedly *not* looking across the road at the pleasure house, which stood uproariously bright in the growing dark. The boatswain had placed Nate between himself and the building, and he kept his eyes averted all the way up the steps and through the door of the tavern. Nate dully recalled Marcus teasing Novachak about something involving the madame, and added that to the list of petty revenges he might someday take against the people who had spent the day whipping shells at his head.

Inside the tavern, flickering candles on the walls provided a spiteful bit of illumination, but that did not stop Novachak from moving swiftly between the tables and the pirates that inhabited them. The tavern was far more crowded than it had been earlier in the day, and while it lacked the wild abandon of the pleasure house, there were tables full of men and women laughing and talking and arguing over bowls of food. It was hard to pick out the aroma of the boar stew over the stale smells of sweat and spilled rum and ale, but it was there, and Nate's stomach rumbled loud enough for him to hear it over the din. He set off after Novachak, the coin from Dax clutched tight in his hand.

The table Novachak had chosen was already occupied by familiar faces: Marcus and Eric were there, along with Xander and Rori. Nate avoided the couple's gaze, but that meant facing Marcus's amused appraisal. He took in Nate's rumpled clothing and the nicks in his skin, and his left eyebrow arched high enough to warp the white Darkbend tattoo on his face.

"Just how bad with a sword are you?" Marcus asked, and he was only half-teasing.

Novachak cut in before Nate could respond. "They let him go soft at that academy," he said, "but don't you worry, we'll have him trained up proper before we set him to watch your backs." He smiled and clapped Nate on the shoulder, but his eyes were hard as ice. "Isn't that right, new blood?"

Nate looked at the boatswain, and then at the others, all waiting for his response. He nodded mutely.

"That's the spirit," Novachak said. He tugged out a chair and pressed Nate into it. "How's the food tonight?"

"Not bad," Marcus said with a shrug.

"He's had five bowls," Eric said. "I'd hate to see him with *good* food."

Novachak laughed with the others before waving down a man carrying a tray of bowls and requesting one for himself. Nate checked the coin Dax had given him, and ordered three more.

"Don't model your appetite after Marcus," Eric warned. "You're still a good-looking lad, after all."

Marcus made an indignant comment that had the others laughing again, and Nate forced himself to smile along with them. He would much rather tell them all the secret of his Skill to spite Arani for taking him away from his friends, even if it was for training, but he dared not with Novachak sitting next to him.

Nate was too tired and hungry to follow much of the conversation as it bubbled up around him. When the stew came, Nate barely tasted the first bowl, he ate so fast. Somewhere in the middle of the second bowl, as his stomach filled and his foul mood faded, Nate glanced around the table, at the smiling faces of his friends, and he had the sudden realization that, someday, he was going to rip himself out of their lives, and he wasn't going to come back. His heart gave a soft pang at the thought of walking away from the first genuine friendships he'd had in a long time.

It will be better when I go back, he told himself. He'd master his true Skill and be able to serve the empire in the navy, just as he'd always wanted. He'd forge new friendships among the ranks of the imperial wind workers and finally have their respect. He'd wear a naval uniform with silver buttons down the coat and earn a salary that could pay back his debts to the empire. He'd make his family proud. And he *wouldn't* stand on a beach while someone threw sharp bits of debris at him all day.

But Nate still felt a little guilty as he rejoined the conversation, and his heart sagged heavily as he recalled his earlier, only half-serious idea of using his Skill to track Arani on behalf of the navy. He looked at the faces of the friends he'd made aboard the *Southern Echo*, and had to admit that he wouldn't be so eager to hunt pirate ships after all, no matter how many shells the captain had thrown at him.

CHAPTER ELEVEN

Sharpen the Skill

NATE WOKE ON THE beach the next morning while the sky was still dark. Xander, Marcus, and Eric snored softly on his left. He had a vague memory of sitting in the tavern for a few hours, then stumbling outside with the others and relishing the relative coolness that had finally arrived with the night. Rather than spend money on a room or stuff themselves back into the hold of the ship, they did what many others had done: collapsed on the beach above the high tide mark, and fallen asleep under the stars.

As far as Nate's memories went, it wasn't an unpleasant one, but he would have preferred to wait a few more hours before having it. Perhaps when the sun was up and it made sense for him to be awake.

The insistent hand on his shoulder had other ideas.

Groaning, Nate sat up, only to be shushed by the quartermaster. Dax gestured to the others and pressed a finger to his lips. Nate scrubbed his face with the heel of his hand, then remembered that he was supposed to be focusing on his Skill training that day. That brought him to his feet. He was not eager to acquire more nicks and bruises, but he was determined to make sure that the time he had to spend away from his friends was not wasted. He yawned as he stretched and brushed sand off of his clothes, then eagerly followed Dax across the beach.

Nate and Dax were not the only ones awake at that early hour, but no one paid them any mind as they headed back to town. It seemed there was always someone awake and about on Spider's Nest, no matter how dark the hour, and the two of them were given nothing more than a few disinterested glances as they picked up an oil lantern and headed off. Despite his exhaustion, Nate could not help but marvel all over again at how different Spider's Nest was from Sunthrone City. The pirate island may have rested in Solkyrian waters, but its citizens and visitors shared none of the superstitious Solkyrian dread of wandering about without the benevolent eye of the sun overhead. While most citizens no longer worshipped the sun as something deserving of tributes, they still preferred to live their lives in its light and avoided being caught out by the dark as much as they could. Skilled or clean-skinned alike, no one on Spider's Nest seemed to share that aversion. For his own part, Nate had always found peace in the night after the unmarked citizens had retired, and he'd shaken off the relics of the old religion in his younger days when his Skill mark was still fresh and healing.

The sky was just beginning to lighten in the east when Dax took Nate back to the covered path that led to the secret beach. They went slowly, with Dax stepping carefully along in the flickering lantern light and offering warnings of treacherous footing. Nate followed the quartermaster's silhouette without a word.

When they came out on the beach, the sky was light enough for Dax to extinguish the lantern. The wind was salty and pure off of the calm water, a little too cool for the early morning but it would be a pleasant relief as the sun rose and baked the world. Nate took a deep breath, savoring the clean scent.

"Go ahead and get yourself ready," Dax said. "We'll be starting as soon as Rori gets here."

Nate frowned, confused. "Why is she coming?"

"She volunteered to help after hearing about how yesterday went."

A flush crept up Nate's neck as he remembered the number of shells and pebbles that had bounced off his head the day before, capped off by Arani's growing disappointment as she'd found and tested the limits of his tracking abilities. He'd hoped to redeem himself a little and show the captain that he could push past his own limitations, but having to perform in front of Rori Goodtide with her solemn eyes and rare but bright smiles...

Nate feared she would be more of a distraction than a help, even after he'd learned about her and Xander.

No sooner had the thought formed than something small but determined smacked into his head and began to wrestle with his hat. Nate yelped and swatted at the bird, which gave him an irritated chirp in response. Nate froze, and the bird fluttered to a clumsy rest on top of his head, tiny talons hooking into the worn fabric of his hat. Nate groaned.

"Can you not control this demon spawn?" he asked tiredly as he turned around to face Rori as she stepped off of the path and joined them on the beach. The bird wobbled and slapped his wings against Nate's head.

"I can get Luken to signal the riggers and run codes from the captain to the helm," Rori returned coolly, "but that's his job. He's free to do as he pleases in his off time."

"Does that include excreting on unpleasant gunners?" Nate asked as he removed his hat and shook the bird loose. He said the words before he'd thought better of them, and he tensed, uncertain how she would react to the jest.

Rori's mouth twitched into the smallest of smiles as Luken glided back to her shoulder and settled himself. "He wouldn't have done it if it didn't please him," she said.

Nate felt a wild rush of relief, and his own lips tugged into a grin.

"What's this now?" Dax cut in, glancing back and forth between the two of them.

"Nothing," Nate said quickly, in case that petty bit of vengeance went against the crew's code.

Rori adopted a placid expression and said nothing.

Dax did not look like he believed them, but he did not press the matter and instead moved Nate into position at the center of the beach. Nate had a pretty good idea of what to expect, given Luken's presence for his training session, and while he wasn't looking forward to trying to dodge the bird, at least Rori wouldn't be lobbing rocks and shells at him.

"Ready?" Dax called. He'd positioned himself downwind of Nate, to minimize the risk of distracting Nate's perception.

Nate didn't think that was necessary, but he supposed it did not hurt matters. He signaled his readiness to Dax and started to turn away from Rori and Luken. He paused when he saw the sour expression on her face. She was looking out to sea rather than at Nate, but he suddenly recalled his last conversation with her. She had not liked the idea of him using his Skill at all.

His stomach gave an unpleasant clench as he wondered if Rori had come to cause trouble for him. Perhaps he'd misjudged her, and her willingness to see Jim Greenroot get his comeuppance was rooted less in making Nate feel better, and more in amusing herself. If that was the case, would she truly help him, or try to sabotage his training and keep him from unlocking his full potential?

The thought squirmed unpleasantly in Nate's mind as he turned his back to Rori and Luken, and reached for the wind.

Distracted, Nate did not perform well at all. It took three attacks on his hat before he finally gathered himself enough to connect to the element, and several more before he managed to dodge Luken. Even then, the bird had to start closer to Nate and fly slower, and that was far from something to be impressed about. Dax gave Nate a few encouraging words before he left to see to his duties for the day, but it was clear from the quartermaster's expression that the captain would not be pleased by his report of Nate's progress.

Left alone with Rori, Nate resolved to try harder. He forced himself to focus, to reach into the wind and watch for the shadow Luken's wings cast as he flew at Nate's head, continuing his bizarre mating dance with his hat as the Goodtide stood by and did not say a word. Irritation clouded Nate's mind. By the time Rori called an abrupt halt to give Luken a few berries and a handful of seeds from her pocket, his frustration had crescendoed into a swirling storm. He stalked to where Rori sat with the bird by a bit of driftwood, letting Luken rest in the shade while he ate. She did not look at Nate as he approached, and he did not try to keep the acid out of his tone when he asked, "Are you going to stop wasting my time and help me train, or no?"

Rori did not look at him immediately, but her shoulders tensed and her fingers curled in the sand. When she finally turned to him, her deep blue Goodtide tattoo flooded his vision.

"I didn't ask you to come here," Nate reminded her before she could speak. "Dax said you volunteered.

Was that to help me, or just to send your bird to attack my lowly Nowind head and have a laugh?" His shoulders tightened as he realized that he had just referred to himself as *Nowind* in front of a Goodtide. It would not be long before she spread that name through the crew, especially in the wake of his nastiness.

But Rori did not so much as flinch. She just kept staring at Nate with her hard, dark eyes. "I'm not laughing," she said quietly.

Nate blew out an exasperated breath. "Then why are you here?"

A moment passed before Rori asked, "Did you really mean it when you said that all you've ever wanted is to use your Skill?"

He frowned at her. "Yes," he said warily.

"That's stupid."

Rankled, Nate turned and stomped away.

Rori would not let him go so easily. He heard the sand whisper off of her clothes as she jumped up to follow him. "You have the chance for something different," she called after him, "a life that the empire doesn't get to define."

"I ran away to be a pirate," Nate snapped, his words all the harsher because he had to lie. "The empire has nothing to do with this."

"It has *every*thing to do with it, because you think you're only worth as much as your Skill! You left Solkyria behind you. Why are you still so determined to live up to the empire's expectations of you?"

Nate halted, panic rushing in to crowd out his anger. "Well, what about you?" he deflected. "You *refuse* to use your Skill, like you're trying to spite the empire with your fear!"

Rori came up short, her lips parting in shock.

"Why don't you use your Skill, Rori?" Nate pressed. "You're a Goodtide, and a strong one, by the look of your mark. What could you possibly have to be afraid of?"

Rori stared at him in silence for a few moments, her mouth slowly closing as her brows came together. Then she reached up and began to unbutton her shirt.

Nate blinked a few times before he realized what he was seeing, and then his jaw went slack in total confusion. "What are you...?" His brain abruptly slapped his thoughts into some semblance of order and told him to turn away, for the sake of every god above and below, *turn away*, but Rori was faster. She spun and dropped her shirt into the sand, pulling her long hair off her neck in the same motion. Nate found himself looking at the bare skin of her back...

And the seven long scars slashed across her spine.

"I served on a merchant ship for three years before I stole my freedom back," Rori said. Her head was turned so she could send the words over her shoulder, but she was staring out to sea and deliberately not looking at Nate. "Because I am a Goodtide, they demanded that I give my life over completely to the ship. They said I had to see them through every storm, bring the ship across the trade routes faster and faster and faster still, and obey every word of the unmarked sailors around me, whether they were the captain or a cabin boy. Because I am a Goodtide, I was their tool to use freely and viciously, and the day I tried to say no, I was tied to the mast and given seven lashes, and left to bleed until dawn."

The scars ridging Rori's back had long since healed, but Nate couldn't help imagining them raw and weeping red, each one laid deep by the hand that had held the whip. Whoever it was, they had not held back.

The rush of the wind was the only sound as Rori bent and picked up her shirt. Her scars disappeared as she pulled her clothing back into place, but they were burned into Nate's vision now. When Rori turned to look at him again, he saw their crisscrossing pattern in the intricate lines of the Goodtide tattoo on her face.

"The crew knows that I was on a merchant ship before the *Southern Echo* found me," Rori said. "But very few of them know how I got off of that ship. I think a lot of them are too afraid of me to ask, and they're right to be. I had to take my freedom, Nate, savagely and without mercy, and I had to use my Skill to do it." She paused for a moment, as though waiting for a judgement that would not come. "I promised myself I would never do anything like that ever again," she eventually continued, "or that I would let myself be defined by this mark the empire had branded into my skin." Her sigh was all hard edges, but her voice was soft. "I want so much more than that."

"But that's not what I want," Nate said softly. "I *want* to use my Skill. I *want* to be worth something."

"You don't need your Skill for that," Rori murmured.

"Maybe," Nate conceded, "but it's what I have, and I need to find out what it can really do."

She shook her head.

Nate sighed. "Rori, if I'd been born with half of my brother's power, I would have made something of myself a long time ago. Instead, I brought nothing but shame and trouble to everyone in my life. I don't expect you to understand what that feels like, but I finally have the chance to do something that no one ever thought that I could." Nate tried to keep his voice kind when he said, "With or without your help, I'm going to do that."

I have to, he thought, but he kept that desperate bit to himself.

Rori's eyes were sad as she gazed at him. "I can't stop you, can I?"

Nate shook his head. "But if you really would like to help me train, I won't turn you away."

After a long silence, she sighed again, but this time with resigned acceptance. "I'll go get Luken. Try to keep up with him this time." She gave him a wan smile. "He's determined to have that hat of yours for a nest."

Nate gave her a tentative smile back, and then went to ready himself for Luken's next assault on his headwear. As he watched Rori coax the bird onto her arm, Nate decided that Marcus was right about Rori. Her horrible taste in pets aside, she was a good friend to have.

A WEEK PASSED WITH Nate training and Rori, Dax, and Novachak all rotating through his exhausted blur of mornings and afternoons. There was no rhyme or reason as to who was serving as his primary instructor at a given time, although Dax's duties as quartermaster made him the scarcest of Nate's instructors. Nate did not mind that so much as there wasn't a lot of overlap between their two weather working Skills, but Dax asked Nate to think and speak about his magic in ways no one ever had before. Nate often came away from those sessions with ideas in his head and a swirl of determination in his gut.

As to Rori and her bird, their exercises were straightforward and unchanging, and Luken never seemed to lose his special interest in Nate's hat, but Nate was getting better at sensing when the bird was approaching. Eventually, he was able to dodge a few of Luken's swoops, but only if the bird came from upwind. Still, he was excited to realize that he was making progress, right up until Rori signaled for Luken to come at Nate from his peripheries and even downwind when his back was turned. It was impossible to sense the bird at that point, with the wind smearing around him and Luken's shadow casting in the wrong direction, but this was what Arani wanted him to be able to do. Nate had serious doubts that it was possible, but if he was going to be a tracker of any sort, he had to try.

If he struggled under Rori, Novachak's training proved even more difficult and humbling for Nate. The boatswain made it clear that he would not be able to help Nate with his Skill. He had no magic in his blood, and no time or desire to try to imagine what that would be like. What he did have was knowledge of swords and pistols, and a new pirate could only benefit from learning about those. Nate saw the wisdom in that and agreed, but after his first sparring session with the boatswain, new bruises were blossoming on both Nate's body and his ego.

"I'm not looking for you to dance your way through some fancy imperial sword form," Novachak said as he hauled Nate to his feet after a particularly hard blow with the heavy practice sticks they used in place of edged weapons. "That kind of stuff doesn't work so great on a moving ship, anyway," the boatswain mused as he slapped sand off of Nate's shoulders. "But you need to get your stance settled and learn how to swing one of these faster than your enemy can. You do that, and you'll be fine in most fights. Not many merchant sailors can do more than that, anyway, and if you're ever fighting someone with actual training, that means we've probably run into the navy and have much bigger problems to worry about."

Nate rubbed a sore spot on his ribs where Novachak had whacked him earlier. "Isn't that something we *should* be worried about?"

The boatswain shrugged. "Captain knows how to avoid 'em, and the *Southern Echo* is faster than most of their ships. The ones that could keep up with her are all caught up in the war, and they're not expected back in Solkyrian waters any time soon."

Nate rolled his shoulders and winced, as much from his muscles twinging as his mind reminding him that his brother's ship had been back in Sunthrone City's harbor not too long ago, but he kept the thought to himself. Novachak pulled him back into another sparring session, and soon Nate was too busy trying not to get hit to think about anything else.

In the evenings, Nate returned to town and spent the last few exhausted hours of the day with his friends. They'd been paid for their last voyage with money from the sale of Arani's agate cache, and while it wasn't much, it had allowed Eric to buy himself a worn but clean shirt of an elegant cut; Marcus to get back inside the pleasure house, although not up the stairs; and Xander to gamble his way into possession of a new dagger, which he enjoyed showing off almost as much as Eric enjoyed modeling his new shirt. They were in good spirits whenever Nate found them, and they teased him about how poor his swordsmanship must be if the officers were working him so hard.

One night, however, he came back alongside Rori, and Xander's gaze hardened when he saw the two of them together.

"Where've *you* been all day?" the Grayvoice asked the Goodtide as she sat down at their usual table in the tavern.

"Training," Rori said at the same time as Nate, who had been too tired to look up and thought that the question had been for him. He glanced up then and saw Xander's narrowed eyes, and his blood chilled.

"I volunteered to help," Rori said before Nate could speak. "He really needs it."

Xander locked his eyes on her. "You're not our best sword fighter," he said.

"Neither is Nate," Rori quipped, drawing a laugh from Marcus. "And I could use the practice," she added with a shrug.

"Maybe you *should* join him for those training sessions, like Arani suggested," Eric said to Marcus. "Gods above know that you haven't been getting any exercise at the pleasure house."

Marcus dramatically laid his hand over his heart and swayed with mock injury. "How dare you, *sir*?"

That pushed the conversation in a new direction, with Marcus and Eric playfully arguing over which one of them would win in a duel, peppered by a few colorful remarks about coming out on top, and then they were off on a discussion about wrestling contests of a very different sort. Rori rolled her eyes and advised the two Darkbends to go throw themselves in the ocean. That brought on a whole new debate as to who the better swimmer was, as illustrated by several past experiences that were both triumphant and embarrassing, the best of which involved one very ill-tempered dairy goat that had once broken free of its cage and terrorized the *Southern Echo*'s main deck for the better part of an hour.

Nate and Xander and Rori all laughed along with the stories, but the Grayvoice did not look entirely placated. More than once, Nate caught Xander watching him with a calculated gleam in his eyes that a quick smile did not entirely mask. Nate would have tried to avoid being alone with Rori after that, but she'd apparently caught Xander's distrustful looks, and she made a point of coming to the secret beach to help Nate with his training even more.

"He doesn't own me," she said when Nate asked her about Xander. "And he should know me better than that."

Finally, in the early afternoon of their eighth day on Spider's Nest, when Rori and Novachak were both with him on the beach and they'd called a halt for a rest and a quick meal of fruit and dried meat, Nate felt a strange flicker in the wind. He was sprawled in the sand, so drained that he was barely tasting the food on his tongue. The gold ring on his hand was anchoring him well, and he had not felt a brush of the Skill sickness since that first day on the ship, but that did not save him from physical exhaustion. He had his head tilted back and was trying to work up the willpower to order his aching muscles to go back to work. The steady wind from the sea was playing over his sweat-dampened skin when something new smeared across the edge of his awareness. It wasn't particularly strong, but it was strange enough to make Nate sit up and squint out at the horizon. The moment he tried to grasp the wind element, the feeling slipped beyond his grip. He frowned at the familiar frustration, but let it go with nothing more than a soft sigh. He'd caught Rori's attention, however.

"Is something out there?" she asked, her dark eyes riveted on Nate. That brought Novachak's attention to Nate as well, and he squirmed under their sudden interest.

"Sorry, it's nothing," he said, reflexively trying to slip out of their notice the way he would have on Solkyria if a higher Skilled and a citizen had found a reason to pay him any attention. He frowned again, this time at himself. Then he turned to face Rori and Novachak. "I thought I felt something in the wind coming in off the sea."

Novachak squinted out at the horizon. "I'm not seeing anything..." he mused.

Nate felt a small rush of embarrassment. "It's probably nothing," he said again.

"Was it big or small?" Rori asked.

Nate blinked at her before offering a vague shrug.

"High or low off the water?" she pressed.

"I didn't get a strong read on it," Nate admitted. "I just felt something new in the wind. I don't know what it was."

"Could you find it again?" Novachak asked. He was on his feet now, tugging the brim of his hat low against the high sun. "Or at least point to where you thought it was?"

Bemused, Nate lifted his arm and gestured out to sea, off to the left. It wasn't directly into the wind, but it was close, and Nate caught another shiver on the breeze, a shadow of something out there.

Novachak followed his direction and pulled a tarnished spyglass from his belt. He extended the instrument to half its length and made a slow sweep of the horizon, then let the glass out further and took another look. He completed three full sweeps before he suddenly froze, and then his hands worked the spyglass out to its full length. The boatswain frowned, lifted his eye away from the spyglass to squint out at the horizon, and then dipped back into the distant view. "Miss Rori," he said after a long moment, "your eyes are younger and sharper than mine. If you would?"

Rori was on her feet and accepting the spyglass from Novachak before Nate had realized she had moved. The boatswain murmured something to her, and Rori sighted along the instrument before peering out. She took considerably less time to find whatever it was that had caught Novachak's attention, but spent several minutes fiddling with the focus on the glass, her lips pressed into a thoughtful line.

Finally, she lowered the spyglass and nodded. "It's a ship. Looks to be heading right for the island. Can't say who it belongs to, but off that bearing, I'd guess a crew coming in from the hunting waters." She cut a glance to Nate. "Come see what you've found."

Nate quickly joined the others and accepted the spyglass. It was lighter than he'd expected it to be, and the spots of tarnish were cool and rough under his fingertips. Rori and Novachak flanked him, each pointing out at the horizon and directing his gaze. Novachak gave the spyglass a gentle nudge as Nate peered through the glass, sending the water rushing across his vision in a dizzying blur, but Nate caught a glimpse of something white in the field. He slowly moved the glass back, fumbling a little to catch the right spot and adjust the focus, but he was ultimately rewarded with the sight of sails. Based on the shape of those sails, it did not look to be a large ship, certainly not a treasure galleon or an imperial man-of-war. Perhaps it was a frigate, but it also could have been a cutter or a brig similarly outfitted to the *Southern Echo*.

When he lowered the spyglass, Nate found that Rori and Novachak had retreated a few steps away, and were speaking in low voices. They stopped when Nate turned to them, and Novachak flashed a big grin before Nate could say anything.

"That ship is a ways out there, new blood. Don't know how you caught it, but consider me impressed."

Rori nodded in agreement. "You're terrible at tracking Luken, but that—" she gestured out at the horizon, "—more than makes up for it."

Nate handed the spyglass back to Novachak, but he cast another look out to sea, where he'd seen the approaching ship. "I still don't understand why the captain wants me tracking birds if I'll be helping you hunt for ships. They don't cast the same kinds of shadows at all."

Neither the boatswain nor the Goodtide responded, and Nate had to look over his shoulder again to be sure that they were still on the beach with him.

Novachak had the spyglass to his eye again, his fingers tight around the metal and his mouth turned down in a sour grimace. Something was wrong.

"Is it the navy?" Rori asked anxiously.

"Worse," Novachak said as he lowered the glass and snapped it closed. "That's the *Dragonsbane*. Seems they slipped the enforcers same as us, and then managed to find themselves a nice, fat prize, if they're riding that low in the water. That ought to put our captain in a *wonderful* mood."

This last bit was grumbled, but Nate and Rori both caught the words, and the Goodtide gave him a wry smirk.

Novachak turned with a sigh and gestured for Rori and Nate to follow him as he started for the path that would lead them inland. "Come on, we've done enough for today, and I think telling the captain that the new blood caught a whiff of the *Dragonsbane* before we could even see it on the horizon may take the bite out of the news."

"And if it doesn't?" Rori asked.

"I suppose I make peace with the life I've lived, and try not to blame the captain too much for stabbing the messenger."

THEY FOUND ARANI AT the tavern, emerging from a meeting with Spider and looking to be in a surprisingly upbeat mood. Novachak groaned, dreading breaking her good humor with the news of the rival crew's success.

Nate was far from familiar with the politics across pirate crews, but during the trek back into town, he had recalled that it was the quartermaster of the *Dragonsbane* that Arani had been dueling when Nate had first stumbled across the pirates. And someone else from that crew had shot her.

The captain may have been making a steady recovery from the wound and evading infection, but Nate was beginning to understand why Novachak made a point of taking careful note of all of Arani's visible weapons before he approached her with the news of the *Dragonsbane*. Nate and Rori made to hang back, but Novachak pulled them both after him.

"I outrank both of you, and that means I don't have to do this alone," the boatswain growled.

"If you're hoping she stabs one of us instead of you," Rori whispered back, "that's a bad plan. She wants to use Nate's Skill, and I'm the only competent navigator we have."

"That's why you're going to stand in front of me," Novachak returned.

Despite the promises of violence and human shields, it was Novachak who approached the captain first, stepping up to speak softly in her ear. The man called Spider looked amused by this attempt at secrecy, and flashed a wicked grin at the boatswain.

"Ah, Mr. Novachak," Spider said in his deep, sonorous voice, "wonderful to see you again. I was beginning to think that you had eschewed our little paradise for more time on Captain Arani's lovely ship.

Madame Silverdale will be thrilled to know that you've set foot on the island once more."

Novachak winced, but Arani cut in smoothly, "She'll need to wait until our next visit, I'm afraid."

The captain turned her gaze on Nate, and he saw that she was indeed far less happy than she had looked a few moments ago. She did not make good on Novachak's predictions of stabbing or other forms of violence, but all the same, Nate recoiled a little when she stepped towards him.

"Mr. Novachak tells me you spotted the *Dragonsbane* making its way to Spider's Nest," she said, giving Nate a searching look.

Nate hesitated, noting the way she'd sidestepped referencing his Skill. Over her shoulder, he saw Novachak dart a careful glance around the room, taking stock of the pirates at the tables who may have been listening. They all looked far too interested in their food and drink to be paying much attention, and one table erupted in riotous laughter in the wake of Arani's words, but Nate took his cue from the officers and nodded.

"Hmm." Arani switched her attention to Rori. "And the bird?"

"Not as much as you'd hoped," the Goodtide said, "but for sighting that ship, we know he has sharp eyes."

Nate blinked at the oblique language, but held his tongue, even when Arani said, "I suppose that's better than nothing."

Those words stung more than Nate would have expected. After Novachak's and Rori's reactions to his detection of the ship, Nate had almost felt proud of himself.

Almost.

"Well," Arani said, shifting her demeanor to something crisp and businesslike, "we have enjoyed our stay, but it is time we took our leave. We have our heading." Her eyes flickered to Spider at this, and they shared a small, knowing smile.

Novachak, for some reason, looked even more displeased when he heard that.

"Fair winds, Captain Arani," Spider said before turning his gaze on Nate and letting his eyes trace over his Lowwind tattoo. "Though I think you'll have those in your favor from now on."

Arani said nothing, but she was fighting back a triumphant grin as she led the way down the stairs. Novachak and Rori followed, but a hand on Nate's arm held him back. He turned to see Spider still smiling at him, not unkindly but far from comforting.

"You're going on a grand adventure, my boy," Spider murmured. "Try to live long enough to tell me the story on your return." Then he gave Nate a gentle nudge and sent him after Arani and the others.

Nate was very aware of Spider's eyes on him all the way out the door.

Chapter Twelve

Set Sail

It took the better part of the day for the crew to trickle back to the *Southern Echo*. They had been expecting the call to sail from the beginning when Arani and Dax had set the week-long limit on their stay, but a good many grumbled over leaving Spider's Nest and all its offerings behind. They all came willingly, however, and most had depleted pockets and a grudging excitement at the prospect of a new prize that shifted to earnest eagerness as the sun began to set and final preparations were made.

All hands helped where they could, Nate included, and he jumped between whatever menial tasks would free up the more experienced members of the crew. Between coiling ropes, tying and untying knots as needed, and loading supplies into the cargo hold, Nate had his hands full, but he still managed to watch with an amazed sort of wonder as Xander and the other riggers scampered up and down the thin ropes, checking the sails and getting the *Southern Echo* ready to hunt. They paid no heed to the specter of death lurking beneath them, waiting for one misplaced foot or a grip slicked with sweat to send them plummeting, and it was both hard to watch and exceedingly difficult to look away. The gunners had an easier time, although Nate did not envy them the task of safely securing cannonballs and gunpowder. It struck Nate as a dangerous enough act while the ship was in port. He could not imagine handling those things while engaged in battle on the open sea. Although, he was likely to witness that firsthand soon enough.

Not long after sundown, Dax saw to it that every member of the crew received a sturdy meal finished off with fruit brought fresh from Spider's Nest, and then Novachak had them draw lots to see who would take the worst of the night's watches. Nate came up lucky, and he joined the other lucky ones below deck for a full night's sleep in their hammocks. If he had been less exhausted from the relentless training followed by manual labor, Nate might have been too excited to fall asleep. As it was, he shut his eyes a little after the ninth bell, and then opened them what felt like a minute later, when a shrill whistle and shout roused the crew just before dawn.

"On your feet," Novachak barked as he moved between the hammocks. "We've got ourselves a prize to catch."

This was met with subdued but happy murmurs, and then the ship was swarming with activity. Exhausted and bleary-eyed, Nate let himself get swept up in the flow. Before he knew it, the anchor was raised and Spider's Nest was a retreating patch of darkness off the *Southern Echo*'s stern, the dawn not yet strong enough to illuminate the land. By the time the sun was fully up, the island was small on the horizon.

After breakfast and a short time of relief for the night's watchers, Arani called the full crew to a meeting. She took up position at the rail of the elevated poop deck, overlooking the gathering on the main deck. Dax and Novachak were below her on the quarter deck, flanking the wheel of the helm and looking appropriately determined for the occasion. The *Southern Echo* was coasting at a slower, sedate pace, but the wind whipped Arani's voice over the gathered crew, carrying her words cleanly to every ear.

"I won't ask if you all enjoyed your time on Spider's Nest, as I've seen what you lot get up to when there's coin in your pockets and time on your hands." She smirked, and several of the crew whooped in agreement. More than a few others looked considerably less pleased, and Nate noticed that Arani made a point of allowing her gaze to linger on the unhappy ones. "I know we didn't have as much coin to play with as we expected," she continued, "but I mean to fix that now.

"I've word from Spider of the *Talon*, a small merchant ship coming in from the Leviathan Sea. Not a great enough prize to pay off our boatswain's debts and see him to retirement—" the crew chuckled a bit more earnestly at this, and Novachak gave a lopsided shrug, "—but more than we were able to get for our agate cache. And," Arani added with special stress on the word, "this one lacks a proper escort."

Nestled between the shoulders of Marcus and one of the riggers, Nate felt the crew shift forward. Their attention was fully fixed on the captain now, and Nate felt their excitement pulsing through the air.

"The *Talon* is taking a direct route to Solkyria," Arani continued. "They mean to rest and resupply at the Coral Chain Islands, but their draft is too deep for the northern reefs. They have to take the southern route around. That puts them right in our path, if we can get to them before they have a clear line of sight to the islands." She paused here, and gave the rigging of the *Southern Echo* an exaggerated glance. Nate and several others followed her gaze, taking in the square sails of the foremast and mainmast, carefully set to let the wind bleed out and keep the ship at a calmer pace. The bright cloth shivered in the breezes, as though eager to snap itself taught and turn that wind into raw power. Nate looked down to see Arani flash another wicked grin at the crew, and her voice was clear and proud when she said, "I rather like our chances of that. What say you?"

The crew laughed and cheered. Nate felt a small thrill as a smile stole across his face. He had yet to see the *Southern Echo* at her top speed, and he found himself looking forward to roaring across the sea, the wind bright and pure all around him and the sun glittering on the blue water.

Then the rigger nudged Nate and said conspiringly, "Ought to be our easiest hunt yet, with a proper wind worker on our side." He grinned at Nate's tattoo and then went back to cheering.

A pit opened in Nate's stomach. He glanced at Marcus, but the Darkbend was cheering with the rest of them, and had not heard the rigger's murmur.

Arani dismissed the crew after that, and Dax and Novachak stepped forward, barking out fresh orders that would see the ship gather speed and properly begin the hunt. The rigger next to Nate disappeared without so much as a glance in his direction, and Marcus gave Nate a slap on the back before leaving to see to his own duties.

"Don't look so scared," Marcus advised him before he left. "This is the fun part."

"I thought getting paid was the fun part?" AnnaMarie the gunner asked as she passed by.

"That's the *best* part," Marcus returned, and he and the gunner laughed as they broke away and headed for their respective tasks, oblivious to Nate's distress.

He felt his knees start to buckle as he thought of the crew staring, wondering why he wasn't working the wind to their advantage, calling him useless.

But he wasn't useless, he realized with a lightning strike of clarity. He'd sensed a ship on that beach. Surely, he could do it again on the water, if they could line up the wind just right.

Nate quickly sought out the captain, and he kept his eyes on Arani as she descended the steps back to the main deck. She disappeared for a moment, but he shouldered his way through the dispersing throng and found her easily enough. He saw her exchange a quick word with Rori before heading off along the railing, making her way for the hold.

"Captain!" Nate called.

Arani turned at Nate's voice, frowning a little as he caught up with her. "Mr. Lowwind," she said by way of greeting.

"Captain, I'd like a word," Nate said, not quite keeping the eager hope out of his voice.

Arani tilted her head and quirked an eyebrow at him.

Nate managed not to throw a surreptitious glance over his shoulder, but he did drop his voice and take a step closer when he said, "I would speak with you regarding my Skill."

The captain's gaze hardened. "Come with me." She quickly led him below deck and to the stern of the ship, where the captain's cabin was housed. She waved Nate inside and shut the door behind them.

If Nate had expected Arani's cabin to be luxuriously decorated and befitting of a naval officer, he would have been disappointed. There were tall windows along the walls that let in sunlight and a view of the sky and sea, and the room was considerably more spacious than where Nate and the rest of the crew slept, but it was spare and lacking in anything but utilitarianism.

Arani had forgone a proper bed in exchange for a hammock not at all dissimilar from the ones the crew used. It hung meekly in the corner, cast aside in favor of a large table surrounded by chairs. A writing desk holding ledgers and journals stood on the other side of the room, next to a great sea chest with a sturdy lock. Everything was clean and uncluttered, almost to the point of disturbance, and Nate did not quite know what to make of it all.

Arani did not seem inclined to give him a tour. "All right, my boy," she said as she took a seat at the head of the table. She leaned back in her chair, injured arm out of its sling but still moving tenderly, and drummed the fingers of her other hand on the smooth wood. "I'm pleased you had the sense to bring this up quietly, but I thought we were clear on the matter of your Skill, and my direct order not to bring it up at all."

Nate drew himself up to his full height as he said, "Yes, but isn't it time that I did?"

Arani's eyebrow flicked up again. "I don't recall ever saying that."

"The crew expects me to help us catch the *Talon*," Nate pressed. "They think I can fill the sails with wind."

The captain shook her head. "I can't stop them from talking, but it's against the code for them to make any move to force you. That will save you from the worst of it, but you'll need to endure their words for a while longer. They'll grumble, but they all know well and good that we've chased down plenty of prizes without a wind worker."

Nate brushed his thumb against the gold ring he wore, feeling the points of the sun crest beneath his finger. "But I *can* help," he said. "I sensed the *Dragonsbane* back on Spider's Nest. I could do it again with the *Talon*, if we're downwind from it."

"The *Talon*," Arani said, each syllable slow and pointed, "is following the trade routes. We know exactly where it's going to be, and we don't need to dance around the water and waste time lining up with the wind so you can show off."

Nate began to respond, but the full meaning of Arani's words settled over him, and his heart stuttered in his chest. "Show off?" he repeated dumbly.

"From the moment you stepped on this ship," Arani said, "you've wanted nothing more than to prove that the mark on your skin is wrong, and show everyone what you can really do. I've told you that you need to wait, and I say it again now. Be patient, and *wait*. Now is not the time."

"But isn't this what you wanted me for?" Nate blurted, frustration heating his voice. "Tracking down treasure ships?"

Arani met his gaze coolly. "I never said you'd be tracking ships."

"What, then? What am I supposed to be doing?"

"For now, following orders." Captain Arani stood and planted her hand on the hilt of the sword belted to her waist, promising Nate that even with one arm recovering from injury, she was not someone to be trifled with. "You may be new blood for a while yet, but the first thing every person on this ship learns is that when it comes to chasing prizes and waging battle, my word is law. It's as the crew decided, and all of them, from the quartermaster down to the cabin boys, know not to go against me when there is ruin and plunder on the line. The entire worth of your Skill depends on you respecting that part of our code. You, more than anyone, fall under my law, so when I tell you to keep quiet and wait, you'll do exactly that, or face the consequences."

"And what would those be?" Nate growled.

"Three lashes," Arani said without hesitation. "As is fitting of defiance of direct orders from your captain."

In spite of his anger, the memory of Rori's scarred back flashed across Nate's mind, and he swallowed his next words. Some of his rage went down with them, leaving him deflated.

The captain held his gaze for a long moment. Nate was the first to look away, and he heard her sigh.

"If we take the *Talon*," Arani said, "we'll have what we need for the next step." She paused for a heavy moment before saying, "I need to be sure you're ready for that."

"Perhaps I could be," Nate said, and he could not keep the pitiful note of desperation out of his voice, "if you told me what it is I'm supposed to be doing."

For a moment, Arani looked like she would finally tell him what she wanted him to track. She regarded him thoughtfully, and idly ran her thumb along the long chain she wore around her neck, as Nate had often see her do when she was thinking hard on a matter. Then she dropped her hand and the moment passed. "We will speak after we've taken the *Talon*," she said. "*If* we've taken the *Talon*. If we haven't, then..." She grimaced, but shook the thought away. "I haven't forgotten what I promised you, and I understand your eagerness to use your Skill. But I mean it, Nate. Wait." Another silence filled the cabin before Arani turned and moved to her writing desk, her back to him in clear dismissal. "Get yourself topside, Mr. Lowwind. I believe Mr. Novachak has work for you."

The deck creaked softly under Nate's feet as he retreated from the cabin.

NATE DID NOT FORGET Arani's sharpness, and his own disappointment was bitter on his tongue, but he was kept busy enough to push both to the back of his mind. With the *Southern Echo* on a direct intercept course with the merchant ship *Talon*, Novachak graduated Nate from coiling ropes to helping the crew rig the sails with the aim of grabbing every last scrap of wind they could. The work was far more physically demanding than anything Nate had done before, and his clothes were plastered against his chest and back with sweat by the time the sails were stretched taut. The wind raced to fill his lungs as the *Southern Echo* leapt over the water, and Nate felt giddy with the rush of all that pure, salt-touched air.

He did not have long to revel in it, as Novachak pulled him on to weapons duties minutes later, and he and a few others checked over the ship's stores of pistols and cutlasses and other equipment. They mostly cleaned the weapons, making sure they were in as best condition as they could be prior to engaging the *Talon*. The work was tedious but went by steadily, and soon enough, Nate was topside again, ready to help the riggers as they needed him.

Unfortunately for Nate, the riggers had the ship well in hand, and what little they wanted help with, Nate could not do.

"The wind off the starboard side could be a little stronger," Liliana remarked as Nate held a rope taut while she secured a special knot. It was almost an offhand comment, but she stared at Nate as she said it, and her voice was pitched to cleanly carry over the wind.

Nate tried to look very interested in the knot the rigger was finishing off. When she was done, he quickly set off in search of something, anything else to do, but he felt Liliana's hard frown following him.

It wasn't long after that the grumbling started, and Nate caught a few irritated stares in his direction. No one said anything directly to him, but Nate could feel the freeze setting in among the riggers as sure as he could feel the wind against his skin, and he silently cursed Arani for ordering him to secrecy. But he remembered Arani's harsh words, and he kept his head down and tried his best to keep up with the rest of the crew as they coaxed the last bit of speed out of the *Southern Echo*'s sails. It wasn't enough. People started stepping in to take his place, claiming that their more experienced hands were needed even on the menial tasks.

Nate could not argue with them, and he settled for trying to make himself as small and unobtrusive as possible.

Novachak was less than pleased by this development. The boatswain cornered Nate against the starboard railing and demanded to know why he wasn't assisting with the rigging as he'd been ordered.

Nate gave the man a bleak, tired look. "They say they have it all in hand," he explained, "unless I can work the wind for them."

The boatswain's stare did not so much as flicker, and Nate was surprised that the man's teeth had not popped out of his jaw with the way he was clenching it. "You're lucky Miss Rori is in need of assistance today," Novachak said. "You'll find her in the navigation room. Help her with whatever she needs, even if that sees you hanging from the mast and sending signals in Luken's stead." He rounded on the rigging crew. "And you lot! If you have time to groan about the wind, then you have time to catch more of it! Captain Arani wants this ship at top speed, so get to it!"

The riggers grimaced but moved faster with Novachak bearing down on them, giving Nate the chance to slip away.

He hurried over the deck but paused before entering the navigation room. No one was paying him much attention, focused as they were on keeping the *Southern Echo* sprinting across the sea. Nate moved to the railing, took a quick, deep breath, and turned his face into the wind. He reached for the element, but as always, control danced just beyond his fingertips. The familiar frustration kindled in his gut, but he smothered it before it could take hold. He thought back to that day on the beach, when the shadow of the *Dragonsbane* had slipped across his consciousness, and how it had disappeared when his academy training had kicked in and he had tried to focus hard. When he'd first sensed the ship, he hadn't been trying to reach for the element at all, just enjoying the feel of the wind through his hair and over his skin. He did the same now, withdrawing his awareness from everything but the sensation of the wind as it whipped around him.

It was harsher than it had been that day on the beach. It ripped at his clothes, frenzied by the way the *Southern Echo* split the natural currents of the air as the ship raced across the sea, although it lacked the wild, raw power of a storm. That was good, Nate thought. It gave him a strong wind with no distractions, and in spite of the disruptions of the *Southern Echo*, there was a smoothness to the wind that soothed Nate. It blew around him with a steady, pure rhythm, clear of snags and catches, perfect and clean and—

There.

Something smeared across the wind on Nate's left, casting a shadow of tangled air against his skin. He shivered a little as he turned instinctively towards the object, but he had to stop himself from reaching for it. Instead, he pulled his awareness back and tried to let the feeling wash over him. It was tricky, as trying to keep himself from focusing too hard was in direct conflict with his desire to read the wind more clearly, which left him with a vague impression of *something* on the edge of the horizon. He had no idea how big or small it was, the shape or the weight, but he thought that it was close to the water line, much the same as the *Dragonsbane* had been. Had he found the *Talon*, then? Could he learn more if the wind kept whispering its secrets across his skin in that frustrating elemental language that he almost but could not quite understand?

He never found out.

Something bumped hard against his shoulder, sending Nate spinning and stumbling. He nearly fell, his footing still a little unsteady out on the rolling sea, but he caught himself on the railing and regained his balance.

"Watch yourself," his assailant growled, and Nate looked up to see Jim Greenroot glowering at him. "Not the best spot for you to be daydreaming."

"I wasn't," Nate replied heatedly. "I was trying to—" he broke off as his gaze drifted over Jim's shoulder, and he caught a glimpse of Arani striding across the deck, steady and determined as she observed the labors of her crew. "Never mind," Nate said.

Jim scoffed and stalked away, hoisting a crate full of wadding for the cannons on to his shoulder. It was not a light load, and Nate was certain the gunner did it to demonstrate how he was pulling his own weight, unlike the Skilled on the ship. Disgusted, Nate went to find Rori.

As Novachak had said, the Goodtide was stationed in the navigation room. Rori had taken full advantage of the table inside to spread out several charts, the corners weighted down with small stones. There were a few instruments on the table, most of which Nate could not identify, but Rori's compass was out and the needle was wobbling against the motion of the ship. Rori was bent over one of the charts, making marks on the parchment in ink, and she did not seem to have noticed that Nate had come in. Luken, however, did, and he squawked and launched himself off the table, arrowing straight for Nate's head.

Nate had no choice but to engage the bird in their all-too-familiar dance. Nate had more than a few nicks in his fingers by the time he ripped his hat off and flung it away, snarling, "Fine, keep it!" Luken dove after the hat, leaving Nate to shake his hair out of his eyes and tug his shirt straight. He looked up to see Rori watching him with mild surprise on her face.

"I really have no idea why he has such an obsession with your hat," she said apologetically.

Nate huffed out a hard breath. He had no desire to speculate on avian obsessions with his headwear, and based on the way Luken was fluffing up his feathers as he settled against the fabric, it did not seem like it would be a problem as long as he did not try to reclaim his hat at any point in the future, near or far.

"What are you doing in here?" Rori asked as she turned back to her charts.

"I'm here to help you," Nate said as he stepped up to the table. His gaze ran over the charts, and he was instantly enthralled by the delicate line work. He could not hope to read the charts in any capacity, nor understand the complicated crisscrossing of the lines over the open water, but it was the islands that drew his attention, all those places that he had never seen before in his life. Nate had seen maps during his early, basic academy lessons that had shown Solkyria at the center of the world and imperial and enemy territories stretching into the east, but these sea charts brought things into focus. These were the places he had dreamed of going as a young boy, always imagining the deck of a navy ship beneath him and the proud Solkyrian flag snapping in the wind overhead. These were the islands whose sands he had long since given up hope of ever setting foot on, let alone seeing with his own eyes. This was the world, spread out before him as something knowable and touchable, and it was finally within his reach.

Rori's voice startled him out of his reverie.

"Nate?" she said, and her tone made it clear that it was not the first time she had tried to get his attention. "I appreciate the gesture, but I don't know what you think you can do here." She followed his gaze, which had wandered back to the maps of the seas and the islands. "You told me that you can't read, right?" she asked, her tone softening as she said the words.

Nate shook his head, his eyes still riveted on the jagged edges of the ink-drawn islands and the rivers and the trees that flooded them. "Novachak sent me," he said. "He said you needed help and I was to provide it."

Rori made a displeased noise. "And what were you doing before this?"

"Helping the riggers." He winced a little. "They started wondering out loud if I could work the wind for them."

Rori's expression soured, and her eyes narrowed as she glared down at the maps. "I suppose I could use a runner between me and the helm," she finally said. "Nothing complicated, just speeds and wind directions so I don't have to keep going out to get them myself."

Nate tore his eyes away from the charts and nodded. That much he could do. He could do more if Arani hadn't ordered him to stay silent, but it occurred to him that Rori already knew that. She was helping him train. It couldn't do any harm to speak to her.

He still worried his bottom lip between his teeth before he finally decided to plunge ahead. "I think I sensed the *Talon*," he said. "There was a shadow on the wind, a little off the port side. It was low on the water, like the *Dragonsbane* was."

Rori stared at him for so long, Nate began to wonder if he had sprouted a second head, but finally she motioned him over and lightly ran her fingers over a line on the chart in front of her. "We're heading due east at the moment, and we should hit this current within the hour. That will push us a little north and increase our speed, and we should catch the *Talon* here." She tapped a spot on the map, next to a bit of scrap paper scribbled over with notes and calculations. "I suspect that lines up nicely with what you sensed."

Nate stared at the place on the map, and tried to imagine where that would be on the horizon, but he had no understanding of navigation to give him a reference point. He sighed quietly. "I suppose Arani is right, and you don't need me to hunt prizes after all."

"Don't do that," Rori said. "That ship should be even further out than the *Dragonsbane* was, and as much as I know my calculations are correct, it's nice to have some confirmation that we're not going to miss our target before we can even see the sails."

Nate blinked and felt something ease its grip around his heart.

Rori glanced at him, and then she gave a quiet sigh of her own. "But don't do *that*, either, and go against the orders Arani gave you."

Nate nodded, a little sheepishly. "I just don't understand what she wants my Skill for," he said, "and she won't tell me."

Rori gave a small shrug. "She has her reasons." She frowned at the maps for a long moment. "I don't like how intent she is on your Skill, but I've known her for a while now, and believe me when I say that you should trust her. She protects her own, and she knows that secrets can keep us Skilled safe from all sorts of dangers, including the ones we never expected."

Nate turned away from the charts and crossed his arms. The gold ring with the Solkyrian crest flashed on his right hand, and Nate found himself staring at it when he said, "I think I'd be a little more prepared if she wasn't trying to keep my own Skill a secret from *me*." He sighed again and reached up to tug his hat over his eyes and his Lowwind mark, only to grasp empty air and remember that he had finally given the thing up to Luken. He glanced at the bird and decided he had at least made the right decision in that regard. Luken looked more content than a cat curled up in a patch of sunshine, and if birds could purr, his would have rattled the ship.

"I understand," Rori said. On some level, Nate knew that she truly did, but he wasn't in much of a mood to admit that. "You should still be careful," she continued. "Soft words echo loud on a ship like this, and you never know who may be listening."

"And we can't trust the rest of the crew?" Nate asked.

"With your life, you can," Rori said. "With your secrets, absolutely not." She returned her attention to the charts on the table and lifted a pen. "If you could, get our current speed from the helm, and tell them to expect that current soon. The riggers will need to adjust the sails when we hit it, and it's best if the helm can prepare them for it."

Nate nodded and set off, but he was troubled by Rori's words. He turned them over and over in his mind as he stepped out of the navigation room and closed the door behind him, worrying at the thought. Arani had certainly decided to trust part of the crew with his secret, and while that did not include Nate himself, her circle did include the navigator, the boatswain, and the quartermaster. He did not like being on the outside of that ring, and wondered if he could form his own.

"You two are certainly spending a lot of time together," a voice snapped out.

Nate stumbled, nearly missing the first step on the stairs that would take him up to the quarter deck and the helm. He spun around to see Xander leaning against the wall of the navigation room, arms crossed and a knowing look on his face. For a moment, Nate only gazed at the Grayvoice blankly, trying to fathom his friend's displeasure. Then he remembered the look that Xander had given him when he'd learned that Rori and Nate were spending time together on Spider's Nest. A lot of time.

"It's not what you think," Nate blurted out.

Xander quirked an eyebrow and a slow, insincere grin cut across his face. "Oh?"

"I'm helping her."

"Are you, now?" Xander's grin disappeared, replaced by a sharp and dangerous stare. "Used to be that Rori came to me whenever she needed some *help*." The Grayvoice let his eyes slip south on Nate's body. "She returning the favor, or got you caught in a one-sided exchange?"

Nate flushed and fumbled for a response, but all he could manage was to open and shut his mouth like a fish caught out of water.

Xander let him flounder in panicked embarrassment for a moment before his scowl evaporated in a laugh. "Easy, Lowwind." He pushed off from the wall and joined Nate at the stairs, suddenly relaxed and easy. "I'm only teasing you. Get ahold of yourself before I laugh so hard I piss myself." His wicked smirk returned. "Besides, Rori doesn't like to go for a roll in the spare sails and let the whole ship know what she's getting up to. She's not the quiet sort."

Nate nearly bit his own tongue in his desperate attempt to swear that he was not trying to come between Xander and Rori.

"Forget it," Xander said, still smirking. "Everyone gets a little jumpy before an attack. Thought I'd try to loosen you up a bit, and get to watch you squirm for my troubles."

"Thanks for that," Nate grumbled.

The Grayvoice shrugged. "You're sweating enough to fill the bilge twice over. Are you that nervous about taking your first prize?"

"No, I..."

Nate thought back to Arani's sharp warning, and Rori's cautioning, and how they both knew more about his Skill than Nate himself. It was easy to resent them both for that. He wanted his own circle to confide in and vent his frustrations, and why should Arani be the one to decide who could and could not be trusted with his secrets? Xander was rough and crude, but he was also a Grayvoice, and he had been the first to reach out to Nate and pull him into friendship.

Nate glanced about to make sure that no one had paused to listen in on their conversation. Everyone was keeping busy, and their shouts across the deck easily could have masked Nate's words, but he still dropped his voice low and leaned a little closer to

Xander before asking, "How much do you know about wind working?"

Xander's smile vanished. "Enough to know that it doesn't make you better than me," he said quietly, but there was a dangerous edge to his voice and the bright humor from a few moments earlier was completely gone. "Maybe Rori's excited to finally have another weather worker around, but you won't be shiny and new forever." The Grayvoice took a step up so that he was standing above Nate when he said, "And it didn't take *me* eight days to figure out how to use my sword."

Nate stared into Xander's eyes, and thought back to their first meeting, when Xander had called him a wind snob and tried to get Nate's gold ring in exchange for a small bit of agate. Then he thought of Rori's hand wrapped around Xander's wrist and the willing eagerness on the Grayvoice's face, and that hard look he'd given Nate on Spider's Nest when Nate and Rori had entered the tavern together that one night. Nate finally saw the depths of the cracks forming in the friendship between him and Xander.

"Understood," Nate said softly. "Sorry."

Xander smirked again before descending the steps and heading off for his rigging duties. With him went Nate's desire to confide in the Grayvoice, in *anyone*, about his Skill.

NATE WAS ON HIS way to complete his fourth run between Rori and the helm when a lookout spotted sails on the horizon. The cry went up across the ship, and Arani and the officers had spyglasses out and trained on the distant water before Nate had time to turn around. Several pirates swarmed to the railings, straining to get a look at the *Talon* as the *Southern Echo* closed in on her prey. Nate let them wash around him, edging his way towards the mainmast and that suddenly empty area of the deck. He took a breath and tried to let his focus blur with the wind, but his heart was pounding hard and he failed to take anything from the gusts but the taste of salt.

After the run-in with Xander, Nate's nerves had stretched taught. He had not told Rori about what the Grayvoice had said, thinking it would be better if he kept that exchange to himself. It sat heavy in his mind for a while until thoughts about the upcoming attack on the *Talon* crowded in alongside it. Now Nate's insides were twisting over themselves, and he felt almost as sick as he had his first day aboard the pirate ship, when he had taken his ring off and invited the Skill sickness into his body. By the time Captain Arani confirmed that they'd found the *Talon* and the crew loosed a wild cheer, Nate was on the verge of meeting his breakfast for the second time that day.

Arani informed the crew that they would bear down hard on the *Talon*, never mind if that signaled their hostile intentions and sent the prey ship running. The *Southern Echo* was the faster ship, and with the Coral Chain this close, speed was more important than stealth.

Nate wasn't sure if he should be happy that his first true trial as a pirate would be over soon, or dread the very real chance that he could be hurt or killed within the next few hours. Pirates were vicious and deadly, but Nate was barely familiar with the proper way to hold a cutlass without guaranteeing blisters on his palms. He was sweating badly by the time Dax sought him out.

"Pull yourself together and come with me," the quartermaster ordered. "There's a bit more training for you before we come upon the *Talon*."

Nate's legs shook as he followed Dax belowdeck. Halfway down the stairs, he suddenly remembered what he'd been doing before the *Talon* was spotted. "Rori has me running messages to the helm," he called.

"I think she'll manage just fine from this point on," Dax said with a rueful smile. "You, my boy, are another matter entirely."

Dax took Nate out of the way of the rest of the crew as they prepared the *Southern Echo* for battle. Orders were shouted from the gun deck and feet thudded across the main deck overhead, but somehow, Dax was able to ignore all of that as he checked over Nate's cutlass. "I'm not giving you a pistol for your first run," the quartermaster remarked as he squinted down the length of the sword. He gave a satisfied nod and handed the weapon back to Nate. "You're shaking so bad, you'll likely shoot yourself before any of the enemy."

Nate tried and failed to swallow past the lump in his throat.

Dax had Nate practice with his sword in the confines of the hold. He let Nate move at his own pace, a considerable mercy given the pitch and roll of the ship. "It'll be easier once we've bled some speed out of the sails," the quartermaster said, "but you may not get lucky enough to keep yourself topside in a fight. Get used to moving through these tighter spaces."

Nate did as he was told. The movement and the need to concentrate on where he put his feet and his sword helped him shed some of his fear, but enough was left that he accidentally stabbed the bulkheads more than once. Dax kept a close watch on him the entire time, calling out corrections and encouragement. Eventually, he halted Nate and asked how he was feeling.

"Like I may start screaming and never be able to stop."

"Good," Dax said. "Do that. Let them hear you on the *Talon*. Shake them as badly as they've already shaken you."

Nate was too nervous to feel any shame at the jab. "Could you do what you did that night on the beach?" he asked, and his voice wavered enough to take off any edge there might have been to the request. "Calm me down a bit with your Skill?"

Dax shook his head. "You feel that blood racing through you? You'll want that. It'll carry you much further than you've ever gone before." He regarded Nate for a moment. "And as it stands, we're unlikely to actually fight anyone today."

That put a bemused look on Nate's face.

The quartermaster shrugged. "Usually, the captain will have us approach our target at a slower speed, so we can get close to them before they suspect anything. Most of the crew will hide below and wait. Then, when we're in hailing distance, we'll bring up the black flag and swarm the top deck, surprising the enemy with our numbers and wild roaring." He grinned a little at that. "Sometimes, that's enough to make the other ship surrender on the spot. Other times they'll try to run, and other times still, they'll put up a fight, and then we go in and make things bloody."

Nate's stomach performed a complicated feat of acrobatics.

"This time," Dax continued, "we're chasing them from the start. They'll know we're pirates long before they can make out our flag. They'll try to run. Most merchants do, but given the size of the *Talon*, she's not likely to be carrying any great prize, and a ship like that will have insurance on its wares. If the *Talon*'s captain is smart, they'll put up a white flag and sit quietly while we take our plunder."

"And if they're not smart?" Nate managed to ask.

Dax nodded at the cutlass in Nate's hand. "You have that for a reason. Keep a sharp eye about you, and you'll be all right. Now, put the blade away and run up and down here. Work on your balance."

"So I don't accidentally stab the bulkheads?" Nate asked with a weak smile.

"So you don't fall into the sea when you run across a plank to the enemy ship," Dax said.

A whole new wave of fears wormed through Nate's mind, but he did as he was told, praying to every god he knew all the while.

CHAPTER THIRTEEN

The Talon

IT DID NOT TAKE long for the *Southern Echo* to catch the *Talon*.

As so many had said, theirs was the faster ship, and the merchant vessel came into sharp focus long before there was any chance of it seeking refuge among the Coral Chain islands. It did seem that the *Talon* would try to run at first, swinging around on a sharper heading and making a desperate attempt to fill its sails, but the merchant ship—not much bigger than the *Southern Echo*—lacked the square rigging that made the pirate brig so fast, and it was barely an hour before the *Talon* was flying white flags and visibly slowing down. Arani had the *Southern Echo* respond with her own black standard: a bone-white dragon head devouring the Solkyrian sun. The dragon's jaws snapped closed on the yellow sun as the wind whipped the flag about, and two blue flags with yellow crosses were strung up beneath it, followed by a solid red flag.

With no need to disguise their numbers, Nate was above deck with the majority of the crew. He'd ended up near Xander and a few other riggers. Still stinging from his earlier encounter with the Grayvoice, Nate avoided his eye, but from their spot on the deck, they both had a clear view of the flags as they went up, and Xander made a displeased noise.

"Captain's signaling that she's willing to give quarter as long as they behave." The Grayvoice pointed at the two blue-and-yellow flags, then nodded across the water at the *Talon*, which was quickly hoisting two crossed flags of its own beneath the white flag. "And they've agreed." He sounded almost bored.

Nate, on the other hand, was giddy with relief until Xander quipped a sharp smile.

"Maybe they're trying to trick us and planning an ambush as soon as we're aboard," the Grayvoice mused.

"What happens then?" Nate asked before he could stop himself.

Xander gave him a cool smirk as he pointed up again, this time at the red flag. "Blood will be spilled."

Nate swallowed hard and went back to praying to every god above and below that he could name. He did not join in the wild shouting of the rest of the crew as the ships came within hailing distance, and he was still silently praying as he began to pick out the individual sailors aboard the merchant ship. They were grim and silent, many standing as rigid as the stone sentinels in the watchtowers on Solkyria. Others were tossing their weapons into a pile on the deck, some quick and unsteady with fear, others slow and deliberate with clear anger. A man dressed in a pristine coat and large hat waved the merchant crew on, his eyes riveted on the approaching pirate ship even as he urged his sailors to unload their weapons at greater speeds.

The *Southern Echo* slowed as she came alongside the *Talon*, bleeding wind out of her sails until the two ships glided over the water at a sedate pace. Hooks flew from the pirate ship to the deck of the merchant vessel, and their ropes were pulled taught to lock the ships together. A few of the more daring members of the *Southern Echo*'s crew swung from the rigging to the deck of the *Talon*, leading the charge, but Arani was the first up on the narrow board that was thrown down to bridge the two ships. She seemed to float across the makeshift walkway, so light and sure were her steps, and she had her sword drawn and a pistol out before her boots touched the deck of the merchant ship. She moved with a direct purpose, seeking out the captain of the *Talon* and shepherding him to the center of the deck. The pirates with her followed suit, brandishing cutlasses and pistols at the sailors to herd them away from the weapons pile and into a tight group that the pirates easily surrounded.

Nate had just enough time to notice that there were considerably fewer merchant sailors than there were pirates, and then he was caught up in the next rush. He barely registered his own forward momentum before he was up on one of the walkways, two pirates flanking the board and holding it steady while they cheered their fellows on. The thin wood shook and bent under the weight of Nate and the others that were arrowing across to the *Talon*, and below them, the water glimmered blue and hard under the midday sun. Nate hesitated, but pirates surged behind him and pushed him forward, and his heart escaped his chest to pound wildly in his throat, and then his feet were moving and he shuddered and felt himself listing to the side as though the sea had grabbed his arm and begun to pull, and then he was jumping down on to the solid, reliable deck of the *Talon*, and he wasn't sure if he felt sick or terribly alive.

All around Nate, pirates swarmed and cheered, brandishing weapons as they pressed the crew of the *Talon* into a submissive huddle. Arani was at the forefront of this, but she stood with one hand raised in a fist over her head, and gradually, the roar of the pirates subsided to a gleeful murmur. The air was charged with anticipation, but the pirates held themselves back, obeying the captain's silent command.

Arani's voice carried clean and clear when she addressed the merchant captain. "If any of your crew are not here, whether they hide in fear or ambush, I give you one chance to call them up. If we find them ourselves, we will give no quarter."

The captain of the *Talon* could not help glancing about as a low growl rippled through the pirates, but to his credit, he drew himself to his full height and nodded respectfully to Arani. He took a quick count of the crew huddled about him. "We are all here," he said in a steady voice. "We offer no resistance." He made a careful gesture to the sailor behind him, who stepped forward and offered a thick, heavy book to Arani.

Arani slowly lowered her arm. Her expression betrayed no emotion as she accepted the book and thumbed through the pages, coming to rest at one marked off by a ribbon. Nate could not see the page from where he stood, but he did see Arani run her finger back and forth across several lines before giving a satisfied nod. She handed the book off to Dax and ordered a survey of the cargo hold. The quartermaster called on several pirates to follow him, and they disappeared into the belly of the ship.

A few tense minutes passed in silence, during which Arani stood in front of the merchant captain and stared the man down. He looked back at her with a deliberate calm that did not quite hide all of his nervousness.

"I assure you," the man said at one point, "the cargo is all accounted for."

Arani said nothing, and the silence resumed.

Nate felt his own nerves start to scrape together again. He lightly nudged the pirate next to him and asked as loudly as he dared, "What is she waiting for?"

The pirate glanced at Nate long enough to make him feel foolish for asking the question. But the man leaned a little closer and murmured, "The quartermaster is checking for ambushes."

Nate blinked and surveyed the small merchant crew. "Their captain said they were all here."

The pirate snorted. "And never has a man lied before."

Nate did not speak again after that.

Finally, one of the pirates Dax had taken below emerged to call out that the ship was clear, and they were beginning the survey of the cargo hold. Arani managed to relax without dropping any of the stoic danger in her expression.

"Wise of you to be an honest man," she said to the other captain before turning and beginning a slow walk around the merchant crew, peering into each of their faces. Many of them looked away. "How does your crew see you, I wonder?" She stopped in front of the first sailor to hold her gaze, a wiry young man who puffed out his skinny chest and clenched his narrow jaw. "What kind of man is your captain?" she asked.

"A great one," the young sailor said without hesitation. "One of the finest in these waters, and far too noble to ever become thieving pirate scum." He spat this with such vehement disdain that Nate expected to see at least three cutlasses embedded in his chest within a few moments, but Arani gave a wry smirk.

"Quite a man he must be," she said with exaggerated wonder. "I imagine that when he breaks wind, it reeks of flowers and fills the sails and blows the *Talon* all the way home." She glanced about at the pirates surrounding her and the masts of her own ship towering over their heads, and shrugged. "Seems to have failed him this time."

A low chuckle ran through the pirates.

The wiry sailor stared at her with open outrage. "We will see you hanged for your crimes against Solkyria, long may the empire shine!"

"Mmm." Arani turned to the next sailor, who looked to be even younger still. He dropped his eyes the moment Arani drew near, and sweat broke out on his skin. "And you?" Arani asked, making it clear who she was addressing. "What say you on the matter of your captain's character?"

The boy could not quite look Arani in the eye, and his voice wavered when he spoke. "He is a good man, ma'am. Stern but fair. We do well under him." A soft murmur of agreement went up from a few others of the merchant crew.

Arani turned a thoughtful eye on the captain of the *Talon*, who looked to be regaining some of his confidence. "A fair captain, these two say. I wonder if he is a different captain to the one with the Lowwind mark."

Startled, Nate scanned the merchant crew again. This time, his gaze snagged on the light blue tattoo on the brow of one of the sailors. She'd had her head down until Arani had picked her out, and Nate had not seen her mark. He saw it now, a curling design more elaborate than his own but nowhere near the level of a Highwind, and he recognized the woman it adorned. He did not know her name, but she had been at the wind working academy for a while alongside Nate, though she was at least two years older than him. She had changed much, growing thinner in her time away from the academy, almost dangerously so, and there were dark circles under her eyes. Nate recalled that she had been one of the more spirited Lowwinds at the academy, full of determination and energy. He did not remember her as one of his tormentors. She might have been one of the indifferent ones, too busy with her own training to care much about Nate's progress, or lack thereof. Her time at the academy had certainly ended on a good note with placement on a Solkyrian merchant ship. Even if she looked worse for wear, she was a Lowwind the empire could be proud of.

"How is your life under this captain?" Arani asked as she came around to stand in front of the Lowwind sailor.

The woman swallowed and her breathing quickened, but she held Arani's gaze. "I..." She shifted a little, and looked to be very aware of the eyes of the unmarked merchant sailers suddenly trained on her. She shuddered visibly under the glower of her fellow sailors, and Nate saw the merchant captain give her a far harsher look than the man had used before, his lip curling as he stared at the Lowwind. There was a warning there, one that Nate recognized all too well.

None of this was lost on Arani, who tilted her head and turned her body a little, opening up more of a view to her crew of pirates, and specifically to Marcus Darkbend, who gave a cheerful wave. Nate saw the merchant Lowwind's eyes widen as they caught on Marcus's tattoo, and her lips parted as she began to search the faces of the other pirates. She picked out Eric Darkbend off to her left, looking elegant as always, and then Xander Grayvoice above her, where he'd joined some of the pirates in the lower ropes of the *Talon*'s rigging to watch from above like a flock of predatory birds. Awe turned to cautious excitement in the Lowwind's eyes, and she spun to take in the rest of the crew, ignoring the angry stares of her own crew and captain. She had just opened her mouth to say something more when her gaze passed to Nate, caught on his Skill-marked face, and froze.

For a moment, time seemed to stop, and everything hung in perfect balance, yet ready to tip into something bright and new.

But a moment was only a moment, and the Lowwind's gaze hardened as recognition bloomed. Nate had not expected her to break into joyous song and dance at the sight of him, but he'd thought that seeing a fellow Lowwind would be the final push she needed to step away from her life on the *Talon* and turn pirate. He offered her a small smile and lifted his hand in greeting. In response, her expression turned dark and angry, and she turned from Nate with open disdain.

Nate felt the pirates around him shift and throw bewildered glances at him, but he could not take his own eyes off of the Lowwind as she gathered herself to her full height and faced Arani again.

"I serve my captain faithfully, and use my Skill for the good of the empire," she said. "I may not have been born a Highwind, but I know my place, and I do what I can with the taint of magic in my blood."

Arani's slight raising of her eyebrows was the only indication that she was surprised. The captain kept her face perfectly blank otherwise. "That is not what I asked you," she said.

The Lowwind swallowed hard and shut her eyes for a moment. Clear regret passed over her face, and then she opened her eyes again and gave Nate one final, scathing look. "It matters not who my captain is," she said. "My Skill belongs to Solkyria, and I am proud to serve. I also know that I am exactly where I am meant to be, as any place with Nathaniel Nowind is no place of mine."

Nate's gut coiled in on itself, and heat seethed uncomfortably beneath his skin. More pirates were looking at him now, along with several of the *Talon*'s crew, and confusion was plain on their faces.

Arani, too, was frowning when the Lowwind turned back to her and intoned gravely, "My life for the empire."

For the first time, the pirate captain seemed at a loss. She gave the Lowwind a slow, searching look from head to toe, taking in her too-thin frame, sunken and exhausted eyes, and limp clothing before turning her frown on Nate. The Lowwind followed her gaze and shot a look of smug superiority at him, but it suddenly fell away to be replaced by shock.

A hand came down on Nate's shoulder and gently pushed him aside. Rori stepped forward into the empty space. Her fingers tightened in a light squeeze on his arm, but her eyes were hard and her jaw set as the Lowwind gawked at her Goodtide tattoo, the only high Skill mark among either crew. Rori slipped past Nate without a word and threaded her way to the front of the crowd, which parted respectfully to let her pass. When she was before the crew of the *Talon*, Rori planted her feet and stood with one hand on the sword at her hip, her chin tilted up in a firm challenge to the Lowwind.

The merchant sailors and the Lowwind gaped at her.

"Seems to me this stupid fool has her mind made up, Captain," Rori said without taking her eyes off of the Lowwind. "Best let her throw her life away as she wishes."

"Indeed," Arani said, at the same moment that the captain of the *Talon* let loose an angry cry.

"You stole a Goodtide?" he snarled, all submission melting away in the face of this revelation.

Arani's spine was rigid when she turned back to him, and Nate caught a dangerous flash in her eyes. "One does not steal a person," she said. "She is with us of her own free will."

"The Skilled do not have wills!" he barked, and Nate was shocked to see him take a step forward. "They belong to the empire. How dare you claim *any* as your own, especially a high Skill?"

Tension grew across both crews then, with anger flaring in the eyes of many of the *Talon*'s sailors, and its mirror rising among the ranks of the *Southern Echo*. The Lowwind from the *Talon* dropped her eyes to the deck and said nothing, but the crew around her began to nod and growl in agreement.

The merchant captain's face turned red under the weight of his self-righteous fury. "I'll see you hanged for this," he shouted at Arani. He swung and pointed viciously at Rori. "And I'll flog *you* myself!" His hand reached for a sword that was not on his hip. He fumbled with the empty air, but that did not stop him from fixing his murderous gaze on every Skilled pirate he could find, Nate included. "I'll flog all of you!" he snarled. "I'll see the skin flayed from your backs and the emperor's seal burned into your chests!"

Nate's throat was very dry, but he felt the protective press of the pirates around him, and his grip steadied on his sword. The pirates weren't looking at him now, but at the merchant captain and his sailors, and they were ready to move. Rori even had her cutlass drawn and had started towards the screaming man.

But Arani held up her hand, catching the Goodtide before she could rush the merchant captain. Then Arani reached into her sash, drew a pistol, and calmly put a bullet through the captain's heart.

Everything was very quiet in the wake of that gunshot. Smoke drifted silently away on the wind, the

Talon's sailors flinched and lost their voices to shock, and even the thud of the captain's body as it hit the deck was muffled.

Arani slowly, deliberately put the spent pistol away and straightened her coat before turning to address the merchant crew. "Does anyone else have something to say?" she asked.

No one did.

Arani had them leave the body of the merchant captain where it had fallen, blood pooling dark beneath it. She set a guard over the *Talon*'s crew, and had Xander and the other riggers begin cutting and slashing their way through the merchant ship's rigging, crippling the vessel. It was too slow to serve as a proper pirate ship, she said, and irreparably tainted by bad captainship. Arani set the rest of the crew, Nate included, to transferring plunder from the *Talon*'s hold to the *Southern Echo*'s. Nate helped move crates of furs and semi-precious gemstones along with barrels of sugar, gunpowder, and rum, and tried to understand how he was feeling.

Fear and relief warred in his mind. The former was all-too familiar from his experiences with Solkyrian citizens looking down on the Skilled, and the latter was new and odd in the wake of seeing a pirate captain, *his captain*, silence a man forever for his open disdain for Rori and the others. The man had been happy to surrender his ship to Arani when he'd thought them simple pirates, but seeing a high Skill among their ranks had changed everything. And the crew had pressed in around him protectively, even as that other Lowwind scoffed at Nate.

While Nate helped move the cargo, he kept glancing up at the flags flying from the two ships' masts. Arani's black standard, with the dragon devouring the sun, looked as fearsome as ever. But as Nate stared at the merchant ship's flag, blue and white with the sun crest of the Solkyrian Empire blazed in gold, it began to look like the more unwelcoming of the two.

Nate shook his head and tried to scatter such thoughts, but his heart would not let them go so easily.

CHAPTER FOURTEEN

A Proposition to the Crew

IRIS STOOD IN HER private cabin aboard the *Southern Echo*, watching the *Talon* recede in their wake. The merchant ship was already small on the horizon, but she knew that the *Talon*'s new captain would still be struggling to get the rigging repaired and the ship underway once more. It would be at least a day before the *Talon* could sail again, and the *Southern Echo* would be long gone by then.

All things considered, the raiding of the *Talon* went about as well as could have been expected, but Iris was still disappointed. While they hadn't grown the crew's numbers, they had not lost anyone either, and had things gone better, Iris would have let that captain sail away on his own ship with no harm to him or his crew. He would have been down some insured cargo and struggled a bit to keep the *Talon* under control following the maiming of its sails and rigging, but he could have kept his ship as thanks for his cooperation. Instead, he'd gone on that tired, awful tirade about the Skilled, and Iris did not tolerate that kind of talk. The Solkyrian Empire may have viewed the Skilled as tools to be worn and abused to the point of breaking, but that was not for her, nor was it for her crew.

It had stopped surprising her a long time ago how the Solkyrians treated their rare magic-users. Solkyria was the only island to produce such phenomena, and its ruler squeezed the life from them. Having lived as a daughter of one of Solkyria's conquered islands and knowing the extent of the empire's greed firsthand, Iris had not expected much of Solkyrians to begin with. It was an odd sort of irony that she was the captain of a pirate crew with a good number of Solkyrian sailors, Skilled and un-Skilled alike, but stranger things were known to happen.

The reaction of that Lowwind on the *Talon*, for instance.

Iris had come across that kind of brokenness in the Skilled before. From the moment their magic manifested, it was drilled deep into their minds that they were meant to serve the empire and its recognized citizens, and to dare to hope for more was treason of the highest sort. Some of the Skilled absorbed that teaching into their very being, and confused its heaviness for armor instead of chains. Many others resigned themselves to a learned helplessness and kept their heads bowed and their mouths shut in an attempt to fade as far into the background as they could. And others still—the ones like Dax, Xander, Rori, Marcus, Eric and even Nate, as much as the boy did not want to admit it to himself—had a spark of rebellion in their hearts just waiting to be fanned into a fire. Iris had seen that in the Lowwind on the *Talon*. But the Lowwind had caught sight of Nate, and her defiance had transformed into spite. Rori had been correct in her assessment of the Skilled merchant sailor; the woman had made up her mind and would not be swayed.

That had been another surprise, the way Rori had stepped forward when that Lowwind had insulted Nate. Rori often preferred to hang back on raids, not out of cowardice but because the sight of her Goodtide tattoo could incite extreme reactions. Most of the crew still didn't quite know what to make of her, and she had been sailing with them for the better part of two years now. But seeing someone sneer at Nate had brought Rori out, and she'd been ready to fight. Iris wondered if Rori would have stepped forward for any of the *Southern Echo*'s Skilled, or if it had been Nate in particular that had stoked her protectiveness. She was mulling this over when a knock sounded on the door.

She turned to see Dax step inside with Nate in tow. The new pirate had done well enough on his first raid, Dax had informed her earlier. The boy had been a bit shaky, but he had gone across the water and played his part without protest. He did not even seem all that upset over Iris shooting the *Talon*'s captain. No, what bothered Nate was the way that Lowwind had reacted to him.

What did that foolish woman call him? Iris wondered. *Nowind?*

Whatever it was, it had cut Nate deep, and his steps were heavy as he made his way across the cabin to stand before her. He did not look at Iris, instead keeping his gaze turned down in a subservient manner.

Annoyance prickled along Iris's skin, but she bit back on the sharp command to look her in the eye and schooled herself into calmness. Her voice was level when she said, "Thank you for bringing him, Dax."

The quartermaster nodded. He would remain present for this private conference between her and Nate, taking up position by the door to intercept anyone who came seeking the captain.

Iris placed her attention back on the young man before her, who was still doggedly not looking at her. She gave an exasperated sigh. "Enough of this self-pity," she said. "It's time we tell the crew what you can really do."

That was enough to drag Nate's eyes off of the floor. "I can't *do* anything," he said. There was no heat in his voice, only exhaustion and resignation. "You don't need me to track ships and I can't help the *Southern Echo* sail any faster, although I suppose now we can say that I make other wind workers choose dying for Solkyria over sailing with me."

So he had determined that much, Iris mused. If nothing else, at least he wasn't stupid.

"It was her choice to remain on the merchant ship," Iris said. "It was a foolish one, but one that she was free to make."

"She would not have made it if it had not been for me," Nate said.

"Which is why I called it a foolish choice," Iris returned.

The young man shook his head. "If I wasn't in your crew, you'd have yourself a proper wind worker now."

Iris placed her hands on the back of the chair in front of her and drummed her fingers on the polished wood. "Perhaps," she agreed. "I won't deny that it would be an advantage to have a wind worker who could do what you can't—" she watched Nate wince at this, "—but that's not what I *need* right now. It's certainly not why I asked you to join us."

The boy gave her a puzzled frown, but he sat down when Iris gestured for him to take a seat. She sat across from him and thought about how she wanted to begin this discussion with him.

"What do you know of Captain Ava Mordanti?" Iris finally said.

"The thief?" Nate asked.

Iris's jaw tightened, but she kept her voice level when she said, "That's the one."

Nate frowned again and looked down at the table, as though he'd find answers in the grain of the wood. "I know she's from an old myth," he said slowly. "I think the story says she stole something from the gods and they sank her ship and trapped her at the bottom of the sea as punishment?"

"So the Solkyrian version goes," Iris said mildly. She was a little impressed that Nate had used so much tact in his description of Mordanti, given that Solkyrians knew her as Mordanti the Thief, the arrogant Veritian villain who'd stolen from the gods because she could not make her fortune on her own merit, and been struck down for her foolishness. That was the legacy the Solkyrian Empire had allowed to exist, and Iris felt an angry thrill at the idea of tearing it to shreds. "Veritians tell the story quite a bit differently."

She gave Nate the historical account of Captain Mordanti's privateering attacks against the Solkyrian Empire's early expansion efforts, and how the Veritian captain had, indeed, taken a treasure from a Solkyrian ship and hidden it away before she'd died in combat defending Veritia against imperial invaders.

"To us, she was a hero," Iris finished. "Someone who endured against even the worst odds, and she left more than just a legacy for us to follow." She paused for a moment, gauging Nate's interest in the story. The boy was leaning forward in his seat, his attention locked on Iris as she spoke. She smiled a little. "Mordanti also left a map. To most, it's a map to the greatest treasure the world has ever known." Her smile turned rueful. "I don't expect you to understand this, but to me, that map is a chance to finalize history and bring back some of the greatness Veritia lost when Solkyria conquered us. It's a complicated legacy, but it's one that the empire hasn't managed to erase. Not yet. I aim to keep history alive."

"A map," Nate repeated skeptically after several silent moments. "You don't mean the one from the legend, do you? The one that Mordanti burned into the wings of a dragon?"

Iris ran her thumb along the chain around her neck. "That would be the one," she said quietly.

Nate stared at her, and it was clear he was trying to decide if she was serious or not. He gave a nervous laugh. "Dragons are extinct," he said. "They haven't been seen since—"

He broke off as Iris pulled up the chain around her neck, revealing the black scale at the end.

"What's that?" he asked in a small voice.

"A scale from the black dragon with Captain Mordanti's treasure map burned into its wings," Iris said.

She lifted the chain over her head. Her neck felt strange without its weight. She bunched up the chain and slid it across the table. It unspooled as it went, trailing the black scale behind it until it came to a stop in front of Nate. He seemed almost afraid to touch it, but he picked up the chain. The black scale swung and glimmered lazily in the air, smoke swirling across its surface.

He shook his head as he stared at it. "This must have come from a sea serpent," he said.

"It's too sharp for a serpent," Iris said, "even a deep-sea one."

"So where did this scale come from, then?"

"From the dragon," Iris said simply, "the night I met it." She smiled as Nate fixed her with a stunned, open-mouthed stare. She crossed her arms and leaned her weight on the back of the chair.

She was familiar with all of the arguments and doubts, and she had answers to each of them, and she had the vivid memory of her brief, chance encounter with the dragon on the Leviathan Sea, when a storm had caught them both unawares and thrust them together before tearing them apart, leaving Iris with a scar on her arm and a dragon scale clutched so tightly in her hand, it had drawn blood.

"Look at the colors," Iris insisted, "look at the patterns. I promise you, that is a scale from a dragon the color of wildfire smoke, alive and flying somewhere out there with Captain Mordanti's map burned into its wings." She reached across the table and held her hand open. "A dragon that lives and breathes as sure as I do, and one that I intend to find."

Nate stared at her for several long moments before he dropped the chain with the dragon scale into her hand. The edges of the scale dug into the familiar, calloused places on her palm as Iris closed her fingers around it.

"You're mad," Nate said. He whipped around to include Dax in the accusation. "Both of you."

"What the captain says is true," Dax said.

"Have *you* seen this mythical beast?" Nate asked.

The quartermaster pursed his lips and said nothing.

"Right," Nate said, swinging back around to Iris. "This goes beyond madness into... into..." he threw up his hands. "I don't know *what* this is, but it's nothing that anyone in their right mind would even think of doing."

"They tend to say the same of anyone who would defy the Solkyrian Empire," Iris remarked.

Nate looked at her sharply, and a new kind of fear was creeping into his eyes. The kind of fear someone learns when their captain orders them to sail into a hurricane. This was no hurricane, however. This was the stuff of legends, made solid and ready for the taking, and Iris needed Nate to help her find it.

"Even if that's a real dragon scale," Nate said, "how could it possibly be the one with Mordanti's map? The legend says she sailed hundreds of years ago."

Iris gave him a wry smile. "That's one of the more fascinating things about creatures that have their own magic. They tend not to die unless something intentionally kills them."

Nate's disbelief deepened. "So how do you know *that* one is still alive?"

Iris dangled the scale between them once more. "Your people hunted these dragons to near extinction, but they had the sense to write down a few things as they slaughtered the creatures. For instance, dragon slayer records note that every time they killed a beast, its scales faded to white, destroying their colors and patterns. I don't pretend to understand how a dragon's magic works, but as long as this scale stays black, I know that the beast is still alive."

Nate was visibly struggling against accepting what Iris was claiming, but he kept looking back at the dragon scale, and pieces of Mordanti's legend were falling into place. "If that's true," Nate said slowly, "how would you even begin to find the dragon?"

Iris let her silent gaze on his Lowwind tattoo answer his question.

Nate's eyes widened. "Oh." He shook his head. "I can't."

"You can," Iris returned. "You're the *only* wind worker who can."

Nate shook his head faster. "This is an impossible thing."

"It's not impossible," Iris said. "It just hasn't been done before." She was the one who leaned forward this time. "It's going to be difficult, easily the hardest thing you've ever done, but we're going to keep training your Skill. Dax and Novachak and Rori all say you've come a long way since you started." She waited until Nate was looking her in the eye again. "I think you can go further. Do you want to try?"

She held her breath as she waited for Nate's answer. She needed him to say yes, to help her find the dragon. She could not do it without him. They had a long way to go before he'd be able to sense something far enough out on the wind to be helpful, and it would need to be upwind of him, based on the reports from his training sessions, but Iris could practically see the wake of Mordanti's ship spilling out before her, carving an ephemeral trail across the seas with an open invitation to follow. She had to set her own ship and crew on the track before it disappeared.

Nate sat for several moments, silently fiddling with the gold ring on his right hand. "You really believe I can do this?" he finally said.

Gods above, I hope so, Iris thought. But she responded with a firm nod of her head.

Doubts warred across Nate's face with his willingness to believe her, and for a heart-stopping moment, Iris was afraid that he would say no.

But then he said, "I'll try."

Iris stopped herself from sagging with relief, but the breath she was holding escaped in a quiet rush. She smiled at the boy. "I plan to reveal your true Skill to the crew, let them know the real reason you won't help them with the sailing, and what you'll be doing from now on instead." *And,* she added silently, *to keep them from prying further into that 'Nowind' name that woman called you.* Aloud, Iris said, "I think a demonstration of your Skill would go a long way towards convincing everyone, if you don't mind?"

Nate nodded, still turning the gold ring around and around on his finger. There was a dazed expression on his face, but something like hopeful awe was beginning to ignite behind his eyes.

"Good," Iris said. "Best go prepare yourself. We'll be using Luken to show them what you can do."

Nate rose and drifted out of her quarters without another word, and without looking at Dax as he stepped past the quartermaster. The door clicked softly closed behind the boy, and Iris allowed herself to sit back in her seat and let the relief wash over her.

They had a lot of work ahead of them, but Iris was finally following Captain Mordanti. She felt the moment stretch out before her, heavy with promise.

It was interrupted when Dax cleared his throat. "I noticed you didn't mention anything about the Court of Sirens," he said as he came to stand before her.

Iris winced a little, but made herself look Dax in the eye. "I don't intend to share that bit of information with anyone."

"Iris…"

"The crew would never vote for this if they knew what was coming next," she said. "You know they wouldn't."

Dax held her gaze for a long moment. "They deserve to know."

Iris shook her head. "They can't, but I will keep them safe."

Dax gave her the sidelong look he usually reserved for the moments when she'd said something particularly outrageous, and he intended to tease her for it. There was no humor in his eyes now.

"I am prepared to buy their safety," Iris promised before he could say anything. "Whatever the cost, we will come out of this alive."

He did not look placated.

"Please, Dax," she said softly. "I'm so close. *We're* so close."

The quartermaster sighed and ran a hand over his tattooed head. "No more secrets after this," he said, pulling his tone of command into his voice, and once more, Iris glimpsed the impassable distance their respective roles had placed between them.

"No more," Iris agreed. "This is the last."

THE WIND WAS GENTLE on Iris's face as the *Southern Echo* moved stately over the waves. The sun was warm in the cloudless sky and the ocean stretched all around the ship, nothing but pure blue to be seen in every direction. Iris loved days like this, and the calm familiarity edged with anticipation helped untangle the knot of worry in her chest. The excitement for what she was about to do surged like lightning through her blood, but first she had to convince the crew to chase a legend with her. They were already gathered below her, their expectant faces filling the main deck and dotting the lower rigging as they waited for her to speak.

"I'm sure you've all noticed by now that we're not making our way back to Spider's Nest with our usual haste," Iris began. She allowed a small pause for the pirates to nod in agreement and exchange curious looks. "That is because I have a proposition for you all. It will seem mad and impossible to some of you. The rest of you will remember that we're pirates, and know that those are words meant to turn away the faint of heart." She smiled. "That's not us."

A cheer went up across the crew, but as she had expected, several of them were more bemused than enthusiastic. These were the ones that Iris would need to work hardest to convince.

"As your captain, I've led you to take many prizes," she continued. "We've had our share of misfortunes and brushes with danger, but we've come out stronger and wiser, and with fat purses that the lot of you keep spilling into Spider's coffers, but you come back drunk on pleasure and fine rum, ready for your next adventure."

The shouting this time was louder and more sustained, and Iris felt a small wash of relief that the crew had short memories when it came to dry spells. Reluctantly, she had to admit that Dax had been right about letting them loose to enjoy Spider's Nest before setting out once more, though she would never tell him that.

Iris waited for the crew to settle before she spoke again. "Now, we could sail back to Spider's Nest, and we could line our pockets with payment for what we've taken from the *Talon*, and we could lie on the beaches and drink Spider's rum and see how far a silver mark will get us in the pleasure house." The crew clapped and cheered again, but she did not let them gain momentum this time. "Or," she said, raising her voice to carry over the noise, "we could do far better than that.

"I come before you now with the offer of a new hunt. It will be long and difficult, and you will need to place your trust in me as you never have before, even when your very lives were on the line, but I promise you this." Iris paused, allowing curiosity to nibble at the crew and pull them closer still. "If you sail with me, I will give you the adventure of your lives, and a treasure to last you the rest of your years."

This piqued the interest of even the most cynical of the crew, and Iris could have cut their anticipation with her sword. This, unfortunately, would be the tricky part. They knew Mordanti's legend well, as it was one of the favorite stories told on calm nights when the crew gathered to bond and music wasn't readily available, but she was about to ask them to put their disbelief aside, and accept something dangerously new.

Slowly, Iris reached up and removed the thin chain around her neck for the second time that day. She wrapped the chain around her fist and let the dragon scale hang freely. It fluttered and danced in the wind, gleaming in the sunlight. So close to the scale, Iris could see the smoke that swirled across its surface, alive and mesmerizing even at this small size. For a moment, her vision was eclipsed by the memory of the dragon in full, the patterns of smoke shifting across its entire body visible even against the storm. She blinked, and the dragon was gone, replaced by a crowd of faces straining to see what she held before them. She raised her fist higher, and swept her eyes over her crew.

"Over two hundred years ago, Captain Ava Mordanti captured a juvenile mimic dragon, and branded its wings with a map to the greatest treasure ever known before setting the beast loose to live its long life as it saw fit. Years ago, I met that dragon, and now I intend to find it again."

A taut silence stretched over the ship, but before it could take hold, Iris came down the steps to the main deck and strode forward, the dragon scale held over her head. "I have seen the black dragon," she said as she began to move among the crew, and she let her passion raise and sharpen her voice. "I thought it a dream or a trick of my own eyes at first, but it left me with a scar and a scale." She did not bother pulling her sleeve up to reveal the scar on her arm. Most of the crew had seen it already, and it was not the thing that would impress them. Iris turned in a slow circle, making sure that every eye on the *Southern Echo* had a chance to see the dragon scale. "The legendary beast is real, and so is Mordanti's treasure."

She lowered her arm, letting the pirates closest to her reach out and touch the scale, seeing for themselves how smoke twisted across its surface, and feeling the sharp edges that time had not managed to fully dull. Doubt began to give way to wonder in those that handled the scale, and it began to ripple across the crew.

"I've held this scale close to my heart, waiting for the right time to follow its promise to the dragon that shed it. Now is that time." She ascended back to her place on the quarter deck, sweeping up to the railing and overlooking the crew once more. She raised the scale again, letting it spin and catch the light. "Sail with me, and I will show you a living legend."

"And how will you find it, Captain?"

The shout came from the middle of the crowd, where Iris had instructed Novachak to take up position and wait for his moment. Right on cue, he asked the question before the wonder could fade and the doubts could find a firm handhold. As planned, the pirates around the boatswain nodded in agreement, their thoughts accepting this as the biggest obstacle to her wild proposal.

Iris took a moment to replace the chain around her neck, but she let the dragon scale hang freely outside of her clothes now, where the crew could see it. It was strange not having its sharp warmth against her skin, but it was a small price to pay for what was to come.

"Our take from the *Talon* will buy us the information we need to begin our hunt," she said. "And our newest member will give us the means to track this dragon as no one could before." She scanned the pirates gathered on the starboard side of the ship. She quickly picked out Dax and, next to him, waiting exactly where he should have been, Nate Lowwind. Iris raised her hand and beckoned him forward.

Nate glanced at the quartermaster, who gave him an encouraging nod. Slowly, the boy came forward, making his way to the stern of the ship.

When he was standing next to her on the quarter deck, Iris placed a hand on Nate's shoulder. "I'm sure you've all noticed by now that Nate does not use his Skill to work the winds to our advantage."

Several of the riggers shot dark looks at Nate, who dropped his eyes to the ground. Iris gave his shoulder a gentle squeeze, but her gaze was hard as she focused on the riggers. One by one, they glanced away.

"There is a reason for that," Iris continued, "and it extends beyond what it says in our code. Nate has actually chosen to use his Skill to help us, but not in any way that you've seen before. He is a tracker, and while he cannot turn the wind, he can read it and follow a trail." She released Nate and drew out a thick strip of fabric from her coat pocket. She bade Nate to turn and let her tie it around his head, covering his eyes. He obeyed without protest.

"Nate bears a Lowwind mark," Iris said as she finished the knot, careful not to tie the blindfold too tightly. She did not want to interfere with Nate's Skill for this next bit. She wasn't even fully sure that he'd be able to do it, but Dax had reluctantly agreed that the boy was ready for this kind of exhibition, and even Novachak had seemed confident, as long as they turned the *Southern Echo* into the wind for the duration of the demonstration. "If the Solkyrian Empire had understood the true gift of his Skill, Nate would have been branded as a Highwind without hesitation."

Nate's head swiveled towards her, and his lips parted as though to ask a question, but he closed his mouth again. His surprise at her confidence in him was clear, even without any words. He turned easily when she touched his shoulder and had him face the crew again.

"To help you all understand," Iris went on, "I think a demonstration will do far more than words ever could." She glanced about the crew again, deliberately searching a few faces before finding Rori on the port side of the ship, exactly where she was supposed to be. Luken was ready and waiting on her shoulder. "Rori," she called, "if you and Luken would be so kind?"

The navigator made her way forward. She did not pretend to be curious about her role in this show, but she did at least keep her expression neutral. "Yes, Captain?" Rori said when she was at the front of the crowd.

"Let's have Luken stretch his wings a bit. No set patterns, let him do as he pleases."

This would keep any of the crew from suspecting that they had set Nate up with instructions on Luken's trained signal flights, and make them believe Nate's Skill for what it truly was. Iris had scoffed at the thought of anyone thinking that she was foolish enough to try to dupe them into chasing after a flying creature with no way to track it, but she had heeded Dax's warning and agreed to let Luken fly free.

Rori ascended the steps to come stand on Nate's other side, and she gently plucked the bird from her shoulder. She gave Luken an affectionate brush with her fingers, then tossed him into the air. Luken's wings snapped open, the trailing pennant feathers flashing a brilliant turquoise against his black body, and he flapped off in a joyful loop. The *Southern Echo* was moving slowly enough that Luken could outpace the ship, and he flew confidently over the side.

"All right, Nate," Iris said, taking a step away from him and motioning for Rori to do the same. "Please track the bird on the wind."

For a moment, Nate was still, and Iris feared that they had all been wrong, and he would not be able to do it. But then he turned a little into the wind and lifted a hand. He allowed his head to droop a bit as his hand began to trace Luken's path through the sky, slowly at first, but gaining speed as he found whatever trail it was that the bird left in the wind.

It wasn't all that impressive, Iris had to admit, as Luken was keeping a straight path and all Nate had to do was keep his arm a little steady. But then Luken cut to the right, and Nate's hand followed without hesitation, and Iris heard a soft murmur start up among the crew. Luken began to play in the wind, dipping and surging as he pleased. He swerved through a few loops and cut back and forth across the bow of the ship, and even swooped down to the water line. Nate seemed to lose him then, his hand falling still when the solid wood of the ship's deck came between him and the bird's trail, but when Luken shot back up into the sky, it only took Nate a few moments to find him again. By then, the murmurs had gained an appreciative edge. Every pirate was watching Nate and Luken with great interest, and Iris was almost giddy with relief. Satisfied that the crew had seen enough, she nodded to Rori, who raised her hands and signaled for Luken to return.

The bird spent a few more moments playing on the wind before he flipped himself around and darted back to the *Southern Echo*. He came fast with the wind behind him now, and Iris frowned as she realized that Luken was not angling himself towards Rori, but Nate. She almost called out a warning, but she saw

Nate tense, and then he dropped to the deck moments before Luken would have smacked into his head. Luken chirped and circled back to land on Rori's arm, and a laugh went up from the crew. Nate's face was red as he tugged the blindfold off, and he shot a sour look at the bird and at Rori, who offered him a bewildered shrug in return.

Iris did not give the boy time to dwell on that small embarrassment. She reached down and pulled Nate to his feet, then raised his hand above his head, as though presenting a prize-winning fighter to the crew. The pirates erupted into cheers, and the shame drained out of Nate's face to be replaced by something not entirely unlike awe. He looked at Iris as though he did not believe what was happening before him. Iris gave him a firm nod and a pat on the shoulder.

"Well done," she told him, and she meant it.

She sent a somewhat dazed Nate off to the side with Rori before raising her hands and calling the crew's attention back to herself. "So you see," she said, pitching her voice to carry, "we can track a flying prey. I have proof of the black mimic's existence, and I swear to you, we will find this dragon, and the map kept secret in its wings. And now, as our code demands, I ask for your support." She took a deep breath and planted her feet squarely on the deck. "Who votes aye to seek the black mimic and Mordanti's legendary treasure?"

Iris was pleased to see several hands immediately rise along with hers, but there were far more looks of skepticism than she would have liked, even in the wake of Nate's demonstration. She felt a flutter of fear in her heart, but kept a steady gaze on the crew.

Slowly, more hands began to rise. When Dax raised his and then Novachak's went up a few moments later, they each brought along additional waves of support.

Up in the rigging, Xander Grayvoice thrust his hand up. Iris caught the sharp gaze he trained on Nate as he did so. Oddly, it seemed almost resentful, but Xander's vote pulled several other riggers' hands into the air. When Iris looked about, taking a more earnest tally of the vote, she could not help but smile at the number of hands in the air, and her smile broadened more when she saw that Nate had joined the supporters. When Iris lowered her hand, the rest of the crew did too.

"And the nays?" she asked.

She needn't have, really, as it was clear where the majority lay, but it was good to give everyone a chance to make their vote known. She took careful note of the dissenters, who were mostly the older members of the crew that were a little too jaded by their years at sea to believe that long-lived dragons still inhabited the world, but some of the gunners did not look thrilled to see how the vote had carried. She would have to watch them in the coming days. Iris had the crew's support and a good number of them were fiercely loyal to her, but if things did not progress as she hoped, she could lose her captainship as sure as the winds could change. But for now, she reveled in her victory.

"The ayes carry," she said, and the vast majority of the crew gave a wild cheer. She let them indulge for a few moments before calling their attention to herself once again. "I ensured that we were stocked for a long voyage before we left Spider's Nest," she went on, "so we may begin our hunt immediately. If you have questions or doubts, you may speak them to me freely. I will hear you out."

Several of the crew nodded, and some of the gunners looked ready to take her up on the offer.

"I meant when I said that this would not be easy," Iris said, "but the greatest things in life never are. Now, let's hunt ourselves a legend!"

The crew stamped and cheered again, and Iris smiled and touched the dragon scale that hung around her neck.

Finally, she thought, and looked with bright hope at the horizon.

CHAPTER FIFTEEN

Responding in Kind

THERE WAS A VERY different charge to the air around the *Southern Echo* following the crew's vote on Arani's proposed treasure hunt. Nate was still giddy from the thrill of seeing people actually smiling after he used his Skill, let alone applauding, and his head felt light. It was a nauseating contrast to the heavy feeling in his stomach.

Captain Arani wanted the crew to hunt down a dragon, and follow the map in its wings to a treasure so steeped in legend, no one could fully agree on what it was. Nate heard murmurs of speculation among the crew, with some insisting that Mordanti's treasure was heaps and heaps of gold and jewels that would dwarf the *Southern Echo*, and others claiming that it was an artifact left by the gods. Others still, Nate included, wondered if there was really anything to find at all.

He thought it a rational doubt. Dragons still plagued Vothein and its nearby islands in the east, but they were squat, ugly creatures that spat acid from their jaws and did not fly. The species that had existed in the western reaches of the archipelago—the kind from Mordanti's story—had been extinct for hundreds of years, the last one hunted down long before Mordanti had sailed the seas. According to Solkyrian history, they had once roamed the islands as freely as imperial ships, with a territory that stretched from the equatorial islands all the way to the Pod in the north. They had not enjoyed the cold much, drawing their upper limit at the edge of the Aurora Sea, but they had been numerous and breathtaking to behold, or so said the historians. Those same historians claimed that the elegant western dragons had used their magic to imitate the sights they'd found most pleasing in the world, staining their bodies and wings with sunsets and waterfalls and other natural wonders, which had given them their subspecies name. The idea that Captain Mordanti had captured a juvenile mimic dragon before it had colored its scales, and then burned a map into its wings and released it back into the world for Captain Arani to meet hundreds of years later...

Historians did agree that mimic dragons had been long-lived creatures, their lifeblood revered for its ability to heal as readily as it could kill. But given the focus of his education, Nate had not learned much else about dragons, although he recalled seeing the bones of one a long time ago. The museum in Sunthrone City boasted the most complete mimic dragon skeleton of anywhere in the known world. Nate had seen it when he was young and learning about the historical glory of Solkyria, and what his role as a wind worker would be in the empire's future. He remembered the dragon skeleton being quite large, but nowhere near the size of the sea leviathan in the next room of the museum, and *those* were not extinct and still caused a lot of trouble for ships, and anyway, the bones of dead things all tended to look very much the same. Nate wished that he had paid better attention in the museum, but his head had still been full of certainty that he would one day sail with the imperial navy and bring glory to the empire with his Skill, just like his brother and sister.

He shook his head clear of the memories. Nate wasn't certain that he entirely believed the legend, but he was a little giddy with the thought that he was going to do something far, far grander than Sebastian or Lisandra ever had done. If the scale Arani wore really had come from the fabled black mimic, then he was about to embark on a journey that would change not just his life, but the world. If he found a supposedly extinct species, *and* helped recover a treasure stolen so long ago it had been given up for lost and nearly forgotten, surely *that* would win him back a place in the empire's good graces, and grant him the life he'd always dreamed of.

He hoped the black mimic was real.

And if his doubts ever began to overpower his hope, Nate had only to find the captain.

Arani wore the black scale openly now, and let anyone take a closer look whenever they asked, and even handle the scale if they still needed convincing. She kept a firm grip on the chain the entire time, but she made no move to press the authenticity of the scale upon the crew, and instead let them draw their own conclusions.

The scale did have a wondrous quality to it that amazed Nate every time he saw it. It was fairly large, fitting neatly into the palm of his hand, and it swirled with dark, ashen colors that seemed to move the longer Nate looked at them. The scale felt warm when he touched it, and while not sharp enough to cut him, its edges were far from dull. His rational mind tried to convince him that such a scale could have come from a serpent, perhaps even a deep-sea leviathan, but those he had studied more readily than dragons, and he knew that their scales ranged in color from silvery-blue to green and were both rounder and flatter than this black scale. He could think of no other creature that would have shed the black scale, and he threw himself back into his training with vigor.

With the secret finally released, Nate openly practiced his Skill on the main deck of the ship. Dax and Novachak took turns getting him set up, but their duties called them away each day, and Nate was on his own for the most part. Rori, too, was scarce, as her tasks as navigator required much of her attention, which also meant that Luken was occupied more often than not.

Still, Nate was determined to hone his Skill, and he felt the crew's attention settle on his shoulders as he worked. Each day, pirates came to the main deck to watch Nate train as a few eager volunteers lobbed objects back and forth across the deck for Nate to track. He got very good at sensing small items sailing across the air behind him, with the wind casting their shadows against his skin, but none of them left readily identifiable prints in the breezes, and Nate struggled to understand what, exactly, he was sensing in the wind. Eric tried to help him with that in particular, testing out objects of various shapes and sizes to see if Nate could tease out their identities, but aside from vague impressions of their shapes, Nate could not say what they were with any authority.

What was more, without Luken, Nate's training was confined to the length of the ship, and he knew that his distance tracking was not growing at the rate Arani wanted it to. He could see that whenever he found her watching him. She frowned far more than she smiled, and Nate sensed that she was running calculations in her head that became more unpleasant with each day that his Skill did not improve. Arani said nothing to the crew, and Nate followed her lead, not once letting slip to the others that he was as likely to find them a flying boar as he was a mimic dragon, but the thought grew heavy on his mind, and he began to wonder what would happen if he failed, if they found themselves stranded out on the open sea with their food run out and nothing to show for their efforts. Would the blame fall on Arani, or would it pass to the Skilled who had failed to lead the crew to their promised treasure?

Nate knew the answer to that question far too readily. Anxieties and fears began to nibble at his nerves, but after his last run-in with Xander, Nate did not think he could trust anyone with his secrets, unless they already knew.

So he sought out Rori, and he explained the problem, and asked her to let him train with Luken more. She reluctantly agreed, which meant that Nate needed another set of eyes for his training. With Luken now the sole owner of Nate's old hat, the bird was less inclined to dive at Nate's head, although he still flashed that mischievous streak every now and again. The majority of the time, however, he flew easily alongside the ship, and Nate stood blindfolded on the main deck, trying to track his movements. Marcus and Eric took turns watching Nate during these trainings, partially to make sure that he was actually following the bird, but mostly to keep Nate from crashing into people and parts of the ship as he stumbled after Luken. But even with Luken there to test the limits of Nate's distance tracking, his frustrations grew. He could still only track the bird and objects when they were upwind of him, and given that a sailing ship benefitted most from having the wind at its back, Nate was very aware that his tracking field was limited to the places the *Southern Echo* had already left in her wake. If something tried to sneak up on them, he'd likely be able to help, but anything in front of them or off to the side Nate would only be able to see with his own eyes, same as everyone else on the ship.

That was the heart of the problem. No matter what he did, Nate could not find a way to do the impossible, and track something downwind of himself. Nate lost Luken every time the bird moved ahead of his position on the ship. One day, when Luken had slipped his focus yet again, Nate pulled off the blindfold and glanced up in frustration. He saw two riggers in the lines above his head, watching him closely. Their expressions were not kind, and it occurred to Nate with a small surge of panic that the riggers, who spent so much time orienting the sails to catch the favorable winds, just might recognize the shortcomings of his Skill.

There has to be something I can do, Nate told himself desperately. *Cross winds or something that I can use. Something!*

But out on the sea, the sails taut with strong winds, Nate's senses were washed out by the dominant gusts. The gold ring on his hand grew warm as Nate strained against the limits of his magic, and he felt everything slipping through his grasp once again.

That afternoon, Eric came to the main deck, ready to volunteer his idle hours to help Nate train. The elegant Darkbend stopped short when he saw Nate's face. For a moment, neither of them said anything. Then Eric motioned Nate over to the railing of the ship and invited him to lean against it, saying, "You need a break."

Nate shook his head. "I need to keep going."

"No," Eric said, "you're starting to wear yourself out."

"I'm fine," Nate said, fighting the urge to look up into the rigging again. The two riggers who'd been watching him had long since gone, but he couldn't shake the feeling of their eyes on him. "I don't have time for this."

Eric raised an eyebrow, pushing his Darkbend tattoo towards his hairline. As always, Eric made such a simple gesture into something elegant. Nate found himself thinking that his life would have been infinitely easier if he'd been born with light magic in his blood instead of wind magic, bending sunlight to entertain nobles while he lived in their homes and ate their food. The frustrations of all of Nate's years of training were piled high on his shoulders, and it was easy to feel a flash of resentment towards Eric, whose future did not hang by a thread that was only as strong as his Skill.

"You either help me train or you find someone else who will," Nate said. "Either way, I'm not stopping."

"All right," Eric said slowly. He pushed himself off the railing and stepped back to Nate's side. "At least tell me what's bothering you. You look like someone caught you gazing amorously at the dairy goat." He grinned wickedly. "You weren't imagining it was Rori, were you?"

Nate made a disgusted noise and turned away.

"Sorry, bad joke," Eric said quickly, stepping around to stand in front of him again. Concern was plain on his face now, and Nate's skin itched under that look. "Really, what's wrong?"

"You wouldn't understand," Nate grumbled.

"You may be surprised," Eric said gently. "You feeling some pressure under your Skill?"

"As if you'd know," Nate snapped. "All you light benders ever have to do is look pretty and make things sparkle."

Eric stared at him for a stunned moment, and then his eyebrows came together in a harsh frown. His gaze became sharp as a knife, and a muscle at the side of his jaw twitched. But the Darkbend said nothing.

Nate turned away with no intent to apologize. He did not like himself in that moment, but he did not understand why anyone with the cushy life of a light bender would have fled the empire. Nate knew that he'd been right, though; Eric would not understand. What was more, he knew that he couldn't tell Eric about the true depth of his troubles for fear of letting slip his ultimate goal of returning to Solkyria. Nate held on to that like a lifeline as he tugged the blindfold back on and went back to training. When he paused for a break some time later, he lifted the blindfold to see that Eric had gone and been replaced by Liliana, who smiled prettily but was clearly bored after watching Nate point at Luken for the better part of an hour.

She was not the only one who was growing less and less enamored by the idea of Nate's tracking Skill. In the wake of the riggers watching Nate struggle, it didn't take long for the crew members who had voted against the dragon hunt to start wondering aloud if Nate really was all that Arani had claimed. They were ignored at first, but the murmurs grew louder and began to spread, and after a few days, even some of the supporters were beginning to wonder if they should find a different wind worker for the dragon hunt.

The idea that Nate may not be strong enough to help them find the dragon spread like fire across the ship, somehow never reaching the officers' ears but circulating among the lower crew just fine. Nate felt it in the glances that touched his face when he sat down for dinner that night. His stomach curled, and he stared at his food rather than eating it. Salted pork and pickled vegetables gazed back at him with bland disinterest. There was a biscuit, too, but those were starting to go stale and were hard and uncompromising unless soaked in beer, which Nate had not yet developed a taste for. Nate pushed his food around and stewed in his own worries.

It took him several minutes to realize that someone had sat down across from him, and he raised his head to find Marcus studying his morose mood. Xander sat next to the stout Darkbend, chewing methodically and pointedly not looking at Nate.

"Come on now," Marcus said, reaching across the table to tap on the edge of Nate's bowl, "it's a sight better than what they fed us at the academies."

Xander snorted. "Nate was at the wind working academy. He ate far better than we did."

"How would you know that?" Nate asked tiredly.

"They fed you every day, yes? Then you ate better than the animal speakers."

Marcus shot Xander a look of open horror. "You serious?"

Xander pulled a drowned biscuit out of his mug of beer and tore savagely into it with his teeth, keeping eye contact with Marcus all the while.

"You poor bastard," Marcus murmured. He turned back to Nate. "All right, so the food's not great and the work is hard, but everything will taste better once we have the dragon."

Nate dragged his eyes up from his food. "You really believe that beast is out there?" he asked flatly.

Marcus gave him a surprised look, but Xander cut in before he could say anything.

"If Arani says it's there, it's there."

It was Nate's turn to send a surprised glance across the table.

Xander ripped off another hunk of biscuit and spoke around the mouthful. "I've been on the *Southern Echo* for going on three years now. We've had our lean times, but Arani's always sniffed out the fatter prizes and kept our pockets lined with coin. It's why she's still captain and almost no one's jumped ship. She's not stupid enough to throw us or the ship away on a fool's hunt, and if she was going to go completely mad, she'd have done something a bit more drastic than ask us to vote on whether or not to seek another score, outlandish as it may seem. So if she says she's got a legendary treasure on the hook, I'll follow her to the end of the world for my cut of it. And if she leads me to a pile of dirt instead of gold, I'll be the first to keel-haul the stubborn bitch."

"Up until that last bit, that was the sweetest thing I've ever heard you say about anyone," Marcus observed.

Xander shrugged and lifted his beer in salute to the decks above their heads, where the helm was situated and Arani was taking her own shift guiding the *Southern Echo* while the majority of the crew ate and began to settle in for the night.

Marcus shifted his attention away from the Grayvoice back to Nate. "I saw Eric earlier," Marcus said gingerly. "Thought he was supposed to be helping you with training today, but he seemed a touch upset, and he wouldn't tell me why." He paused for a moment, measuring Nate with his eyes. There was a guarded note in the stout Darkbend's voice when he asked, "What did you say to him?"

Nate sighed under the weight of his cracking friendships. "Something stupid," he said. "I got frustrated with my Skill and lost my temper with Eric."

"That much I'd figured out," Marcus said. "You going to apologize to him?"

"Next time I see him," Nate said, and he meant it.

"He'll appreciate that," Marcus said. "Just don't let it sit too long."

"I won't," Nate promised.

"Why are you frustrated with your Skill?" Xander asked suddenly.

Startled, Nate glanced up to see the Grayvoice watching him intently, that same calculating look in his eyes as the day he'd tried and failed to take the gold ring from Nate. After Xander's reaction the last time Nate had tried to talk about his wind working Skill, Nate never suspected that the Grayvoice would be the one to bring it up again. The man had gone cold and angry, and said that being a wind worker did not make Nate better than him. Then Nate thought of how he'd spoken to Eric earlier that day, and with a guilty start, he realized that he could have had more tact around his friends.

Humbled, Nate dropped his voice and leaned in closer to Marcus and Xander. "I'm having a lot of trouble," he confessed. "I think Arani may want something impossible from me."

Xander's eyes narrowed, but Marcus shook his head emphatically.

"Come on, Nate," the Darkbend said. "Two months ago, I would've said it's impossible to read anything in the wind, but I've just spent the last several days watching you track a *bird* while *blindfolded*."

"Only when it's upwind of him," Xander said around the mug of beer he lifted to his lips.

Nate shot him a sharp look, but Xander quirked an eyebrow as an open challenge, and Nate released a hard breath and looked away.

Marcus elbowed the Grayvoice lightly in the ribs before saying, "The captain has a lot of faith in you, Nate. She's trusting you to get us to where we need to be."

"That's the problem," Nate said. He shifted uneasily and dropped his voice lower. "I don't know if I can."

Marcus glanced at Xander, but the Grayvoice had gone pensively still and did not take his eyes off of Nate.

"My Skill has never been strong," Nate murmured, all the old doubts and failures catching up to him. "Arani thinks I can use it to find a dragon, but this entire crew has been set up for disappointment, her included." And Nate himself most of all. He shook his head bitterly. "It's the wind working academy all over again, and what's Arani going to do when she realizes that the tool she picked up isn't actually useful?"

Marcus frowned and opened his mouth to argue, but Xander tilted his head and cut a sharp grin across the table at Nate. "Now you're getting it, Nowind."

It took a moment for Nate to realize what Xander had just called him. Surprise quickly gave way to pain, and Nate made to push himself up from the table. Then, in the closeness of the room, Nate felt something cut through the air off to his right, heading straight for his face. He flinched, fully aware that he had not gotten out of the way of the object, and that it was going to hit him, and that there was a very good chance that it was going to hurt.

The object slapped against skin with a solid *whap*, but it was not Nate's face it had hit. Xander's hand had shot out to catch the thing. Nate barely glimpsed rock-hard bread clutched in the Grayvoice's grip before Xander was on his feet and staring at the other table, which had several of the gunners seated along it, AnnaMarie Blueshore and Jim Greenroot among them. Silence fell as Xander locked eyes with the group, but the other pirates looked far more amused than concerned.

Jim shrugged nonchalantly. "Just wanted to see if he could dodge something other than a trained bird. So far, his Skill's been about as useful as yours, Sheep Lips."

Xander looked at Jim, then at the biscuit he'd snatched out of the air. He turned the stale bread in his hands, and then, without warning, hurled it at the gunner. The biscuit hit the man square in the nose, knocking his glasses askew as he yelped and flailed into the pirate behind him. Xander calmly walked forward, and there was a sudden flash of metal in the Grayvoice's hand: the dagger he'd won on Spider's Nest. Nate rose to his feet at the same time as the rest of the gunners at the other table, and then the shouting began, and then Xander was ducking under punches as he went after Jim. Bowls went flying when the table was upended, and the shouting grew as the other pirates present called encouragement or groaned at the disruption.

"ENOUGH!" a heavy voice roared over the din. Novachak shouldered his way through the crowd, thrusting pirates aside as he barreled his way to the heart of the fight. He ripped Xander away from the gunners and sent the Grayvoice stumbling backwards into Nate and Marcus, then swung around to snarl at everyone in the room, "What frost-touched nonsense are you idiots fighting over now?"

"An insult was thrown at us," Xander said mildly, catching his balance against Nate. "I responded in kind."

"You came at me with a blade!" Jim said, his voice thickened by a bruise spreading across his nose, but whether that was from the biscuit or someone's fist, Nate could not say. The gunner had lost his glasses at some point, and his eyes were small and squinting without them.

Novachak's interest sharpened at Jim's statement. "Did you now?" he asked Xander, his voice suddenly quiet.

In response, the Grayvoice held up his hands. His dagger had vanished.

The boatswain was unimpressed. He snatched Xander by the collar of his shirt and yanked him forward. The boatswain slapped his hands over Xander's clothing, seeking a concealed weapon. Xander submitted with an expression of mild boredom.

Nate held his breath as he waited for the inevitable to happen, for Novachak to find the dagger and dole out punishment to Xander for daring to attack one of his fellows. Such things were forbidden on the *Southern Echo*, and according to the crew's code, the instigator could lose a hand for their aggression, or even their life. He could not begin to understand Xander's calmness as Novachak searched him.

But then the boatswain stepped away from Xander and ducked his head to peer under the tables and around everyone's feet, and Nate realized that Xander had somehow made that dagger vanish.

When Novachak failed to find the weapon, he shoved the Grayvoice back into place between Nate and Marcus. The boatswain fixed a harsh glare on Xander, who returned the gaze calmly. Novachak did not appear ready to believe that Xander was innocent, but he turned away all the same. "You all know the code," he barked at the pirates, "and what we do to those who break it. I suggest you think long and hard on how much you like your own extremities the next time you move to strike your own crew mates." He abruptly rounded on Jim. "And you," Novachak snapped, "just earned yourself a spot on the dead night's watch."

The gunner started to protest. Novachak thrust his shoulders back, broadening his already formidable frame, and pinned the man with his icy gaze. Jim ducked his head and mumbled, "Aye, sir."

Satisfied, Novachak picked his way over the fallen bowls and their spilled contents. He paused in the doorway and gave a sharp wave at the floor. "Get this mess cleaned up." He raised his eyes and glared directly at Xander when he added, "All of you."

With some grumbling, the pirates fell to the task. It wasn't long before the upended table was sitting on its legs again, the bowls picked up and the food swept away. Several people were upset at the loss of their dinners, and they went to see if they could cajole more out of the cook, which Nate knew was unlikely and would only put them in a worse mood. As soon as the last trace of the fight had been cleared away, he excused himself and went topside.

It was quiet on the deck of the *Southern Echo*, and even the steady wind and the splash of the waves against the hull were soft. The sun had set, and the twin moons glowed softly against the black sky, outshining the stars. Nate leaned on the ship's railing and looked up at the moons, thinking about how at this time of year, the faint glow of the northern auroras would just be visible from Solkyria. It wouldn't be long until they filled the night in the north, and the Dancing Skies Festival began. Nate had never had much reason to look forward to the holiday, but he felt a pang at the thought of missing it this year. They were sailing south, and each day brought them farther and farther away from the things Nate had known all his life, replacing them with balmy nights and strange stars.

With a sigh, Nate brought his eyes down from the sky and looked out across the dark water. He imagined a dragon out there, soaring and dipping through the sky and swooping down to snatch fish from the water before climbing high on the winds again, its scales twisting with smoke and wings branded with a pirate captain's wild greed. A dragon he could not see and could not sense, because he could not read that angle of the wind. Idly, Nate turned the gold ring on his hand, sending the sun crest rising and setting between his fingers.

Footsteps sounded on the deck a moment later, and he turned to see Xander approaching, his black Grayvoice tattoo stark against his skin under the moonlight. For a moment, Nate considered trying to avoid Xander, but that would solve nothing, and Nate was growing tired of pushing his Skill between himself and others. He waited for Xander to draw closer before hailing the Grayvoice.

"Thanks," Nate said as he quickly slid his right hand behind his back, hiding the ring from Xander's sight. "For... you know."

Xander grunted and took up a place next to Nate, leaning on the railing and staring out into the night. "Thought it'd be easier for you to use your Skill if your face wasn't bruised."

Nate huffed a soft laugh and tilted his head up to the unfamiliar constellations overhead. He longed to tell Xander everything, from his time as the weakest wind worker at the academy to his wild idea of returning to Solkyria to serve in the navy, but knew that Xander would not welcome hearing any of those things. Instead, he confided his doubts to the Grayvoice.

"I really don't know if I can find the dragon," Nate said. "I mean it."

Xander made a thoughtful noise before reaching his hand towards Nate's hip. Confused, Nate reflexively moved away, but the Grayvoice was faster, and his hand slipped inside Nate's pocket and withdrew something that Nate hadn't noticed was there until its weight was gone: the dagger from the fight. Xander let the moonlight play along the blade for a moment. Then he winked at Nate. "I know you mean it." The blade disappeared into the folds of the Grayvoice's clothing, and then Xander returned his attention to the dark horizon. "I expect you to try anyway." He was silent for a few moments before asking, "Was that what you and Rori were doing on Spider's Nest? Training your Skill?"

Nate nodded. "That was all."

Xander gave a pensive murmur. He did not look relieved.

Nate pressed the ball of his foot into the *Southern Echo*'s deck. The dryad wood was hard and unyielding against the bottom of his boot, one solid thing in the middle of a vast nothingness. "Did you really mean it when you said you'd follow Arani to the end of the world?" he asked.

Xander shrugged. "If she says there's treasure there."

"You have a lot of faith in her," Nate observed.

"I have faith in her record as a pirate captain," the Grayvoice returned. "She's been on the account for years, and she's always kept her crew's pockets lined with coin. She hasn't taken a Solkyrian treasure galleon, but she hasn't swung from the gallows, either. My last captain, Bluehill... he can't say the same."

"Oh." Nate shifted awkwardly, unsure of what more to say. "I'm sorry."

Xander looked at him with genuine confusion. "The man could barely catch a prize moving so slow, it may as well have been dragging its ass on the seafloor, and his crew was so sickeningly enamored with his soft, bleeding heart that they followed him all the way to the gallows. They were terrible excuses for pirates, the lot of them, and they all got what they deserved when they danced at the end of a short rope." There was no anger or remorse in Xander's words; he stated them as simple facts.

"What about you?" Nate asked quietly.

Xander shrugged again and returned his attention to the night. "I've been satisfied with my take from the *Southern Echo*'s voyages thus far." A sardonic smirk cut across his face. "Though none of Arani's officers trust me much, given that my departure from Bluehill's crew was only a few days before pirate hunters mysteriously caught up with his ship on the open sea. They think I sold him out."

Nate regarded the Grayvoice for a long moment. "Did you?"

"Of course not," Xander said. "That would imply I got money out of the deal." He let that hang in the air before he glanced at Nate and burst out laughing.

After a moment, Nate joined in, nervously at first, and then relieved to finally have some release after all the stress of his Skill training. They were still chuckling when Rori came up to them, yawning and stretching after her last turn at the helm and council with the captain on their bearing. Luken chirped softly on her shoulder, for once too tired to have any interest in bothering Nate.

"What are you two laughing about?" Rori asked.

"The past," Xander said.

Rori hesitated long enough for her silence to become noticeable before saying, "You may want to start thinking a little more about the future. We're coming up on the doldrums."

"Gods below," Xander groaned. "I was hoping we would avoid those."

Rori shrugged. "Captain says her source on the dragon will be waiting on the other side. This is the fastest way to get a starting point for Nate." Her eyes cut to him when she said his name, and she regarded him frankly. "Are you ready?"

"No," Nate answered truthfully.

The Goodtide sighed and moved towards the railing, taking up a place between Nate and Xander. The three of them stared out at the dark horizon and said nothing else for a long time.

Chapter Sixteen

Dead Wind

The next day, not long after the sun had cleared the horizon, the wind died.

It happened far more suddenly than Nate expected. His earlier training at the academy had informed him that the doldrums surrounding the equator were prime areas for wind workers to serve their crews and push ships out of the dead zones, but nothing in those lessons had prepared Nate for what it would feel like for everything to simply cease.

For as long as he could remember, the edges of his awareness had been full of the whispers of breezes and the murmurs of the gusts. In the doldrums, the element's voices went silent, and a vast emptiness filled Nate's head and heart.

It hit him like a hammer, and as the *Southern Echo*'s sails went slack without a scrap of wind to fill them, Nate felt as though his lungs had shriveled in his chest. Choking, he fell to the deck, his body and mind reaching for something that was no longer there, and his vision swam and began to darken. He was dully aware of shouting around him and a pair of rough hands rolling him on to his side as the world faded, and then something broke loose in his throat and he sucked in air like a starving man falling upon a feast. He coughed and sputtered on the richness of it.

After several minutes, he was able to sit up, and he found the crew standing in a ring around him. Some bore open concern on their faces, others were confused, and others still whispered to each other and looked at Nate as though he had failed a test he did not even know he was taking.

And it was so, so quiet.

Nate only realized he was shaking when Novachak's hand closed over his shoulder and steadied him.

"All right there, new blood?" the boatswain asked.

Unsure of the answer, Nate did not respond.

A commotion started up near the back of the crowd, and the crew shifted out of the way as Captain Arani came forward, Dax and Rori following in her wake. They all came to a halt when they saw Nate kneeling on the deck.

"What happened?" Arani demanded. Her voice cracked out like a whip in the silence.

Novachak waited a moment, but when Nate did not move, the boatswain offered a cautious shrug. "He went down when the wind died. It was like he almost died with it."

Dax drew in a sharp breath and exchanged an even sharper glance with Rori. Arani stepped aside as the Goodtide surged forward. Luken, nestled in his usual spot on Rori's shoulder, chirped indignantly before taking off in a burst of brilliant feathers.

It was like an explosion in Nate's vision, bright and searing at this close range. He gasped and fell back as Luken climbed into the sky, each flap of the bird's wings leaving a churning of air behind that was so strong, it was like looking at footprints left in fresh sand, if those footprints were on fire. Nate shut his eyes and his awareness reflexively reached out to follow Luken's trail, and what was once blurry was now crisp and focused as his connection to the element roared through his body and mind. He still could not turn the wind, but he could see everything so, so clearly.

Nate shot to his feet and nearly fell into Rori. She caught him and helped him steady himself, and Nate gripped her arm with a ferocity that surprised even him. Rori tensed but she did not pull away, and Nate managed to lift one hand and trace Luken's flight path as the bird shot out over the water, dipped down to the waves in a playful dive, then cut back to the ship and made a few circuits around the deck before settling on one of the gently swaying rigging ropes. Nate did not lose track of him once.

His hand still pointed at Luken, Nate peeled open his eyes and looked at Rori, and he suddenly understood how it must feel to be a Highwind or a Goodtide, and to have that strong of a connection to an element. Rori's breath was a soft cloud as it stirred the air between them. Nate felt the formation of the sharp, pointed voids that pierced the stillness as the crew drew in small gasps, and then the hard bursts of wind as they gave triumphant yells at the sudden, drastic improvement in his tracking abilities.

Rori's eyes locked with his, and he saw the exact moment she realized what he had; he'd finally unleashed the true potential of his Skill. But instead of the pure, raw joy that Nate felt, her gaze was wary, and she looked almost afraid for him.

Then the crew was on Nate, and several pirates were slapping his back and cheering, and they did not stop until Arani barked out that they all had other things to do now that the wind was gone from the sails. She put herself in front of Nate as they dispersed.

"That," Arani said, "is what I am looking for. Keep going. I want that Skill ready to do far more than track a bird."

Nate felt a surge of satisfaction, and he straightened to his full height. "Aye, Captain."

He did not see Rori slip away, but she was gone when he turned around.

THE JOURNEY STRETCHED TO a slow crawl as they crossed the doldrums, even when the faintest whispers of wind teased through the sails and nudged the *Southern Echo* a little further along. The ship mostly coasted on the ocean currents that Rori kept a close watch over, and although she never once used her Skill, the Goodtide was exhausted by the time they were nearly to the equator. She moved across the deck like a storm cloud, and everyone gave her a wide berth.

Many others, Nate included, were in much lighter moods. With the *Southern Echo* cruising along at a sedate pace and no real winds to speak of, the pirates were free to rest and enjoy the leisurely sail. Nate sought out and made amends with Eric, and he was intensely grateful when the Darkbend forgave him. Together, they joined the crew in their fun. They all played games, traded stories, and gathered to sing along to the lively tunes Marcus played on his fiddle in the evenings. They also gathered to watch Nate train with Luken, and now that he had the clear connection to the wind, Nate did not mind having so much attention on his shoulders.

There was no place Luken could hide from Nate in the doldrums. Everywhere the bird went, Nate could suss out his trail through the air, even when Luken drifted further and further away from the ship. He did not go terribly far, as he could only keep himself airborne for so long. Rori was quick to intervene whenever she felt that the bird was being pressed up against his own limits, often swooping in to reclaim Luken before stalking off to the navigation room again, so Nate's training returned to blindfolded tracking of tossed objects. It became something of a game for the crew as Nate's Skill improved. Guessing what was being thrown based on the sizes and shapes of the disruptions he perceived was tricky at first, but as Nate grew more familiar with the things that could be found and tossed about with relative safety on a ship—from coins and shells to bundles of clothes and even someone's false eye—he began to recognize the trails they left behind. He learned to differentiate between all of them as they streaked through the air, and even when the faint winds of the doldrums picked up every now and then, Nate could still tease the trails out from the background noise of the breezes. He got quite good at the game, and by the time the equatorial crossing came, spirits were far higher among the crew than Nate had ever seen.

On the day of the crossing, Nate was rounded up with the few other sailors who were also about to enter the southern hemisphere for the first time. Nate had heard stories of Solkyrian crossing ceremonies during his academy days when naval wind workers had come to observe the young trainees, although with a Veritian captain and several non-Solkyrian crew members, Nate was not certain what he should expect from the veterans of the *Southern Echo*. It turned out to be considerably tamer than the wild stories, thanks in large part to Nate demonstrating day after day that there really was something to his Skill after all. None of the previously initiated members of the crew were feeling particularly vindictive after witnessing his improvement. They rode high on waves of hope.

When the passing of the equator came, a Solkyrian sailor led the prayer to the goddess of the sea, doused those that had not yet crossed the line with clean seawater rather than water from the bilge, and then made the marks on their foreheads with the yolk of an egg instead of the blood of a chicken. Then came the trials of penance, and the crew had great fun calling out different animals for the newly initiated to imitate while serving the midday food and drink rations. Eric in particular managed to come up with several challenging animals, from the squat Vothenian lizards to the wriggling eels of the Pod, which were distinctly devoid of arms and other limbs that would have made serving food considerably more efficient.

Finally, Nate and the other initiates were held upside down by two of the stronger gunners over a bucket of seawater, and made to recite the Solkyrian oath of loyalty to the empire, though with the words changed to replace the empire with the *Southern Echo*, and the fickle, dangerous seas in place of the ruling Goldskye family. Those who stumbled over the words or forgot a line were dunked in the bucket and then made to start again until they had recited it perfectly. Nate, who had said the words every day at the academy, fumbled once in the beginning when he forgot that he was supposed to say the ship's name, and then sailed through it cleanly on his second try.

"The *Southern Echo* is my life," he finished to a roar of triumph from those around him. "My life for the *Southern Echo*."

The crew cheered wildly as Nate was placed back on his feet, given an extra ration of beer, and welcomed to the ranks of the equatorial initiated.

The rest of the crossing day was spent in revelry and celebration, and Nate, Marcus, Eric, and Xander were all pleasantly drunk by the time the sun had set and the crew had sung away much of the night, many of them falling asleep on the deck under the stars rather than in their hammocks.

It did not occur to Nate until he was almost asleep that Rori had not participated in the crossing ceremony at all, and had somehow managed to avoid the entire thing, even with Xander leading the roundup of the uninitiated.

NATE WOKE THE NEXT morning to a dim sun clawing its way up into a hazy sky. The world felt as fuzzy as his head, and judging by the stiffness in his back and neck from sleeping on the hard deck, his training with Luken was going to be particularly unpleasant. Nate sat up with a groan and stretched, trying to keep his face turned away from the sun. Broken as it was by the clouds, its light was still creating an unpleasant pounding in his skull.

"On your feet, the lot of you," Novachak's rough voice rang out. "Line up for your morning rations, Kai's bringing them around since I don't trust any of you to make it down the stairs. Once you've eaten, bring out the rain barrels. Captain's aiming to catch the edge of a storm before we move on."

Nate rubbed the sleep grit from his eyes and tried to push his awareness out into the faint breeze taunting the sails, but the effort brought a wave of nausea and he quickly released the element. Yes, his training today was going to be excruciating. Bitterly, he wondered how he'd managed to get drunk off of a drink he did not even care for.

When he cracked open his eyes and moved to line up with the others along the railing, Nate discovered that he did not need his Skill to know that a storm was coming. He could taste the rain clearly on the air, and when he looked off of the starboard side of the ship, he saw a large, dark gray smear on the horizon. The light gusts were coming from that direction, but they didn't feel like the raging winds of a bad storm. More like a quick, passing rainfall that would leave them drenched, but no worse for wear.

His guess proved accurate. By the time the rain barrels were in place with the canvases stretched to funnel as much fresh water into them as possible, the *Southern Echo* was dancing a little faster over the waves, but the winds weren't strong enough for the ship to pick up any real speed or to threaten the sails. The rain came in a solid curtain of gray, falling hard and heavy on the crew, thundering off the deck and the canvas of the rain catchers. It was warm rain, far from refreshing, but that did not stop several pirates from stepping out on to the deck and cupping their hands, and they drank as deeply as they could from the sky.

Nate meant to wait for the water from the rain barrels after the storm had passed, but Eric appeared at his side and hauled him up the steps.

"Better if you get some in you now," Eric advised him. "You too, Marcus."

The stout Darkbend grumbled something that Nate did not catch and tried to pull away.

"No," Eric said firmly, "I'm not going to leave you alone, and no, I'm not talking too loud, you just can't hold your liquor. Let's go, both of you."

Nate's head was too full of cotton for any sort of protest to form, and he went topside with Eric to drink from the storm. He was soaked through immediately, but after a few mouthfuls of rain water, he was starting to feel a little better, and he found that after the long stretches of silence in the doldrums, the presence of the wind around him once more was a very pleasant feeling. He stood for a long time with his face turned to the sky, letting the rain drum against his skin.

The storm ended as abruptly as it had started, and the haze burned away in its wake. Under the midday sun, Nate's clothes dried quickly, and the sunlight no longer seared through his head like an iron spike. That was why he noticed the tension running through Dax and Novachak and even Arani as they moved to gather the crew and assign new tasks, although the captain's nervousness was underscored with determination. Nate pushed his awareness out again, and while his head offered a weak protest, he was able to read the wind more clearly. He felt a thrill at how easy it was for him to reach further out beyond the ship than he ever had before, but he made himself focus as he searched for some sign of danger. He found nothing. There were no other storms to threaten the *Southern Echo*, and Nate could not sense anything coming towards them, either through the sky or over the water. He had no answer as to why the officers were on edge.

But when Nate went to help move some of the freshly filled rain barrels, he passed the helm, and saw the grim set of Rori's jaw as she steered the ship. Her hands were clutched tight enough on the wheel to turn her knuckles white, and she glared out at the sea with a mixture of anger and fear.

Nate hesitated, and then slipped up the steps to her. "You all right?" he asked.

"I know where we're going," Rori said. Her voice was a soft growl, and Nate had to strain to hear her. "I don't like these waters."

"Why?" Nate asked. "What's happening?"

Rori's jaw clenched. She shook her head and kept her eyes on the sea. "I hope Arani knows what she's doing," she muttered.

Before Nate could ask her anything more, a shrill whistle came from the middle of the ship, where Dax had boosted himself up on a crate to address the crew.

"We're coming up on the meeting point," the quartermaster shouted, making sure his voice carried to every sailor on the deck and the ones up in the rigging, too. "We need the plunder from the *Talon* brought up to the main deck. Everyone except the riggers and the helm is to help move the cargo topside. Once you've done that, store your weapons and then come see Mr. Novachak. He'll give you a length of rope long enough to anchor yourself to the ship."

A confused murmur went up in answer to this, but Dax had nothing more to say, and the pirates moved to follow his orders.

Nate glanced at Rori, who looked nearly sick with worry now.

"Tie a good knot," she advised him, and tugged at a line of rope coiled around her waist that Nate had not noticed until now. It stretched behind her to loop through an iron ring on the deck, and was tied off with three distinct knots, each more complicated than the last.

With that warning hanging over his head, Nate hurried to help with the plunder and get his lifeline from Novachak.

The pirates made an efficient chain to pass the items taken from the *Talon* and move them topside. Exotic furs, semi-precious stones, barrels of sugar, and a small chest of coins passed through Nate's hands to be piled on to the main deck. It wasn't long before the pirates in the hold called out that they'd handed off the last of it. Nate and the others filed back upstairs to get the ropes from Novachak, who had the two cabin boys measuring and cutting lengths from a long coil. Everyone was given their bit of rope and a stern instruction on where to anchor themselves. They were being kept away from the railings, Nate noticed, with the majority of the crew being directed to the masts and the rest going for the iron rings drilled into the deck that were typically used to secure the topside cannons the *Southern Echo* carried. Nate was told to take a position at the mainmast.

"Tie three knots," Novachak instructed him. "And have your neighbor check them to make certain you're secure. This is no time for pride."

"What's happening?" Nate asked.

Novachak's icy eyes narrowed but he shook his head. "Move along, new blood. Not much time left."

Nate found that he wasn't the only one at the mast feeling anxious. Most of the pirates were like him, confused and nervous as they fumbled with the ropes and tied off their lifelines on the pegs that ringed the mast. A few speculated about what could possibly have the entire ship preparing for a disaster on par with a devastating storm.

The guesses ran wild, from crossing the Rend into the realm of the gods to this being some twisted form of punishment for something that had offended the captain in yesterday's crossing ceremony. Nate's neighbor—who, much to his displeasure, turned out to be Jim Greenroot, but who also thoroughly checked over Nate's knots and confirmed the security of his lifeline—thought that there was a bad storm coming. Nate told the man that he did not sense anything on the wind, but Rori had said that she did not like these waters.

Jim stared at Nate for a long moment, clearly working something through in his mind. Then his eyes went wide behind his spectacles. "Bleeding gods below," he breathed as he turned to stare out at the sea.

Nate followed his gaze, but his attention caught on Captain Arani.

She was the only one among them who had secured her lifeline near the railing. She stood with her hands resting lightly on the smooth wood. She stared down into the water, and did not raise her eyes when she called, "Mr. Malatide, are all hands secured?"

The quartermaster pounded on the deck, and shouted for them all to pull on their lifelines. They obeyed, and no one came loose. Dax whipped his attention across the ship, letting his gaze linger just long enough to confirm that they were all safe. "All hands secured, Captain!" he called back.

Nate watched Arani take a deep breath, and then she reached into her pocket and withdrew a single bright coin. It flashed in the sunlight as she tossed it into the sea.

An eerie quiet descended on the ship. Jim Greenroot had his eyes shut and his hands clapped over his ears, and he was getting puzzled looks from some of the pirates around him. Others, however, had horrified understanding blooming across their faces, and they too tried to close their ears. Nate was just beginning to think that he should follow their example when a soft, haunting voice came floating up from the sea. It was beautiful, and Nate felt his breath catch as the melody reached into his very soul and filled him with wonder and warmth. Another voice joined the first, and then a third, and then Nate stopped noticing things as he strained against the rope digging into his waist. He had to know what was making that beautiful sound. He had to, and if he could only reach the source, his life would be rich and blissful and he could rest, for if he didn't find out soon, his heart was going to burst.

CHAPTER SEVENTEEN

The Court of Sirens

TO IRIS, THE CALLS of the sirens scraped high and harsh against her ears. Her teeth clenched, something almost like pain went through her spine, and her nails dug into the wood of the *Southern Echo*'s railing. She hated the thought of inflicting even such a small bit of damage on the dryad-infused ship, but she had to keep her shoulders back and her ears clear. Spider had warned her that plugging her ears to the sirens' song would have been a great offense to them, never mind the pain and danger that accompanied their magic. If she wanted to barter for information, she had to start by following their rules.

The same courtesy had to be extended by the rest of the crew, otherwise Iris would have ordered them to plug their ears with whatever they could find. As it was, she had to settle for the lifelines, and hope that the men and women who were currently straining against their ropes had not tried to keep any of their daggers or other bladed weapons against Dax's orders.

She spared a glance at the crew, picking out Novachak and Dax, both slack-jawed and pawing at the air as they pulled against their lifelines. Not far from them, the gunner AnnaMarie kept stumbling as she tried to run closer to the railing and the sea than her lifeline would allow. At the helm, Rori had her hands wrapped tight around the wheel, wincing at the pain of the siren song, but that did not dull the furious glare she'd fixed on Iris. Later, if the navigator was feeling brave, she might have some choice words about Iris's decision not to tell the crew where and who she was getting her information from, but that had been supported by the quartermaster, albeit reluctantly, and Iris did not dwell on the idea. She quickly scanned the rest of the ship's deck, finally picking out her tracker in the huddle around the mainmast. Nate was straining hard against the ropes, but his knots held firm, and he was as safe as he could be.

With that small comfort, Iris turned back to the water, and tried not to flinch too badly as the sirens' voices crescendoed into a shrieking mess. Even over their song, she heard the groans of longing that went up among the affected crew, but no one came pitching forward, all lifelines holding secure.

The siren song ended abruptly, cutting into a silence so merciful, Iris could have wept with relief. She allowed herself one deep, steadying sigh before addressing the creatures in the water below. "I am Captain Iris Arani of the dryad ship *Southern Echo*," she said, and her voice sounded strange in her own ears after the harsh song. "I come seeking to barter with the court."

Spider had assured Iris that, as she would be dealing with the Western Court of Sirens, she herself would be safe against their magic. Had she been dealing with the Eastern Court, it would have been a very different story, but with the Western Court, Spider had promised that there was no risk to her and the others among her crew who were exclusively attracted to men, if they felt any sexual attractions at all. Iris had not been entirely willing to trust Spider's word alone, hence the lifelines on every member of the crew. And yet, even with confirmation of Spider's assurance still ringing in her ears, she was not eager to untie herself from the *Southern Echo*. The sirens had stopped singing, but they looked plenty dangerous even with their mouths shut and sharp teeth hidden away.

The faces of the three sirens turned up to Iris were pale against the water, their scales glinting in the sunlight. Two of the sirens were blue in color, their heads crested with fins that shaded towards the blackness of the deep ocean. The other's scales had a grayish hue, but with brilliant white running under its chin and down its neck, not at all unlike the patterning of the sharks that roamed these waters. All three sirens stared at Iris with unblinking eyes that seemed too large for their pointed faces. There were small bumps where there ought to have been noses, and another crest of fins on the sides of their heads in place of ears, but they still looked uncomfortably human to Iris. That made the working gills on their necks and shoulders all the more unsettling.

The shark-patterned siren moved forward, and Iris glimpsed a long torso giving way to a longer tail beneath the waves. Its mouth peeled open to reveal sharp teeth. "What do you seek?" the siren asked. Its voice was a harsh whisper, and Iris was shocked that she could hear it so clearly with the distance between them.

"Only information," Iris called back. She was uncertain if the siren's magic amplified her own voice back to the creature, but it did not flinch at her volume. "I bring treasures unknown to your people in exchange."

The two blue sirens shifted eagerly and pushed themselves a little further out of the water to reveal thin arms and bodies corded with muscle, but the shark-colored leader stayed where it was. "Show us," it hissed.

Iris nodded and loosened the knots on her lifeline, letting the rope fall away from her waist. A nervous thrill ran through her as she turned from the railing and moved to the stack of goods piled on the ship's deck. She felt the crew's eyes on her as she selected a few of the semi-precious stones and the pelt of a small animal common in the east, but nonexistent on this side of the Leviathan Sea. She did not risk glancing at the crew as she gathered her choices and strode back to the railing. She had to look calm and confident in front of them, even if she felt anything but. She was glad she had years of practice under her belt as she tossed the stones and pelt into the water.

The two blue sirens dove beneath the waves as the stones hit, blurring out of sight as they chased after the sinking gems. The animal pelt remained floating for a bit, but the lead siren made no move to reach for it, or even look at it. The siren simply stared at Iris and waited for the other two to resurface. When they returned, they had the gemstones cupped in their webbed hands, and worked together to shovel them into large sacks of woven seagrass they wore around their middles. The animal pelt disappeared into a sack a few moments later. No words were exchanged among the sirens, but the blue escorts fixed twin looks of anticipation on the leader, who kept staring at Iris. And then, without so much as a signal, all three sirens ducked back beneath the water. Their powerful tails came up to lash at the surface, and then they were gone, racing back into the depths.

Iris could not stop herself from going rigid, but she turned the sudden jerk of her shoulders into a casual stretch, and then leaned on the railing with her arms crossed as though the three sirens suddenly disappearing was unsurprising. Spider had warned her to be patient and expect strange behavior, but she could not help but think that one party abruptly vanishing from the negotiations did not bode well, especially before any real offers had been made.

She wondered if the sirens were expecting her to throw more treasures into the water. She was tempted, but the haul from the *Talon* was not a vast trove of wealth, and she needed to keep as much of it in reserve as she could for the actual bartering. If it came to it, she was ready to use all of the plunder to pay for information on the black mimic, but she would not show weakness to the sirens, and especially not to the crew. They were murmuring quietly behind her now, trying to figure out what was going on, but fear of the sirens kept them away from the edges of the ship, and that was all Iris wanted of them for the time being. They were her crew, but this was her deal to make, and her legend to chase and finally secure.

Her patience had worn brittle by the time a few bubbles formed on the surface of the water. That was the only warning she had before a dozen sirens burst to the surface, sending small geysers of water into the air. These sirens were considerably bigger than the first three, with thicker bodies and teeth that jutted over their thin lips. Many of them had wicked harpoons in their hands, topped with barbed tips cut from rock and coral. Their coloring ran duller, pulling more into grays than those of the scouts. This made the leader stand out all the more.

Covered in bright bands of pink, red, white and black around a column of creamy yellow scales running along the front of its body, the lead siren was larger than its fellows by far. It bore the same crested fins as the others, but long spines fanned out along the leader's head, back, and arms, adding to their already impressive size. Iris had the feeling that, if she met this creature on dry land and it held itself upright on its braced arms, it would be nearly as tall as her. In the sea, where it could stretch out to its full length, it may well be three times her size.

Iris managed to stare at the siren leader for only a moment before sweeping her hat off of her head and offering a low bow. Spider had not been able to say for certain whether or not the sirens recognized human courtesies, but erring on the side of the overly polite was unlikely to hurt matters when attempting to get something from sea monsters notorious for luring sailors to their deaths. When Iris straightened, she could have sworn that the banded siren leader looked amused. She chose to take that as a good sign.

"Fair tides to you, Greatest of Swimmers," Iris called down. "I come seeking information, and the promise of safe passage through your territory. I have treasures to give in return, both enduring and ephemeral, as the sea sees fit to take them." Iris had rehearsed the flowery words tirelessly, but they still felt inflated and clumsy on her tongue.

If the sirens noticed, they did not let it show. Instead, three of them swam to the *Southern Echo*. Their arms came out of the water and hooked on to the side of the ship, and the sirens looked up at Iris expectantly.

When Spider had told her what to do at this point, she had nearly swatted him across the face, so certain was she that he was having fun with her. But Spider had been deadly serious, and his somberness did not break as he explained that the sirens would need to see her full offering with their own eyes. And so, Iris bent down and lifted the long coil of rope at her feet, one end already anchored to a cargo ring on the deck next to her, and dropped it over the side of the ship.

The sirens did not flinch as the rope unspooled and swung towards them, even when it plopped heavily into the water mere inches away from one of them. They grabbed it and hauled themselves up the side of the ship hand-over-hand. They moved unsettlingly fast for creatures that spent all of their time underwater, not hampered in the slightest by their own weight or the unsteady sway of their tails.

Iris moved aside as the sirens reached the railing, finally risking a look at the crew. Most of them looked confused, but when the first siren slipped over the railing and thudded on to the deck, their expressions changed to horror. Once more, Iris's crew strained against their lifelines, but this time, they were trying to press themselves as far away as possible.

The siren flicked its gaze over the pirates, taking in their terror with fish-bright eyes before catching sight of the pile of plunder sitting on the open deck. It looked pleased, and let loose a single high-pitched screech. The two sirens behind it sped up their efforts to get aboard, and light splashing came from the water below.

"We will take these treasures," the banded leader said from the water below, its voice clearer and stronger than that of the shark-colored scout. "What is it you wish to know, Land Dweller?"

Iris watched the three sirens pull themselves across the deck of the ship. Their tails slipped after them, leaving long trails of salt water and a few glistening scales behind. They began to pick over the plunder from the *Talon*, and seemed particularly pleased with the bits of agate Iris had thrown in from the *Southern Echo*'s stores.

Perhaps this would go smoothly after all.

Iris leaned over the railing to address the banded siren leader again. "I seek the home of the black mimic."

The leader hissed. Its entourage tensed and pointed their weapons, and the three sirens aboard the *Southern Echo* sent several pieces of agate clattering to the deck.

"You cannot afford such knowledge," the leader growled. "For asking, we will take a price."

At that, a few rolled up animal pelts went sailing over the edge of the *Southern Echo* and splashed into the sea. One of the leader's remaining siren guard dove under to catch them.

"Seek something else," the leader said.

Iris shook her head. "I seek the home of the black mimic," she repeated. "Nothing else."

The leader bared its long teeth. "For refusing, we will take a price."

Two of the sirens on the ship came forward, dragging the small chest of coins between them. They lobbed it over the railing, and it landed with a thunderclap in the water below. Another siren disappeared from the leader's group.

"Something else," the leader insisted, "before you can no longer afford safe passage out of our waters, Land Dweller."

Iris gestured to the pile of plunder on the ship's deck. "You may have it all, if you give me what I seek."

Another hiss came from the banded siren. "It is not enough."

Damn you, Spider, Iris thought before turning her mind to the ship's hold, and the things she could afford to part with that would pique the sirens' interest. She thought of the guns in the armory, and while part of her railed against the idea of shorting the amount of weapons available to the crew, the rest of her hummed with anticipation. She was so close to finally obtaining the location of the black mimic. What were a few guns and swords to a living legend? She reached up and touched the black scale hanging from the chain around her neck. "I will pay more," Iris said, "after you give me what I ask."

The siren leader allowed itself to sink further into the water, but it did not look away. A few tense, pensive moments slipped past. Then the leader rose up again, and Iris saw its tail swish powerfully in the water beneath it. "We will take our price," the leader said, "and you will have what you seek, and safe tides to carry you away."

Iris's heart gave a mighty leap. She struggled to keep her voice calm as she said, "I thank you, Greatest of Swimmers."

The siren leader did not look particularly pleased, but it came forward and took a firm grip on the rope dangling down the side of the *Southern Echo*. It hauled itself halfway out of the water and stopped there, and Iris had the feeling that her earlier estimate was correct; this siren was easily three times her length. She swallowed her fear as she moved closer to the creature, stopping only when she stood directly above it. She did not like how close its face was to her own.

The siren glared at her with black eyes that glittered like onyx. "Long ago," the leader informed her gravely, "hunters came on ships for the mimic dragons, seeking those beasts with scales the colors of the skies and blood that cured as readily as it killed."

Iris nodded as though this was new and fascinating information to her, and tried not to let herself be distracted by the shower of semiprecious gemstones that went soaring over the railing off to her right.

"The hunters who sought the dragons chased them across our waters," the siren leader continued.

"Sometimes, the hunters would stop and turn their weapons on us, and we learned to sing to save ourselves. This made the hunters think that we had great treasures to hide, and the price to drive them out of our waters was too high." A shudder ran along the leader's spines before they fanned out wider, making the banded siren look even bigger. "We would not have those hunters return to our waters. Do you understand, Land Dweller?"

Iris's nod was slower this time, but earnest. If she captured the black mimic and showed the world that this wondrous species of dragon still existed, it could trigger another hunt for their rumored miracle blood. Iris had no intention of bringing mimic dragons back to the world, however, if there even were any mimics beyond the black one. She would get the map, and then she would be on her way, and the black mimic could live out the rest of its lonely life as it saw fit. The world did not need to know how or where she'd found it, nor was it likely to care once she'd followed Mordanti's trail to the end and recovered the legendary treasure, proving once and for all that the Veritian side of history was the one that rang true. So Iris nodded and agreed and waited patiently for the three sirens behind her to throw more of the plunder from the *Talon* into the sea.

"To find the black dragon," the siren leader said, "you must go west, to the island where nothing grows. You will not be welcome."

Iris frowned at the siren when it did not offer more. "I was hoping you could be a little more specific." A crate of exotic furs sailed over her head. "Considering the price."

The siren leader did not say anything for a long moment, but amusement flickered in its black eyes. "Go west for seven days and nights, and south for two.

You will find the dragon." The siren bared its teeth. "Or the dragon will find you."

It was vague, but it was far more than Iris or anyone else had ever had to go on. "You have my thanks, Greatest of Swimmers," she said, and she meant it.

The siren leader lowered itself back into the water. "Our price is still to be met," it reminded her once it had rejoined its fellows.

"It will be," Iris assured the siren, ready to push a cannon over the side of the ship if that was what the leader demanded of her.

"We know," the leader hissed. "We always take our price."

Iris paused, her body half-turned from the railing and warning bells sounding in her mind. She did not like how the leader had said that. She suspiciously watched one of the plundering sirens as it dragged another crate across the deck and tipped its contents over the railing before hoisting itself up and dropping down into the water. She turned to look for the other two, intending to ask them to wait while she gathered some additional items from the ship's stores for them to choose from, and found that they had moved to the foremast and were looking thoughtfully at the crew huddled there. Alarmed, Iris started towards them.

Then the horrible, screeching singing came again, so much louder and harsher than before, and Iris gasped and fell to her knees under the sudden pain and pressure in her head. She slammed her hands over her ears, but that did not save her from the sound. She grit her teeth and looked up just in time to see the remaining two sirens on the *Southern Echo* grab one of the riggers—Billy Yellowrock—as he lunged forward, eyes distant and hungry for the source of whatever blissful melody he was hearing. One siren held Billy tight. The other snapped its jaws closed on the taut lifeline, sawing at the rope with serrated teeth. It frayed and came apart, and with one harsh tug, the rope snapped.

Iris scrambled to her feet as the sirens moved. She should have been able to catch them. They were out of the water and she was on her own ship, by all the gods above and below, it was *her ship* and Iris knew every knot in the boards and every rolling pitch of her rhythms, but the sirens moved so much faster than they had before, and they went over the railing, dragging Billy with them.

Iris dove after them. She had time to draw one fast breath before she crashed into the sea. The salt water stung her eyes, but she forced them open as she began to swim, tiny bubbles swarming all around her. She kicked hard and raked her hands through the water, but even as she swam as fast as she could, some part of her knew that she was already too late. She just managed to catch a glimpse of Billy before the sirens dragged him down into the dark. He looked terrified, now that the song was gone. And then he, too, was gone.

Iris slowed to a stop. Her breath had already turned stale in her lungs, but she hung there in the water, even as the rest of the sirens drifted around her at a much more sedate pace. She couldn't be sure, but she thought that they were laughing as they dove back to their home.

The leader was the last to go. It swam in a tight circle around Iris, nearly brushing her with its spines and looking far too pleased with itself. Its tail lashed through the water, powerful and graceful and deadly. The siren leader came to rest facing her, and for a terrible moment, it looked as though it was considering taking Iris into the depths, too. She had voluntarily come into the water, after all, even if it was not a song that had pulled her in.

But then the leader smiled, and Iris longed to plunge her sword into its chest. "Our price is met," the banded siren said, and beneath the water, its voice was deep as thunder. It flipped away and lashed its tail and vanished into the darkness below.

Iris's lungs burned all the way back to the surface, and her clothes threatened to drag her back down as she broke free of the water and drew in deep, coughing breaths. She tread water for a few moments, not sure if she was hoping for the sirens to return or not, but the only thing that met her was the call of the pirate who spotted her from the ship. More cries went up, and Iris saw that a good part of the crew had removed their lifelines to rush to the railing. She clenched her teeth with anger and worry as she struck out for the ship. She had to get them out of here.

They had lowered the rope ladder for her by the time Iris swam the distance back to the *Southern Echo*. Her soaking clothes were heavy as she pulled herself up, and she was panting hard by the time she reached the railing. Dax helped her over and on to the deck, his expression grave as she bent over to catch her breath. She knew what he and the rest of the crew were waiting for, but she allowed herself a moment of respite before facing all of them. One last deep breath, and then she straightened up. She shook her head, and she saw what little foolish hope had remained drain from their faces.

It was going to be a somber funeral that evening.

Iris squeezed water out of her hair and clothes. "We got what we came for," she said, making sure her voice was steady and carrying across the ship. "Miss Rori?"

"Aye, Captain?" came the navigator's subdued reply from somewhere back by the helm.

"Set a course for due west. We have a dragon to find."

For a moment, no one moved. They simply stared at her, or at each other, or down at the water.

Then Novachak's rough voice began to bark out orders, and the crew drifted away to their tasks. Dax stayed with her, one hand on Iris's shoulder as she recovered her breath and glared daggers at the sea.

Before long, the *Southern Echo* had left the Court of Sirens in her wake, along with the plunder from the *Talon* and one of her own.

CHAPTER EIGHTEEN

A New Heading

THE EVENING BREEZE WAS light but steady during the funeral for the taken sailor. It was an odd sort of thing for Nate to be standing in the crowd, listening to Dax speak about the man—Billy—in a voice heavy with genuine sadness. Nate had seen Billy about the ship plenty, as it was impossible not to come across nearly everyone from the crew at least once a day, but they had never spoken. Nate could not remember if they had even shared a glance, or if they had just shuffled past each other, too focused on their own tasks to think much of the other.

Nate did not know how to feel as he watched the crew gather as close as they could to the railing. For burials at sea, the body was wrapped in a spare bit of sailcloth with a cannonball at the feet to weigh it down into the depths, uniting the deceased with the sea for the rest of eternity. But the sirens had already done that, so Dax came forward with the dead man's personal possessions: an old hat, a worn but well-cared for cutlass, and a cheap wooden flask chipped and faded with use. The quartermaster passed them to the captain, who held them over the side of the ship and murmured a final blessing and beseeched the goddess of the sea to have mercy on the soul of their departed brother. Then Arani opened her hands, and the sea received the old items and the sorrows of the dead man's surviving crew.

Dinner that night was muted, with voices pulled low and far less laughter than there normally was when the men and women of the *Southern Echo* gathered to fill their bellies. Someone raised a toast to the taken sailor, and Nate joined in mechanically.

It was shocking how quickly life aboard the *Southern Echo* returned to a semblance of normalcy the next day. There was still a pall hanging over those who had known Billy best, but they set about their tasks and found ways to fill the hole his absence left. Soon enough, it was like the man had never been there at all.

Nate's morning training session with Luken went much the same as it always did, and then Marcus and Eric both had duties to see to, so Nate went off on his own for a couple of hours. The sun was unrelenting that day, and Nate went below seeking shade and cooler air. He made his way to the hold, intending to rest a little before his afternoon session. He was not alone, as several others had come down the steps with the same idea, but orders came that pulled a few of them to other parts of the ship. The rest settled in among the supplies and were snoring softly before long. A nap sounded good to Nate, and he put himself in the last unoccupied, out-of-the-way spot he could find, under the stairs. It was fairly comfortable there, and pleasantly dark, and Nate felt himself begin to drift off. He jolted awake when footsteps slammed near his head. Two pairs of boots came to a halt, and one of their owners shushed the other. Deeper in the hold, someone grunted and rolled over in their sleep, but no one came awake at the sudden intrusion.

"This is the best I expect we'll find," the first pirate whispered.

"Fine," came a quiet growl that Nate recognized as Xander's. "Now say your piece, Ethan. I've got things to do."

"You know my piece," Ethan snarled back, somehow managing to keep his voice soft even as it burned with anger. "I just don't understand why you don't share it."

"Because unlike you," Xander returned calmly, "I can see past the end of my own nose. If one pirate is what the sirens wanted in exchange for the black mimic's location, I'd call that a fair bargain. Better him than me."

"Billy was one of us," Ethan hissed.

"And?" Xander said. "Would you have preferred to go in his place?"

Nate heard the creak of the step as Ethan shifted uncomfortably. The rigger was still whispering, but with more confidence when he said, "Mark me now, Grayvoice, Arani is going to pay for this treasure with our lives. I don't fancy being the next one thrown to sea beasts."

"Then take care not to look too appetizing," Xander said flippantly.

"I don't see how you can joke about this. If those sirens had been three steps to the left, they would have taken *you.*"

"But they didn't," Xander said, "and now I know to hang back when everyone else charges forward."

"You would watch the others die that readily?"

Nate could almost hear the shrug in Xander's voice when he said, "The fewer pockets to line when we do get that treasure, all the better for everyone still standing. All I have to do is outlive the stupid ones."

A small pause played out before Ethan said, "That may be harder than you think."

"And if you think *that*," Xander said, his boots turning and starting back up the stairs, "maybe you're not fit for a longer life."

Ethan followed Xander, but Nate stayed down in the hold for a long time after that, letting those words roll through his head as he listened to the snores of the pirates around him and the creaking of the *Southern Echo*'s hull.

He swallowed past the small lump that had formed in his throat. He wasn't entirely surprised to hear Xander talk like that, given his proclaimed willingness to follow Arani to the end of the world for a legendary treasure, but as Ethan had said, Billy Yellowrock had been a rigger, one of their company. It was strange to think that Xander could dismiss someone who should have been a friend so easily. Nate spent a few moments considering Xander's volatile temper and their own tenuous friendship, and he wondered how secure any of his relationships with the people of the *Southern Echo* truly were. Perhaps he had let himself get too comfortable in a ship full of killers and thieves.

Survive this, Nate told himself. *Survive this, and return to where you belong.*

But he thought of the genuine laughs he'd shared with Eric, of the rare smiles he'd been able to draw out of Rori, and of the pure joy in Marcus's eyes when he played the fiddle and set the crew to dancing. Nate thought of card games played in idle hours and stories traded over meals and even Arani's reserved but genuine praises, and his heart offered up its rebellious question once again. It bothered Nate that he was afraid of the answer.

ONCE NATE STARTED LISTENING, he began hearing conversations like the one between Xander and Ethan every day. Some were whispered, and others were more boldly stated, but the underlying thought was the same: how high was the price Arani would pay for this treasure?

This wasn't like the pirates' other hunts. They accepted that danger was a constant presence in their lives, and taking a prize was always fraught with problems that could turn fatal. But those were real, tangible things that everyone had understood when they'd signed the code and pledged their loyalty to the *Southern Echo*'s flag. Hunting for dragons and unknown treasures was another matter, especially now that they all knew that their lives could be forfeit in situations well beyond their control.

The *Southern Echo*'s pirates understood the navy coming after them. They understood merchant sailors putting up fights. They understood the rolling threat of bad storms and dangerous waters and yes, even the leviathan sea serpents that ruled the south. A captain who would barter their lives in exchange for information on a fable was not something they could comprehend, and even the ones who were quick to point out that Arani had dove into the sea after the sirens and tried to save Billy did so with shadows in their eyes and their mouths turned down unhappily.

A crew mate lost in an honest fight against an enemy or to a storm was acceptable. A crew mate lost on the captain's whims was not.

No one spoke of outright mutiny. They seemed willing to wait and see if there really was a dragon at the end of the trail Arani and the sirens had set them on, but the crew's breaths grew hard as tension coated the ship from bow to stern.

And Nate, who was very aware that Arani had put them on this path only because of his Skill, threw himself even deeper into his training. If the crew overthrew Arani, he was certain that he would be caught up in the damage.

When the ship finally passed out of the doldrums, the wind filled the *Southern Echo*'s sails once again. It was a more gradual onset than their abrupt absence had been, and Nate found that while Luken's signature was blurry once more, he could more readily pick it out from the surrounding gusts. What was more, the doldrums had given Nate the chance to understand pure air currents more intimately, and he shouted with triumph when he discovered that he could track the bird flying downwind. But his jubilation was short lived when Nate realized that he could only track Luken in that direction if the bird had originally begun his flight from an upwind point, and that would not do for hunting dragons.

So, every morning after the meeting with the sirens, Nate woke well before the sun was up. He collected Luken from his perch next to Rori's hammock, and after a few protesting squawks, brought the bird topside to continue their training. Luken did not hesitate to let Nate know that he was irritated over having his sleep disrupted, and he dove at Nate's head again and again until he had worked out the worst of his avian grudges. Nate let him do it, using this aggressive ritual as a warmup exercise for what came next.

He found that he got the cleanest readings of Luken's downwind flights at the bow of the ship. The sails caught most of the tailwinds that pushed the *Southern Echo* along, so Nate only had to contend with the air disrupted by the ship and the occasional rogue gust from the sea. He stood at the foot of the bowsprit, his eyes shut and his lips partly open to let the taste of the wind into his mouth and lungs. Slowly, the shape of the wind would come into focus, and fill in more and more as Nate extended his awareness, feeling out each current and breeze and prying out the patterns of their motion and strength. When he found Luken in these moments, the bird's trail was a series of smeared flashes caught in the disturbed air, somehow both muted and too bright against the background noise of the natural wind. Then the bird would slip too far away, and Nate could not follow him.

Frustrated, Nate came out of the element and squinted into the dim pre-dawn light, finally picking out Luken's darting form in the distance. He watched the bird fly for a bit, trying to get a sense of his patterns. It was cheating, in a way, but Nate had to learn how to extend his reach and find Luken from a distance, and he needed to do it when the bird was already downwind. He'd never be able to track a dragon otherwise.

Nate remembered his academy training, and all the ways it had failed him. He thought with wry amusement of what Tobias Lowwind would tell him to do to further his connection with the element, and took a moment of self-indulgence to imagine the look of total shock that would settle on the head instructor's face if he knew what Nate was up to now. He could almost hear Tobias's old lessons: *Pull the wind to you. Bend it to your will. You must control the wind, for that is the true purpose of your Skill.*

But Tobias had been wrong. So very wrong.

Nate thought for a moment, and then took a deep breath of sea wind and shut his eyes again. He let the element wash over him, feeling the patterns and the shapes of the gusts as they naturally were. He felt his own shadow in the breezes, smeared and tangled with the air. He let a particularly strong gust catch his awareness, and shepherd it off the bow of the ship.

Nate made no effort to resist. He let the wind carry him further and further on his search for Luken, and slowly, the world began to change. Though his eyes were shut, Nate gradually became aware of color all around him, mostly blue but with tangles of green and purple threading through. They aligned themselves with the winds, and he could clearly see the colors ribbon in and out of each other, tracing fresh patterns in the sky. His shadow and that of the *Southern Echo* were dark smears behind him. Ahead of him, sparking and dancing on the wind, was a pinprick of light. Nate reached for it, riding the wind closer and closer as the light grew brighter and brighter until he could reach out and touch it. The gold ring on his hand burned hot, and Nate's skull erupted with pain.

With a gasp, he fell out of the element and against the ship's railing. It took a long time for Nate to catch his breath and for the headache to subside to a dull pulse, but his heart was soaring. He'd done it. He'd ridden the wind to Luken.

"Are you all right?" the concerned voice of Eric asked. The elegant Darkbend held a small wooden carving that Nate recognized as a fiddling project he worked on in his spare time. He must have come to sit with Nate at some point, but Nate had been too engrossed in the wind to notice. Eric stood next to Nate now with his carving and whittling knife in one hand and his legs braced, as though he expected Nate to faint at any moment.

Nate put his hands on the ship's railing and nodded slowly, hiding a small wince as the heated ring pressed harder against his skin. It wasn't enough to burn him, but it was undeniably hot, and further proof that Nate had stretched his Skill further than he ever had before.

"I think I just did the impossible," he said, his voice breathy.

Eric gave him a sidelong look, slowly straightening up as the moments slipped past and Nate proved to be steady on his feet. "You followed Luken downwind?" the Darkbend asked.

"No," Nate said, "I *found* him downwind." His heart raced with excitement. "I have to tell the captain!"

He made to run off, but Eric stopped him with a hand on his arm. "Hold on," he said, and the raw concern in his voice was enough to make Nate pause. "I don't know what you just did but..." He stared at Nate, and his eyes were wide beneath his white Darkbend tattoo. "It looked like it hurt."

"A little," Nate admitted, "but I'm fine." He gave his friend a broad smile, unable to contain his happiness and awe. "I found him *downwind*, Eric," Nate whispered. "I thought it was impossible, but I *did it*."

Eric looked at Nate for a long time before offering a cautious smile, but a line of worry was creased between his brows. "I'll go tell Arani," Eric said. "You stay here and be careful."

Nate grinned and waved the Darkbend off. He felt another rush of excitement as he thought of what he'd just done. He needed to do it again. Nate returned his attention to the horizon, and went back into the wind to test the limits of his magic and the edges of the pain he'd felt, and see how much of it he could take.

THE CAPTAIN WAS ALMOST as excited as Nate was by the breakthrough he'd made with his Skill, and with her encouragement and praise bolstering his spirit, Nate pushed himself even harder. The headaches became part of his routine, and the throbbing in his skull fell to a persistent rumble that refused to fade even during sleep. Morning after morning, day after day, night after night, Nate grit his teeth against the pain and tossed Luken back into the air, and sent his awareness out along the winds again.

On the seventh day of sailing after leaving the doldrums, the world went dark as Nate tangled himself with the element. The wind smeared itself around him, scattering wild strokes of blue and green and purple and now red across his awareness. The sails and the masts of the ship were dark, looming things behind him, and his own breath was a spot of pale blue that smudged into nothingness after it left his lips. His head burned with pain, but he would not let go. Not yet. He could see the sparks in the distance, could feel the sporadic pattern of wind crashing against Luken's body and wings as he flew over the sea, and if Nate could just push further, a little further...

There.

The bright burst of a wingbeat, casting a shadow into the wind and sending a hot throb of fresh pain into the space behind Nate's eyes. It faded to a dull burn after a few moments, present but not unbearable, and Nate pushed himself again. The pain came again, but it was drowned out by the roar of excitement and determination that echoed in his heart, and he held his own breath so that it would not interfere with the things he saw ahead, and if he could go further, he could join with the element as no wind worker ever had before, and then—

"ENOUGH!"

The shout ripped across the wind, sharp and angry and red. It speared through Nate's head and severed his connection to the element, sending him reeling back into his own body with enough force to stagger him. The pain erupted nearly tenfold in his head, and almost threw Nate to his knees. Someone caught him before that could happen. They grunted under the effort, but refused to let him fall.

When Nate's legs had stopped shaking, he peeled open his eyes to see Rori bracing his weight against herself. She was struggling, but her eyes were soft.

"Gods below, Nate," she murmured, "enough."

Nate forced his legs to cooperate and pulled his weight off of Rori. Something like shame wanted to rise up in him, but his head was too full of that persistent pain to give it any room. He settled for turning away and trying to catch his breath. Rori's shadow flickered across Nate's eyes as she raised her arm and signaled to Luken, who was flying erratically in front of the ship. The bird caught sight of the motion almost immediately, and he darted back to the *Southern Echo*, arrowing straight into Rori's arms. He climbed up on to her shoulder, buried his head under his wing, and trembled his way to sleep.

Nate had not realized how tired Luken was until he saw the bird curled up, and the look Rori was giving him made his blood run cold. The softness had evaporated completely from her gaze. In spite of the bird's harassment of his head, Nate felt a genuine pang of guilt for exhausting Luken. He offered Rori a soft apology.

"He's not the only one you're going to kill if you keep this up," she said. "When's the last time you've eaten anything?"

"I'm fine." Nate shook his head, and winced at the way his headache clenched at his temples with the motion. "I'm finally making progress," he gritted out. "I can see Luken in the wind. If I can just go further, I can track this dragon. I know I can."

"Is that worth dying for?" Rori asked, and Nate was startled by the sharpness in her tone, but he held her gaze more readily this time.

"I'm not going to die," Nate said, "but yes, it would be worth it. For the first time in my life, I finally understand what my Skill can do, what *I* can do. Having this magic in my blood actually means something. I'm not going to let that go."

Rori's eyes hardened, but she said nothing, only turned to stare out at a horizon gone fiery with the sunset. Nate looked at it too, trying to find peace in the beauty that came with the death of the day. He only felt a rolling anxiety that accompanied the knowledge that the ship was turning south, and would soon be near the place the sirens had told them to go. He had to be ready before then, so he could track this dragon and show the empire, his family, *himself* what he could really do.

"I finally know what it's like to have a Skill like yours," Nate said, his voice soft and awed.

Rori jolted away from him. "My Skill destroyed my family," she hissed. "Then it chained me to a boat that sailed into the Forbidden Sea with the intent to cross the Rend."

It was Nate's turn to give a startled jerk. The Forbidden Sea bore its name for a reason, filled as it was with dangerous creatures and the supposed tear in the fabric of the world that left it exposed to the realm of the gods. All the stuff of superstition and children's stories, really. The Forbidden Sea was a vast expanse of nothing, with no place to seek refuge when a ship's supplies ran out. The empire's attempts to cross it had been in vain, and the ships that had returned did so with fully depleted stores, their survivors starving and bearing tales of some of their dead mates succumbing to intense thirst and drinking seawater, the rest carried off by hunger and exhaustion and sickness. For a captain to have deliberately sailed into it...

The haunted look in Rori's eyes suddenly made a great deal of sense.

"When my Skill first manifested," Rori growled, "I prayed and I wished and I hoped that there had been some mistake, that I didn't have a Skill and I would have the freedom to choose what I did with my life, that I did not suddenly belong, body and soul, to the empire. My family helped me hide it for years, long enough for me to start thinking that maybe I could be a free Goodtide." She bared her teeth in sudden disgust. "I actually started to *like* my Skill. I thought it a gift from the gods, even if I had to keep it hidden. Then my secret was found out, and everything was torn apart, and I came to understand what a curse a Skill truly is." She took a shuddering breath and turned her eyes out to the reddening sky and sea. "A Skill will destroy everything you hold dear before it destroys you. You're letting yours do that now. I see it every time you try to control the wind. We weren't *meant* to control these things, Nate. It's not our place."

"But I'm not trying to control it," Nate said softly. Rori's gaze narrowed into a glare, but he kept his tone gentle, as he would with a wounded animal he wanted to help. "I'm reading the wind in ways I never thought possible. Ways no one ever *realized* were possible." He gazed out at the horizon, already reaching again for the winds that danced around the ship. "I'm not turning it to my will like every other wind worker. I'm letting it take *me*."

Rori drew in a sharp, quiet breath. "That sounds dangerous, Nate."

It probably was. He shook his head anyway. "I'm not afraid."

"You should be."

"I'm not going to hide from my Skill," Nate said with a frustrated sigh. "I'm not like you, Rori."

Rori bristled. "I'm not hiding," she said. "I choose not to use it."

"And I choose this."

Rori stared at him for a long moment, and Nate was surprised when tears came into her eyes. She did not let them fall. "I won't get in your way, then." She shoved a bundle of cloth wrapped around something hard into his hands and turned to leave, but added over her shoulder, "If you're really going to throw away your life over this, you can do it without taking Luken with you."

Nate did not watch her leave. Instead, he watched the sun fall below the sea, and it only occurred to him as the stars began to emerge that his splitting headache had dulled. He looked at the bundle in his hand, and slowly peeled the corners of the cloth away. He found himself staring at several pieces of agate, some of them quite large. When he touched one of the pieces, a band of cool relief stretched across his forehead, quieting his head pain for a few blessed moments before it sulked its way back to the edges of his mind, nowhere near as intense as it had been before.

He considered going after Rori. He did not. Instead, he gathered himself for another union with the wind element.

TRUE TO HER WORD, Rori would not let Nate train with Luken anymore. Arani was initially displeased, but Dax intervened on Rori's behalf, pointing out that they did use Luken for communications across the ship, and if they kept overworking the bird, they were likely to lose him. Most of the crew were neutral on this issue, but there were a few who thought that a single bird was a small price to pay for a dragon. They'd already paid with a man's life. A bird's was nothing compared to that.

Dark whispers followed Rori about the ship. In return, Rori promised to cut the throat of anyone who tried to take Luken from her. That seemed to stave off any actual attempts to steal the bird, although Nate noticed that Rori kept Luken far closer than she had before, and took to sleeping in the navigation room rather than her hammock. Nate worried for her, but their last exchange weighed on his mind, and he kept his distance. Besides, he knew that Rori could take care of herself. According to Xander, she kept her sword and three loaded pistols with her, and would not let anyone in to the navigation room except the quartermaster and the captain, once Arani had sworn she would not send Luken to his death.

While Luken may have been gone from his routine, Nate's head remained under constant attack, this time from overexertion of his Skill. The agate Rori had given him certainly helped, but his magic was proving too strong, and he rapidly surpassed the strength of the anchors. Nate's gold ring burned on his hand, and the agate grew hot under his touch as the power of his magic grew and grew.

He kept pushing himself anyway. He did not want to admit that Rori may have been right to warn him, but he did not have much time left as it was, so he drove his way through the pain as best he could, and tried to pretend that his lack of sleep at night was from excitement and determination. The dark rings that formed under his eyes and the exhausted pull of his muscles told another story. Nate gripped agate in his hands and focused on the wind, and did everything he could to drown out his own body's protests.

Without Luken to focus on, the wind was a pure, wild thing all around Nate. He sorely missed having something to give context to the sweep and flow of the gales; without that, it was dangerously easy to get lost in their currents and drown. He had to work even harder to keep himself tethered to the element without letting it drag him into oblivion, which left him so tired he could barely lift food to his mouth at dinner. Eric and Marcus took to bothering him at meal times, trying to get him to send more food into his stomach, but Nate did not want food. All he could think about was the freedom of the winds. He paid with physical pain to ride them, but Nate had magic no one else did, and his excitement over going ever further was what allowed him to wake up in the mornings even as his exhausted body begged for sleep.

On the fourth morning after his argument with Rori, Nate dragged himself topside, placed himself at the bow of the ship, and connected to the wind. As always, the shadows of the masts and sails loomed behind Nate, and the air in front of him was a clean sweep of nothingness for the wind to play with as it saw fit. Nate picked a direction, and let the wind carry his awareness farther and farther away from his body aboard the *Southern Echo*, sweeping him off to open skies over calm waters. The pain that hammered like a spike through his head grew faint as he left his body behind, fading to a dull little bit of unpleasantness that tethered him to his mortal self. Nate knew that the further he went, the more it would hurt when he returned, but he did not let himself turn back. He wanted to go even farther than he had the day before, when exhaustion had broken his concentration and swept him out of the element. He was about to gather himself for another push when a different air current cut across the one he rode. It was steadier and warmer, and had a strange, sulfuric tang to it. With a heave, Nate shifted his awareness from the cool ocean breeze to the hotter one, and he was distantly aware that miles away, a gold ring was burning against his skin and his body was sweating as it stood on the rolling deck of the *Southern Echo*.

Nate followed the new wind, feeling it grow hotter as he went. He wanted to trace it all the way to its source, but he was so tired by then that the best he could manage was a frustrated lunge towards the horizon. A dark, blurry mass took shape on the water, and Nate had the sense that the hot, steady air was coming from it. From what Nate could tell, the mass was not moving, and while it was a good ways away, he knew that it was very, very large. An island, perhaps, given the steady shadow it cast as it pushed the wind aside and threw its heat into the sky. He wondered if this was where the sirens had told them to look for the black mimic.

The thought made Nate linger longer than he should have, searching for a sign that he'd found the right place. Even this far outside of his body, he was beginning to feel dizzy, and if he did not release his hold on the element soon, he felt it would rip him apart. But he forced himself to hang on even as the world grew unsteadier and blurrier around him, and so he was there to catch the trace of a wind shadow not entirely dissimilar to Luken's. He could not make out the shape or guess at the size, but he knew the pattern as wing beats.

Nate's hold on the wind element slipped, and he went crashing back into himself. This time, there was no one to catch him when he hit the deck, but the jolt that went through him on impact barely registered under the waves of pain and stress that crashed over him after exerting his Skill for so long. It took him a long while to get his eyes open and claw his way to his feet, and by that time, a few people had paused to frown at him. Nate looked past them, raking his eyes over the ship, and saw Arani on the stairs that led up to the poop deck. He began to stumble after her.

"Captain," he tried to call, but his voice was weak in his throat, and his lips were dry. He sucked in a breath, coughed, and tried again. "Captain!" He fumbled his way along the railing, nearly falling into a few pirates as he went, but he was gaining momentum and his legs were starting to cooperate a bit more. "*Captain!*"

Arani stopped as the shout ripped clear of Nate's throat, and she turned to see him all but crash into the base of the steps.

Nate tried to find the words, but he was panting too hard, and he had to settle for swinging gestures that left Arani puzzled. She descended a couple of steps, then froze as Nate desperately locked his gaze with hers. His voice still failing, Nate willed the words into his expression, hoping Arani would understand. She did. Her eyes widened, and her brows lifted in a silent question.

Nate nodded his answer.

Arani's smile could have cut the sky.

CHAPTER NINETEEN

Dragon Wings

THE *SOUTHERN ECHO* RIPPED across the water, her sails stretched to catch every last scrap of wind. Nate stood at the bow with Captain Arani, who had managed to get Luken away from Rori once more. The Goodtide was at the helm, as far away from Nate as she could be, but he had no trouble imagining the brittle look in her eyes as she watched for Arani's signals from the bow, ready to redirect the *Southern Echo* with a touch of the wheel.

Arani was silent as Nate threaded his awareness through the winds, but he could see the excited burst of her breath with even more clarity than the flying creature they approached. Whenever Nate murmured a correction to their course to keep them on a straight shot to the creature, Arani sent Luken into the air a moment later, her gestured commands to the bird smearing on Nate's peripheries. Luken would do as he was trained, and dip and soar on the corresponding side of the ship, adding flashes of his wings and their long pennant feathers to send additional information to Rori at the helm. Nate found the bird's motions distracting as he could not begin to understand their complicated meaning, but without fail, after each of Luken's performances, the ship would turn and head straight on the line Nate had picked out. With each course adjustment, the excitement of the crew swelled, until it felt like a wave looming behind Nate, ready to crash down on his head and sweep him away. Nate felt their eyes on his back like so many pins driven into his flesh, and he prayed to every god above that he was not leading them to a large bird. He wasn't sure he'd survive their disappointment.

As the ship sailed on, more details revealed themselves about the creature in the wind.

It was much larger than Luken, though Nate could not guess at its true size without further context. It flew in lazy circles over the ocean, weaving back and forth in no discernible pattern until it would abruptly tuck its wings and dive, vanishing as it collided with the water. A few moments would pass, and then it would burst from the sea and climb back into the air, its shape obscured by the water streaming from its body. Nate was fairly certain the beast was fishing, but what struck him was the way it would spin and triumphantly thrust out its wings after every dive. It was not unlike the way Luken flashed his wings to signal the helm. Nate was baffled as to why a creature would do that without prompting.

He got his answer when the *Southern Echo* finally caught up to it.

They were close enough by then that its shape was much clearer to Nate. He was afraid to say aloud what it was. His head knew that was foolish, but his heart feared that speaking the words would shatter everything, and thrust this creature back into the realm of impossibilities. So Nate withdrew from the wind element, pressed a bit of cooling agate against his temple, and leaned heavily on the railing as he watched Arani lift her spyglass to follow the distant shape in the sky.

"It's not the black mimic," she finally said, and Nate felt his heart drop. His spirits lifted cautiously when

Arani smiled and offered her spyglass to him. "But it *is* a promising start."

As Arani signaled for the ship to bleed some wind out of the sails, Nate peered through the spyglass. He wasn't as adept with the instrument as the captain was, and his exhaustion added an extra tremor to his arms, but he eventually picked out the creature in the distance, and his heart gave a mighty leap in his chest.

It was a dragon. Not the black one, as the captain had said, but unmistakable in its sinewy grace. He could not quite make out the color of the creature, but he thought it might have been yellow or pale orange, certainly a bright color that stood out against all the blue around it. It flew in lazy loops over the water, and Nate was mesmerized by the easy shift and lean of its body as it rode the wind. As Nate watched, the dragon tucked its wings and dove for the water, arrowing straight into the waves with a far smaller splash than he expected. When it erupted out of the water a moment later, however, it did so with a massive heave of its wings and an explosion of glittering spray. A silvery fish was clamped in its jaws, and the dragon gulped it down as it climbed back into the sky. Then the dragon did that strange spin and flex of its wings again, and Nate forgot how to breathe as he finally got a good look at the beast's coloring.

It was the color of a day as it began its slow descent into twilight, when the sun bathed the world in gold and softened the shadows with dreamy splendor. Its body was a rich, gleaming yellow from nose to tail, but its wings blazed with all the colors of the softest hours of the day, a thousand shades of gold streaking across their lengths. The dragon beat and flexed its wings, showing them off in all directions before falling back into its slow circles above the ocean.

"It's beautiful," Nate breathed as he lowered the spyglass.

"It is," Arani agreed. She took the instrument back and gestured out to sea. "Let's see if you can find another one."

Nate wished they could have sailed closer to the golden dragon. He longed to see its brilliant colors up close, but he knew that Arani was right; they were not looking for a gold mimic.

By then, most of the crew had found and passed around other spyglasses and glimpsed the golden dragon in the distance. One of the gunners made a pointed, sour remark about the dragon's non-black colors and mapless wings, which prompted Jim Greenroot to cuff the man on the side of the head and snatch the spyglass out of his hands.

"That boy just led us to a *dragon*," Jim snapped, the wind carrying his words to Nate's ears. "He'll keep working the wind and find the black one yet."

A thrill ran through Nate, and joy pulsed through his veins as more excited praises drifted up from the crew as they observed the dragon. They shouted congratulations and encouragement to Nate, and he rode high on the wave of their happiness. But it wasn't for the crew that he returned his awareness to the wind, and reluctantly pulled himself away from the first living dragon he had ever seen. He did it for himself.

Reconnecting with the wind meant enduring that searing pain all over again, but Nate kept himself focused, and before long, he was rewarded with not one but two more dragons casting their wind shadows over the ocean as they hunted together. Nate pointed off the bow to where the dragons flew, and Arani sent the *Southern Echo* bounding after them.

Neither of these dragons were the black mimic, either, but they caught sight of the ship and broke off their fishing long enough to drift closer. Nate realized that the creatures were easily twice his size, but he was too awestruck to feel any sort of fear in their presence.

One of the mimics was the deep violet of evening, its wings spangled with emerging stars and the last glow of sunset. The other was all the colors of sunlight playing off tropical, turquoise water, its body and wings edged with the darker and truer blue of the deeper sea. Their bodies were slender and graceful but with a powerful curve to their chests. Their two legs were tucked neatly up along their tails, wings stretched out proudly at their sides. As the dragons drifted closer, Nate could see three flexing talons on their main wing joints. Their heads were crowned with long, shining horns, and their faces were all graceful angles and points.

The dragons kept their distance from the ship at first, bobbing and tilting off the starboard side as they eyed the vessel curiously. The pirates stared right back, and Nate heard their calls of excitement and wonder as they watched the dragons. Those calls grew to shouts as the turquoise dragon drifted closer and twisted itself in the air to flash its full wingspan at the ship. It seemed pleased by the reaction it drew from the crew, and it bobbed playfully through the air as the pirates laughed. Not to be outdone, the evening-colored mimic angled itself higher into the sky and glided closer to the ship's topsail. It kept pace with the *Southern Echo* for a few minutes, catching the same wind that filled the sails and putting its starry wings on display for the crew on the deck. Those up in the rigging got an especially good look at the evening mimic, and would later describe how its scales shimmered in the sunlight and its eyes watched them with bright intelligence. Eventually, the two dragons grew bored with the *Southern Echo* and they arced away to resume their fishing, but not before they each offered one last dazzling display of their wings.

"Oddly friendly, these mimic dragons," Dax said as he came up to the bow. He was as transfixed as the rest of the crew on the receding dragons, but Nate caught a hard note of wariness in his tone.

The warning seemed to break whatever spell Arani had fallen under. The captain's joy faded beneath a thoughtful expression, and she drew back from the ship's railing to hold herself straight and formal once more. "Between the sirens and the lack of dedicated hunters, I imagine those two haven't seen a ship before," Arani replied.

The quartermaster cast a sidelong look at the captain. "And what do you think one that *has* seen a ship will do when it spots the *Southern Echo?*"

Arani scraped her hand across the back of her neck and frowned at the now-distant mimics. Luken chirped softly on her shoulder and nipped at her fingers. "I don't know that a dragon would be able to pick out where we keep the powder kegs, but best get those secured, and have the crew ready to douse the deck and sails with seawater."

Dax nodded and slipped away.

Nate watched him go, and felt a strange flutter in his gut as he realized that he had seen three dragons, and had completely failed to be afraid of any of them. He had the nasty feeling that that was not an intelligent way to react to a creature that was twice his size, had very sharp teeth, and could breathe fire. "They're so beautiful, it's so easy to forget that they're dangerous," he murmured.

"Some of the most dangerous things in this world are also the most beautiful," Arani said. She glanced at him for a moment. "I'd have thought those who'd enjoyed the sirens' song would understand that." Her gaze wandered over her shoulder, to the pirates on the deck who adjusted the sails and chattered excitedly about the dragons. "Maybe they do," she said thoughtfully. "Maybe they appreciate the beauty all the more for its danger." She shrugged and faced the sea again. "All in all, a dragon wouldn't be the worst last thing to see, but I intend to see a lot more than a few dragons before I die." She thrust her chin forward. "Anything else out there?"

Three more times, Nate sensed mimic dragons on the wind, and three more times, the crew was treated to a spectacular display of colors when the dragons came to see the strange vessel that had crossed into their territory. While none of the other dragons dared venture as close as the turquoise and evening-colored mimics had, one of them did loose a plume of fire from its jaws. The display was angled towards the water, but the warning was clear, and Arani had the ship turned away from the dragon and sailing off before the beast could take their presence in its territory as a greater threat. That shook Nate and the crew a bit, adding a good dose of wariness to their gazes as they watched the next dragon approach. This one was not hostile, however, and it was easy for the wonder to return. The final dragon, colored the soft pinks of a sunrise, danced well ahead of the *Southern Echo* for a long while, as though escorting the ship to the small chain of islands that appeared in the distance.

Arani raised her spyglass, and confirmed that those had to be the islands the sirens had directed them to. "We have a clear heading in sight now, so you could rest if you'd like," she said to Nate. She tilted her head and held his gaze for a moment. "Or, if you'd like to keep searching...?"

Nate nodded determinedly. Tired as he was, he did not want to stop, not even in the face of that awful pounding in his head. He did not have to range as far to sense the dragons now that they were close to the mimics' islands, and he knew that he could push through and keep searching, even with his borrowed supply of agate anchors overheated and the gold ring burning on his hand. He wanted to see this through, to be the one who pointed Arani to the dragon she had spent so many years waiting to meet again. He could endure a little more pain and push through a little more tiredness for that.

The true problem, however, was that Nate did not know how to even begin to figure out which trail would lead to the black mimic. He could not tell a dragon's color from its wingprints in the wind. There had to be an answer, unless Arani was determined to sail the ship in circles until they chanced upon the one dragon they were looking for. Nate tried to shake a solution loose, but between his headaches and exhaustion and the steady presence of the dragons flying around the islands, concentration eluded him. He had to content himself with sitting up in the bow, staring at the approaching islands, the smallest of which threw smoke into the air. That would be the one he had sensed earlier in the day, Nate thought dully.

Indeed, as the *Southern Echo* drew closer, Nate could feel the subtle shift in the air as the sea winds clashed with the heat from the island's active volcano. He did not purposefully try to connect with the wind element, but he was so exhausted that he couldn't completely stop himself from slipping into it with a semi-lucidity that left him giddy, even as he understood that he teetered on the edge of tumbling so completely into the wind that he risked coming untethered from himself. He was dimly aware that his breathing was shallow and growing lighter with each passing moment, and he giggled when his brain offered up, *The empire is my life, my life for the* Southern Echo.

Then a bucket of seawater crashed down on his head, soaking him through, and someone slapped his cheek with enough force to whip his head about. He barely felt the impact. The next slap was much the same, but the second bucket of water brought him sputtering back from the edge. He gasped and found himself sprawled on the ship's deck. He did not remember falling.

"All right, Nate, you're all right," came the warm voice of the quartermaster.

Nate blinked blearily up at Dax and found he did not have it in him to respond. Over the quartermaster's shoulder, Marcus stood clutching two empty buckets, his eyes wide against his Darkbend tattoo.

"He needs to stop," Dax said to someone off to his right. Nate rolled his head to see Arani standing there, arms folded as she gazed at Nate like he was some sort of puzzle that she could not solve.

"I asked him if he wanted to rest," she said. "He said he was fine."

Dax shook his head. "He's done. He can't go on like this."

Arani's eyes narrowed slightly as she continued to stare at Nate. "We're so close," she murmured, softly enough that Nate wasn't quite sure he'd heard her correctly. Her voice was clearer when she said, "What say you, Nate? Do you want to continue?"

"Captain," Dax growled, low and warning.

"I'm asking the boy," Arani said. "Do you intend to continue?"

In that question, Nate heard every person in his life who had ever asked him if he truly thought that his

Skill could be worth something. And he answered the way he should have answered every last one of them: "Yes."

"You're going to kill yourself," Dax said sharply.

Nate looked at the anger in the quartermaster's eyes, and then at the fear on Marcus's face. "I can do this," Nate said, and slowly pushed himself up.

"Nate—" Dax began, but Arani cut across him.

"You heard the boy," she said. Her voice was soft but heavy with command. This time, when Dax turned a furious stare on her, she looked back at him with stoic calm.

The quartermaster scowled as he rose to his feet. "I won't watch him die for this."

"You won't," Arani agreed, "because *he* won't." She cut her gaze back to Nate.

"I can do this," he repeated.

Dax shook his head and stormed off, grabbing Marcus and hauling the Darkbend after him. Marcus stumbled along in Dax's wake, and the fear was not gone from his face.

Arani offered her hand and helped Nate to his feet. She took a firm grip on his shoulder as he swayed and caught himself against the railing. "All right?" she asked.

Nate took a deep breath and nodded.

"Good." She gestured for him to retake his place at the bow. "Find me that dragon."

Nate obeyed, slipping back into the wind element. It felt like stumbling down a steep slope, each step promising to rip his feet out from under him and snap his bones if he wasn't careful. Dax's warning echoed softly at the back of Nate's mind, but he could not give up or rest yet. He had to find the black mimic.

He picked up the trails of lots of dragons flying around the islands. Some fished off the coasts, others played in the breezes, and others still were just moving from point to point. All of them flew with that graceful dip-and-rise motion that showed off their brilliant wings to their fullest capacity.

With the dragons dominating the skies, Nate did not see many other creatures, although he picked out a few straight trails that he thought belonged to birds that must have shared the islands with the mimic dragons. They were easy to parse from the dragon's trails, so different were the shapes of their wind shadows. And with the hot air billowing out of the volcano, the wind prints were far sharper. Nate ignored the straight trails in favor of the dragons' tracks, trying to find some discerning pattern in their motions that would signal the black mimic among them. He had no idea what to look for, as the dragons all flew with those same looping, flashing movements. His attention caught briefly on a small knot of mimics that suddenly jerked and scattered on the winds, but they calmed and resumed their easier flights soon enough. The thing that had frightened them flew in a straight, focused line, and Nate suspected it was a large bird that had caught the dragons off guard. His head was throbbing again so he did not try to focus on it, and instead went back to lightly scanning the dragons. The bird kept coming straight for the *Southern Echo*, however, and Nate found its growing wind shadow difficult to ignore. Especially as it came closer and closer, and Nate finally realized that it was not a bird at all.

Gasping, Nate fell out of the wind element and thrust his finger towards the rapidly approaching shape. He tried to say Arani's name, but his voice failed him. The captain's hand closed on his shoulder a moment later, however, as she quickly stepped up next to him. Once Nate was steady, she locked her spyglass against her eye, her muscles still with tension. When she lowered the spyglass, there was a strange expression on her face, with her jaw clenched in a grimace but her eyes bright with unbridled anticipation. Her hand strayed up to the dragon scale she wore on the chain around her neck, and Nate thought he heard her whisper, "Found you."

Then she was moving quickly away from the bow, bellowing orders to soak the ship's deck and furl the sails. "Dragon fire incoming!" she shouted.

The warning whipped the crew into a frenzy, and Nate found himself mesmerized by the sudden efficiency that was the line of pirates that formed to haul buckets of water up from the sea and splash them across the deck. Riggers darted up and down the lines, securing the sails and passing more buckets up to douse the canvas. Water rained down and thundered over the decks of the *Southern Echo*, pooling into a mirror sheen under the sun.

"Nate, get away from there!" someone called, and Nate turned to see Eric hurrying towards him, sea water sloshing over the rim of the bucket in his arms. "It's coming right for you!"

Nate did not know what to do with that bit of information. His head was fuzzy and heavy, and he still could not quite catch his breath, and there was just so much churning up the air on the ship now. He fell back against the railing and looked away from the chaos on the decks, and a line of coldness thrashed its way across his mind.

There was a dragon coming, low and fast and very dark against the sky. It did not flash its wings or try to show off the shimmer of its scales. Instead, it flew straight and hard, and as Nate watched, it opened its jaws and screamed.

The sound tore at his ears and drummed up the pounding in his head until it rivaled the fiercest of thunderstorms. Nate may have cried out himself, he wasn't sure, but Eric was there with his hand on Nate's arm, and the Darkbend pulled him away from the bow. Nate finally understood that he needed to *move*, and he tried to push his legs to run. He stumbled into Eric, sending both of them tumbling to the deck. The air above them boiled with sudden heat, and then the dragon's wings clapped like thunder and it was past them, roaring fire on to the deck of the *Southern Echo*.

Men and women screamed and threw themselves out of the way as the dragon shot over the ship, veering off sharply before it could crash into one of the masts. Steam and smoke began to rise, and Nate saw that the dragon's fire had almost immediately evaporated the water the crew had thrown on to the deck. Another pass, and it would set the entire ship ablaze.

The dragon screamed again as Nate pushed himself up. It twisted in the air and turned its body back to the *Southern Echo*, ready to charge in again. For the briefest of moments, Nate clearly saw the parchment color of its wings, marked with charcoal-black lines. Then it was diving for the ship again.

"No guns!" Arani shouted from somewhere near the mainmast. Nate saw her rip a rifle out of a pirate's hand. "You kill it, we lose the map!" She whipped around, cupped her hands around her mouth, and screamed, "Marcus! Eric! To me!"

Next to Nate, Eric scrambled to his feet and took off running. He wove his way deftly through the chaos of the deck, and Marcus caught up with him halfway there. They were sprinting to the captain without any hesitation, and the only thing that stopped them was Dax suddenly appearing and tackling them both to the deck. More screams came, and then there was another blast of fire as the dragon shot over the ship again, its body an arrow of black.

This time, the flames lingered on the *Southern Echo*, and the ship gave a deep shudder as patches of her wood burned. Not all of the pirates had escaped, either, and at least three were moaning in pain now. Arani herself was slapping violently at the sleeve of her coat, which smoked and threatened to do far worse if she didn't get it under control. Her attention, however, was on the two Darkbends.

Nate's relief at seeing them both unharmed was a sluggish thing as his exhausted mind struggled to keep pace with everything happening around him. He saw Arani hurry to their side, and pull them and Dax to their feet. Her mouth moved furiously as she said something to the Darkbends and pointed at the dragon, which was already turning and coming for yet another pass. Around them, pirates were scooping up the wounded and dragging them out of the way as others came in with more water to douse the fires on the deck. People screamed and shouted at each other. The air boiled with dread.

Nate shut his eyes and tried to silence the thundering in his skull, but the dragon roared again and when he looked up, Nate saw Marcus and Eric moving in unison, calling upon the joint power of their Skills to refract the sunlight and send it into the dragon's eyes. Between the two of them, they could only bend a thin sliver to their wills with precision, but that was all it took. The creature hissed and thrashed its head when the light seared its vision, and Nate watched in awe as it pulled up short and turned away from the ship, finally offering a clear view of its wings as it shifted. Nate wasn't the only one who gasped when he saw the distinct lines of the legendary treasure map. The dragon twisted away before anyone had time to get a good look, smoke streaming from its jaws as it moved further out over the water.

For the first time since he'd sensed it, Nate saw the dragon take up the slow, looping flight of the rest of its species as it cleared its vision and regathered itself. His foggy mind managed to notice that, unlike its brilliantly colored counterparts, the black mimic kept its wings angled down, as though determined to hide the map. When it snapped around again and darted back towards the ship, Nate only saw its smoke-colored body, and nothing of its wings.

Marcus and Eric were ready for the dragon. They bent another harsh beam of light into its eyes, and this time, the dragon's roar of fire passed between the fore and main sails. It burned clean through the ropes, but it missed the ship and the canvas, and the dragon arced away, shaking its head as it tried to clear its vision. Nate saw the angry, frustrated heave of its wings as the creature abruptly angled itself into the sky. It shot up, disappearing into the glare of the sun. Nate tried to follow its path with his eyes, but the sunlight burned his vision, and he had to turn his head away.

He wasn't the only one who'd made that mistake. Several people called out that they could not see it, and they strained to peer into the bright sky. Marcus and Eric stood tense, arms raised and waiting, but they kept their eyes locked on each other, and not on the sky.

Nate was too exhausted from overexerting his Skill to panic in that moment. Instead, he groaned against the next wave of pain in his head, did his best to ignore the heat of the gold ring on his hand, and slipped back into the wind element.

The dragon was high overhead, positioning itself with the sun directly behind it. It hovered for a moment, then tucked its wings into two sharp blades and dove, slicing through the winds straight for the ship.

"It's coming back!" he screamed, and he had no idea if anyone heard him. He lunged forward on his hands and knees and pointed into the sky, up at the sun and the falling dragon.

More shouts went up, and Nate pulled himself back from the wind element just in time to see Eric and Marcus send another sunbeam back into the sky. They shot this one wildly, whipping it back and forth in a desperate attempt to hit the dragon, and were rewarded with another scream from the black mimic. Nate felt the snap in the wind as it lurched to the side, and instead of slamming into the ship, the dragon hit the water and disappeared under the waves.

A fraught silence fell as everyone waited, casting uneasy looks at the sea around them. It was not unlike the terrified waiting they'd done when they'd met the sirens. The dragon, however, did not make them wait long.

It burst out of the sea and sent the *Southern Echo* rocking, a heavy spray of water falling down on to the deck. The dragon pumped its wings furiously and climbed away from the ship, screaming as it went. It paused once to turn and glare at the ship, and then it cut away across the wind, heading back for the smoking island with no further fanfare.

Nate watched it go, only realizing that someone was coming up behind him when their boots hit the deck next to him. He looked up to see Captain Arani step to the bow and stare after the dragon the way a starving person would gaze at a lavish meal just out of reach. When she turned to face the crew, her eyes were bright and wild, and she made no effort to hide her excitement.

"We have our heading," she said. "We make for the island."

It took a moment for the crew to respond. When they did, it was without protest, but it was without any cheering, too.

For his part, Nate managed to stay awake long enough for Dax to help him down the steps and through the ship to his hammock, and then Nate fell into the darkest sleep of his life.

CHAPTER TWENTY

The Black Mimic

IRIS WASTED NO TIME. The wounded were taken below for treatment, and Iris had the riggers up among the sails before the last of the injured had disappeared. As soon as the *Southern Echo*'s rigging was repaired, she ordered the ship to the island, and stood alone in the bow as they approached. She would have liked for Nate to be up there with her, too. Without the boy, she never would have found the black mimic again, but he'd gone below to rest. According to Dax, Nate had fallen into an impenetrable sleep as soon as he'd been bundled into his hammock. Iris felt a pang of guilt at that; Nate had told her that he could keep going, and she'd trusted him to know his own limits. Perhaps that had been a mistake, but they'd found the black mimic, and she could not pretend to be disappointed in the least.

The dragon was just as she'd remembered, fierce and terrible in its beauty, smoke twisting across its scales and the map branded clear on its wings. Iris clutched the scale she wore around her neck and felt her anticipation swell with each wave the ship pierced.

As the *Southern Echo* drew closer to the islands, more mimic dragons came to investigate the ship. The crew was significantly less enamored with the beasts after the black mimic's attack, and Iris herself felt a taut ball of nerves form in her gut whenever one of the dragons flew in for a closer look. But Marcus and Eric beautifully performed the task she'd set for them, and they bent narrow beams of sunlight into the eyes of any mimics that came too close for comfort. The dragons snorted and tossed their heads in annoyance, and then went away to do whatever dragons normally did, which appeared to be flying at the best angles to show off their wings to their fellows, or occasionally descending to sun themselves on the beaches of the three scruffy islands.

The black mimic, on the other hand, did not show itself again.

Iris did not think it had gone far. It had landed on the smallest, darkest island, and Iris was certain that if it had taken off again, it would have launched another attack on the ship. All was quiet as the *Southern Echo* anchored in a shallow harbor, and Iris laid out her plan to the crew.

"I need Dax here to watch over the ship and assume command should something happen," she told the gathering of the uninjured pirates on the *Southern Echo*'s deck. "Marcus and Eric, you're to remain here and use your Skills to drive off anything that comes too close. The safety of the ship and the wounded are in your hands. As to the rest of you, I'm willing to let you choose, but I need twenty brave souls to come with me to that island, and capture the black mimic. It needs to be alive. If it dies, its colors will fade and Mordanti's map will be lost forever." There was a chance that, since the map had been branded on the dragon's wings in place of its natural color staining, it would endure after the beast's magic had faded, but Iris was not going to take that chance. They would take the black mimic alive, or not at all. She pointed at the black sand beach that stretched before them, and the rocky slopes that rose up against the blue sky. "Who will come?"

The pirates looked at the island, looked at each other, and looked at her in silence.

Iris gripped the pommel of the sword on her hip and tried to temper the anger that flared in her heart. She tried, and she failed.

"We come this close to Mordanti's legend," she fumed, "and your courage fails you now?" She glared at the crew, and several of them dropped their eyes to the deck. "After everything we went though, enduring the doldrums and losing one of our own to the sirens and *several* of your brothers and sisters burning so *you* could have the chance to walk across a beach and bring them back a legend, you would stop here and let their pain and sacrifice go to waste?" She stormed across the deck, the heels of her boots slamming through the silence. "I have not sailed this far for nothing. None of us have. So I ask again, who will come with me?"

Silence reigned in the wake of her words.

Iris's lip curled in disgust. She had seen these men and women charge headlong into gunfire, beat back swords, and face the fury of cannonballs without hesitation, all for prizes far less valuable than what they could find today. But no, now they quailed at the thought of the very same kind of danger presented in the form of a dragon. Yes, the beast could fly and breathe fire, but that wasn't so different from the flash of gunpowder and the deadly eruption of a cannonball that could shatter a mast and tear limbs from bodies. Cowards, the lot of them. Iris would find this dragon herself if she had to, and get Mordanti's map. She was not going to let someone else's fear stand in her way. And based on the looks some of the crew were giving her, they knew that, too.

Nikolai Novachak was the first to volunteer. He muttered something under his breath, and then stepped forward. "I will go with you, Captain." He looked as far from pleased as he possibly could be, and very much like he wanted to slap her over the head and tell her that she was being a perfect fool, but at least he was with her.

After Novachak, AnnaMarie Blueshore came forward, and two other gunners followed her. Iris found herself glad for their stocky strength. She had a feeling it would prove useful.

By the time the rest of the volunteers had trickled in, Iris had sixteen people coming with her to the island. It was more than she had expected, but less than she had hoped for. It would have to do.

The men and women that had not joined the party gathered at the railing of the ship, silently watching the rowboat descend. Iris was very aware of their eyes on her back as the little boat was uncoupled from the *Southern Echo*, and she knew they would remain there long after her party had begun the final journey to shore.

Iris, however, had far more pressing matters in front of her, and by the time she and the others were splashing in the surf to drag the rowboat out of the water and up on to the beach, her thoughts were centered once more on the black mimic.

"All right, Captain," Novachak said once they had the rowboat above the high tide mark. "We've come with you to the edge of the world. What now?"

Iris nodded towards the rocky slopes, and the mouth of a large cave a little ways up from the beach. "That's big enough to house a dragon."

"Or any other living nightmare," Novachak grumbled.

Iris ignored him. "What do you notice about this bit of beach, Mr. Novachak?" she asked.

Novachak looked around the island with undisguised displeasure, which only heightened when he glanced up at the smoldering volcano towering above them. He kept his voice low when he said, "That this is the last place I'd like to be right now."

"A sentiment the rest of the mimics seem to share," Iris said.

She watched from the corner of her eye as Novachak glanced about, his bemusement quickly giving way to grim understanding. As she'd said, there were no dragons on this part of the island. A few drifted on the wind nearby, but they purposefully arced away from this place and were careful not to come too close, even when they twisted playfully through the air and sent each other tumbling through the sky. Not even the odd sight of Iris's little group pulling a rowboat on to the beach had been enough to get the better of their curiosity, and from what Iris had seen out on the water, she knew that mimic dragons were not shy creatures.

Their lack of presence in this tiny part of their own world was a loud roar in her ears.

Iris loaded up with the others, hoisting a length of chain over her shoulder and taking up one of the hooks they'd brought in the rowboat, along with the slaughtered chicken they'd pumped full of sleeping draught. The rest of the group did the same, gathering chains, hooks, torches, and coils of heavy rope. Iris's boots sank deep into the dark sand as she led the way up the beach, the others clanking and grunting softly behind her. The pull of the chain against her shoulder made her slow, but she knew that she was carrying less than the others, and she would not allow herself to complain. Not that she would have; with every step that brought her closer and closer to Captain Mordanti, Iris felt the mounting urge to break into a run. The dragon scale she wore around her neck swung steadily with her steps. Finally, the cave loomed over them, high and deep and dark. Iris paused at the mouth long enough to light a torch, instructed half the group to wait several minutes before coming inside, and then stepped into the blackness.

It was cool inside the cave, and the firelight from the torch played off of rough stone walls that bore faint trails of water trickles. The sand underfoot gave way to hard rock, and in spite of walking through the dark with a beacon to announce her presence to whatever lay further in, she felt the need to place her feet carefully, and move as quietly as she could. She was not surprised when the others behind her did the same, falling into silence as they crept forward. Every rattle of the chains they carried sounded like a thunderclap. Before long, Iris's nerves were stretched taut enough to hum.

After several creeping minutes, she held up a fist, ordering the others to halt. She let the natural silence of the cave press down around her, and ignored the race of her heart as best as she could. She shut her eyes and listened, and thought she heard a dry rustle up ahead, just out of the range of the flickering torchlight. When she opened her eyes, she only saw darkness ahead of her, but the feeling that she was being watched whispered up her spine.

Iris handed her torch to Novachak behind her. She slid the chain over her shoulder and gently lowered it to the floor, then hefted the drugged chicken carcass. She swung her arm back and forth a few times, gathering momentum, and then lobbed the chicken into the dark. She heard it land with a soft *whump*. There was a small pause, followed by a distinct dragging sound, and then all was quiet again. Iris waited, but she heard no snapping of jaws or crunching of bones. The silence pressed down.

She still felt like she was being watched.

Iris drew her sword, the only protection she had. The rasp of the blade as it came free brought little comfort, but the weapon was a familiar weight in her hand, and easy to hold. She took the torch back from Novachak and took a slow step forward, and then another one. A few more paces in, and the edge of the torchlight hit the chicken, which had been swept off to the side of the cave and looked to be otherwise undisturbed. Iris swallowed past the hard lump of trepidation in her throat. She focused in front of her again as she lifted the torch higher, and froze as the light caught on two shining eyes, flooding them with firelight.

For a long moment, nothing moved. Iris and the dragon simply stared at each other. Then the black mimic's lip curled back, and its teeth gleamed in the flickering light. It loosed a bone-rattling growl. Iris barely heard the gasps of fear behind her as she lifted her sword. It was all she had time for before the dragon charged.

Iris had half a moment to register the bulk of the dragon as it came into the light, its angled head snaking forward to snap at her. Her body responded instinctively, and she threw the torch and dove to the side. The torch bounced off the dragon's head and clattered to the ground, but the beast did not slow. It barreled past Iris, clipping her with the edge of its wing, and made for the crew. She heard Novachak shout, and then the dragon reared back, its chest swelling as it gathered air, and then came a roar of brilliant fire that lit the cave with harsh clarity.

It was easy for Iris to see Novachak throw himself to the ground in time to avoid more than a singe to his clothes. The pirates behind him followed his lead, hurling themselves out of the line of fire, but luck ran out across the back half of the group.

One man stumbled back in fright, tangling with the woman behind him. Their eyes were wide with terror, and then they were engulfed in dragon fire. They did not have time to scream. Those two caught the worst of the attack, but another three did not escape unharmed. They howled as the dragon fire licked across their arms and backs. They lurched away from the heat before falling hard to the ground, too stunned from the pain to rise again. The smell of burning flesh caught up to Iris then, and her stomach roiled as she breathed in the horrible scent underscored with the sulfuric tang of the dragon.

When the dragon's roar stopped, the cave went dark again, and it took several moments for Iris's eyes to adjust to the much fainter light from the guttering torches dropped to the ground. The dragon was a dark mass in front of her, but she saw it draw in another breath, and she knew it would roar again.

She leapt to her feet and brought her sword down in a vicious chop, hoping she'd judged the posture of the dragon correctly. She meant to distract it, not kill it. Her sword hit something hard and unyielding with enough force to jar her shoulder, but its downward motion brought the blade scraping against a more tender area further down the dragon's body, and the scales gave way.

The dragon screeched and whipped around to face Iris. Fire glowed in its throat, and Iris swung her sword up in a desperate attempt to bat the dragon's head aside. She knew that she was not fast enough, and the beast would kill her. Its eyes shone with pure hatred, and its jaws began to open. But then it swept a wing into Iris, driving the breath from her lungs and sending her sailing through the air. She cracked against the cave wall a moment later, and the world went even darker around her as she slid to the floor.

The dragon's next roar and the screams of the crew were muted against the ringing in Iris's head. Her vision swam and threatened to desert her, and precious moments slipped away as the heat of the dragon fire and the smell of more burning skin washed over her. Her stomach finally rebelled, and vomit burned through her throat. She heaved twice, and the sharp, acrid taste pulled her back to her senses. Her head was throbbing and when she touched the back of it, her fingers came away wet, but there wasn't time to think about that. She pushed herself to her feet, looking about wildly for her sword. She had no idea where it had fallen, and a frantic glance did not reveal it to her. Her head whipped around as she heard shouting from the crew, and she was shocked to see Novachak still alive and fighting. He and the remaining crew wouldn't stay alive for much longer, even as the other half of the group came charging in from the mouth of the cave, desperate to help. The dragon pressed them all back, leaving more and more bodies on the floor as it advanced.

Iris's gaze caught on a length of chain on the cave floor, dropped and forgotten in the battle. She ran for it, and managed to snatch it up without pitching face-first into the rocky floor. The chain was heavy in her hands as she threw herself at the dragon, and she let her body slam into its neck. The end of the chain snapped up and crashed into the dragon's head, stunning the beast and sending it stumbling. It hissed in pain and anger, but Iris did not give it time to recover. She hauled the chain over the dragon's shoulders and looped it around the beast's neck, and the weight of the links made the dragon teeter. A wing shot up and flung Iris away again, but she did not land as badly this time, and her vision was clear as Novachak ran forward with another chain.

He threw his over the dragon's shoulder, dragging one of the wings down and pitching the creature to the side. Novachak shouted for the others to help, and before long, chains and ropes were slung across the black mimic in a haphazard web. The beast bucked against the restraints, but the weight was too much, and it stumbled.

Iris came forward and grabbed one of the ropes, pulling it hard. "Bring it down!" she roared.

Novachak and the others obeyed. They took up the ropes and chains and wrestled against the dragon's strength, and finally, the beast fell. It sprawled on the cave floor, hissing, and Iris ripped off her own belt as she rushed to the dragon's head. The beast saw her coming, and slid its head over the floor. It used the last of its strength to lift its neck and draw back like a snake, and then it shot forward and opened its mouth wide. Iris could count every last razored tooth. She spun to the side at the last second, and the dragon's jaws closed on nothing. She flung the belt around the dragon's muzzle and pulled it tight, sealing the beast's mouth closed. Novachak and AnnaMarie hurried to help, and they held the dragon's head while Iris looped the belt around its jaws again before securing the leather through the buckle. When that was done, Novachak pressed the dragon's head to the floor. The beast did not resist, and Iris fell back, panting hard as she stared at the black mimic. It looked back at her with hatred, but it was subdued. They had won.

And Iris, sweat plastering her clothes to her skin and aches beginning to make their presence known throughout her body, closed her eyes, and smiled.

WITH THE BLACK MIMIC secured, more of the crew came ashore to help bring the dragon out of the cave. It wasn't a safe operation. Two people sustained nasty cuts on their arms from the sharp claws on the dragon's thrashing legs, and the beast's tail knocked Dax clear off his feet when it slipped the grip of the pirates holding it down. They eventually figured out that they could lash the dragon's legs together and then bind them to the tail. From there, they managed to rig up the chains and ropes in a way that let them pull the dragon out of the cave, on to the beach. They needed the sunlight to read the map; the torches threw unsteady light at best and Iris would not risk losing any details to unreliable illumination.

Out on the sand, they adjusted their haphazard netting again, rolled the dragon on to its back, and spread its wings. The dragon grumbled its protests and tried to shake loose from the pirates, but with their weight added to the chains and ropes, it could do little more than tremble and growl around its makeshift muzzle. Finally, Mordanti's treasure map was revealed in all its glory.

The dragon's left wing had been branded with lines of latitude and longitude, with only a few islands picked out across the vast ocean. A trail of sea currents led along the spines of the wing, coming to an end at the tip of the wing, at a cluster of islands that Iris did not recognize. The right wing showed what looked to be one of the strange islands in more detail, and promised that Mordanti's treasure was inside a cave on that island. Tempted as Iris was to drink in all the details of the right wing, she found herself puzzling over the left one and the wider map it bore.

"Do you recognize these islands?" she asked Rori.

The Goodtide navigator had come over from the ship armed with a leather-bound journal, some sticks of charcoal, a fine-tipped pen, a pot of ink, and a scowl she did not try to hide. "No," she snapped, barely glancing at the place where Iris pointed on the dragon's wing.

It was harsh enough of a reply that it easily could have warranted discipline, but Iris was too focused on the map to pay it much mind, and her heart somersaulted with excitement and joy even before the crew's wariness. She had not expected Rori to be this upset by the sight of the black mimic chained down on the beach, but the sooner the Goodtide finished copying the map, the sooner they could let the beast go. Ideally with a large helping of sleeping draught forced down its throat so that the *Southern Echo* had the chance to put some distance between herself and the island before the dragon was ready to unleash its fury. So Iris left Rori to the work, and slowly walked back and forth along the edge of the dragon's wing, frowning over the details.

As with all maps, this one would not do much good if they could not figure out where it was meant to begin. Mordanti had not been concerned with including a compass rose on the map, although given that she'd branded it on to a dragon's wings, it was amazing she'd been able to include as much detail as she had. Iris could not imagine that this dragon would have held still for the branding. She felt a pang of sympathy for the creature, but it passed quickly. As soon as the map was copied to completion, Iris would leave this poor beast alone for the rest of its life.

Pirates murmured to each other as they stole forward for peeks at the map. Iris let them, though few of them were willing to stand so close to the dragon after the number of lives it had taken in the cave. The crew had paid a heavy price for this, and the air was somber as they came forward to gaze upon Mordanti's map with their own eyes and satisfy their curiosity before stepping away again, rubbing their arms and throwing unhappy glances up at the cave where many of their mates lay dead. They'd gathered what they could of their friends' remains and taken them back to the ship for a burial at sea, but the dragon's fire had not left much behind.

Iris would address that later. For the moment, she kept her attention on the map. She walked all the way around the wing, careful not to tread on the membrane as she turned her head this way and that, frowning down at the islands spread along the delicate lines. There was something familiar about them, she thought, but she could not place it. She kneeled at the dragon's shoulder, trusting the men she'd assigned to hold the beast's head and neck down, and peered at the islands gathered near the wing joint, where the membrane bunched and stretched with each flex of the dragon's wing. There were three islands branded there, each one smaller than the last. There was a dark, blurry smudge above the smallest one, but as Iris looked closer, she realized that the mark was intentional, meant to show smoke rising from its mountain.

"Oh," she breathed. She surged back to her feet and spun around, kicking up black sand as she turned to look at the other two islands rising up out of the sea some distance away. "It's here," she said, and she felt everyone's eyes lock on to her. "Mordanti's map begins right here."

An unusual choice for someone who had wanted dearly to conceal the location of their treasure, but Iris remembered the battle inside the cave. Mordanti had good reason to be confident that not many people would have much success obtaining her map, let alone surviving long enough to read it.

"Are you certain, Captain?" Dax asked from across the dragon's length.

Iris nodded and returned her attention to the map. "If she started here, then..."

She moved along the wing, tracing out the currents that ran to the next island on the map. It was larger than any of the three in the volcanic chain, but it rested alone in the ocean. If there was truly nothing else around it as the map suggested, that was a terrifyingly easy landmark to miss. And beyond it, at the edges of the wing, there was another cluster of islands of varying sizes that fanned out in a distinct arc.

Iris thought about the islands north of this barren little chain where they'd found the black mimic. None of the islands she could pull into her mind's eye looked anything like this, which could only mean that Mordanti's map extended south. Based on the orientation of the starting three islands, Iris knew the map went east as well, not west into the Forbidden Sea. She felt a small wash of relief at knowing that Mordanti had not been *that* daring, but it was a short-lived respite. South and east of these three barren islands, at a scale the map depicted...

"It's the Ice Hook," Iris said.

The legendary pirate captain Ava Mordanti had hidden her treasure in the Ice Hook, a frozen wasteland even more unforgiving than Novachak's northern home. Explorations nearly three hundred years ago had first revealed the Ice Hook's existence to the world, but with no resources to offer and dry, bitter winds threatening to freeze the sails of any ship that overstayed its welcome, no one had felt the need to explore it further. Especially not now, with the war between Solkyria and Vothein holding the attention of the inhabited world.

Iris raised her eyes from the map to see Dax, Novachak, Rori, and a few others staring at her.

"We are not prepared for a journey like that," the quartermaster said quietly.

Iris agreed. "We'll need to get enough provisions, and warm clothes for the crew. We may be able to find what we need with the Leviathan Sea Traders, if we're lucky."

"Captain," Dax said as he came around the dragon, speaking in a tone that made him sound like he was trying to soothe a wild animal. He kept his voice low, pitched only for her ears as he drew up next to her. "If we sail that far south, we'll be completely at the mercy of the gods."

Iris normally scoffed at the idea of leaving her fate in anyone's hands but her own, but she understood that Dax's concern was less of a religious one, and more of a practical one. Even sailing fully stocked from the southern islands in the Leviathan Sea, the Ice Hook was a long, perilous journey away, and nothing but an eternal winter would greet them at its end. And yet, ships had made the crossing before, and returned to tell the tale. Iris had come too far to give up now. They all had.

"People have died for this, Dax," she reminded him quietly. "Would you let their sacrifice be for nothing?"

"Of course not," he said sharply. "But if we do this, more of us are going to die. Would *you* ask that of the survivors?"

"I would," Iris said. "I ask nothing more every time we leave port to hunt a prize. We will not abandon this now."

Dax gathered himself as though he were about to challenge her right there on that beach, in front of the crew and the black mimic alike.

But Rori called softly from the dragon's right wing, and motioned for Iris to come look at something. Whatever the Goodtide had found, it had deepened her scowl even more.

Iris moved to Rori's side, Dax following behind her. Novachak came to join them, but the two men held back to let Iris have the first look at the spot where Rori was pointing. She'd found a bit of text tucked into the corner of the dragon's wing where the membrane joined with the body. The letters were warped and stretched by the shape of the wing, but Mordanti had written them in old Veritian script, and Iris slowly read:

The greatest treasure gifted from the gods
lies forever hidden behind a wall of ice
that will only yield to dragon fire.

Dragon fire.

Iris shut her eyes and breathed out a long, frustrated huff. She felt Novachak press into her shoulder as he moved in to read the text. Dax, however, had to rely on Novachak's translation.

"Gods below," the quartermaster swore after a moment.

"We have to take the frost-damned beast with us," Novachak said.

As one, the three of them turned and looked at the dragon's head, which had tilted towards them as they'd studied its right wing. It fixed them with a smoldering eye the color of live embers, and Iris could have sworn that the beast looked spitefully pleased.

Chapter Twenty-one

All Kinds of Chains

AFTER A FEW HOURS of blissful sleep, Nate's headache returned. It woke him just in time for him to haul himself topside and watch with morbid fascination as the pirates dragged a sleep-drugged dragon down the beach to the surf. There had been some debate as to whether or not a rowboat would actually be able to support its weight, let alone if they could even get the creature inside, but they had decided to try. The gamble paid off; the rowboat was dangerously overburdened as two lone men labored to bring the dragon back to the *Southern Echo*, but they made it with only one near-capsizing experience. Then the dragon was bound to the rigging that raised and lowered the rowboats from the water. Nate stood back while the others heaved on the ropes, and slowly, the black mimic was swung on to the deck of the ship. The dragon groaned and gave a few bleary blinks when it came to rest on the wood. That was enough to push everyone away, and they regarded the dragon warily even as its head slumped against the deck, a tired sigh heaving through its sides.

They'd all heard what had happened inside the cave, and they knew the names of the men and women who were not coming back from that island. No one wanted to join them.

"Thought we didn't need the dragon for the map," Nate heard someone grumble, and he recognized Jim Greenroot's sour voice. "Why are we bringing this godsdamned beast on the ship?"

"We need it," Novachak answered. He'd come back ahead of the dragon to get the ship ready to receive the beast, and he regarded the black mimic grimly now. "Can't get Mordanti's treasure without dragon fire."

"We have plenty of gunpowder," Jim growled. "Don't need a dragon for that."

"It wouldn't be enough," Novachak said tiredly. "Captain says that southern ice isn't natural. I've seen enough frozen miracles not to argue with her."

"But why take it with us now?" Jim pressed. "We could come back for it when we're ready."

Novachak leveled him with an unimpressed stare. "We lost nine people catching this demon. You want to release it, let it get its strength back, and then try to catch it *again*? Or better yet, give *another* one of those dragons reason to attack us with no guarantee we'll be able to take it alive?" The boatswain shook his head. "Best keep this one with us, and with a heavy dose of sleeping draught in its belly."

The dragon was lashed to the main deck in front of the navigation room at the stern of the ship, as out-of-the-way as it could possibly be without dragging it up or down any of the ship's stairs. Everyone gave it a wide berth, taking care to step far away from the beast when they went to raise the sails. The dragon grumbled and slept, and Arani called for volunteers to administer the sleeping draught to the dragon as needed. When no one stepped forward, the crew drew lots, and Eric Darkbend wound up in the rotation, slated to dose the dragon that night.

While he pitied his friend, Nate was glad that he himself had not come up in the draw. He meant to help with the ship however he could now that his Skill was no longer needed, but he was so weary, he barely made it through the funeral ceremony for the pirates who had died on the island. As soon as it was finished, Dax sent him below to go back to sleep, and Novachak backed up the order. Nate was very conscious of the pirates laboring hard around him to bring the *Southern Echo* about and send the ship north again, but outside of the two officers, no one paid him much mind at all. Everyone else was either watching the sleeping dragon with apprehension, or talking dreamily about what they were going to do with their shares of the treasure once the voyage was finally over. Nate took their imagined futures with him to the berth, and they filled his mind as he fell into a troubled sleep.

He woke hours later, when it was dark and most of the crew were in their bunks. He lay in his hammock for a while, listening to the sounds of their sleep and wondering when they had all started dreaming of the futures they intended to buy. Nate fiddled with the gold ring on his hand. He pressed his thumb into the crest and felt the jagged lines of the sun rays against his skin.

He could go back to Solkyria now. He could track enemy ships for the navy, giving them an unstoppable advantage in the war against Vothein. He could finally make his parents proud. He could be so much more than Sebastian.

But he wouldn't see this voyage to its end. If he was going to return to Solkyria, he needed to leave the very next time the *Southern Echo* put into port. He'd found the dragon for Arani; she didn't need him anymore. None of the crew did. He could slip out of their lives as easily as he had come into them, and he could finally claim the fate he had always dreamed of. But he would never see his friends again.

Nate turned the ring on his finger and tried to find peace between the certainty that he could finally have what he had always wanted, and the doubt blooming in his heart. He knew that the longer he stayed with the pirates, the harder it would be to convince the empire that he had been taken against his will. The idea of lying about Arani and her crew put a bitter taste in his mouth, but he would have to do it. It was the only way the empire would pardon his disappearance and accept him back. He'd show them what he'd learned about himself and what his Skill could do. He'd carve a place for himself in the navy. He would track Votheinian ships.

Or pirates.

The thought was unwelcome, but he knew it was true. The empire could just as easily place him on a pirate hunting ship as it could a war vessel. He'd even imagined as much, not so long ago. Now, he wondered what he would do if he really did have to track the *Southern Echo*, and because of him, Eric, Marcus, Rori, Xander, and all the others met their ends with nooses around their necks.

He couldn't do that to them. But he couldn't stay with the crew, either. They all had dreams that they intended to buy with their shares of Mordanti's treasure, and Nate did not fit anywhere into those schemes.

The ship creaked around him, and the air suddenly felt too close.

Nate swung out of his hammock and pulled his boots on. He was still tired, but his head felt much clearer after the second rest, and he made it up the steps to the main deck without trouble. He drew in deep breaths as he moved to the railing. He almost reached for the wind element but stopped himself, not wanting to invite the pain and exhaustion from his Skill use back into his body. Instead, he listened to the whisper of the sea against the *Southern Echo*'s hull, and the shifting of the sails in the wind. The stars overhead were more familiar now, and he had the sudden thought that he may never see these southern skies again.

Filled with a melancholy he did not fully understand, Nate slowly wandered down the length of the ship. Even this far south, the pirates' instincts for stealth ruled, and there were very few lanterns lit to illuminate the deck. Under the bright stars and the twin moons, that did not matter so much, and Nate easily picked his way along. His feet turned him towards the stern of the ship, where he would find the sleeping dragon. A small wash of fear touched the back of his mind, but it was buried under the desire to see the dragon up close. He hadn't gotten a good look at it yet.

As he drew nearer and could follow the rise and fall of the dragon's spine against the darkness, he caught low voices on the wind. He almost turned around, but he recognized the speakers, and he circled around the dragon to find Eric and Marcus sitting on the steps leading up to the quarter deck, talking quietly. Nate's sudden appearance startled them, but they relaxed and beckoned him over. The stairs creaked under Nate as he settled two steps below them, his back pressed to the carved banister. The dragon murmured softly and shifted in its sleep.

"Shame you weren't here earlier," Marcus informed Nate. "Eric was giving the dragon the sleeping draught, and it was quite entertaining."

"You only say that because you weren't the one who had to stick his hand down the beast's throat," Eric responded primly.

"You didn't do that, either," Marcus said. "Liliana held the mouth open and you poured the draught in while standing as far back as you could manage." He leaned closer to Nate and murmured, "The fool nearly soaked poor Liliana with the sleeping draught, he was shaking so bad."

"Yes, and Marcus was a perfect help through all of that," Eric said wryly. "Sitting right here and laughing the whole time. Lily nearly put a bullet between your eyes."

"Hardly," Marcus said. "The woman can barely aim straight when she's sober. You can be certain she was properly drunk before she put her hands anywhere near that dragon's head." His teeth flashed white as he grinned at Eric. "And I think you've finally found the way to ease her infatuation with you. She wasn't happy when you refused to help her open its mouth." Marcus lounged back on the stairs as though he had not a care in the world, but Nate saw him glance at the dragon, and he heard the quick, shallow breath Marcus took when he looked at the beast. "Strange, though," he murmured. "No matter how much I see it, I still can't believe that the black mimic is *right there*, on this ship with us." He was silent for a moment. "Nothing about this feels real."

"Everything about this is *too* real," Eric said, and the sudden fervor in his usually mild voice charged the air. "We've all paid a heavy price to get here, and it's going to be worth it. It has to be."

Nate glanced up in time to see Marcus brush his hand over Eric's and grip his fingers. The gesture only lasted for a moment, but there was an intimacy there that spanned a lifetime.

"It will be," Marcus murmured. He saw that Nate was watching them and offered a lopsided grin. "We've had big ideas ever since we first joined the crew."

"Long before that," Eric corrected. "We knew what we were going to do before we left Solkyria."

"Well, we certainly dreamed about it," Marcus agreed. "Then we started taking it seriously when we joined Arani's crew." He cast another look at the dragon, one that was a mix of unease and hope. "This is the first time we can actually plan for it." The hope grew on his face as a smile emerged.

Nate shifted his weight on the step. He'd never heard Marcus or Eric talk about their hopes for their lives beyond the *Southern Echo*, at least with not any seriousness. The future had seemed too uncertain for that, but it struck Nate in that moment that he had never asked them, either. He'd been too wrapped up in his own fears and dreams to think about theirs. "What is it you plan to do?" he asked after a moment.

Marcus blinked at Nate as though just remembering he was there. Eric was a bit more composed and answered for both Darkbends.

"We're going to one of the islands in the Sunrise Sea," he said with total certainty. "Far enough away from Solkyria that we won't ever have to worry about the empire again, but not too far from the finer things life can offer." He gave Marcus a pointed look. "Autania has wonderful food and folklore theaters, I've heard."

Marcus rolled his eyes, but his smile flashed in the starlight. "It's also at the ass end of the Trailing Chain, and has terrible droughts in the summer. I'm not sacrificing a bath for some puppet show."

"Please, you've foregone a bath for far less, and that was long before you became a pirate."

The Darkbends fell into a familiar pattern of teasing, and Nate felt an ugly twinge of envy as he watched them, but it faded as he realized that he was genuinely happy for his friends. He was glad that they, at least, would get to see this journey to its end. He hoped they would forgive him, after he'd left. He was going to miss them.

"So you don't plan to go back to Solkyria?" Nate asked when a lull fell.

The question killed the Darkbends' mirth.

"Why would we ever?" Marcus asked. "The empire took everything from us. We're only just now getting it back."

"But it was your home," Nate said.

Marcus's frown deepened into genuine anger, but Eric stopped anything he might have said with a hand on his shoulder.

"He's a wind worker," Eric said softly. "He doesn't understand."

Marcus's dark expression did not clear, but he pressed his lips together. He tipped his head back to stare up at the stars, refusing to meet Nate's gaze.

Nate blinked in confusion. "What don't I understand?"

Marcus shut his eyes as his breathing became hard and tense. Eric placed a hand on his knee and murmured a soft reassurance before turning to Nate.

"We learned how to use our Skills at the light bending academy," Eric said quietly, "but our education did not stop at looking pretty and making things sparkle." Nate winced at the words, remembering when he'd flung them at Eric earlier in the voyage. He started to apologize again, but Eric waved him off. "We're not like wind or tide workers," the Darkbend continued. "We don't have a steady, practical use. Most of us usually go on to serve as entertainment for the upper class and nobility." He hesitated a moment, and a slump came into his shoulders. "That includes our light bending abilities, but we're meant to serve beyond that, and allow our lords and ladies the opportunity to indulge their more... carnal pleasures." He sighed quietly. "Our training and our service doesn't stop at our Skills. It extends to our bodies, too."

Nate looked at his friends with growing horror. "They make you do that?"

"It's what's expected of us," Eric said. "Especially if we're blessed with particularly good looks, and not particularly strong magic."

"And if we're not that pretty," Marcus spat, "they teach us things to supplement our attractiveness, like painting or singing or... playing the fiddle."

Nate went cold as he thought of all the nights Marcus had stood before the crew, filling the air with joyous music. "I had no idea," he murmured. "I'm so sorry."

Marcus grimaced before letting out a soft sigh. He brought his face down from the sky. "I do actually like the fiddle," he admitted, as though shamed by it. "I didn't want to like anything the empire taught me, but..."

Eric looped his arm around Marcus's shoulders. "It's all right," he whispered.

"It's easier with the crew," Marcus said. "With them, I know that they just like the music. They don't ask for anything else." He shifted uncomfortably. "I like playing for them."

Nate did not know how to ease his friend's pain. Awkwardly, he said, "I think they appreciate it."

A moment passed before a smile tentatively shaped itself on Marcus's face. "I know they do."

Nate was the first to break the short silence that followed. "So, Autania," he said. "It's nice there?"

"Nice enough," Marcus said, and the tension released itself from his body.

"It's beautiful," Eric said firmly. "Totally unlike anything this side of the archipelago."

"And they welcome the Skilled?" Nate asked, suddenly wondering if he, too, could find a life there, but he thought of his parents and that squashed the next question he might have asked before it could form.

Eric looked thoughtful for a moment before exchanging a shrug with Marcus.

"They're not known to be hostile towards us," Eric said, "but more importantly, they're no where near close enough to be friendly with Solkyria. If you want to get away from the empire, you could do far worse."

A soft laugh cut through the night, and Nate turned to see Xander standing next to the dragon, regarding the beast as it slept. Nate had not heard the Grayvoice approach, and judging by the surprise on their faces, neither had Marcus nor Eric.

"Why bother trying to get away from the empire?" Xander asked. He took a few slow steps around the dragon, though what he could be looking for on a black dragon at night was beyond Nate. "Solkyria may just win the war and expand east, eventually taking Autania." He shoved his hands in his pockets before finally turning to the others. "It's a stupid plan you two have," Xander said.

"And what's yours, o' mighty font of infinite wisdom?" Marcus demanded.

Xander seemed genuinely surprised by the question, but his smile slowly split the night. He started up the quarter deck's stairs, stopping only when he could look Marcus dead in the eye without lifting his head. "I'm going back to Solkyria," Xander said.

Nate was glad the Darkbends were as startled as he was; it helped cover up the hopeful surprise that gripped him at the thought that he might not need to sneak back to Solkyria alone, after all.

Then Marcus snorted and began to laugh. He stopped as Xander continued to stare at him. "You're serious?" the Darkbend asked.

Xander nodded, and Nate almost spoke up, but the Grayvoice said, "I'm going to go back to Solkyria, and I'm going to make certain that everyone on that godsdamned island knows who I am." He tilted his head back and glared up at the stars. "They'll whisper my name on the streets, and if they don't learn to respect me, they'll learn to fear me. They won't be able to kick me to the side and ignore me ever again. I'll make sure of that."

Nate's heart withered into silence as he stared into a darker mirror of what he'd wanted for himself. After learning what Marcus and Eric had been through, he couldn't help but wonder what Xander's animal speaking trainings had consisted of. He wasn't sure that he wanted to know. But Xander's resentment of Nate's status as a weather worker made a great deal more sense to Nate now, and he felt foolish for even thinking that anyone but him would want to return to Solkyria and rejoin the empire.

My life for the empire, Nate thought as he turned the gold ring on his finger. It still felt hot against his skin after anchoring him against so much magic use. Months ago, Nate had felt unworthy of bearing the Solkyrian sun crest. Now, he wondered if he even wanted to.

"They'll arrest you," Eric finally said, "the moment you set foot on Solkyrian soil. They won't care how much money you have. You can't buy your way back into the empire's favor."

Xander shrugged. "I never had it to begin with. And I don't aim to put any money into the emperor's pockets. I'll be purchasing quite a few guns and hands to wield them on my way back to the empire." Another fiendish grin crossed his face. "And I've got friends that would love to do quite a lot of damage to Solkyria's fleets."

"What friends?" Marcus demanded.

Xander lowered his eyes, but he looked out at the black waters instead of at anyone in the small group. "You wouldn't know them."

Marcus threw up his hands. "And he called *our* plan stupid," he grumbled to Eric.

"Mmm." Eric frowned at the Grayvoice for a few moments longer before shifting his attention. "What about you, Nate?"

Nate froze. "Me?"

Eric nodded, and both Marcus and Xander glanced in his direction.

A small wave of panic crashed over Nate. "I haven't really thought about it," he lied.

"Come on," Marcus pressed. "You escaped Solkyria and you've never once thought about what you'd do with that freedom?"

Nate was spared having to answer when the door to the navigation room abruptly banged open, startling them all and even making the dragon murmur and shift in its sleep.

"He didn't break free from Solkyria," Rori said as she stepped outside. She hesitated at the sight of the dragon, and a strange but unafraid look came into her eyes before she shook herself and faced Nate and the others. "Weather workers are never free," Rori continued. "We're a threat to Solkyria if we're not under its thumb. You three may be able to figure out a future for yourselves outside of the empire, even if it wins the war, but not Nate, and certainly not me. Our marks are dangerous. We'd always be trying not to get captured or killed, and no matter how far we go, there'll always be someone who will know what we are, and try to hurt us for it, or force us to work, or catch us and sell us back to the empire." She lightly scraped her boot against the bottom step, but she did not come up the stairs. "We don't get to dream the same as you do."

Xander crossed his arms. "You looking for pity, Goodtide?" he asked acidly.

That did not surprise Nate. He knew firsthand how unkind Xander could be when he had any reason to speak of his Skill, especially when in comparison to someone else's.

Rori looked up at Xander without any affection or trepidation. "If I was," she said, "I would never come to you." Her gaze shifted past him to rest on Marcus and Eric. "I mean it. Don't push Nate on this."

Marcus shifted awkwardly. "I didn't mean anything by it," he said.

"I know you didn't," Rori said. She sighed tiredly and leaned against the railing, her back to the sea and her eyes on the sleeping dragon. "Soon, everyone on this ship will be richer than they ever dared hope, and it's all because of one poor soul branded with someone else's dream."

"Very poetic," Xander said mildly.

Marcus leaned forward and cuffed him lightly on the shoulder.

"Rori," Eric said delicately, "what would you do, if you didn't have to worry about the empire?"

The Goodtide threw a slow, sardonic glance up at him.

"No, really," Eric said. "Just for a moment, forget about the empire and the tattoo on your face and the magic in your blood. For one moment, be totally and completely free. What would you do?"

Rori took a long, slow breath and scuffed the heel of her boot against the step again. "That's a dream for someone else, Eric."

"But have you thought about it?"

She was quiet for a few moments. "No," she finally said.

Nate had the distinct feeling that she was lying.

Chains clinked together softly as the dragon shifted in its sleep.

THE NEXT FEW DAYS of the *Southern Echo*'s journey north melted away at much the same pace. Pirates worked on the ship in familiar rhythms disrupted only by the sleeping dragon at the stern of the ship. In their off time, they talked of the things they would do with their shares of the treasure, from spending it on food, drink, and the finest pleasure houses to buying estates and setting up farms. They all looked forward to the future, including the ones who had not wanted to go after the dragon in the first place. Nate listened whenever these conversations sprang up around him, but he did not join them, and no one pressed him. Either Rori's warning from that night with Xander and the Darkbends had spread, or the others were too wrapped up in their own fantasies to notice Nate's lack of participation. He did not think it was the former.

Nate helped where he could with the ship, but he slept away a good part of the journey, and could only perform simple tasks when he was awake. No one complained about this, as Dax was not shy about reminding them that Nate had earned his rest by finding the black mimic. But exhaustion plagued Nate, and his hands were clumsy even with the simplest tasks. The crew began to turn away from him once more. It wasn't out of malice; they simply knew that they could perform the jobs better than he could, and it was easier for them to keep him out from underfoot and away from the ship's key operations than it was to let him make a mess and then sort it out. They relegated him to easy chores at the corners of the decks, and he watched the crew laugh and trade their excited versions of the future without him.

He would have preferred their malice. At least then, he would not have been pushed aside and forgotten. Not even Jim Greenroot could be bothered to pay Nate much mind, distracted as he was by his dream of buying up land for a grand estate. So Nate faded into the background, and tried to be happy for his friends whenever they talked about their plans for the future, but Rori's words weighed heavily on his mind. Nate was at a loss for what he could do beyond returning to Solkyria as he'd originally planned. He'd never imagined anything else.

This lasted until the ship reentered the doldrums, and then the real trouble began.

The drop in the wind hit Nate again, but knowing what to expect helped temper the effects. He made sure he was below deck when the ship crossed into the wind-dead zones, and he spent the worst of it in his hammock, dozing as he waited for the dizzy spell to pass. It took some time for him to feel up to coming topside once more, but when he did, he found that without the constant roar of the wind in his ears, his head felt clearer, and his headaches finally began to subside. That meant he heard every word clearly when Arani and Rori began to argue about the speed of the ship.

Unlike the rest of the crew, Arani's nerves were drawn taught. She wanted to get back to Spider's

Nest—the only truly friendly port open to them—and restock as quickly as possible, so they could set out again and follow Mordanti's map. It was not an unreasonable want, but she did not like how long it had taken for the ship to return to the doldrums. She sought out Rori to tell the navigator as much, and did not seem to care that Nate and the others swabbing the deck could hear them as they argued at the helm.

"The wind was at our backs when we were sailing south," Rori pointed out. "It was against us going the other way. We did the best we could."

"There was more that could have been done," Arani said. "You know that."

Nate's mop slowed as he watched Rori frown in confusion.

"I put us on the most direct heading, Captain. If I'd cut us any further north, we'd have been at a standstill."

Arani jabbed a finger into Rori's chest. "But *you* could have lifted our speed and seen us here two days ago."

Rori opened her mouth to protest, but froze when she realized the same thing that Nate had a moment earlier: Arani wanted Rori to use her Skill. The Goodtide slowly closed her mouth and shook her head, dark anger coming into her eyes. But Arani leaned in closer to Rori and said something too softly for Nate to hear, and the Goodtide's fury quickly gave way to unease.

"Do you understand, Miss Rori?" Arani asked as she drew back.

Rori nodded wordlessly.

"Good," the captain said. "I'll allow you the rest of the day to gather your strength, but tomorrow, you call upon the tides to see us out of this place."

Rori's jaw clenched and she looked ready to fight, but she kept her hands on the ship's wheel and nodded instead. "Aye, Captain," she growled.

Arani held her gaze for a few moments longer before turning on her heel and stalking away. Nate waited for her to move well past him before he laid down his mop and told the others he would be back in a moment. They stared distractedly after Arani and waved him off.

Nate hurried to the helm, and found Rori clenching the wheel so hard, her knuckles had gone white. "You all right?" he asked, although he already knew the answer.

"No," Rori confirmed. Her eyes were fixed ahead, on the horizon, and she did not so much as blink.

RORI DID NOT TELL Nate what the captain had whispered to her, and she remained quiet and withdrawn for the rest of the day. Nate found himself glaring at Arani whenever he saw the captain, although like the rest of the crew, she seemed to have less inclination to pay him any attention now that his part in the treasure hunt was done. He found himself hating Arani a little, not just for his own sake, but because she'd asked Rori to do what the Goodtide had sworn off forever. What had happened to the captain who had promised a choice to the Skilled among her crew, who had promised she did not treat the Skilled as tools?

Nate got his answer the next day, when someone noticed that the dragon was awake.

The morning began as many others had, with clear skies and weak winds, and Nate had eaten a quick breakfast and gone to help haul the ropes that would furl the sails, if the riggers would let him. Work proceeded as usual, with the exception of Rori, who was at the center of the ship and standing with her eyes closed and legs braced against the *Southern Echo*'s gentle rocking. Nate was not the only one to stop and watch as Rori began to work her Skill and command the waters beneath the hull. Her arms were spread, and she used far less motion than Nate had expected of a tide worker, but there was no mistaking the shudder that ran through the ship. The deck lurched under Nate's feet as the waves changed and the *Southern Echo* began to gather speed. The current Rori called up did not measure up to the ship's speeds when the wind was filling her sails, but there was no mistaking the steady breeze that began to blow from the bow of the ship, and when Nate peered over the side, he saw how the waters around the hull churned with energy.

"Could've used that the first time we were here," one of the riggers grumbled, and the statement was met with louder agreement.

"Quiet," Nate snapped, not bothering to check who he was silencing. He could only watch Rori as a light sweat broke out on her brow, and her breathing began to quicken. He wondered when it was that she had last used her Skill.

"Doesn't look like she's gonna last very long," someone else noted.

Nate turned to face the speaker, his hands clenched into fists, but a cry of alarm went up from the stern, and everyone's attention snapped to the back of the ship, where the dragon rested.

It had almost become possible to forget that the *Southern Echo* had a dragon chained to her deck. The creature had started to become a piece of the ship, albeit one that no one wanted to lounge or step on, but the crew had grown used to its quiet presence and some of the fear had subsided. Now, however, the dragon shifted listlessly beneath its chains, and blinked blearily at the pirates that scrambled away from it. The creature did not manage to do much more than that, but based on the sudden wave of panic that washed over the ship, Nate would have thought that the thing had thrown off its restraints and taken a bite out of someone's leg.

"Enough of that!" Arani called before anyone could find a more extreme reaction. She appeared at the railing of the poop deck and surveyed the crew below her with stern anger. "Supplies are running low, and that includes the sleeping draught for the dragon. We have enough to see us back to Spider's Nest if we ration it properly, so that's what we'll be doing." She cast a meaningful glance at the black mimic as it grumbled and settled once more. "The beast will be more alert for the rest of the voyage, but it's locked down, and with Rori hastening our speed, we should make it out of the doldrums without any trouble." She turned her head as Dax stepped up next to her. He did not look pleased.

"The captain is correct," the quartermaster called out. "We will be safe, but we will need to use our supplies carefully. That goes for food as well."

A groan went up from the crew as Dax informed them that they would be giving up eggs for the rest of the journey, as the chickens were needed to feed the dragon. They would hold off on sacrificing the dairy goat for as long as they could, but there were no promises about that. However, with Rori using her Skill, the captain and the quartermaster were confident that they would be out of the doldrums soon, and then it would be smooth sailing back to

Spider's Nest, where they could safely restock. No one looked placated by this, and Nate came to understand why as his meals changed from already thin soups to hardtack biscuits popping with weevils and tough, salted strips of meat that dragged against his teeth and put a raging thirst in his throat. The rum and beer ran low, too, and the water that was left in the caskets was slimy and difficult to swallow. No rains came to replenish the supply. Attempts at fishing yielded few catches that were too meager to feed the full crew, and there was nothing else to be done.

The crew grew sluggish under the poor diet, and tempers ran hot throughout the ship. Dax and Novachak prowled the decks, breaking up fights before they could begin, but the real savior was the hope that everyone held on to like a lifeline in a storm: their dreams of what they would do with Mordanti's treasure. Nate heard the pirates talking to their friends, their shift mates, themselves, anyone who would listen to all the things they planned to do when they were finally rich men and women. And if the dream began to falter, if someone began to doubt, they would go and look at the dragon on the deck, and remind themselves that there was a map in the creature's wings and a fire in its belly that would open the future for them.

Rori was the clear exception to all of this. She exhausted herself under the weight of her Skill, a tired slump coming into her shoulders and dark rings forming under her eyes. She could only control the currents beneath the ship for a few hours at a time before she needed to stop and recover what little strength she could, and her skin and clothes were constantly damp with sweat. She never seemed able to fully catch her breath.

Nate hurried to return the borrowed agate to her, but they were nothing but cold stones at that point, burned clean through by Nate's overuse of his own Skill. Rori had to rely on what agate she had left from her personal collection, which she wore up and down her arms under the sleeves of her shirt. Nate suspected that their anchoring support was already wavering, but Rori would not say. He offered to let her borrow his gold ring, but Rori took one look at the Solkyrian crest and snarled her refusal.

Nate retreated, and watched her struggle with a tightness around his heart. He wondered if this was what he had looked like when he had been tracking the dragon. He asked Eric, who gave Nate a grim look.

"Watching you was damn terrifying, and you were barely aware of anyone around you when you were working your Skill," the elegant Darkbend said before nodding at Rori. "So yes, it was about that bad."

Nate doubted that; he had only been reading the winds, not trying to bend the ocean to his captain's will. And even then, he had burned through the agate anchors Rori had gifted him. With guilt heavy on his shoulders, he volunteered to run Rori's meals to her. His lax schedule allowed him the job, but he did it partly to have an excuse to check on his friend, the gods below take Xander if he had a problem with it; and partly to apologize for burning through Rori's extra agate without so much as a thank you.

For her Skill work, Rori was afforded a small mercy in the form of special meals that contained a few bites of chicken. The rest of the bird went to the dragon, its meat concealing the diluted sleeping draught, but Rori was given a piece of the meal to help keep her strength up. It seemed almost farcical to Nate, given how much her Skill was taking from her, but even that meager recompense drew envious eyes, particularly from the

Solkyrian members of the crew who did not bear any Skill marks. Nate was working with the riggers when he overheard two of them talking about Rori in low voices.

"The princess is finally doing her job," one of them glowered. It was Ethan, the man from that secret conversation with Xander before they'd found the black mimic. "About time Arani put the Goodtide bitch to work. She's been coasting with us long enough."

"You know she gets special meals now?" the other rigger said. Davy, Nate remembered, that was his name. "Fresh meat for working so hard."

"*We* work hard," Ethan said. "I think we deserve that as much as she does."

"More, I'd say," Davy said. "We have to put up with the Goodtide's smell, after all. She *reeks* these days. Almost makes me regret still thinking about pushing her down and spreading her legs."

They laughed then, and Nate felt something cold and dark take hold of his heart.

In retrospect, Nate probably should have gone to Dax. The quartermaster would have known how to handle the situation peacefully, but Nate had not wanted peace in that moment. Instead, he'd launched himself at Ethan and Davy, and come away with a bloody nose, extra rotations on swabbing duties, three strikes from the ship's flogging stick, and a stern warning from Novachak to never do that again. So, needing someone more experienced to bring retribution down upon the riggers, Nate thought about the night a gunner had thrown a biscuit at his head, and then he went to Xander. The Grayvoice listened to Nate's account in silence, and then walked away without a word. Less than an hour passed before a scream of "Man overboard!" ripped across the ship. Ethan and Davy, who both turned out to be terribly poor swimmers, had to be fished out of the sea before they drowned. It was a close thing. Ethan coughed up enough seawater to nearly fill a bucket, and it took Davy two full minutes to start breathing again. Dax and Arani immediately wanted to know how the riggers had gone overboard in clear weather in the middle of the doldrums, and when Rori wasn't even using her Skill at the time. Davy, shaking badly and eyes wide with clear terror, swore that he had been careless and slipped coming down from the rigging, and Ethan clenched his teeth and nodded in silent agreement. Nate picked Xander out from the small crowd gathered around the soaking pirates. The Grayvoice met his gaze impassively, and gave Nate a small nod. Dax and Arani watched Xander suspiciously after that, but with Ethan and Davy insisting that they'd gone overboard through their own fault, the officers had to let the Grayvoice be.

After that incident, murmurs about Rori quieted for the most part, and the crew left her alone. When she wasn't on the main deck working her Skill to push the ship through the doldrums, she was in the navigation room, looking over the charts and making certain that she had the *Southern Echo* on the right course. At least, that's what she seemed to be doing. More than once, Nate found her slumped over the desk, her cheek flattened against the charts and her breath fluttering in an exhausted sleep.

On the third day after Ethan and Davy had gone overboard, Nate let himself into the navigation room, a small plate of steaming chicken scraps held tightly in his hand. Rori was once more asleep at the desk, but Luken was nestled in the nape of her neck, and the bird chirped at Nate as he shut the door.

"Hey there, demon spawn," Nate murmured to the bird as he stepped to the table.

Luken chirped again and ruffled his feathers. The two of them had come to a sort of truce while Rori was suffering, and mostly left each other alone now, although Luken was still in possession of Nate's old hat and showed no signs of ever letting it go.

Nate surveyed the mess of charts and quills spilled across the table before he moved a pot of ink aside and gently set the plate down. Rori stirred at the soft sound. Her eyes fluttered open and she blinked blearily at Nate a few times before a ferocious yawn overtook her. Ignoring Luken's protests, she sat up and scrubbed her hands over her face, leaving a smear of ink across her chin.

"How long was I asleep?" she asked. Her voice sounded sticky in her throat.

"Not sure," Nate answered honestly. "We're into the second afternoon watch."

Rori groaned and rubbed at her eyes again. "I need to get back out there."

"You need to eat," Nate said, "and not be a complete idiot. That's my job around here."

That earned him a weak smile. "No, you're a special kind of idiot. When we were sailing south, the only time you stopped for a break was when you actually passed out." Her expression darkened. "Gods below take the fools on this crew who think I'll do that to myself."

Nate cast a pointed look at the small puddle of drool Rori had left on the table.

"I'm out of practice," she said once she saw what he was looking at.

Nate carefully pushed a few charts out of the way before perching on the table. "When was the last time you used your Skill?" he asked softly.

Rori's gaze wandered to the meager plate of chicken in front of her. "Not since the merchant ship," she murmured. She reached out and took a piece of meat from the plate and turned it slowly between her fingers. "Do you know the strangest part of all this?"

Nate tilted his head and waited, sensing that she did not need his prompting to talk.

"I actually *missed* using my Skill," Rori said. Her voice caught on the words, but she forced them out. "I loved my magic when I was a child, but after what happened to my family and what I did to the *Godfall*..." A haunted look came into her gaze. "I told myself I wasn't going to use it again. And I didn't, until Arani ordered me to do it, and I hate her for it, but part of me was glad to have the excuse to use that power again." Rori tore the chicken meat apart in her hands. "I didn't fight her because I wanted to taste that power again. I'm a really strong Goodtide, Nate, and I remember what it was like when I could control the currents and the tides. I'm terrified of it." She dropped the uneaten food back on to the plate and fell back in her seat. Her spine popped with the abrupt movement, and Nate winced in sympathy. "The last time I used my Skill, I tore the *Godfall* apart and killed everyone on that ship."

"Is that why you've been holding back now?" Nate asked.

She gave him a startled look.

He hooked his thumbs into his pockets and shrugged. "I've seen tide workers use their Skills before. They use their hands and their arms a lot more than you do. Even Dax does it, and his work is with blood, not the tides. When you use your Skill, you look like you're fighting against your magic." He held her gaze for a long moment. "Tell me I'm wrong."

Rori stared at him for a while longer, then shut her eyes and leaned back with a heavy sigh. "You're not." Luken chirped and hopped into her lap, and Rori reflexively ran a light touch along his feathers. "It was so easy to do what I did to the *Godfall*. I'm scared I'll do that to the *Southern Echo* if I'm not careful."

"You think you could?" Nate asked. "You said yourself you're out of practice."

Rori's expression hardened, a deep frown cutting across her brow. "Practice *controlling* it, yes. The power is still there. I can't let it out."

Another silence fell over them. Nate broke it by nudging the plate of chicken closer to her, and she reluctantly began to eat, chewing slowly and without any joy.

"I used to dream about summoning and taming storms," Nate said. "I wanted my Skill to have that kind of raw strength. I still kind of wish it did. But you know, after tracking the black mimic and seeing what you're doing, I think I understand why you'd rather be without a Skill."

"But you'd still keep yours?" Rori asked as she chewed mechanically on another bite.

Nate hesitated, thinking over the question hard, and about everything he'd heard and seen from his Skilled friends once he'd started to look beyond himself. Then he nodded. "It's part of me. And if I could figure out what I *want* to do with my magic instead of throwing myself at what everyone else thinks I *need* to do with it, maybe I'd be able to love it."

Rori smiled sadly. "It's a dangerous thing, to love your Skill. Count yourself lucky that you never did."

Nate did not know what to say after that.

"I have thought about it, you know," she suddenly blurted. "About what I'd do if I could be completely, totally free." She bit her lip and pushed the remains of the chicken around on the plate. "When I was a young girl, I wanted a ship of my own that I could sail wherever I pleased, and I'd use my Skill to quicken the currents as they took me around the world. I still want that, even though it's foolish. I want to see more of the world." The frown returned to her face. "But I don't want any chains on me when I do it."

Nate crossed his arms. "That sounds pretty good to me," he said. "Better than what I thought I'd do." He considered telling her about his horrible plan to run back to Solkyria and throw himself back under the empire's control. If nothing else, maybe it would give her a reason to laugh. But Nate had the sense that Rori, somehow, already knew. "Maybe I'll borrow that dream, if you don't mind."

"It's pretty," Rori said, "but it's not for weather workers. It's a dream for someone else."

"Probably not," he agreed, "but it'll give me something to hold on to until this crew disbands and I have to figure out what I'm going to do when there is no more *Southern Echo*." He watched Luken preen one of his wings, and wondered what Rori would do with the bird once they were done. He'd be shocked if she did not keep him. "We could try it, you know," Nate said idly, giving himself the chance to get caught up in fantasies of the future, just like everyone else. A future that, for the first time in Nate's life, did not include the Solkyrian Empire. He felt a rush of shame at the thought, but it was quickly washed out by a bright wave of hope. "With our shares of Mordanti's treasure," he said, excitement seeping into the words, "that would be more than enough for a ship, and we could do what Dax did and disguise our marks."

Rori stared at him for a moment. "You'd come with me?" she asked softly.

The question startled him, and he flushed when he realized that he had been making plans for the two of them without even thinking about it. His excitement burst, but he still felt that warm bubble of hope in his chest. "If you wanted the help," he said hastily. "I mean, I'm not much of a sailor so you'd need your own crew, unless you got a smaller boat, but then you wouldn't really need me at all, I suppose, and I don't think you'd really be able to see as much of the world as you'd want..."

He broke off when he saw that Rori was smiling at him sadly.

"It's a kind offer," she said, "but it wouldn't work. Can't think of many people who would sail under a Skilled captain, and as to the tattoos... Well, there's a reason Dax doesn't go anywhere near towns under Solkyrian control. He knows he's safe from a distance, but if you know what to look for, you can see his mark." She let out a hard breath. "And that's with a simple Malatide mark. That's a lot easier to hide than this." She gestured at her face and the complicated Goodtide tattoo that decorated her skin.

Nate could not disagree with her. Plain and simple, it was an option that Rori did not have. Even if Nate successfully covered up his own mark, he'd still be branded by Solkyria, and the world would still be looking at that spot on his face, and they would know that a Skill mark was there.

A dream for someone else.

They sat in silence for a few minutes longer while Rori finished her food, both of them trying hard not to think about the future that had to come after the *Southern Echo*. Then Rori pushed herself to her feet, murmured a thanks, and went to put her Skill to use once more.

"WHERE IN THE SIX hells are we?" Arani snapped.

Three more days had passed, and despite all of Rori's efforts, the *Southern Echo* still had not cleared the doldrums. Even at their widest, the ship should have cleared the doldrums half a day ago at most. But the wind had not come, and it was past the point of unnerving the crew.

As their navigator, Rori had never failed the crew before, but that was when she was able to rest and not throw away every last scrap of her strength trying to find an impossible balance between the raw power of her Skill and her fear of unleashing it. Nate knew that, and he would have been astonished to learn that Arani was oblivious to it, but the fact remained that the ship's sails hung limp from the masts and the *Southern Echo* could only crawl over the waves when Rori was not there to push the currents. The crew was growing nervous as the supplies continued to dwindle and the black mimic groaned and shifted beneath its chains, and the captain had come seeking an answer.

Nate had found Rori resting uneasily in her hammock that morning, forgoing the navigation room in favor of something that would sway with the ship and ease the turmoil of her exhaustion. He'd brought her another plate of chicken, this one considerably smaller than the last; there was only one bird left, and they would need the rest of the meat for the dragon's sleeping draught. She'd choked down the food and been gathering her strength to rise to her feet when Arani and Dax had found them. The captain had some of the charts from the navigation room in her hands, and she waved them like a battle flag as she demanded to know where and how they'd gotten lost.

Rori pressed her hand against her forehead and heaved a deep sigh before reaching for the charts. "Let me see," she said.

Arani handed them over, and Rori peered blearily at the sea maps. It took her several minutes to piece together the navigational information, and Nate saw the glassy sheen to her eyes as she struggled to put her thoughts in line. She finally shook her head.

"I don't know, Captain," she said, defeated. "We're on a straight course, that much I know I've been able to do. We should be out of the doldrums by now."

"Then where is the wind?" Arani demanded.

Rori shook her head again. She sounded as though her heart had cracked. "I don't know."

Arani moved to take the charts back from Rori, but stopped with one hand on the paper. She frowned hard at the chart, and then whipped around to Nate. "Have you felt the wind at all?"

He shook his head sheepishly. Between the slow recovery from his own Skill overuse and focusing on Rori, he had not paid much attention to the scarce, weak breezes in the doldrums. He'd also been eager to lose the feeling of being shunted to the side, like a tool that had already served its purpose.

"Unless we've let ourselves sail in circles, we should have the wind back," Arani said. She kept her gaze riveted on Nate as she spoke. "I doubt we've failed to notice the sun rising and setting in the wrong place, so we have to be out of the doldrums. What could possibly keep the wind from us outside of that place?"

Nate frowned in confusion for several moments, and then he had a terrible thought that sent panic surging through his blood. He turned and ran for the stairs. He heard the captain shout for Dax to stay with Rori, and then her footsteps thundered behind Nate as he raced topside.

Gods above, let me be wrong, he prayed frantically as he threw himself across the deck. His shoulder collided with someone's chest and nearly sent them both sprawling, but Arani caught Nate by the elbow and hauled him back on balance. They surged to the railing, and Arani tore out her spyglass to scan the horizon.

The sky was pale and hazy that day, with a patch of clouds clustered in the distance. The ocean was empty all around the ship, the winds quiet.

Far, far too quiet.

Nate shut his eyes and opened his awareness to the wind element. He braced himself for the flood of air currents... which never came. There was a faint tickle of a breeze caused by the *Southern Echo*'s slow forward crawl, but all around them, the wind was gone. Unlike the first time they'd gone through the doldrums, there wasn't even a flicker of motion for Nate to follow.

A shiver ran up his spine. *Gods above, please.*

He pushed his awareness further out, ignoring the fresh flare of pain as he sought something, anything, in a world gone silent and dark all around him. This was not natural. He knew that beyond any doubt, and yet he still beseeched the gods to let him be wrong, to let the wind come rushing back like a mischievous child that had strayed too far from home and only come running when they'd known they were in danger of punishment.

The gods ignored his prayers.

When Nate finally found the wind, it felt warped and wrong against his consciousness. It bent away from the *Southern Echo* at unnatural angles, forming a massive void all around the ship. Beyond that, the wind romped and blew as it pleased, save for the steady rush that came from the northeast, cutting an oblique line against the natural patterns. Nate could not pick out any details beyond that, but he did not need to. There was only one thing in the world that could have done this.

"Highwind magic," Nate murmured as he pulled himself back from the element. "Very strong."

"Are you certain?" Arani asked, but there was no desperation or hope or even fear in her voice. She simply needed to know that he was sure.

Nate nodded and pointed across the sea, at the patch of clouds on the horizon. Had they grown larger since he'd last looked at them, or was that his own distress exaggerating their size?

Arani pointed her spyglass at the clouds and said nothing for a long time. There was no shake in her hands or tremor of any sort in her body. The only traitor to her calm revealed itself when she lowered the spyglass, and Nate could see the grimness in her eyes.

"I can't see a ship, but that bank of clouds is coming towards us," she said. "It's low on the water and moving fast. No way there aren't a couple of Highwinds pulling those clouds along to hide a ship." She grimaced. "It seems the Solkyrian navy has been looking for us."

"How do we escape?" Nate asked.

"We don't," Arani said. She snapped her spyglass closed and turned away from the railing. For a moment, she looked about the ship with a sad sort of fondness, and then her eyes alighted on the dragon chained in front of the navigation room. She changed immediately, thrusting her shoulders back and drawing herself up to her full height. "Enemy approaching from the northeast," the captain roared, and the entire ship came to a sudden halt. "All hands prepare for battle!"

Bewildered looks were exchanged and directed off the starboard bow where Arani had indicated, but a new alertness came to the men and women of the *Southern Echo*, and they went to work.

Nate, however, stared at the captain in horror. "You can't fight the navy," he said.

"They've taken the wind and my tide worker is exhausted," Arani growled back, "and surrender is not an option." Her gaze returned to the dragon. "This will be bloody," she murmured, "but this ship and this crew will fight to the end." She suddenly turned her attention on Nate. "I need you to monitor that ship as it approaches. I want you to tell me how far out it is every time you see me, even if I just walked past you a minute ago." Her hand gripped his shoulder. "They think they can surprise us, but if we do this right, we'll hit them first. I'm counting on you, boy."

Nate hesitated for the briefest of moments, a lifetime of idolization of the Solkyrian navy gathering at his back. Then he nodded, his voice stuck in his throat. His friends' lives were on the line, and Nate would guard them however he could.

Arani squeezed his arm before pulling away.

"What about Rori?" he blurted before he could stop himself.

Arani glanced back at him, and her eyes went soft with regret. "She rests, and we pray to every god we know that she has enough of her strength back when we need it."

The captain strode off, and Nate turned back to the approaching clouds banked low on the water. Another shiver went through him, but he steadied his breath, and began to work.

CHAPTER TWENTY-TWO

Battle Tides

"STEADY," ARANI GROWLED AS she paced up and down the length of the ship. Louder, she called orders for the crew members on the deck to adjust the sails and try to find the nonexistent wind before the fog boiled over them, pretending as though this were a strange but natural occurrence and she was simply trying to get her ship clear of the mists. The crew responded quickly, and the uneasy glances they threw at the looming fog easily could have been mistaken for reluctance to be caught in poor seeing conditions.

For his part, Nate sat huddled beneath the port railing, ducked down and as out of sight as he could be. He read the wind as best he could from that spot, and he'd managed to tease out the position of the navy ship from the strong gusts the Highwinds kept in its sails. He relayed the information to Jim Greenroot every time the gunner drew close enough for Nate to speak softly to him, which Arani ensured happened often by calling conflicting orders and changing her tactics to try and find the wind for her sails. With danger closing in, all animosities were suspended, and Jim willingly found reasons to pause long enough to listen to Nate's report, and then he would move to the stairs that led below. He would not descend, but instead pass the information to the pirate waiting on the steps, and they in turn ran to tell the gun crews. With the gun ports closed, the gunners had nothing else to base their aim on, and it was a wild, desperate hope that when the signal came, they'd be able to throw open the ports, fire immediately, and manage to hit something vital on the navy ship. With as close as the enemy vessel was coming, it would be almost impossible for them to miss entirely, but as Arani had said, they had one chance to damage the navy ship past the point of retaliation. If they failed, they were dead.

That was why Arani had the *Southern Echo* flying the colors of a trade ship from the Coral Chain. It was a flimsy disguise, as only the poorest of captains would have let their ship wander so far off the trade routes, but Arani took that as an opportunity to make herself and her crew look like they had absolutely no idea what they were doing. The stacks of crates they'd piled around the black mimic and the canvas tarp they'd thrown over the entire array would hopefully bolster that perception. Caution had prompted Arani to order an extra dose of sleeping draught for the dragon, which kept the beast quiet but had cut into the last reserves of the drug. Novachak had informed Arani and the rest of the crew that there was just enough to see them back to Spider's Nest, but it would be a close thing, provided they came out of this fight alive.

As the chaos swirled on the main deck, Arani came to the port railing and stopped next to Nate. He looked up to see her give the fog a defeated look before turning her back to it and surveying the frantic crew. Her expression changed immediately, to a hard determination completely at odds with the slump she intentionally put into her shoulders for any navy sailors that happened to glimpse her in the next few moments. "Go now," she ordered.

Nate scrambled forward and darted for the steps, all but falling down them in his haste to get below. The woman waiting halfway down the stairs caught him and helped him find his footing again before looking at him expectantly.

"It's time," Nate confirmed, and the pirate disappeared into the ship.

Nate hesitated before following, risking a final peek across the main deck. He looked up just in time to see the fog part like curtains, and reveal the naval frigate.

It was not the largest ship in the empire's fleet, not even close, but it was bigger than the *Southern Echo*, and the main deck was nearly half a level above that of the pirate ship. The Solkyrian flag waved from its three masts, the golden sun proud and dangerous against the misty backdrop, and the ship was close enough that Nate could see the uniformed men and women standing at the railing, rifles raised and at the ready. His heart leaped into his throat at the sight of so many guns.

There was no way Arani's plan would work.

"Nate?" someone called softly from below.

He looked down to see Dax waving him away from the top of the stairs, and Nate quickly descended to join the pirates that hid below, which included all of the Skilled. Arani had ordered them out of sight, for a merchant ship from the Coral Chain colonies with a Veritian captain would not have a single Skill-bearing sailor among its crew, no matter how friendly its owner was with their Solkyrian rulers. Blades shone dully in the faint light as Nate joined them, every pirate armed and silently waiting for whatever came next.

"It's a frigate," Nate murmured to Dax.

The quartermaster nodded grimly. "A small blessing from the gods above."

Nate wasn't so sure about that. "Why haven't they fired on us yet?" he whispered.

Dax held his hand up, and in the following silence, Nate and the others heard the authoritative call from the naval ship.

"Identify yourself and your cargo immediately," the frigate's officer demanded, sharp enough for the words to carry clearly to Nate and the rest of the pirates below the main deck.

Arani shouted back a false name and a brief manifest of goods from the Coral Chain.

"And how did you come to be so far from the trade routes?" the officer called.

They heard Arani say something about an unlucky combination of bad weather and losing their navigator to a fever not long after they'd set off.

If the naval officer responded, they did not hear it.

"They suspect us, but they're not certain," Dax murmured with a nod. His eyes were riveted on the ceiling, and there was a tautness to his voice that Nate did not like.

"Is there any chance they'll let us go?" Nate whispered into the quiet.

"No," Dax said.

The room held its breath under the silence. Nate waited for gunshots to ring out and bodies to hit the deck above their heads, but the quiet remained, almost taunting in its persistence.

"By order of Emperor Cadmus Goldskye," the naval officer finally shouted, "we claim your ship and all its cargo for the Solkyrian Empire. Do you surrender peacefully?"

"We're already sailing for Solkyria," Arani called.

"Do you surrender peacefully?" the officer snarled back.

Arani put a clear note of resignation in her voice when she said, "Aye. Come aboard, then."

Faint sounds of wood thudding against wood and the scrapes of grappling hooks on the deck came moments later.

"Here they come," Dax murmured. There was no relief in his voice, even though Arani's plan was working thus far. The next step depended entirely on Dax. The quartermaster's eyes were already unfocused as he stepped away from the group and tapped into his Skill, reaching out his awareness to the heartbeats of the navy sailors as they crossed the gap between the ships. It was up to him to determine when enough navy sailors had come over and the critical next point in Arani's plan came, and the Malatide had insisted that he was more than up for the task. The crew had faith in Dax, but unease rippled through the pirates as unfamiliar boots began to pound on the deck overhead.

Nate glanced around, catching a grim but determined nod from Eric, a calm and steadfast look from Marcus, and an angry but eager gleam in Xander's eyes. Then Nate saw Rori a few paces away, breathing hard. The few hours of rest had not been nearly enough for her to recover her strength, but she had insisted on joining the fight. Looking at her now, though, Nate saw the wild panic in her posture. Her nerves were stretched to the breaking point.

Nate threaded his way to her side and quietly asked her if she was all right.

"They're not taking me back," she breathed. "I'd rather die."

Nate could not shake the feeling that they were all going to die in the next few minutes, but he did not want Rori's final thoughts to be wrapped in fear. She deserved better.

"What's the name of your ship?" he whispered to her.

Rori's hand shook as her grip tightened on her cutlass.

Nate gently touched her arm, and she stilled. "I know you've thought about it. Maybe it *is* a dream for someone else, but that doesn't mean you can't have it, too. So what's the name of your ship?"

Unshed tears were bright in Rori's eyes, but she took a deep breath and held them back. "*Tide Song*," she whispered.

Nate nodded and covered her hand with his. Her skin felt cold beneath his touch. "Then think of the *Tide Song*," he said, "and don't stop."

Rori took another shuddering breath, but the shaking in her hands began to calm.

A moment later, Dax's shoulders rippled, and he pulled himself out of his Skill with a gasp. "Now!" he shouted, slamming the pommel of his cutlass hard against the side of the ship. "FIRE!"

Nate heard the gun ports slam open, and the scrambling of the gunners as they pushed the loaded cannons into place. Calls of outraged surprise came from above as the navy sailors saw what was happening, but they were drowned out by the roar of the cannons and the splintering crashes of the cannonballs finding the side of the naval frigate. If the gunners had done their part well, that close range would have let them hit the frigate's cannons and destroy the navy ship's ability to retaliate with its port side guns. There was no time to wait and see if they'd succeeded. Dax was leading the charge up the stairs, and the pirates surged forward with a roar.

When Nate broke topside again, it was into a world of complete pandemonium. Gun smoke mingled with the fog as navy sailors and pirates alike fired on each other, and there was fresh blood on the *Southern Echo*'s deck. Swords clanged and rasped, and men and women screamed with bloodlust and pain. A few pirates had already gone down, but there were more navy sailors lying dead on the deck.

Arani's plan had worked, and they had taken the navy by surprise.

Nate kept to the edges of the fight, less by choice and more by his inability to handle a sword well enough to cut his way into the thick of the fighting. A grim navy sailor appeared before him, and their swords traded blows. The impact of steel on steel rattled Nate's teeth, but he tightened his grip on his cutlass and pushed back. His opponent grabbed his arm, and Nate snatched at the navy sailor's sleeve. They grappled and heaved against each other, and Nate could feel that he was outmatched in a contest of raw strength. His boots skidded on the deck as the navy sailor forced him back. Nate bared his teeth and tried to find his footing before the sailor could knock him down. Then his attacker screamed in pain, and he released his hold. Startled, Nate jumped back to see the tip of a cutlass poking through the sailor's gut. The blade was wrenched back with a sickening squelch, leaving a hole and a rush of blood in its wake. The sailor fell to the deck, and Xander gave Nate a quick salute with his bloody sword before rushing off, already looking for another kill.

Before Nate could recover himself, Dax flashed past him, and Nate saw the quartermaster clench his hand and drop a sailor with his Skill as she pointed her pistol at him. Her skin went pale and she clutched at her chest before she went down and did not rise again.

Nate allowed himself one deep breath, and then he plunged back into the fray.

He somehow found himself fighting alongside Arani not long after that, near the stern of the *Southern Echo*. The captain was handling two attackers to Nate's one, but the numbers were starting to tip in favor of the pirates. Arani knew it, and there was triumph on her face as she pushed one of the navy sailors back and slashed at the other. She kept glancing up, though, and Nate knew that she was watching the sniper she'd posted in the crow's nest.

The sniper was meant to find and stop the Highwinds. The *Southern Echo* was the faster ship, and if they could get the wind back, they had a chance. As Nate glanced up, however, he felt his heart sink.

The sniper was on his fourth rifle out of the pre-loaded six guns up there with him, but he had not managed to shoot the Highwinds yet. As the sniper fired off another shot, Nate used his Skill to tracked the path of the bullet as it sliced through the air, but a sudden strong gust from the Highwinds pushed the bullet aside, and it missed its mark. The sniper reached for the next rifle, but before he could get the shot off, a bullet from the navy ship slammed into his heart, and he fell. His body crashed into the deck below with a sickening thud, and the triumph in Arani's eyes faded away.

With a snarl, the pirate captain drove her sword through the gut of one of her attackers, and then pushed the other one violently away before turning on the man Nate fought. Her sword bit into his side, and he fell back, giving Nate and Arani a brief moment of respite.

"We have to break the Highwinds," Arani growled, more to herself than to Nate, but he knew she was right. The *Southern Echo* was not going anywhere without full sails. Arani cast a wild look across the battle and focused on the first decent shooter she found. "Xander!" she called, and the Grayvoice finished off his opponent before acknowledging her. "Get up there and take out those Highwinds!"

"Aye, Captain," Xander called back. He ran across the blood-slicked deck, jumping over the bodies of navy sailors and pirates alike as he made for the ladder that would take him up to the crow's nest.

Nate did not think that Xander would have any better luck than the first sniper, and he would be an easy target for the navy's pistols and rifles as he scaled the ladder. Most of the guns had already been fired at the beginning of the fight, but if anyone had reloaded, the Grayvoice was in trouble. Arani had to know that. They needed a different plan if they were going to take out the Highwinds.

Arani did not seem to have one. She kept fighting, even as more sailors swarmed over from the navy ship, and the battle began to turn against the pirates. There had been more pirates than navy sailors to start, but the navy was far better trained in combat, and more and more pirates were falling to the deck, dead or too injured to continue. Nate saw Marcus take a nasty slash across his arm before Eric lunged in to help, and Ethan the rigger was on the deck with blood spilling out of a deep gash in his leg.

In a moment of brutal clarity, Nate understood that they were not going to win this fight.

His captain did not seem willing to acknowledge that, even as her crew fell around her. Nate could not fathom why until one of the naval officers came to engage Arani directly.

Nate was fighting another sailor, but he had a clear view of Arani and the officer as they crossed swords. The blows they traded were quick and angry, each of them going for the kill, but neither finding the upper hand. Arani had been in the battle longer, however, and she finally started to flag as her endurance wore away.

The officer sensed his advantage, and he pressed in with a hard stab of his sword. Arani parried the attack, but the officer landed a savage kick to her middle that sent her stumbling backwards. She hit the crates stacked in front of the navigation room and fell, landing squarely on the dragon hidden beneath the canvas. A deep growl came from the creature as the entire bundle shifted beneath her, and Nate saw something in Arani's eyes that he had never seen before: panic. She scrambled to her feet, and in her haste pulled part of the canvas with her, revealing the snout and bared fangs of the black mimic. Arani flipped the canvas back in place as quickly as she could, but it was too late.

The officer who'd been attacking her halted, his gaze snagged on the dragon as it hissed its displeasure before succumbing to the sleeping draught again, and Nate's own opponent stopped at the sound and turned to stare. Nate cut the woman down before she could recover. He looked up in time to see Arani bare her own teeth, her panic giving way to absolute rage. She launched herself at the naval officer, slashing viciously at him. He fell back, his movements slowed by surprise, but he blocked Arani's attacks with enough skill for Nate to know that Arani would not break through his defense. He knew it as much as he knew that she would not let that dragon go, and would fight to the death to keep it. Not just her death, though. Everyone's, from Dax, Rori and Novachak to Marcus, Eric, Xander, and even Jim Greenroot. They'd all perish before Arani let anyone take Mordanti's legacy from her.

Nate looked across the deck to the navy ship, and spotted two people standing apart from the others, arms raised and seemingly oblivious to the battle that raged on the *Southern Echo*. The wind swirled about the two Highwinds, bent entirely to their wills to keep both ships in place. If they fell, the wind would return. Nate glanced up at the limp sails above him, and he knew that there was only one way the *Southern Echo* came away from this fight, and took everyone he cared about with her. Nate knew what he had to do.

It was a terrible, desperate idea, but it was the only one he had.

His gaze snagged on Rori as he turned to go, and their eyes locked for a moment. Blood was smeared across her forehead and stained her shirt, but she was still standing, and Nate intended to keep it that way.

Get yourself that ship, he thought as he looked at her.

She frowned and looked like she would start towards him, but another sailor closed in, and Rori whipped up her cutlass to block the attack. She grit her teeth, and Nate turned away. He ran for the stairs that would take him up to the poop deck. A hand caught him before he hit the first step.

"Where are you going?" Arani snarled. Her eyes were wild from the battle, and desperation rolled off of her in waves.

"To do what you need me to," Nate said. "I'm going to use my Skill one more time."

Arani blinked.

Nate bared his teeth at her in a bitter smile. "It made no difference in the end, if I was with the empire or with you. We Skilled are all just tools, aren't we? So I'm going to do what you need me to, but you'd better let the rest of them decide for themselves, like you promised."

Anger and determination swirled through Nate as he looked past Arani to the fighting crews. He picked out

Rori once more, still alive and struggling, and beyond her, Dax helping Eric defend Marcus. Novachak was holding his own, but Xander was halfway up to the crows's nest, completely vulnerable to an attack. More pirates were falling to the deck, dead and dying. Nate had to go. He looked back at the pirate captain one last time. Her mouth was hanging open in shock, and she seemed to be at a total loss for words.

Nate was not. "My life for the *Southern Echo*," he said, placing his hand over his heart in a mock salute. Then he ripped his arm free and scrambled up the steps to the poop deck.

The raised level put him just above the main deck of the navy ship, and Nate allowed himself to hesitate just long enough to brace his feet and gather his strength. *Don't think,* he told himself. *Just go. Now!*

Nate pushed off as hard as he could and exploded forward in a wild sprint. He leapt up on the railing and launched himself across the narrow gap between the ships. He barely saw the flash of water beneath him before he hit the railing of the navy ship, the wood bruising his ribs and driving the breath from his lungs. Nate clawed at the railing and pulled himself over. He rolled on to the deck of the navy ship, the wood cool and unfamiliar beneath his hands, and then he shot to his feet, cutlass drawn and his Skill tracing out the shape of the wind around him.

He'd caught the two navy sailors in front of him completely by surprise, and that was the only thing that let him swing his sword into the hip of the first man. The blade bit deep and the man went down howling. The second one recovered enough to block Nate's next attack, and he managed to scrape his sword against Nate's arm, but Nate barely felt the pain as he swung his own weapon around again. This time, he hit the sailor in the shoulder, hard enough to send the man sprawling, and then Nate was off, running as fast as he could across the deck to where the two Highwinds stood, using their combined magic to hold the wind back and keep the *Southern Echo* locked in place.

Someone shouted at Nate as he raced across the navy ship, and he felt the squeeze in the air as a gun prepared to fire. Nate dove to the side, and a bullet ripped through the place where his chest had been less than a moment earlier. He dodged around another navy sailor, just barely getting his sword up in time to turn aside a blow that would have taken his arm off. Nate dropped his cutlass under the force of the hit, but he could not go back for it. He kept running and ripped out the dagger on his belt. The Highwinds were just ahead of him, both facing away as they worked the wind and kept the *Southern Echo* and his friends' lives locked in the navy's grasp, but the closer one heard him coming.

Time seemed to slow for Nate as she turned to face him. He saw her eyes widen as he barreled towards her, but she recovered and swung one of her arms around in a vicious slice. Nate sensed the wind gather behind her and coalesce into a sharp arch as she launched it at him in a blazing gust. He threw himself into a forward roll, diving clean under the hard burst of wind. As he came back to his feet, he kept running, and hurled his dagger as hard as he could. The blade somersaulted through the air before embedding itself in the Highwind's shoulder. She shrieked in pain and clutched at the injury. Then Nate was past her, and he barreled into the other Highwind's back, tackling the man to the deck. They struggled together for a moment, but Nate had the upper hand, and he pinned the male Highwind beneath him, pressing his face into the deck and twisting his arms behind his back.

There was a sudden lull as the Highwinds' forced air currents were released.

And then the true wind came with a roar.

It was strong enough to send both ships lurching, although the *Southern Echo* was angled to catch more of it. Her sails filled and the pirate ship leapt forward, tugging the tethered navy ship off kilter. Nate heard the surprised shouts of outrage from the naval officers, and those that were aboard the frigate redoubled their efforts to try to get to the pirate ship before it broke free. A battle cry went up from the *Southern Echo*, and though Nate could not see it, he imagined Arani and Dax and the others surging forward, pushing the naval crew back and cutting the lines that bound the ships together.

A cannon fired from one of the swivel guns on the *Southern Echo*'s main deck, and the ball ripped into the mainmast of the navy ship, splintering the massive tower. Nate ducked his head against the shower of wood that rained down around him, feeling a large piece batter across his shoulders before falling away. When he looked up again, the damaged mast swayed dangerously, and for a moment, Nate was certain that it would fall and crush him. Then the wind toppled it backwards, over the starboard side of the ship and into the sea. There were cheers from the pirate ship and more shouting and screaming, and then two navy sailors had Nate's arms locked in theirs, and they pulled him kicking off of the male Highwind.

Nate continued to struggle, but his eyes were locked on the sails of the *Southern Echo* as the ship began to pull away. She was the faster of the two, and with the mainmast of the navy ship down, she could get away. She had to.

"Cannons at the ready!" a navy officer screamed. "Sink that godsdamned ship *now*."

Nate thrashed against his captors but they held him fast.

"Ready," the officer snarled, "and fi—"

The navy ship rocked dangerously as a massive swell of water leapt up between it and the *Southern Echo*, pulled from nowhere by one person's magic and will.

Nate had just enough time to feel a flash of triumphant pride for Rori before the deck pitched sideways under his feet, and his stomach performed several uncomfortable maneuvers as the wave pushed the two ships apart. Nate glimpsed the unsteady weave of the *Southern Echo*'s masts as she fought against capsizing, and then he was clinging hard to a bit of rigging as the navy ship rose up on to the crest of the wave. The gods above only knew how the frigate did not roll into the water. It scraped past the top of the wave and fell down the other side, pitching violently the other way.

Screams of fear ripped across the ship as another wave came and threw it back into the air, and Nate heard the captain frantically trying to get the navy sailors to turn the rudder and keep the ship from being broadsided by the swells. They fought hard for control, and water crashed on to the navy ship's deck three times before the worst was over. By the time the waves had calmed and the ship was no longer threatening to capsize, the *Southern Echo* had disappeared into the very same fog the navy ship had used to disguise its own approach.

"Highwinds," the captain roared, "clear this at once!"

The female Highwind whimpered as she moved to obey. She only had use of her uninjured arm, and her gusts were sporadic. The male Highwind pushed her aside and sent out a spinning wind that cleared away the immediate fog, but the *Southern Echo* was not revealed. He launched a few violent gusts off the side of the frigate, but to no avail. The pirate ship was gone.

Nate released a long sigh of relief. He did not fight this time when the navy sailors grabbed him and shoved him forward, nearly sending him sprawling across the deck.

"Got this one, Captain," one of his captors called.

The officer turned a harsh glare on Nate, which only intensified when he saw the Lowwind tattoo on his brow. But before he could say anything, the male Highwind turned around, and he and Nate both stuttered to a surprised halt as they recognized each other.

"Nathaniel?" Sebastian blurted incredulously.

Nate had never seen his brother so shocked before. That look of horrified surprise was well worth the beating the navy sailors gave Nate before they locked him in a cell below deck.

CHAPTER TWENTY-THREE

The Vote

AFTER THE INITIAL RUSH and the terrifying struggle against the waves called up by Rori at the *Southern Echo*'s stern, the ship raced clear away from the frigate, her sails stretched taut. Iris stared up at those sails, watching them carry her and her crew to safety on the winds Nate had freed. They weren't clear of the danger yet, but now they had a chance, thanks to him.

Iris could not believe that the boy had taken down two Highwinds by himself, let alone gone over to the navy ship to begin with. But the winds were back, and Nate was gone.

Iris listened to the groans and soft voices of the battered crew picking themselves and their wounded fellows up. Hands had already taken up the necessary tasks to keep the sails full and the ship moving forward, but it was a very small part of the crew that had come through the fight unscathed. Many others were injured, some lightly and others terribly, to the point where Iris feared they may not survive the night. And the rest...

The rest lay dead on the *Southern Echo*'s deck, the dryad wood stained dark with their blood. Fallen navy sailors were intermingled with Iris's dead crew, left behind by the survivors who had dove into the water and swam back to the frigate once they'd realized the pirate ship was escaping. Iris supposed she should see all of the dead returned to the sea, although she did not intend to give the same treatment to the navy sailors as her fallen crew. They'd paid the highest price for the freedom of the *Southern Echo*. So many of them were gone.

And one had been left behind.

Iris picked her way over the deck and tried not to think about that. It would have been impossible even if Rori had not come stumbling across her path, her face smeared with blood and one arm hanging limply at her side. She looked at Iris with wide, wild eyes as the wind whipped her hair about.

"Where is he?" Rori asked, so quietly that Iris almost did not hear the words.

There was only one person Rori could be asking about, and from the Goodtide's frantic gaze, Iris had the sense that she already knew the answer.

Iris shook her head.

Rori began to cry. They were silent tears, but they were thick and rolled down her cheeks to drip off of her chin. She fell to her knees on the deck with a heavy thud and began to shake.

Iris did not know what to do in that moment. She was grateful when Marcus and Eric came hobbling over, both of them bruised and bloodied by the fight, but alive. Between the two of them, Eric had suffered the lesser injuries, and he crouched down next to Rori and put his hand on her arm. Rori turned her face into his shoulder and began to sob in earnest, and Marcus stepped closer to rest his hand on Rori's back.

"Captain?" a familiar voice said from behind Iris.

Relief flooded through her as she turned to see Dax, still standing and wonderfully alive. For a moment, the quartermaster's eyes went soft as he gazed back at Iris, and a small, private moment passed between them in the midst of all that loss. But there was work to be done, and Dax straightened up.

"We're taking the official count of the dead," he informed her, "and Mr. Novachak intends to care for the worst of the wounded himself."

He paused, and Iris nodded for him to continue.

"Do we have our next heading?" the quartermaster asked softly.

"We do," Iris said grimly. "We keep on, and get ourselves clear of the danger before turning for Spider's Nest."

A choking sound came from the deck, and Iris glanced back to see Rori trying unsuccessfully to push herself to her feet. Eric steadied her as best he could, but the young woman tried to pull free of his grip, mistaking the help for an attempt to hold her back.

"We have to turn around," Rori breathed. "We can't leave him with the navy."

Eric and Marcus did not say a word, but they both looked at Iris with the faintest glimmer of hope in their eyes.

Truly, being a captain was a heavy burden to bear.

"Nate made a choice," Iris said quietly. "We owe him our lives for that, but we can't go back."

Eric sighed quietly and Marcus dropped his eyes to the deck, but Rori's face twisted with open anger.

"You *coward*," the Goodtide snarled.

That caught the attention of several others, including Xander Grayvoice as he descended from the crow's nest, looking frazzled after dealing with the sudden reappearance of the strong sea winds and the surging of the waves Rori had called up. He took in Rori's distress before crossing his arms and fixing Iris with an alarmed look. "What happened?" he asked.

"Nate went over to the navy ship," Rori said in a rush before Iris could answer. "We left him behind."

Xander cut his gaze to Rori for a long moment before looking back to Iris. "We *are* leaving, right?" he asked quietly.

"Yes," Iris said.

"Good," Xander said.

Eric, Marcus, and Rori all glanced at the Grayvoice sharply. The two Darkbends looked at him in shock. Rori looked at him with raw fury.

"He saved us!" she spat.

"Maybe," Xander said mildly, "but more importantly, *we* still have *that*." Xander gestured to the stern of the ship, where the black mimic slept, still concealed by the crates and sheet of canvas. "We can't give that up for one person. Right, Captain?" He looked to her expectantly, and the eyes of everyone who had stopped to watch the exchange followed.

Iris took a slow breath. "If we go back, we'll lose everything," she said, fighting for calm under Rori's anguished stare. "That frigate still has its starboard cannons. It would tear the *Southern Echo* to splinters before we could ever get close enough to try to save Nate."

"He might not even be alive anymore," Xander quipped.

Rori rounded on him. "He's a wind worker," she snarled. "They wouldn't kill a wind worker."

To Iris, it sounded like Rori was trying to convince herself as much as she was Xander.

The Grayvoice, however, scowled and shook his head. "He's the Nowind. They have no use for him. You know that."

"Stop," Eric said, his voice a low growl.

"You going to tell me I'm wrong?" Xander said, taking a step forward. Eric may have been the taller man, but Xander was broader and stronger, and both of them knew that. "He's not worth it."

"He's our friend," Marcus said quietly.

"We've all lost friends before," Xander snapped. "What's one more when we have a legendary treasure in front of us?" He turned to Iris before anyone had the chance to say another word. "I'm with you, Captain," he said, and Iris could not remember ever hearing Xander Grayvoice sound so earnest. A few murmurs of agreement went up around him.

Iris felt very, very cold as she saw who her strongest supporters were in the wake of the battle with the navy ship. There were so few of them, and her skin crawled under their wild, hungry gazes. The rest of the crew did not protest, but they averted their eyes.

This was not at all how she had imagined it would be to follow Mordanti's legacy. Her crew was supposed to share in her joy and triumph, not feel like they could not even look at her.

Iris felt her heart twist.

Xander left a moment later, taking many of the onlookers with him. Their strides were somber and grim. Iris stood gazing after them, very aware that Rori, Marcus, Eric, and Dax were all staring at her now. With a quiet sigh, Iris turned to Rori first.

Fresh tears were spilling down the Goodtide's cheeks, more from fury than sadness. "You betrayed us," Rori whispered, but the words hit Iris like a blow.

She narrowed her eyes at the tide worker. "I did no such thing," Iris said quietly, putting a hard edge into her voice. "It was Nate's choice."

"But you brought him here." Rori took a step forward, shrugging off Eric's hand. "You brought all of us here, and you promised we would have a choice, but then you made him... you made *me*..." Rori broke off, shuddering. "I swore I'd never use my Skill again, and you knew that," she breathed.

Iris bristled, but any protests she might have spoken in her own defense withered under Rori's accusing stare. For the first time in a very long time, Iris was the first one to look away.

"And you let her do it," Rori said as she rounded on Dax. "You're supposed to represent the crew. *All* of us. Just because you hide your tattoo doesn't mean you can pretend you're any different from the rest of us Skilled."

Iris glanced at the quartermaster, and saw that he was slack-jawed and staring. She wasn't sure that it was fair of Rori to say that to Dax. He'd warned Iris, after all, and she'd ignored him. It had been her choices and her orders, and she'd pushed them forward no matter what anyone around her had said.

That was not what a good captain did.

When Iris looked back to Rori, she saw that the Goodtide had already turned away and started across the deck. Marcus and Eric gave Iris one last lingering look before they both followed her, leaving Iris with Dax by her side and her heart heavy in her chest.

HOURS LATER, CLEAR OF the fog and miles away from the naval frigate, Iris surveyed her beloved, battered ship.

The *Southern Echo*'s deck was dark with blood that needed to be scrubbed away. Her sides were splintered and holed from the few cannon shots the frigate had managed to get off, and they needed patching. And she rode lighter in the water with the lost lives of her crew, but they were finally safe.

Iris was tired, but she could not let herself rest. Not yet. She called a meeting of the surviving crew.

They'd had time to see the dead returned to the sea and tend to the wounded by then. Rough bandages adorned nearly everyone as they slowly gathered on the main deck, called up from their tasks and private mournings. They looked at Iris with exhausted eyes, but they still came, and they listened willingly as she began to speak.

"We lost a lot of good people today," Iris said, and she barely had to raise her voice to carry, the crew was so quiet. "It's thanks to them that we came through that fight alive."

Off to the side, Iris spotted Rori leaning heavily on the ship's railing, holding Luken close to her heart. The bird was the only one who seemed to have come through the fight unscathed, and he chirped softly in Rori's arms, perhaps responding to the intensity of the navigator's grief. Marcus and Eric stood with her, sharing her pain. Xander, however, was on the other side of the ship, with the riggers and some of the gunners.

"Because of their sacrifice, we have a choice before us." Iris hesitated here, a sour taste coming into her mouth. "A better captain would have given you this choice days ago, when we learned what truly lay ahead of us. I am sorry that I allowed myself to fail you in that regard."

The crew shifted, some of them glaring darkly at the deck beneath their feet, but others softened their gazes and looked at Iris with the familiar trust they'd shown her before. She took encouragement from them.

"As we stand now," Iris said, "we have our ship, and we have Mordanti's treasure map, and we have a dragon that holds the fire in its breast that will let us see this journey to its end. But we also have someone that we've left behind. I've gone long enough now ignoring your wants in favor of my own. You are free men and women, and you put your faith in me to see you through everything, and I need to return that trust."

Iris spread her arms and gestured to the two empty crates set up near her. They flanked the murmuring dragon still chained to the deck, which was more alert now than it had ever been since they'd taken it from the volcanic island. Iris had personally checked the binding around its muzzle that kept its jaws closed and deadly flames locked away, but she felt its molten gaze on her back as she addressed the crew.

"We have a choice before us," Iris said. She gestured to the crate on her right, which bore a crude charcoal scribble that roughly resembled the black dragon behind her. "We could stay the course, repair and properly stock the ship with plenty of supplies and sleeping draught for the dragon, and then sail to the end of Mordanti's map, find her lost treasure, and sear our names into history."

A hungry gleam came into several people's eyes. It was muted by their exhaustion, but it was there, bright and burning.

Iris lowered her arm and looked to the crate on her left. This one was plain and unmarked, dull compared to its dragon-branded fellow. "Or," she said, "we could abandon this quest, and sail back into the arms of the navy, in a desperate attempt to free the one we had to leave behind. Nate is a wind worker, and they won't kill a wind worker, no matter how strong or weak his Skill." A flicker of movement caught Iris's eye as Rori and the two Darkbends turned their heads to look across the ship at Xander. The Grayvoice folded his arms and raised his chin, refusing to be chastised. "If the navy catches us," Iris continued, "we won't be able to escape this time, and they'll see us hanged for our crimes against the Solkyrian Empire." She paused, hating the taste of the next words on her tongue. "And if we go back, we need to release the dragon. We don't have enough sleeping draught to see us back to that ship and then beyond, should by some miracle we survive."

Iris very purposely did not look at Rori or Dax or the other Skill-marked members of her crew as she said this, instead focusing on those with the treasure-hungry gleams in their eyes. She drew a deep breath before continuing.

"As I said, I intend to let you make this choice. Cast your vote as your heart tells you." She paused once more as Nikolai Novachak came forward and handed her a scrap of colored silk torn from the Coral Chain flag they'd flown earlier. With her lot delivered, he stepped back to hold the fabric scraps between the two crates, ready to hand them off to each crew member as they came forward to cast their votes in a much more formal process than their usual method of raising hands. Iris felt the occasion merited the ceremony.

"If you'll permit me," she said, "I would cast mine first, so you all know my heart."

A few people exchanged glances, but no one protested.

Iris nodded her thanks, and then turned and threw her scrap of pink silk into her chosen crate without another moment of hesitation. She heard the murmurs from the crew that came in the wake of her public decision, but she'd expected as much, and she did not turn around. Instead, she stood before the black mimic, closer than Dax would have told her was wise, and gazed steadily at the beast, which had begun to rouse itself once again. The dragon lifted its head the little that it could, and blinked its molten gold eyes at her. They locked their gazes as the crew came forward and slowly determined both of their fates.

She thought about Nate as her crew cast their votes in a steady stream. She thought about what he'd said to her during the battle.

He'd said there was no real difference between her and the Solkyrian Empire. No difference between a life of freedom, and one spent yolked and hobbled by an unforgiving ruler. It set her blood to seething the more she thought about it, and for a moment, her eyes left those of the dragon to find the black flag that snapped in the breeze off the stern of the ship, the one that bore her personal emblem of a dragon closing its jaws on the sun.

My life for the Southern Echo, Nate had said.

Mine too, Iris thought.

The sun had nearly set by the time the full crew had voted, and everything was painted in orange light as Dax came forward to count the vote. With a shuddering breath, Iris turned to see what her crew had decided.

As it turned out, Dax didn't need to do much counting at all. One crate had several scraps of colored fabric inside of it, but the other held a pile, and the decision was clear.

Iris breathed a sigh of relief.

They'd voted with her once more.

Chapter Twenty-four

Chosen Fate

ONE OF NATE'S EYES was swollen shut and the pain in his ribs had subsided to a rolling ache by the time Sebastian came to see him. The lack of swagger in his brother's step surprised Nate, and it was strange to see Sebastian keep his eyes lowered and speak softly when he informed the guard that their commanding officer had ordered him to talk to Nate. The guard waved Sebastian on with undisguised impatience, and the Highwind offered the man a shallow bow before slipping past him. As soon as Sebastian was clear, he pulled the arrogance back into his saunter and drew himself up to his full height as he approached the cell. It did not disguise the dark rings under Sebastian's eyes, or the tired slope of his shoulders, or the other signs of Skill exhaustion that Nate could now recognize at a glance.

Nate leaned against the wooden bars and thought that this was one of the sadder things he had seen lately. It gave him a small amount of satisfaction to know that his brother's posturing no longer made him feel small, but Nate was mostly surprised by how much he pitied the man.

Sebastian seemed to realize it, too. A frown briefly flickered across his brow before he schooled his expression back to superiority. He actually tilted his head back a little so he could look down his nose at

Nate before speaking, and Nate could have sworn that his brother had been taller. Had Nate grown in his time on the *Southern Echo*, or had he simply learned to stand up straight?

"I always knew you would be a complete disgrace to our family," Sebastian said. "But you've truly outdone yourself with this betrayal to the empire, Nowind."

The old nickname still made Nate grimace a little, but a strange calm quickly washed away any shame he felt. Nate had tracked dragons and broken two Highwinds' holds on the wind with nothing more than his Skill and his body. Sebastian could not take that away.

"There's no need to pretend that we're still family," Nate said. "We haven't shared a name in a long time, and you've been desperate to distance yourself from me for years now." Nate glanced at the guard, who showed no interest in the words traded between two wind workers, even if one was a prisoner and the other a fellow navy sailor. But *fellow* was too strong a word, Nate realized. "You won't win any favor here by stepping on me," he told Sebastian. "You're too far beneath everyone else for that to work."

Sebastian flushed angrily. "You're beneath us all," he said. "You think that's changed because you ran away like a coward and played at being a pirate?" A cruel gleam came into his eyes. "Could you even help them sail, or were you so worthless that they threw you over to this ship so they could get away? Maybe they saw an easy way to rid themselves of you, Nowind."

"It would've been easier just to gut me and throw me into the sea than pick a fight with a navy ship," Nate remarked. He smiled tiredly at his brother. "And I've done more with my Skill over the last few weeks than you could ever hope to do in your entire life. I've seen more wonders of this world than you ever will, sailing back and forth on a naval patrol boat. Keep your Highwind life, Sebastian. Even if mine ends on the gallows in Sunthrone City, I wouldn't trade it for yours."

It only surprised Nate a little to realize that he meant what he'd said. He was returning to Solkyria after all, and he was going to die there, but he did so knowing that he'd saved the lives of his friends with the wind in his face and the open sky over his head, and it was a fate he had chosen for himself.

Sebastian seemed at a loss for what to say next. He stared at Nate in silence, as though waiting for Nate to break and admit that he was lying. No, that was exactly what he was doing. He'd used this same tactic throughout their early lives, when they'd shared time at the wind working academy and Nate had tried to pretend that his Skill was stronger than it was, that he could keep up with his older brother. Before sailing on the *Southern Echo*, it would have worked. Nate would have let Sebastian's intricate Highwind tattoo flood his vision, and his own insecurities would have broken him to pieces.

Now, he simply looked at his brother's Skill mark and thought about Rori. He would have liked to see her at the helm of a beautiful ship called *Tide Song*. He realized that nothing was stopping him from imagining it, and the idea brought a flicker of warmth to his chest. Even if she kept on believing that it was a dream meant for someone else, Nate could think of her as the Goodtide captain of a ship of her own, and nothing would spoil that for him until the day he swung from the gallows and never had another thought again. He'd keep that close to his heart, the idea of Rori getting her own ship, of Marcus and Eric finding a home in Autania, of Xander maybe learning to let go of his obsession and hate as Nate had learned to do, and all of them staying far away from Solkyria.

"You're going to be executed, you know," Sebastian said. "They know you served those pirates willingly. Your Skill won't save you from a hanging."

"I was just thinking about that," Nate agreed.

Surprise furrowed Sebastian's brow. "How can you be so calm about this?"

Nate shrugged. "It's not something you'd understand."

Some anger returned to his brother's expression, but confusion continued to win out. "You're going to die, Nathaniel."

Nate pushed off from the bars of the cell and moved to the solitary bench built into the wall that would serve as both a seat and a bed for the duration of the voyage. He eased himself down and relaxed against the hull of the ship behind him. It lacked the steady warmth of the *Southern Echo*'s dryad wood, but Nate shut his eyes anyway and clasped his hands behind his head.

Sebastian curled his hands around the wooden bars. "If you gave the empire information about the pirates you sailed with, they may show mercy and let you live out the rest of your life in the mines."

Nate gave a dry laugh. "You think that's mercy?"

"You'd be alive."

Nate tilted his head and regarded his brother for a moment. "I was right," he finally said. "You don't understand."

The Highwind's expression darkened, but he made a visible effort to control his temper, which was a new phenomenon to Nate. "That pirate ship had something on its deck," Sebastian said, and Nate could hear the growl of reluctance in his voice. "Lieutenant Yellowshore swears it was a dragon."

Nate kept his face and his voice calm, but his heart began to pound in his chest. "Is that why you're here?" he asked. "Because someone says they saw something strange in the heat of battle? I'm hurt, Seb. I thought you just wanted to visit with your little brother."

Sebastian scowled, and Nate did everything he could to keep the panicked questions that raced across his mind from showing on his face.

Would the navy go after the *Southern Echo* if they knew about the black mimic? What would happen to everyone if they found the pirate ship? Did the empire believe in or even care about Mordanti's treasure map?

He calmed a little when he realized it did not matter.

The *Southern Echo* was long gone, and once Arani had the ship repaired and restocked, she'd vanish into the south, chasing down the legend. She was too clever to be caught by the navy twice, and with Rori willingly using her Skill once more, they could get away from anything. Nate was sure of that.

"Did they have a dragon?" Sebastian asked. He sounded like he did not know what he wanted Nate's answer to be.

"I think we're both a little old for fairy tales," Nate said.

A moment passed, and then another, and then Sebastian scoffed and turned away. Nate watched his brother swagger off, until he passed the guard again, at which point he dropped his head and shoulders and made himself small before the other man. Nate remembered being intensely jealous of his brother and his position with the navy not so long ago, and he couldn't bring himself to laugh.

After that, Nate did not have much of anything to do, except wait and listen to the snatches of orders he heard from the naval officers as the sailors repaired the ship as best they could before attempting the journey back to Solkyria. The *Southern Echo* had done serious damage to the frigate's port side, and there was a real danger of the hold flooding if they did not patch it up. Nate was glad to be imprisoned on the starboard side of the ship, both because it kept him clear of the spray of the waves as they lapped against the damaged hull, and because it saved him from the attention of the navy sailors when they came to work on his level. They patched over as much of the hull as they could with bits of spare wood and sealed the gaps with hot tar. It was shoddy work but would hold long enough to bring the ship back to land, where they could make repairs in earnest. In spite of the navy sailors' discipline, however, it was long work, and the sun had set by the time they'd finished with the holes in the hull. There was nothing to be done for the destroyed mast, so it was left to the sea as the ship turned north.

They fed Nate at some point by throwing a bit of hardtack into his cell. Nate picked it up and quietly gnawed at it, and knew better than to ask for water to wash it down. He may have been able to finally look his brother in the eye, but Nate was still marked by a Skill, and he knew that if he drew the attention of the unmarked sailors, he'd be inviting another beating. They wouldn't hold back now that he was a criminal and traitor to the empire. So Nate stayed quiet on the bench in his cell, and the worst he had to deal with were the couple of sailors who spat at him when their work brought them past his little prison.

At the eleventh bell, a relief for the guard outside of Nate's cell came and took up the post. The man settled into his seat with a mug of ale and a small book that he read by the light of the lantern hanging next to him, and he never once looked at the cell.

Nate lay down on the bench and tried to sleep, but he felt the rock of the unfamiliar ship and missed his hammock on the *Southern Echo*. He sighed softly into the dark and let his thoughts drift back to Rori, and then to Marcus and Eric, and then on to Xander and Dax and Novachak and Arani and all of the others. He imagined them living their new lives once they'd found the treasure.

A heavy thud startled him out of his thoughts.

He sat up to see the guard's chair standing empty some distance away. It took a moment for Nate to pick out the shape of the guard lying on the deck next to it, breathing but otherwise completely still. He'd fallen asleep, and pitched out of his chair.

That man is a remarkably sound sleeper, Nate thought.

Then he saw a flicker of movement beyond the guard, and three people crept silently out of the shadows.

Alarmed, Nate rose to his feet as the leader of the small group stooped down to the fallen guard's body. The gentle clink of keys on a ring sounded as the leader straightened again. Nate was getting ready to scream his throat bloody and wake the whole ship when something flittered past the lantern and landed with a rustle of wings on the horizontal bar of the cell. Brilliant blue feathers flashed in the dim light, and a soft chirp came from the bird.

"Luken?" Nate asked in disbelief.

Someone shushed him, and Nate looked up to see that the leader of the group had begun to fit the keys into the lock on his cell. A soft click came, and then the door swung open and the leader was gesturing him forward.

"Quick and quiet, now," the leader whispered, and Nate recognized her voice.

"Captain Arani?" he murmured as he came forward. She shushed him again and waved him on.

Stepping as lightly as he could, Nate followed Arani back to the fallen guard. As they drew closer to the two people waiting in the shadows, he recognized Dax and Jim Greenroot, who gave Nate a curt nod before turning to the senior pirates for his next orders. Arani paused next to Dax, her sword drawn as she watched him expectantly. The quartermaster had his hands raised, one over the fallen guard and the other pointed deeper into the navy ship, and he was frowning hard with concentration. After a moment, the quartermaster nodded, and Arani led the way to the stairs that would take them to the gun deck. Jim followed with Nate close behind, and Dax brought up the rear.

As soon as they were on the gun deck, Arani moved to the starboard side and crept her way along the wall. Jim did the same, and Nate followed them to a cannon that had been pushed back from its open gunport. Arani sheathed her sword before climbing out of the opening. She disappeared over the edge.

"Your turn," Jim whispered as he gave Nate a firm push forward. "Be quick about it, and don't fall."

Nate worried that was easier said than done, but there was a rope leading down from the edge of the gunport, and he managed to get outside and lower himself down. Lights from the navy ship glowed above him, and Nate felt a surge of fear at the thought of someone looking over the side of the ship and seeing him shimmying down a rope. It was drowned out by the thrill he felt at the cool night breeze against his skin, and the knowledge that he wasn't dreaming; they had come back for him.

Nate made it down to the waterline and found a rowboat waiting to receive him. No sooner was the boat wobbling under his weight than someone had crushed their arms around him, driving the breath from his chest.

"Don't you *ever*," Rori breathed into his ear, "do something like that again."

"I'll try," Nate said, and he was glad that it was too dark for the others to see the foolish smile that plastered itself across his face.

Jim and Dax came down to the boat without trouble, and Luken alighted on Rori's shoulder as the gunner and the quartermaster picked up the oars and began to row away from the navy ship. Nate heard Rori take a deep breath, and then there was a gentle wave beneath them, carrying them away from the frigate, adding to the speed that Dax and Jim's strength lent to the oars. Nate cast a worried look at Rori, but she was breathing evenly as she called up the soft current. Soon, the naval frigate was a cluster of bright lights in the dark, and Nate's eyes began to adjust to the faint moonlight that came through the cloud cover. He picked out the dark shape of the *Southern Echo* waiting for them, and he could have wept with relief.

"Thank you," he said to the pirates around him.

"You're one of us," Arani said, "and we don't leave our own behind. I won't forget that ever again." She leaned forward and clapped him on the shoulder. "But you compare me to that heathen beast you call an emperor one more time, and I'll have you scraping barnacles off the keel for a year."

Nate smiled as he said, "Aye, Captain."

The familiar sounds of the *Southern Echo* filled Nate's ears as they climbed aboard the ship and brought up the rowboat. Marcus and Eric were there immediately to greet him with hugs as fierce as Rori's, and to slap him on the back with unbridled joy. Several others patted his shoulders and welcomed him back to the ship and the crew, and Novachak came forward to say, "You're mad, my boy, but the frost take me if I've ever met anyone as brave as you."

Nate laughed, and felt his heart swell as he looked around at the faces of the crew.

His crew.

"All right," Arani called, "wind's at our backs and the night's giving us cover. Let's away before that frigate decides to come find us."

Nate ran to help with the sails, and before long, the *Southern Echo* was racing away, the lights from the frigate disappearing over the horizon. When they were clear and away, pirates started coming up to Nate to demand to know what, exactly, he had done to break the navy's hold on them. Nate shared the story, sheepishly at first, but the crew joked and teased the details out of him, and he was laughing along with them by the time he was done.

That was when he noticed that a few of the crew were giving him dark looks, Xander Grayvoice chief among them. Confused, Nate started towards his friend, but Xander turned and stalked away. Nate made to follow him, but came up short when he finally saw that the deck in front of the navigation room was empty, and the black mimic was gone.

"After you freed us, we had a decision to make," Arani said as she stepped up beside Nate. She followed his gaze to where the dragon had been earlier that very day, the creature of legend she had spent years dreaming of. "We were going to run out of sleeping draught for the dragon if we went back for you, so it was either keep the beast, or rescue one of our own. I had the crew vote, and nearly everyone agreed." She nodded at the empty space. "The beast damn near took my hand off, but we let it go."

"That couldn't have been easy," Nate murmured after a stunned moment.

"No," Arani said, "but it was the right thing to do."

Nate shifted his weight across his feet. "I suppose I'll be tracking it again?"

Arani sighed softly and looked with undisguised longing off into the night. "Maybe someday we'll try again, but not today." She shook herself and turned away from the dark, empty sea. "For now, I think we'll focus our attention on something less likely to set the ship on fire." She frowned in the direction Xander had gone. "Not everyone will be happy about that, but the votes were cast, and the choice was made." Arani placed her hand on Nate's shoulder once more and gave it a gentle squeeze. "I'm glad we made the right one. Welcome back, Nate."

"Thank you, Captain," he said.

Arani left him then, and Nate went to find Rori, Marcus and Eric again. The four of them stayed up talking well into the night. By the time dawn had brightened the sky and the crew was tugging the *Southern Echo*'s sails into place to catch the wind, Nate knew beyond any doubt that he was where he belonged.

CHAPTER TWENTY-FIVE

The Next Horizon

LATE THE FOLLOWING NIGHT, when most of the crew was asleep and the *Southern Echo* glided peacefully over the waves, Iris and Dax sat in her cabin, speaking in low voices and trying to make sense of their world once more.

"I still can't believe you let the black mimic go," Dax said.

Iris grimaced. "I can't either, but I think about what that boy said to me before he threw himself on to that ship and I..."

Dax waited patiently, the candlelight flickering over the intricate lines of his tattoos and shining in his dark eyes.

"Well," Iris said after a long moment, "what's a few more years carrying around a dragon scale and never knowing if you're ever going to have the chance to find the end of the legend again?"

"We still have the map," Dax pointed out.

"We do," Iris agreed, "but no dragon to get us past the magic of the Ice Hook. I don't see the crew voting to go chase down another one of those beasts any time soon. Do you?"

Dax smiled wryly and shook his head.

"So my earlier point stands. Although, if there is a next time," Iris said as she rose, withdrew a key from her pocket, and unlocked her sea chest, "we'll skip the part where I make a complete ass out of myself."

Dax snorted. "You're handling this far better than I thought you would."

Iris turned to him, an unopened bottle of rare whiskey in her hand.

"Ah," he said. "Best not let you drink alone, then."

"I'm sorry for your suffering," she said, slipping back into her seat behind her desk.

"And I yours," Dax returned. He watched her break the seal and take a large draught of the burning stuff before offering him the bottle. "For what it's worth," he said, taking the whiskey, "you did win over the crew again, and me, too. We're glad to know our captain values our lives more than her own obsessions."

"Mmm." Iris turned and looked out the windows at the back of the cabin, at the dark waves dancing under the silver moonlight. "Not all of them. Quite a few wanted to leave Nate to the navy and see where that dragon would lead us."

Dax passed the bottle back. "But not nearly enough to vote you out."

"That could change when the navy comes after us again."

The quartermaster frowned. "You think they'll try?"

"We blew several large holes into one of their frigates," Iris mused, "and then stole a prisoner out from under their nose. *And* they saw the dragon. If Trystos didn't have a special interest in us before, he'll have one now." She turned the bottle in her hands. "It was no coincidence that ship found us, you know. They were looking for us, probably because of what happened on the *Talon*."

"You mean Rori?" Dax said softly.

"I do." Iris took a smaller sip of the whiskey, wincing at the burn in her throat but glad for the pleasant warmth when it landed in her belly. "But," she said with false brightness, "if the imperial brat wants us, he's going to have to catch us first."

Dax's frown deepened. "Solkyria's self-appointed pirate destroyer turning his attention on us is not something to take lightly, Captain."

"I'm quite serious." Iris offered him the whiskey again. "We have an incredible ship, and I aim to stay far beyond the reach of Prince Trystos and his hunters." She gave the bottle a little shake, but Dax still hesitated before taking it. "I'm more worried about the crew," she admitted. "They need something to make up for the run of luck we've had the past few months. They may have voted to let that dragon go, but..."

"But what do we do now, if the navy and Trystos are after us?" Dax finished. He took his time drinking and swallowing before passing the bottle back to her.

"Exactly," Iris said. She looked at the amber liquid in the bottle for a moment before replacing the cork. "We're not going to be able to hunt around Spider's Nest and the Coral Chain for a while." Iris rose and replaced the bottle in her sea chest. She turned the key in the lock and listened to the click of the tumblers falling into place. "I suppose we could go east for a bit. See what Vothein's merchants have to offer."

"Do you know of a fence out east who will take our plunder?" the quartermaster asked.

Iris shook her head as she collapsed back into her chair. "Honestly, I wouldn't even know where to begin looking for one, but it's the only idea I've got." She studied the wooden beams over her head. "I really lost it all on this one." Her mouth twisted into a sardonic smirk. "Now I know how Nikolai must feel."

Dax snorted. "No, you outdid our boatswain in a grand way. I've never seen a navy frigate target *him*."

Iris rolled her eyes and let her gaze settle on the ceiling again. "It was never just about the treasure, you know," she said.

"I know," Dax said softly.

Iris ran her thumb under the chain around her neck. There were two scales on it now, the second one found on the deck after the dragon had been persuaded to fly off without torching the ship. It was smaller and sharper than the older one, but they both swirled with black smoke.

"I was finally doing it," Iris murmured. "I was following Mordanti's trail, and I was going to prove to the world that she was more than just some fool from a Solkyrian fable. She lived and she breathed and she fought the empire, all in the name of Veritia." She hesitated, and regret stained her voice when she spoke next. "I lost myself trying to get closer to her. What I did to Nate and Rori..." She shook her head. "I never should have done that."

"No," Dax quietly agreed. "I'm glad you realized that before..."

She brought her gaze down and met the quartermaster's level stare, gesturing for him to continue.

"Before I had to do to you what I did to our first captain," he finished grimly.

Iris was still for a long moment before she nodded. "You would have been right to do it." She meant it.

A long, heavy silence settled over the cabin, broken only by the familiar creaking of the ship around them. Iris and Dax looked at each other, and once more, that familiar chasm opened between them, brought on by their responsibilities to the crew. Then Iris cleared her throat, and she and the quartermaster began to speak of the paths that were open to their crew. They both knew that there would be trouble ahead, and their triumphs would always come at a cost, but they were pirates, and they had committed their lives to danger a long time ago. All that remained now was to keep moving forward, over the next horizon.

Catch the next voyage of the *Southern Echo*:

A Whisper from the Edge of the World

Coming 2023

Sign up for the newsletter so you never miss an update
or release!
Scan the QR code below to sign up:

About the Author

K.N. Salustro is a science fiction and fantasy author who loves outer space, dragons, and stories that include at least one of those things. When not writing, she can be found drawing and painting, designing and crafting plushies, and trying to play video games while her cat paws at the screen.

For updates, new content, and other news, visit:
www.knsalustro.com

Acknowledgments

This is a very special book for me. Not only is it the first installment of the *Southern Echo* series, but it is also my first book as a full-time author. That is a surreal feeling, and I have several people that I need to thank in helping me realize it.

First and foremost, thank you to my parents, who are way more supportive than Nate's. They have been in my corner cheering me on from the start, and when a much younger me told them that I wanted to be an author when I grew up, they took it as seriously as I did. Thank you, Mom and Dad, for your love and support, and for teaching me how to keep parts of the world steady while chasing a dream. There's no perfect formula for that and I'm still figuring some things out, but I know that without you two, this never would have happened.

Next up, thank you to my sister, who made growing up interesting and, again, is way better than Nate's family. We didn't always get along, but once we learned how to be ourselves, we sorted it out, and now we know how to have fun. Thanks for embracing all my weirdness, and for sharing yours. Wouldn't trade you for the world!

Up next comes Ben. I'd need a whole additional novel-length book to say thank you to him in all the ways he deserves. For now, I'll say thank you for being in my life. Thank you for being completely and totally you, and for letting me be unapologetically me. Thank you for the laughs and the tears and the days and the nights. I love crossing every horizon with you.

A huge thank you to my editor, Susan, who helped me dig into this story and its characters and make them the best they could be, and who would not accept "good enough" for anything. Without her, this would have been a very different book. Thank you, Susan! I can't wait to work on the next one with you.

I also want to thank the online game crew. You all are some of the most creative and lovely people I know, and every new adventure is a blast. Quite literally, in our case, as even our stealth missions somehow always manage to include at least one explosion. Thank you all for the wild stories and the even wilder laughter.

Finally, thank you, reader, for coming along on this first voyage. I hope you'll join me, Nate, Captain Arani, and the rest of the crew on the next one.

Books by K.N. Salustro

The Star Hunters

Chasing Shadows
Unbroken Light
Light Runner

The Arkin Races

Cause of Death: ???

Tales from 2020

Southern Echo

The Roar of the Lost Horizon
A Whisper from the Edge of the World*

*Coming 2023

Made in the USA
Monee, IL
28 April 2023

32603612R00246